MW01065497

CREATED OF ONE BLOOD

CREATED OF ONE BLOOD

by

Lloyd Durre

Copyright © 2000 by Lloyd A. Durre

All rights reserved.
No part of this book may be reproduced, stored in a retrieval
system, or transmitted by any means, electronic, mechanical,
photocopying, recording, or otherwise, without written
permission from the author.

ISBN: 1-58820-272-0

1stBooks rev. 9/13/00

Dedication

To my beloved wife Louise

Acknowledgements and Thanks

To the following people who gave encouragement and helpful advice during the writing of this book:

Carol Edgar Martin
Lea Trimble
Harry Styron
Gerald Wardrum
Colleen Tucker
Dayle Michelle

Chapter I
The Abduction of Gabe

Cherokee Nation, Georgia
1838

With a pail of water swinging in her right hand, a mulatto woman trod across a new-plowed field toward three black workers and their Cherokee master who were chopping up the clods of earth in preparation for the spring planting. The laborers straightened their naked backs and brushed the sweat from their brows. They knew Essie brought cool water for their parched throats. She passed by her husband and the other two slave workers and went directly to her master to offer him the first dipper of water. The young Cherokee master straightened himself and leaned wearily on his hoe. As Essie held out the dipper, he reached out to receive it, then stopped shortly, his hand up raised. There was a distant sound of horses running hard and men's raucous shouts. Essie perceived and understood her master's alarm. She thought of the harassment and plundering endured by the Cherokee people. Raiders of marauding white rabble stole their cattle, horses and crops. She remembered how her young master had mourned the mysterious tragedy of his father's death. Her heart pounded as they listened. Were the highwaymen passing by or were they turning into the little road leading into the field?

Suddenly over the hill dark forms of the riders appeared like monsters out of a sea of black earth, silhouetted against the red-streaked sky. The Indian squared his shoulders, gripped his hoe with tight fists and faced the horsemen. Essie drew back to stand by her husband, her trembling hand resting on his wet shoulder.

With a shout the men drew their mounts to a halt a few feet from the Cherokee. In menacing silence six burley men surveyed the situation. Then a squint-eyed ruffian called out, "Hey, Indian, Kevit Tanner ain't cha? We cum t' ask ye a favor. We want t' borrey yer blacks fer a couple o'days."

1

"Can't do that. I need 'em myself," said Kevit.

"But we need 'em a heap worse. Gotta have 'em. It's fer the public good."

"What public good?"

"T' work on the levee. We're gettin' men together t' do it. Could flood a wide area."

"What you payin' t' use my men?" asked Kevit.

"Ain't payin' nothin'. Ever'body's helpin' t' keep from floodin'."

"This here's Cherokee land; you got no right here. Besides, my land's high. It don't flood. I ain't obliged t' help," said Kevit.

"The law sez yu gotta help. Got a order here from Judge Garver. Sez yu gotta furnish yer slaves." The brawny fellow pulled a paper from inside his jacket pocket and handed it down to Kevit.

Kevit took the paper and unfolded it. "Why, this ain't no legal paper. This here's a letter from somebody. Nothin' but a letter from somebody."

"Aw, guess I brung the wrong paper. No time t' get th' other paper. We'll be takin' yer niggers now."

"Now you're talkin', Clem," sneered a grizzly-bearded man. Then with a simper he added, "Didn't know he kin read, did ye, Clem? Want him t' read thet letter fer ye?" There was a loud guffaw from the men.

"Shut up, all of you," growled Clem. "Get them darkies onto thet spare horse. Two kin ride it; th' other'n kin ride yer nag, Joe. Ye kin ride double with Bob, lessen you wants t' ride with the nigger."

Joe dismounted, grumbling. The three black men stood paralyzed in fright. As the horsemen approached, Gabe's fear for Essie spurred him to action. "Run!" he shouted, givimg her a hard push.

Dropping her bucket, Essie raced toward the house. Gabe glanced after her to see her safely on her way. Then he fled with all his might toward the woods beside the house. The squint-eyed man raised his rifle to his shoulder and took aim at Gabe.

2

"Stop, Gabe, come back! shouted Kevit in fear for Gabe's safety. "Gabe, stop now!"

The fleeing Negro halted at his master's command. The other workers gave quizzical glances toward their master who shrugged helplessly.

"Let's go, Clem," called one of the men impatiently.

"You got no right to do this," protested Kevit. The Federal Government gave us a treaty to protect our property."

"Look, Injun," said Clem, "there ain't nothin' yu kin do. The gover'ment don't protect Injuns. It's a white man's gover'ment. B'sides yu gotta clear out o' here and git acrost th' Mississippi like ye agreed to."

"Never agreed t' it. That false treaty was forced on us," responded Kevit. "Chief Ross and our people didn't agree to it."

"All I kin say, boy, is thet ye better not make trouble. Remember how yer paw was kill't."

"Wus Soarin' Hawk this guy's father?" asked one of the men.

"Yeah, an' thet ought t' be warnin' enough," sneered Clem.

Four men dismounted and shoved the three Negroes toward the horses. They began to remount.

"Wait! He's got that house slave. Might as well take her too," shouted one of the men.

"Naw, come on, let's go," growled Clem.

In the Cherokee farmer's kitchen, peeping through a slit in the door, Essie was filled with terror. As she watched Gabe being forced to mount a horse, she had an impulse to run out and cling to her husband, fighting with fists and teeth against those who would take him from her. "Wish they'd take me too," she moaned to Fawn, Kevit Tanner's wife who watched through the crack of the door with her.

"No, Essie, Gabe wouldn't want that. A woman wouldn't be safe with them devils," said Fawn.

They watched the raiders vanish and heard the shouts of laughter and the clatter of hooves die away. Kevit stood forlornly, then he turned, gathered the work tools, and trudged to the house. He slammed the door shut and leaned against it, his muscular body limp as he faced the women.

3

Ooh, Mas'er Kevit, they took Gabe! What we gonna do?" sobbed Essie.

"Yea, they took Gabe, and Sam and Benny. They had no right to. Believe me, Essie, there was nothin' I could do."

"I know," said Essie.

They'd a' taken you too, Essie, if Gabe hadn't pushed you away. I couldn't stop 'em. Even if I'd had a gun, I couldn't stop em. Too many of 'em."

"No gun, Kevit!" gasped Fawn. " Our people can't have guns."

"Why shouldn't I have a gun? We have a right to protect ourselves. It's time Cherokees stood up for their rights. Property stolen, women raped, people threatened, even killed."

Fawn went to him and put her hands on his shoulders. "I'm afraid. Don't take any chances, Kevit."

He broke away from her. He slumped into a chair, brooding. "I'll go t' New Echota tomorrow. I'll tell the old leader of our Council about this."

That night Kevit tossed sleeplessly in his bed, his seething brain reviewing the event of the afternoon. Certain that his workers were irretrievably lost, his anger raged. Tomorrow he would go to make his appeal to the National Council. He would incite his people to seek vengeance. The Council would listen to him: after all, wasn't he the son of Soaring Hawk? For five months now his father had been gone, dead from a violent assault, his horse and wagon stolen. Soaring Hawk had been a peaceful man, often raising his voice before the Council with a plea for reconciliation. Kevit realized it now--his father was betrayed by his own philosophy. His peaceful attitude had been a mistake. The thought tore at Kevit's heart. Soaring Hawk, whose wisdom Kevit had revered, whose council had been so important to him, whose dignity and inner self-assurance had been so beautiful! Soaring Hawk had been wrong! Well, not completely wrong perhaps. He held an exalted position among his people.

Kevit had inherited a farm, house and furnishings, and three male slaves. Gabe Forbes was the foreman over the other two

4

workers. His loyalty and devotion beyond question. Kevit had bought Essie to be Gabe's wife.

In the attic, Essie mourned her loss. Gabe had been her husband for seven short months. He was handsome, strong, and tender. His cheery personality made him a favorite among both blacks and the Cherokee people. Essie had fallen in love with him almost at first sight. She had been in the Cherokee country only a short while, a slave loaned by an owner to a young missionary couple. The circumstances of their union had seemed a miracle to her. Now she gazed about the room searching for things which bore the memory of Gabe's touch. On the wall hung a piece with a very romantic image. She thought about the time he had found it and shown it to her. They had been strolling hand in hand through the forest. "Look," he said, "This puts me in mind of you, so smooth and slender like you, Essie. And see, it almost has your face." Holding a weathered branch up to show her, he put his arm around her and pasionately kissed her.

At one end of the room, on a wooden pegs on the wall hung Gabe's few garments, worn and faded. Essie thought of how she had washed them in a tub in the back yard. What a pleasure it had been! With what tenderness she had laid them across a smooth fence rail, pressing out all the wrinkles with her hands so they could dry in the sun! Tears fell as she thought that she would no longer hang his clothes there. Who would care for him now? She saw also the soft piece of woven cotton cloth hanging next to Gabe's things. It, too, hde been washed and lovingly cared for. She had woven it on Fawn's loom, a fuzzy receiving blanket which would first touch her future new-born child. She had shown it to her husband and let him feel its downy softness, and they had dreamed together.

Now Gabe was gone. Could he ever come back to her? No, people never come back--not black people anyway. Her mother, her father, and her brothers, all gone never to return. She sat in her chair dreaming of her past life.

Chapter II
From Plantation to Cherokee Mission

At the age of ten Essie had grieved the death of her mother. Her father and two brothers had been taken away from her. Heaven only knows where they were now. The frightened mulatto child was taken to the slave market and sold to the owner of the vast Fern Haven Plantation near Decatur, Georgia. There, without family with whom to live, Essie was given over to Leona who trained and groomed her to help in the big house's kitchen. When she was seventeen, tall and comely, she first began serving at the master's table. Thomas Lovell was not remiss to observe the fresh-bloomed womanhood of the new attendant who stood bearing a tureen or a tray while the inveterate servant, Leona, passed about the table serving food and removing used dishes. Feeling the master's stare, Essie attempted to steady her trembling hands. Back in the kitchen Essie asked Leona, "Why do he look at me like thet?"

"Don't pay him no mind, honey," she said, "He likes yo." And then when she saw Essie's timid uncertainty, she added, "He's an old dear! Devilish, thet's fer sure, but an old dear. And they ain't no excapin' him." Leona wore a wistful expression which made Essie wonder whether her devotion to the master had been fostered by some clandestine affair she may have had with him. Throughout the plantation, Essie had overheard vague innuendos that Tom Lovell was a philanderer whose advances were next to impossible to fend off, once his ardor was aroused.

Even though nearly eight years had passed, Essie still remembered the glint in his eye when he first viewed her, a scantily clad, frightened girl, on the auction block at Atlanta. She remembered the sly nod of acquiescence to the auctioneer as he outbid the others in the market place.

Now she studied him as she stood in waiting as Leona served the family. When, on occasion, his eyes met hers she felt the blood surge through her feverish face and wondered whether her mulatto skin was betraying her embarrassment, as it did so often with white folks. Did he interpret her observance of him as an inordinate fascination for him? In truth, she had found him interesting and handsome, an older man with a bearing of genuine aristocracy. Such qualities were bound to arouse interest in a poor slave maiden. But Tom Lovell did not blush, his gaze was steady and constant. How could he do this? thought Essie. Surely Missis Claire, his wife, would see him!

Indeed, the forebearing Claire Lovell, who sat at the opposite end of the table, did not fail to notice her husband's perverse demeanor, but she also knew it was futile to chastise or reprimand him for what she had learned from past experience to accept as his natural weakness. Besides, there were the children to consider. Claire therefore attempted to divert his attention from the comely mulatto by plying him with questions about the operation of the plantation, a subject about which she knew little and cared less. Tom replied with a nod or a grunt, and when forced to it, he uttered a vague, brief comment. Claire turned the conversation to the subject of the children's progress, their education, their deportment, or physical well-being. To her consternation, her husband remained taciturn and distracted. Finally, in a desperate attempt to bring Tom to his senses and to call attention to the fact that Essie was a mere child, Claire said in her most matronly tone, "Leona, I hope you will be able to clear the table by yourself. I would like Essie to go out with the children. They dearly love for her to play their games with them."

Indeed, Essie was a favorite of the five Lovell children, and it was she who rode with them to the church near Decatur on Sunday, and she tended them during the service, occupying a place on the Lovell pews in the family enclosure situated in a prominent position near the front of the sanctuary. It was Essie who, when the building became chilly, went to fetch the mistress' shawl from the carriage, or if it were hot Essie went for the lady's silk fan, or a cool drink of water, if the sermon were long and tedious. And always when Essie rose from the pew and stepped from the family box, closing its glistening white gate behind her, she did it with such grace and decorum that all the congregation watched and felt in their hearts that she made a

8

tremendous contribution toward the maintainence, if not indeed the elevation, of the prestige of the lofty Lovell family.

The parishioners, as well as the very Reverend Dr. Eubanks, were also cognizant that quite often Thomas Lovell turned in his pew to gaze after Essie as she removed herself and returned. The congregation was well aware of the escapades of the community's most prominent citizen and made discrete allowances for his "aristocratic behavior" which was not bound by the moral confines put upon more humble folks. But the Doctor Eubanks was a bold and discerning man.

One bright Sunday morning he chose as his text verses from Paul's letter to Philemon. How the southern hearts thrilled as the doctor related how the apostle had returned the runaway slave to his master! Surely, here was a divine endorsement of the grand old institution which was now under northern verbal and propaganda attack.

Tom Lovell listened with gratification. He had not been an enthusiastic supporter of the Reverend Dr. Eubanks. After all, the minister had been educated in the North and had not until now verbalized his support of slavery. Tom had thought that he had in the past side-stepped the issue, so to speak.

The doctor pressed on in his message, expounding Paul's admonition to Philemon, the slave owner, how he was to receive the slave Onesimus, as his brother in Christ. The good preacher began to expand the scripture text, to apply the Christian principles to slave-holders today. It was then that the message began to lash out and strike at the slave-owning parishioners. Not only did the pastor call for just and humane treatment of Negroes, but he placed upon the masters the obligation to promote the spiritual welfare of the black race. "We are the guardians of their souls," the minister's voice rang out with eloquence and conviction.

Many men winced and squirmed in their pews, all the while feigning nonchalance, of course, each recalling how on some occasion he had taken advantage of his slaves, overworked, punished brutally, canjoled, or sexually assulted a female.

Essie had never heard such talk, and she was overwhelmed by it. She glanced toward Tom Lovell. She recalled a certain light-skinned slave, probably three years younger than herself, who roamed the plantation. "Dat boy's skin ain't light 'cause he got born'd in de light o' de moon," an old babbler had whispered to Essie. "No suh. Hones' t' de Lawd, he were sure 'nuf conceived in de dark o' de moon." She had laughed hilariously. "Dat ar's Massah Tom's boy. Massah Tom don't show him no favorite dealin' though. He ar' jest a no'count slave jest lak' we is."

Tom Lovell sat motionless in his pew. Essie thought how white and cadaverous his face looked, yet how handsome his features and his thick greying hair brushed modishly back. The rector's admonishment to slaveowners struck her as a new concept. "Thy Master, too, is in heaven," he was expostulating, "neither is there any partiality with Him." Essie almost dared not think of it. A master could not do anything and everything he pleased! Never before had such an outlandish, almost sacrilegious, thought occurred to her. "It is the master's moral duty to instruct his black wards in moral virtues and chastity, to denounce promiscuity and illegitimacy," proclaimed the preacher.

Men flinched with notions of perdition. Women felt faint and longed for instant transport from this public assembly to some more idyllic scene. And poor Essie had confused thoughts about her obligation to Master Tom. Would he make the amorous advances that his demeanor, especially his leering eyes, seemed to forebode? The Reverend Dr. Eubanks had disclosed a moral dilemma where she had previously thought she had no prerogative.

As the congregation filed from the sanctuary, each one was greeted by the rector. No one made mention of the sermon. Tom, flanked by his wife and children, shook the pastor's hand with a warm salutation. He himself avoided making any comment about the sermon and evaded the risk of the pastor doing the same by a hasty inquiry: "Dr. Eubanks, I have been wondering about your son Alfie. How is he doing on his mission among the Cherokees?"

"Alfie is doing fine. He seems to have won the confidence of the redmen. His efforts are winning many Christian converts."

"Excellent! That's great news. I would like to make this contribution to his work." He handed the minister a twenty dollar bank note.

Three days later the inevitable dilemma came to Essie. The dinner had been served, and Essie was alone clearing away the dishes. Leona was serving Mistress Claire's meal in her room where she was suffering from an attack of summer complaint. The children had been excused from the table and were outside playing. Essie had just carried a tray of dishes and placed them at the wooden kitchen sink and turned to go back to the dining room to get the table linen when she found herself face to face with Thomas Lovell. He held a glass in his hand.

"Essie," he said in a soft velvet tone, "I have a little indigestion. I wonder if I might have a spoon of bicarbonate of soda in water."

"It's in the pantry," said Essie and she went in to get a stoneware jar. Tom followed her and stood at the pantry doorway. Essie removed the jar lid and took a pinch of soda and dropped it into the glass which Tom had placed on top of a pickle barrel. She picked up the glass. "The water's in the kitchen," she said. Tom stood blocking the exit, his eyes fastened upon her, his mouth formed a carnal smirk. Essie spoke, almost pleading, "Let me get the water for yo, massah."

He took the glass from her and set it down. "Never mind, honey, my stomache seems to have quieted. I don't think I'll need the soda now. But my heart, you make my heart flutter and convulse. Essie, I do believe you are the most exquisite woman I ever seen." Tom moved toward her and placed his hands on her waist and drew her toward him. Essie pulled away. "Listen, honey, I've been watching you fer a long time. I've seen you watching me too. Don't tell me you find me unattractive. I own you, Essie. I bought you because you were a sweet girl, and I knew you would develop into a beautiful woman. I noticed that slave-beatin' bully Van Horn about to buy you. He's a beast to

11

his niggers, women as well as men. I done you a favor when I bought you, honey."

"I guess I is grateful t' yo, Mas'ah Tom. And yo is a handsome man all right, but yo is white, I ain't. Yeah, I do look at yo, suh. I noticed yo in church Sunday, yo listenin' t' thet Reverend Eubanks so intent. Yo was handsome, suh." Essie felt his arms about her draw her closer to him. She was deliriously nervous and insecure. Her only respite seemed to be to talk. "Yeah, yo was real handsome. An' thet Reverend Eubanks, ain't he heavenly! Yo like him too, I could tell. His sermon meant a heap t' yo, I could tell. I'm glad yo ain't no savage monster like some slave masters is. Reverend Eubanks is such a dear to be thinkin' o' us poor worthless colored folks."

Essie's alluring qualities seemed to vanish, and Tom's ardor began to wane. When she began giddily, "Thet Reverend Eubanks sez...," he turned away, mumbling to himself.

He left the room. "Damn that Eubanks," he muttered.

Later at the Wayfarer's Tavern, where several of the plantation owners gathered at a large round table, Tom related his attempted conquest of Essie. "I didn't really struggle with her, ner she with me. She didn't have to; she just rebuffed me with her remarks about Eubanks, and I turned away cowed," Tom concluded his account with a dismayed countenance.

There was a boisterous guffaw among the men. Jake Copeland's great hulk shook with laughter, his huge belly snuggly wedged against the table tottered it until the glasses swayed their contents. "That's rich," he roared. "We was all green with envy over that enchanting wench with the flawless tawny skin. When Tom paraded her into church we was ready to cut his throat an' steal her away for ourselves," boomed Jake with laughter, and he brought his fist down in clamorous delight. "Tom done spoiled his chances with her by exposing her to Eubanks' morality."

With a faint hint of good natured embarrassment, knowing that the joke was on him, Tom said in mock anger, "That Eubanks, damn him, he can't be that holy. 'Course he ain't got no mulatto goddess promenadin' 'round t' tempt him."

"He hit us mighty hard in that sermon o' his," said Jake. "He don't know what it's like bein' master o' a gang o' slaves."

"He ain't human," chimed in another fellow.

"His wife ain't even as much human as he is, judging from her frigid face," remarked still another man. "She's probably just as cold as she looks."

"Aw, now you ought t' have more respect for the reverend's woman. She ain't well, you know. My wife sez she's right poorly," reported one.

"Say, Tom," said Jake, "since Essie ain't goin' t' be useful to you like you thought, lessen you force her, why don't you just donate her to the reverend. Maybe she could bring a little fun into his life, his wife bein' so sick and all. It just might be she could soften him up into a regular human being."

Among the gleeful men, there was a general assent to the proposal, but Tom dismissed the idea with a comment, "Aw, you men are ridiculous." For the remaining time he spent amid his amicable friends, Tom was silent.

He was still in a pensive mood as he rode his horse home. It was a blow to his manhood to think of himself as being unappealing to the Negro slave. After all, she was only a slave. She had no right to wound his pride, to reject him. To be sure, she was young, but black folks learn about lovemaking while they're young. They ain't bound by propriety. They just do what seems good to them. Nobody censures them. White folks don't care how they live as long as they produce children to supply work hands.

Then Tom thought of the Reverend Dr. Eubanks. His business was morality. His continuous employment was how to behave ethically. Tom could not comprehend the pastor's spiritual motivation. Tom, who was bound up in the material world, could not understand ethereal, divine theology. He had no immutable moral standards such as those that ruled the Reverend Dr. Eubanks' life. Tom's behavior was only slightly restricted by what others thought and said. He had learned that, as a general rule, people were willing to overlook scandalous behavior when the offender was wealthy, powerful, and handsome, and he found excitement in flouting acceptable social rules. He chuckled to think of how often he had dared to risk public censure.

Had the Dr. Eubanks ever in his lifetime done anything thrillingly devilish? Suddenly Tom became obsessed with a desire to lure him into some shockingly wicked misdeed. No reproach is more stinging to a social offender, such as Tom, than the example of a saintly person. By his very nature, the saint appears to the rogue to be his adversary. If the saint can be brought low there remains no standard whereby the evildoer can be compared, and thus he appears to be elevated and has obtained a new cohort in wrongdoing. Tom's spirits began to soar as he contemplated the downfall of the reverend. Jake Copeland's suggestion that he should present Essie as a gift to Eubanks began to have cunning appeal to him. Imagine, he thought with satanic glee, Essie in the reverend's household and the Mrs. Eubanks an invalid confined to her bed. How could he resist Essie's charm and pulchritude? Tom's character being what it was, he could not conceive of the clergyman not yielding to such a temptation.

"Why, Tom, what a beautiful magnanimous jesture!" exclaimed Claire Lovell when her husband revealed his plan to present Essie to the Reverend Cedwic Eubanks. While she feigned a congenial smile, Claire thought to herself, "Could it have been only my imagination, Tom's enticement with that mulatto? This is an unbelievable development! Why is he really doing this? Why?"

"Claire, I won't do it without your approval," said Tom. "I know how difficult the management of the household is."

"Leona can train another scullery maid," commented Claire.

"Essie is not just another scullery maid. Why, just yesterday you, yourself, remarked that Essie was the cleverest, best domestic slave Leona has ever tutored. And I can certainly taste her influence on the food," remarked Tom. Suddenly he realized that his words were in opposition to his scheme. "But you are right, my dear. Leona can train another girl. Because Essie is so valuable, that's all the more reason we need to give her to Eubanks. It will be all the more noble of us."

14

Part Two of Chapter II

Claire herself helped Essie pack her clothing into two carpet bags. Essie was confused about the transaction. She was sad to think about leaving the plantation. The manse was small and she knew that she would be lonely there. The ailing Mistress Eubanks would require a lot of attention. What would she be like?

Tom drove the carriage to the manse with Essie sitting beside him. Tom gazed upon her. She was beautiful even in cold sternness and uncertainty. He reexamined his feelings and wondered how he could give her up.

The clergyman came out to the buggy. "Tom, this is the most generous gift I have ever received," he said. "How could you have known the strain I have been under? Essie will be a god's blessing to my wife. But Tom, you needn't have made it a legal transaction. You could have just loaned Essie to us for a short term."

"Nonsense," said Tom. "We want you to know how we value your friendship and ministry."

The plantation owner carried Essie's valise into the manse and bid them farewell. As he drove the buggy away, he glanced behind the seat to the compartment where baggage was carried. He smiled to himself. There sat a small valise filled with Essie's clothes. He had purposely carried only one of the two bags into the house. Later, he thought, he would have an excuse to return and see Essie again. He reached behind, lifted the carpet bag bringing it forward onto the seat beside him. While the horse walked unguided, Tom opened the bag. It was filled with undergarments. Tom grinned mischievously. Imagine, he thought, Essie working around the parsonage while not wearing undergarments. The clergyman's wife was a small woman; Essie couldn't wear her cast-offs.

At first Essie's encounter with Master Tom in the pantry had left her confused. She had had no doubt about what the master's intentions were. Never before had she reacted with anything but submission to his commands. But never before had his desires been anything but routine and ordinary. His authority had been absolute. Now she was puzzled; her station in life came into question. No longer would her life be wholly tranquil with meek obedience. Fortified by the Reverend Dr. Eubanks' words, Essie assumed a faint measure of independence and self-determination. It had all begun with her rebuff of Master Tom. Somehow through it she gained confidence; she began to imagine that she had some control of her destiny. Still, how would she meet Master Tom's next attempt to seduce her? Would she be able to withstand him a second time?

Her questions Had been resolved unexpectedly when she left Fern Haven and became the property of her new owner. Essie was unable to figure out the reason for the change. Would she have been better off to have yielded to Master Tom? Still, he was not one to have freely relinquished his property rights to her.

In her new position Essie was at first uncertain and frightened. She felt lonely in the eight room house occupied only by the minister and his sick wife. She missed her former slave friends of the old plantation. Of course, every Tuesday, Thursday, and Saturday a black girl named Viola came to clean house and cook the evening meal, but she was not very communicative and seemed unwilling to make friends with Essie. But the Reverend Cedwic Eubanks was very considerate and kind. He realized Essie's isolated position and was sympathetic.

However, unable to suppress his curiosity, the clergyman, too, wondered why Tom Lovell had brought Essie to him. Rumors of Tom's philandering had sometimes reached his pious ears, but not desiring to censure the man, he had rejected the scandalous remarks, not willing even to risk defaming any man unjustly. Now, however, he allowed himself to speculate. If Tom were guilty of promiscuity, could it be that now he was thrusting Essie aside as one of his most sensual temptations? In effect, he was practicing a principal of Christ who said, "If thine eye offend thee pluck it out." Glory be! The man had had a change of heart! He conjectured that, perhaps as a result of hearing his sermons, Tom Lovell had become penitent.

Eubanks reasoned that perhaps Essie herself was, in fact, involved with Tom Lovell. She had been an obvious favorite of the Lovell family. Had she somehow fallen from favor? He wondered whether her residence in the manse was intended to be a form of punishment for her. Not certain that such was the case, Eubanks resolved to treat her with the utmost consideration. He urged Essie to join him and his wife in their morning devotions which were subtlely designed to teach Essie Christian morals.

While confined to her bed and too weak to hold a book, Mrs. Eubanks asked Essie to read to her. Essie had never been to school and her meager ability to read she had learned in her early years from her mother who had secretly learned from children she had been assigned to keep. The pastor's sick wife prompted and encouraged Essie so that through the months Essie's literate skill was vastly improved. And through Essie's gentle nursing and cheery companionship, Mrs. Eubanks' health began to improve.

Essie was often homesick. She missed being with Leona and the other slaves. She missed the singing, dancing, and laughter. She longed for the Lovell and her duties there, through which she had found satisfaction and pride.

On one rare Sunday morning when the mistress felt well enough to be left at home alone, Essie was allowed to accompany the vicar to church. Ordinarily, blacks were not permitted in the service, but the pastor had suggested that she might like to watch from the balcony. Not feeling that she had been relegated to an inferior position, she exulted in the splendid view of the whole congregation. Below, in their customary compartment, the Lovell family sat dressed in Sunday array. Deep joy and affinity for them filled her heart. She studied each one, the five fidgety children, the reserved and beautifully proper Mistress Lovell, and Master Tom appearing so noble dressed in his grey frock coat with powder-blue lapels and satin cravat.

At the close of the service as the Lovells passed down the aisle toward the foyer, Tom noticed Essie in the balcony. At once his eyes sparkled. Essie smiled in recognition of the family, while the children bounced with joy at the sight of her, until at last Claire Lovell herded them outside. In a fantasy of nostalgic reminiscence, she stood in the balcony until the building was almost empty of worshipers. She felt least attracted to Missus Claire who was by nature a woman reserved and aloof, but the children were lively, engaging and free-hearted, and Tom had a masculine allurement which seemed special.

Essie, at eighteen, had a woman's natural attraction for men. She thought about Tom's visit to the manse to deliver the second valise containing the rest of her clothes. He had profusely apologized for his oversight, although he offered no explanation as to why it had taken five days for anyone to discover the striped maroon and black carpet bag. Then Tom related how much Essie was missed at Fern Haven Plantation. Casually he suggested that if she wished and if the minister and his wife agreed, some afternoon he would be willing to take Essie for a visit with her old friends. So a time was set for a week from the next coming Wednesday.

Essie was no less thrilled with the prospect of an afternoon at Fern Haven than Tom Lovell was pleased to take her. Looking young and dashing for his forty-three years, Tom drove away from the manse with Essie beside him in her best calico dress. "You have the looks of a real charmer today," said he with a smile. "Leona has baked a large pan of ginger cake for the occasion, and she was grinding coffee when I left."

They rode on in silence. Occasionally each one glanced at the other, and when their eyes met there was a clearing of the throat and a casual turning away. Matter-of-factly Tom remarked, "Oh, Essie, you remember the spot where the spring is, where we had a picnic that time? It's right here not far off the road. I want you to see how beautiful it looks. Rudy brought a crew over and cleaned out the spring and cleared the grounds. It looks like a park." With those words he drove the carriage off the road and across a grassy field. He leaped from the rockaway and dashed around to offer his hand to Essie. The humble slave girl was overwhelmed by such gentle attention. No man had ever shown her such kindness. In fact, she had not had any close contacts with any other man or boy since her father had disappeared. At Fern Haven she had been a house servant. With the exception of two old men, all her fellow domestics were women. She shared a room with Leona who was more than twice her age. Whenever Essie ventured out of the big house, the field hands looked upon her as not being one of them. The black youths observed that the taffy-colored beauty was no ordinary wench. Slave gang leader Spiro, perhaps hoping to save Essie for himself, had announced, "Listen, ye black slouches, thet gal is too highfalutin' for you raven-black niggers." But even Spiro had not dared risk approaching her.

Now as Tom led her into the idyllic rendezvous, Essie's heart sank. What she had supposed would be an outing for a simple social visit was becoming a dangerous predicament. Thoughts of Master Tom's tainted reputation came to her mind, but the gossip was usually light-hearted, and his offenses were spoken as being escapades which entertained rather than shocked the talebearer. She wondered about the women to whom Tom had made love. Had they felt unharmed and not ill-treated? Or were they tearfully remorseful with broken hearts?

Tom was strutting about the grassy plot. "Isn't this the most beautiful spot in the whole country? These ferns along the creek are what gave the plantation its name."

"Master Tom, I shouldn't be here alone with you. I reckon you brought other women here too."

"Don't be upset, Essie," he said soothingly. "You know it's you that entices me." His tone was that of a defenseless schoolboy faced with a temptation beyond his power to resist. He moved to her and attempted to embrace her. Awed by his boldness, she felt weak and unable to withstand her former master. Then, all at once, there was something about him that brought to mind that day in the kitchen pantry. She had rebuffed him then. Now Tom was kissing her on the neck. Suddenly Essie stiffened; she pushed against him with her arms.

"Reverend Eubanks says it ain't right for a woman to give herself to a man she ain't married to."

"Reverend Eubanks be dammed."

"I ain't your slave no more, Master Tom."

"Essie, I gave you to Eubanks. Can't you just this once be good to me as a reward?" he pleaded, stifling his vexation and whispering tenderly. He thought of what a fool he had been to part with her. Dr. Eubanks was an insensitive clod, and Essie was now just as unattainable as she was before. He tore at her dress.

Suddenly a odd sound wailed through the woods. It was a blowing like a hunting horn. Holding Essie firmly, Tom stood still to listen. The horn blasted again unsteadily, an uncertain undulation of tone. Again and again it sounded, closer and closer. Tom relaxed his grasp of Essie and stood in alarm and wonder. Along the path leading to the big house, the bushes stirred.

"Hello, Papa, Hello, Essie." The two Lovell boys burst into the clearing. "What's the matter? You look funny."

Tom removed his hands from Essie. "Nothin's the matter." He became aware that his shirt was partly unbuttoned. Essie's dress was off the shoulder. "Oh," stammered Tom, "Essie fell over that big rock over there. I was just helping her."

"Did you hurt yourself?" asked Ned of Essie. She shook her head in reply. "We come to welcome you."

"Were you making all that noise?" asked Tom.

"Yes," said Ned, who was the older of the two, "me and Simon. He can't blow very good." Ned held up an army bugle.

"Where did you get that," asked Tom, uneasily shifting his weight and brushing a nervous hand across the side of his jaw.

"It was Uncle Newell's. Mamma let us have it to play with."

"But why did you come here with it?" asked his bewildered father.

"Why, 'cause Mamma and all the house slaves is comin' here for the picnic for Essie."

"Here? They're coming here?" Tom muttered vaguely. The disconcerted man felt his wet shirt cling to his sweating body. Was it some kind of a trap?

Essie heaved a sigh of relief. She stooped to receive the warm embrace of the innocent lads who sprang into her arms.

Not until Claire came was Tom able to surmise the answer to the puzzle. "Tom and Essie," she exclaimed, "you beat us here, I'm so glad you knew to come here." It was Claire's way of protecting him. The picnic was her impulsive inspiration which came to her after Tom had left in the rockaway to fetch Essie.

Claire knew Tom well enough to calculate that he would probably take the slave-girl to his Fern Creek hideout. She had sent the boys with the army bugle--Uncle Newell's treasured bugle from the Mexican War--to alarm him and foil his plans.

Essie was given no time to think about Clair's scheme. Her friends crowded around her with greetings. They exchanged news and asked questions. Little wonder that now the impelling memory was so clear and glowing; it had been a happy outing fit to remember. And she had not found it necessary to make any decision about Tom's salacious advances.

There weren't any such good times for Essie at the minister's manse. Because of Alta Eubanks' illness, not many occasions were given over to entertaining. A few relatives came and a few friends, but their visits were brief and gushing with solicitations over Alta's health and comfort. The most gratifying visitor was Alfred Eubanks, the only son of the doctor and his wife. Alfie was a handsome blond of twenty-four. His homecomings were like a tonic for his mother. She called for her mirror and spruced herself with powder and comb. She arose from her bed, put on her dressing gown and went down stairs where she listened with fascination as Alfie recounted for hours his experiences among the Cherokees.

Once when he came, Alfie brought with him a young brave called Shucker. Essie took great interest in the copper skinned visitor whose complexion was slightly darker than her own. His clothing was that of a conventional Georgia gentleman with the exception of Indian accessories, a beaded belt, moccasins and a string of colorful beads. His hair hung in black shiny braids. Essie hovered near, serving refreshments and giving attention to the convenience of the guests. She did not want to miss a single bit of the conversation. Shucker's clear and articulate speech fascinated her. He was a man of education and sensitivity. Always, before, she had observed such refinement only in people of the white race. Now she grasped a new ambition to acquire such admirable traits for herself.

The discussion dwelt upon the plight of the Cherokees whose land was coveted by the white race. Alfie planned to establish a mission school to educate and Christianize Indian

21

children. For days after the two young men had left to return to the Cherokee nation, Essie found Alta Eubanks eager to continue talking about her son and his work. Essie was pleased to learn more, and many cheery discussions followed.

Two months later Alfie came again. His mission school had been established. Even more significant was the news that a new young woman sent from a society in Massachusetts had joined the mission. Julie was the main subject of Alfie's conversation during his entire stay at the manse.

"That son of mine has been smitten mighty hard by that new missionary teacher," remarked Alta with a gentle shaking of her white head. "His good spirits seem to be catching. I think I feel like dressing and going down to sit on the side veranda."

For six years Viola, a black cleaning woman, had been coming to the manse three times weekly. She was a free woman with a pocked face, the wife of a free Negro porter. Her husband had earned money to buy Viola's freedom. The veteran charwoman resented a younger woman coming into what she considered her domain. Viola lambasted the new girl incessantly. A compliment for Essie about her culinary talent or work well done was regarded by Viola equal to a slap on her own chubby jaw. Viola took delight in the thought that she was free and not a slave laborer. She reminded Essie that it was only her shortage of funds which kept her from owning such as her. Essie dreaded the three days a week when the "uppity" worker came.

As Mistress Alta had predicted, when Alfie came home again he brought the missionary maiden with him to meet his parents. Julie was a serious girl with an engaging smile. She spoke sparingly, and with wide brown eyes, gazed adoringly at Alfie who chatted unceasingly about his future plans for the mission and Julie. When the conversation touched upon the Cherokee language, Julie opened up and took charge, ardently attempting to explain the function of the eighty-six characters of Cherokee writing invented by Sequoyah. Then, in turn, Alfie gave rapt attention to his beloved as though he were hearing it for the first time.

Essie's struggle with printed English had, with Alta's support, met such success that now Essie considered this new language an exciting new field of interest.

When Alfie and Julie departed to go back to the mission, plans had been formulated for their wedding upon their return in early June. Julie's aunt and uncle, with whom she had lived in Massachusetts had come on hard times and had left their home to migrate to Missouri. Since they could not be present at the wedding, it fell upon Alta and Essie to serve the bride with helpful attention. Essie stitched and fitted the wedding gown and combed and groomed Julie devotedly. The wedding was a simple ceremony in Dr. Eubanks' church.

After the wedding, the Eubanks' household returned to its humdrum routine with Viola wrangling at Essie. When, four months later, Alfie wrote that Julie was "in the family way" and was suffering with spells of severe sickness, Essie expressed a sympathy saying,"I wish I wus there to help her. Alta, in her distress for the young couple, seized upon the idea to send Essie to Julie. Viola, who was delighted with the prospect of being rid of Essie, promised to take good care of Alta. So with Essie and her baggage aboard, the clergyman drove a carriage northward to the Cherokee mission where Essie would stay until after Julie's child was born. That night Eubanks slept on a pallet on the floor of the mission school and the next morning he made the ardurous journey back home. Essie was bedded down in a niche in the tiny attic, where she endured gladly the stuffy, crowded room, so pleased was she with her new assignment.

Chapter III
Essie in the Cherokee Nation

Essie labored willingly, even eagerly, for the new mistress whom she loved from the very start. Each day she hurried through her household chores so that she could join Julie in the school. The mother-to-be, despite her nausea and frequent dizziness, resisted any suggestion that she withdraw from her duties. Essie stood ready to help. Essie loved the little Cherokee children. As the weeks went by, Essie observed and learned along with the students. Gradually she assumed the role of a supplementary instructor. She took the children outside to romp and play at recesses. She learned a few Cherokee expressions and sought to learn more. Julia assigned additional lessons to the eager slave girl. After a few months Essie had become an essential member of the teaching staff. Cherokee parents were pleased with the progress of their offspring. The school enrollment grew until it was soon evident that more space would be needed.

Volunteers from the neighborhood were called upon to construct an addition. The response was great, but none of the workers had much construction experience. Alfie felt it would be necessary to go to Kevit Tanner and persuade him to send his slave Gabe to be the leader of the crew. Gabe was a big man, a favorite and a respected leader, with a gentle voice and willingness to work and use his expertise.

Trees were cut and logs hauled on an oxen-drawn wagon to the sawmill. Boards were moved to the construction site. Timbers too large to transport to the saw mill were squared with broad-axes to form sills and beams. Whenever Essie had any time, she watched the workmen. She marveled at their dexterity as they worked with saw, auger, and draw-knife. She admired their skillful fitting of the mitered joints held in place with hickory pegs. The workmen removed their shirts during the warm October days. Sometimes they were self-conscious to see the mulatto maiden study them so intently, but they soon realized that her attention was mainly on Gabe. They began to make

25

friendly jests about it to Gabe, who grinned and worked all the harder.

One day at the close of school Essie came out to check on the progress of the builders. The frames for the walls were in place and the ceiling beams were being hoisted into place. Gabe scaled a ladder with an armful of wooden pegs. Against the blue sky his shiny brown skin took on azure highlights. The muscles which capped his broad shoulders moved with undulating waves of rich brown flesh as he raised a mallet and pounded the round pegs through the beam and into the sill. Essie watched; he was, she thought, the most handsome human being she had ever seen.

Gabe had finished securing one end of a joist and was walking across it to the other side. Men on the ground were in the process of raising the next beam into place. A mule pulled a rope which ran through a pulley wheel and was tied to the heavy timber. As the joist was hoisted high above the walls ready to be lowered into place. Suddenly the tree branch to which the pulley wheel was attached broke and tumbled to the ground. Essie screamed as she saw the large timber spin in the air toward Gabe. He ducked his head. The massive beam crashed to the puncheon floor. But as it fell it glanced off the joist on which Gabe was walking. The movement of the the timber under his feet was just enough to throw him off balance. He staggered, as Essie watched horrified. Then he fell. As he tumbled he grabbed at the cross member on which he had been walking. His grip gave way and he pitched to the floor. Essie gasped in terror. She rushed to him and lifted his head onto her lap. The workers gathered around. "Oh, Gabe," she cried, "Can you hear me?" She stroked his face lovingly and ran her fingers over his shoulder.

Anxiously she watched as one of the men passed his hands over Gabe's form. "Ain't no broken bones, near as I can tell," he said. Slowly the dazed Negro opened his eyes.

"Are you hurt?" Essie asked.

"My leg," whispered Gabe, wincing with pain. Carefully the workers moved him into the schoolroom. For three nights Gabe slept in the schoolroom because his leg was too sore to ride a horse to Kevit Tanner's farm. By day he hobbled outside to

26

supervise the Indian workers. At last the building was finished. Gabe returned to work for his master and seldom came around the school.

One day a pair of Georgia militiamen rode up to the school. They dismounted, flung open the door, and strolled into the building. Alfie, Julie, and Essie raised their eyes from the children gathered around them. There was something foreboding about the appearance of Georgia soldiers on the soil of the Cherokee Nation. Why had they come? One of the men advanced to Alfie, surveyed him cooly and asked impertinently, "Are you Alfred Eubanks?"

"Yes."

"Do you have a license to be here?"

"A license? What kind of license?"

"According to the law of Georgia, no white persons are permitted to stay on the Cherokee reservation without a license."

Alfie raised his jaw stiffly. "Sir, I'm a missionary to the Cherokees. I have their permission to be here. This is Cherokee territory. These people have their own government. You have no jurisdiction here."

"I'm afraid you're mistaken about that. I've been instructed to warn you that either you secure a license within the next fifteen days or we'll carry you bodily from the area." The two men turned and walked stiffly toward the exit. At the door one of the men turned. "Fifteen days! Failure to comply will mean a jail sentence."

The next day Alfie called a hasty gathering of the men of the neighborhood to discuss the situation. Already many of the Cherokee farmers were alarmed over the rash of forays by Georgia white men. Along the Georgia border many farmers had suffered the loss of horses, cattle, and crops. They welcomed an opportunity to discuss their problems. The schoolroom bustled with noisy palaver. Alfie presented his dilemma. "I must either resist the soldiers and attempt to stay here without a license or submit to their demands and hustle to Milledgeville to obtain a license." A flurry of outcry spread across the assembly. "In a similar case some years ago the Supreme Court of the United States upheld the Cherokee

Nation's right to govern itself without interference from Georgia. But the State defies the court. Little by little, her government and people violate Indian freedom and independence. The government at Washington does nothing to protect Cherokee treaty rights."

The crowd shouted in agitation. Alfie continued, "It is my personal feeling that your approval of my work, along with what I know to be the Lord's sanction, is enough."

"They may sentence you to prison," warned Alfie's friend Shucker.

"I am ready," said Alfie.

Essie was proud of his stance.

"We don't want them to destroy our school as they did our newspaper," warned Wild Pony.

"If you go to buy a license, we'd be surrendering to them," protested Kevit Tanner. "Still, I don't know what else we can do." He shrugged his shoulders in helplessness. The gathering broke up into small clusters as they discussed and argued together. Over all there were feelings of anger and despair as they dispersed.

"Alfie, you can't risk going to prison. I need you," pleaded Julie when Alfie told her about the meeting. In his unsettled heart Alfie knew she was right.

"The militiamen said they would be back in fifteen days. Surely I could wait till just before the time is up to go to Milledgeville. If I'm forced to get a license, I am not going to appear too anxious. I will do it under protest."

Alfie took no action. The state capital was more than a hundred miles away. He made a mental notation that he should review his decision before the middle of November. Many Cherokees were proud that their white missionary friend was defying the officers of Georgia.

Late one night as Essie slept in her attic loft, she had a nightmare about Tom Lovell of Fern Haven. Once before Master Tom had appeared in one of her dreams as a vile seducer who pursued her relentlessly. However, on this particular night Tom was a heinous blackguard who lashed out with a long cat-o-nine-tails across the bloody back of a male slave. Essie tossed in her sleep, her pity for the victim causing her sharp agony. The wretched Negro writhed in pain. Finally when he raised his imploring face, Essie could identify him! It was Gabe Forbes! Essie screamed and awoke suddenly. She sat up and looked about. The room was dark except for an eerie crimson glow at the window. She leaped from her bed to look outside. "Fire," she shrieked. "The school is on fire!"

Essie threw a dress over her head, slipped her feet into a pair of moccasins and fled down the stairs and out the door. As she went, she shouted the alarm to Alfie and Julie. She sped to the school. Before the building hung a bell on a trestle. She tugged the rope wildly. On the frosty air the distress signal pealed loudly, summoning the inhabitants. Men toted sloshing buckets up from the brook behind the school. In a frantic rush, they pitched water at the flames. But the blaze had already reached the roof top. The desperate attempt soon proved hopeless. The exhausted, gasping firefighters were forced to abandon their efforts. Powerless and dejected, too downcast to speak, the onlookers stood watching the leaping, crackling flames. Together Alfie, Julie, and Essie watched at the edge of the darkness. The night air was chilly, but the radiant heat from the fire warmed their faces. The two young women began to sob gently. "You've been in the cold long enough, dear," said Alfie as he led Julie back to their home. "I've got to take good care of you. Can't take any chances."

Essie thought of the children who would come in the morning and view the smoldering ashes. She knew their hearts would be broken. She shivered in the cold as the flames died down to glowing embers, her face held in her hands. A gentle hand touched her neck and she felt a warm coat laid across her shoulders. It was a cotton jacket, and it bore the poignant odor and warmth of its owner, who now stood before her. "Oh, Gabe," she moaned, "What we goin' to do?"

Gabe took her into his arms, comforting her. He paused as though he were contemplating what to say, then he whispered, "We'll build another school."

"But our books, everything, all gone."

"Don't cry, Essie. Things is goin' to be all right."

Later at his home, Alfie said, "I don't see how we can go on with the school. Not until we can raise more capital to rebuild. I think it would be best for us to return to Decatur and stay there until after the baby comes." He moved restlessly to the window where he gazed toward the ruins of the school and then back to Julie who was relaxed in a small rocker.

"You needn't feel that what we do must be because of me. Lately I've been feeling fine, and I'm able to do anything anyone else can do," said Julie with a resolute tilting of her head.

"Of course you can, my dear. Your energy and stamina are a source of encouragement to me. It's just that--well, now I feel we are helpless to accomplish much here. And I know Mother will be fretting and worrying about us."

"Alfie, Cherokee women have been having babies in these hills for centuries. Conditions here are just as favorable for it as any place back home."

"Yes, but you must admit there's more unrest here. Don't forget just two months ago Soaring Hawk, Kevit Tanner's father, was found slain on the road to Ducktown, his horse and wagon stolen. Nobody ever solved that mystery. The school is gone. People are wondering; most of them convinced, that it was deliberately set on fire. Some families have moved west with Major Ridge and Stand Watie. Maybe next summer, when the treaty deadline comes, all the Cherokees will be forced to leave. I don't have much faith in John Ross' appeal to Van Buren and Congress, no more than he found any mercy in Jackson."

At the mention of Cherokee removal, Julie caught her breath. "Dear God, no!" she gasped.

"I think the wisest thing for us to do is to go back home and wait to see what's going to happen," Alfie continued.

"You may be right. But I'm sick with disappointment. We were making such wonderful progress. I was so happy about it," moaned Julie.

Julie's sorrow was resounded and multiplied in Essie's mournful reaction. In the days following the fire, the two women found little to comfort themselves. Alfie was attentive and made earnest attempts to divert Julie's thoughts from the move which he deemed would soon be necessary. They took short walks around the area to visit their Cherokee neighbors. Alfie had intended that the little strolls would cheer Julie, but every meeting with their friends became a depressing farewell.

Essie's morale was alternately lifted up and cast down by the almost daily visits of Gabe Forbes. Every evening when he could get away from his master's farm, he came to be with Essie. Her spirit soared to see him coming down the rutted clay road, and it sank into despair when he released his lover's embrace and vanished into the blackness of the night on his return home.

Julie discussed with Alfie the melancholy which had befallen Essie. "It's doubly hard for her. She loves the children just as much as I do, and she is heartbroken over the thought of leaving Gabe."

"It's about all a man can stand to see two women so unhappy," lamented Alfie.

"Oh, I'll be all right, sweetheart. I'll have you, and soon I'll be busy with the baby. But Essie..." Her voice broke with emotion.

"Confound it, I've never been one to support slavery. Essie really should be free to do what she wants to do. When I was a boy there was a big movement among southerners to set slaves free. I remember going with Papa to the meetings. Now that the North has become so radical, the South has been forced to defend it's ideology, and the abolition movement down here has become non-existent. If it was left up to me I'd set Essie free."

A light beamed in Julie's countenance. "Oh, Alfie, if only we could! I want no part in separating her from Gabe." Essie was overjoyed when they announced their desires to set her free.

"Then Gabe and me can be married! He's done asked me often."

"But Essie, we don't own you," said Alfie. " I can try to persuade Father, but what if he doesn't agree? I think he will, but what if he has other plans? There could be no wedding. Wait! That's it! If you two were married Father would be forced to give in. 'What God hath joined together let no man put asunder.' Papa would never do anything to break up a wedded couple. Essie, he gave you into my custody. I give my consent

31

to your marriage. Now if Kevit Tanner will just agree for Gabe to have a wife, we can plan for a wedding."

Essie's broad smile vanished. She said, "But if I was to be set free, I can't stay in Cherokee country. Free women of color are not allowed to stay here."

"That's right," said Alfie thoughtfully, "You will need to leave with us or...or...you could be sold to Gabe's master. What about that, Essie?"

"I choose Gabe," she said, her big brown eyes steadily reflecting the unwavering certainty of her decission. "If he's a slave, I want to be one too so's I can be with him."

Essie's wedding was a quiet affair. Kevit Tanner, perhaps more sympathetic because he himself had only recently taken a bride, gave his permission for Gabe to have a wife. Kevit gave his word that he intended to purchase Essie if the price was not exorbitant. Alfie assured him that it would not be. The young missionary assumed full responsibility. He would grant Essie permission to marry, he would persuade his father to sell her to Kevit Tanner, and he would perform the wedding ceremony.

Before the fire, Alfie had used the schoolhouse for Sunday worship services. Now, because there was no suitable place, the wedding was held outdoors. The late November sun was warm, but there was a crisp northern breeze, so Alfie conducted the ceremony protected from the wind by the stone chimney left standing at the ruins of the school. Gathered around was a small cluster of Cherokees, their bodies hunched against the wind and their eyes squinted against the brightness of the sun. When the last word was spoken, cheery cries arose from the onlookers. Several came forward with small gifts, tokens of their esteem for Essie.

With Gabe as her husband, a new life opened up for Essie. At last she found peace and fulfillment. Now she had embraced an existence unlike any she had known since childhood, a life filled with deep sustaining love. Before her union with Gabe, she had been a part of a system built around providing comfort and pleasure for white masters and in which she was an lowly servant. Now there was a new relationship, a sphere of her very own in which she was the nucleus and Gabe whirled about her with unbridled love and devotion.

Kevit Tanner paid the Reverend Eubanks the purchase price agreed upon, and Essie became the Indian's slave. Gabe had lived with the other two male slaves in a little bunk house. Now Master Kevit gave the newlyweds the attic room in his own cabin, and Gabe built an outside stairway up to a private entrance. Essie became the house servant and helper to Kevit's wife Spotted Fawn.

Fawn found Essie's companionship more cordial than that which most slaves had with their their mistresses. However, Essie was so happy and accustomed to her station as a servant that she had no desire to take advantage of Fawn's inclination to treat her as an equal. As the months went by Fawn was delighted to learn that Essie had become pregnant. And a few weeks laters, Fawn whispered with a demure smile, "How wonderful it will be that our two babies will be so near the same age. I hope they will be lifelong friends."

"You, too?" Essie exclaimed joyfully, "Oh, Fawn." The two women hugged each other in a sisterly embrace.

Alone in her solitary attic, Essie thought of Gabe's elation over the prospect of becoming a father. Their happiness had been enhanced; their dreams soared. Now all was shattered by the abduction of Gabe. She mourned, fearing that her husband was gone forever. Even more grievous than fear for herself was her concern for Gabe in the hands of cruel men. What abuse might befall him as a slave of a brutish master. She wept bitterly until sleep overtook her weary soul.

In the morning, she resolved that she would--she must--somehow be reunited with Gabe!

Part Two of Chapter III

Early in the morning Kevit arose to make his journey to New Echota. Fawn watched from her bed as he stretched himself to slip out of the lethargy of sleep. How handsome he is, thought Fawn. Already his skin was darkening from the spring sun. His muscles swelled and rippled as he drew on his garments. He dressed in a blue and white checked tunic made from material Fawn had woven on her loom. She also had made the beaded belt, into which he put a wooden-handled knife, sheathed in leather. Around his thick neck was a necklace of cougar teeth and feathers. He wore chocolate colored buckskin leggings and beaded moccasins. He wound a brightly colored turban around his head. Fawn delighted in the strong features of his face, his firm cheeks, his keen eyes overshadowed by the precipitous brow, his well-sculptured nose and lips. Then Fawn detected the tenseness that drew his lips in rancor, the flare of the nostrils, and the hard furrows across the brow and around the eyes. She knew his bitter thoughts and was worried.

"Don't get up yet, unless you want to," said Kevit. "I will take a couple of corn cakes and go on my way." Bending down, he gave her an affectionate embrace, passing his hand tenderly over her abdomen for a quick measurement of the life within her.

In a few minutes Kevit was making his way to New Echota, capital of the Cherokee Nation. He carried a small pouch, fastened to his belt, in which he had placed several corn cakes. It would be nightfall before he reached his destination, allowing for some time to visit with his uncle on the way. He began with a gentle jog trot, which he could continue for a long time. Passing several acquaintances along the way, he exchanged greetings with them. Only when he stopped to rest did he encounter a friend with whom he chose to visit. Spotted Owl laid his bow across his lap as he sat with Kevit on a rock beside the road.

"I have not been fortunate in the hunt today. My arrow fell short of its mark. A big fat buck escaped from me. With my rifle, I could have brought him down."

"I have no gun either," remarked Kevit. "Now I am sorry that I gave it up. General Wool comandeered Cherokeer guns as military weapons. He promised to protect us with the army. Bah! I think it was only a trick to disarm us so that white men could steal our property. How ridiculous for Governor Schley to denounce us as a hostile people who threaten the people of Georgia! We are the ones who are threatened. Why should we surrender our arms to prove our peaceful nature? We have shown our desire for peace." He became inflamed with rage as he related how he had lost his slave workers the day before.

"Some of my neighbors have lost their cattle to wild beasts. If they had not given up their guns, they could have protected their livestock," said Owl. Kevit rose to his feet.

"I must hurry on my way. I hope members of our Council will hear my plea and can bring justice for our people," said Kevit. As he hurried on his way, he called, "May fortune guide your arrow to the big buck!"

It was a beautiful May morning. Sometimes Kevit stopped briefly at a high mountain lookout to survey the misty forest valley below. As he stood on a lofty promontory, he heard the resounding report of a rifle. Then he saw far below a clearing in the forest. Four soldiers were riding on a mountain trail. He fiercely resented the presence of the army men in his beloved Cherokee land. What right had they to be there and to fire their guns, when his friend Spotted Owl could not have a gun to use in his search for food?   As Kevit approached Red Fox Village, he saw an assemblage of men. Even before he was within hearing distance he could tell by their gestures that they were greatly aroused. He drew closer, unobserved by the ranting crowd. "What has happened?" asked Kevit. The men turned solemnly toward Kevit.

"Haven't you heard? The army has rounding up our people and is putting them in stockades. They took Daniel Nun and Sam Bunt and no telling how many more. Soldiers are roaming around the country searching out our people," said Strong Arm, chief spokesman for the group. "Runners have just come to report it."

"Why? What have they done?" asked Kevit.

"Ain't done nothin'," answered the brawny brave. "Washington is tryin' to get them to enroll to move west. They will put every Cherokee in stockades until we all agree to migrate."

"Some outfits have already gone, three or four, I think. Some went again' their will. Was put in wagons or on barges after they was got drunk. Some couldn't do nothin' else. Lost their land and homes when white men came with lottery claims and forced them to leave," said a young radical with a buffalo skin over his shoulders. "I think it's time to fight back."

"Chief Ross lost his home. Beautiful two story house it was with that fine library of--musta' been over a thousand books," bemoaned an old man with faded eyes and thinning white hair. "Many times I walked with Ross over his land. Such fine barns, herds of cattle and sheep! Peacocks strutted over the lawns. We was proud of our chief's wealth and power! Now look, we're brought down like a vanquished people, in our own land--the land the Great Spirit gave us--where we buried our fathers." The old man's lip trembled exposing his snaggy teeth, tears trailing down his brown wrinkled cheeks. With a heavy sigh he continued, "John Ross fought with me under General Jackson at Horseshoe Bend. Now look at us! Jackson puts his boot on our throats. If I had known he would deal with us with such treachery, I would have felled him with my tomahawk then," railed the old warrior. "John Ridge and Stand Watie, fought at Horseshoe Bend too. Those traitors!" The old sage shook his shaggy head sorrowfully." John Ridge and Stand Watie were among the approximate 300 Cherokees who negotaited independently with a United States government agent for the tribe to evacuate the land and move west.

"But fifteen thousand Cherokees have protested the treaty with petitions," remarked Kevit with incredulity. The men shook their heads. They all knew the story. They knew how Chief John Ross had fought for Cherokee rights, how he had withstood Ridge in the Council, how John Walker, a conspirator with Ridge, had been shot between the eyes after the council meeting, and threats of violence plagued the land.

"How can they force us to leave the land that gave us birth?" asked Kevit.

"By the force of the army, that's how," answered Strong Arm.

"I'm on my way to New Echota to report the theft of my three slaves," said Kevit.

"Three slaves," remarked Strong Arm with an air that made Kevit's loss seem trivial. "Chief Ross lost fifty times as many, I would suppose." The realization of the extreme hopelessness of his position struck Kevit like a crash of thunder. His heart sank in deep despair. He started to leave and then turned back to Strong Arm.

"When will the army be rounding up people in my area near Long Swamp?" he asked.

"Who knows?" replied Strong Arm. "When the stockades are ready, I guess. Looks like we'll all be in 'em 'afore long." Overshadowed by gloom, Kevit left the cluster of men. All the frightening reports he had heard in the past now bore heavily on his spirit. This spring, like all others, he had gone about his work as usual, repairing his fences, cleaning out hedge rows, doing his spring planting, preparing to purchase a horse and a few cattle. Always, the threatening danger had been set aside as not being imminent. The New Echota Treaty had provided for a two year period to be used by the Cherokees to conclude their affairs before their migration. Now the two years were past, and Kevit, like his neighbors, was no more ready than before. It should not have had been inconceivable that the Washington government which had broken treaties for fifty years could now perpetrate such an injustice on a peaceful, law-abiding people. Chief John Ross was in Washington presenting the Cherokee plea to the Congress? Kevit had added his signature to the memorial sent from his people to the people of the United States. Runners had carried the petition to all corners of the Cherokee Nation. Surely the appeal of over fifteen thousand people would not be ineffectual! Also, there were rumors that President Van Buren, more lenient than Jackson, had given an additional two years of grace. Perhaps the day of departure would never come. When Kevit came to his uncle's farm, he sensed there was something strange about the place. There were changes unfamiliar to him. Two fine horses raised their heads to watch him from behind a new-built fence around the field beside the house. New chairs sat on the porch, curtains hung at the window. When Kevit rapped on the door, a middle-aged white woman, in a plaid gingham dress, made her appearance. "I came to see Uncle, Silas Tanner," said Kevit. In inscrutable silence, the woman stepped out on the porch. She carried a broom in her hands, which somehow Kevit thought of as a weapon. For a moment she stared at Kevit, then she leaned her broom against the wall and gave a vigorous jerk on a rope hanging from a large bell mounted on the porch post. The clang of the bell summoned the woman's husband, a stern, raw-boned farmer.

The woman announced in a coarse rasping voice, "This Cherokee's lookin' for his Uncle Silas Tanner."

Taking a deep breath, the man put one foot upon the porch step and assumed a deliberate, menacing stance.

"Silas Tanner don't live here no more. We are the new owners by the Georgia lottery. It's legal and the State of Georgia guarantees it," he said sternly.

"Where is he?" asked Kevit.

"He refused to vacate. The Georgia Guard took him off. I think they put him on a barge at Ross' Landing. He's right smart on his way west by now."

"What about his livestock and ..."

"Look," said the man, "we don't have to say nothin' more." Unnoticed by Kevit, the woman had stepped back into the house and now stood tensely gripping a rifle. Nonplussed, Kevit backed away. He turned to go back to his home. He thought of the uncertainty of his future. Actually, now that he thought about it, he could not recollect a time when there had not been threat of danger. He remembered stories about Uncle Silas, who was often implicated in adventures bordering on violence. When Kevit was fifteen summers old, Silas had gone with Major Ridge to raid illegal white settlements on Cherokee land. Soaring Hawk, the boy's father, had remonstrated before the Council against the sending of a band of horsemen to drive out the white trespassers. Having failed to defeat the resolution in the Council,

Soaring Hawk had endeavored to dissuade his younger brother, Silas, from participating in the escapade. Kevit had gone with his father to Major Ridge's plantation and had seen the sixty braves, their faces and bodies marked with ghastly red and black war paint. Stripped to the waist, they wore buckskin trousers, some with buffalo hides and some with head feathers. They carried knives, tomahawks, and rifles. As they raced their horses about the plantation, they rehearsed their bone-rasping shrieks and howls. Kevit had never seen such a terrifying sight.

Their intentions had been only to frighten away the white intruders. They aroused the settlers, gave them time to collect their possessions, and drove them off. Then they burned their houses and barns. This latter action seemed justified to the Cherokee raiders because the buildings were on Indian-owned land, and if they were not destroyed, the occupants would return to them. But as Soaring Hawk had feared, the results proved disasterous to the Cherokee cause. Newspapers blared, "Indian War in Georgia."

In retaliation, white marauders felt justified in starting new aggression against the "savages". Indian property was looted, cattle stolen, and women raped. Georgia passed a law claiming ownership of all Indian territory. In the litigation which followed, the Supreme Court had decided that the State of Georgia could not take the land in violation of the Federal treaty which had granted the land to the Indians in perpetuity.

President Jackson had refused to adhere to the Court's decision. Instead, he vowed that if a fire were set under the Cherokees, when it got hot enough, they would migrate. In effect, Cherokee sovereignty had vanished eight years ago. As Kevit thought about the atrocities against his people, while he journeyed wearily back to his farm, he suddenly became fearful for the safety of Fawn and his little home. Why hadn't he thought of it before? What if the raiders who had stolen his slaves yesterday were to return? In panic, he began to run, racing with all his might! The sun had journeyed past its midday position, halfway down toward the western hills. Kevit knew that he could not reach home before dark. He sprinted with all his might. Finally exhausted, he stopped to rest and to eat the last of his corn cakes. Still gasping for breath, too hurriedly he attempted to eat the dry corn cake. He began to choke. Not far from the road was a little brook. Panting and coughing, he stumbled to the water, kneeled down, scooped the water in his cupped hands and drank. He sloshed the cool water on his face and paused to regain his strength.

Then he heard the sound of a brisk-walking horse. Looking up, he saw a young blond man in the uniform of the Georgia Guard, a young blond man with a large drooping moustache. The militiaman slowed his horse and turned off the road toward Kevit.

"I got lost from my regiment. Is this the way to Long Swamp?" he inquired. The words "Long Swamp" rang with horror for Kevit. Militiamen near his home! His animosity for the soldiers overwhelmed him. Dear God, he thought, what of Fawn and Essie? He could barely speak, he was so distraught. Unable to reason, he gasped. "Yes, that way." The horse moved toward the water, stretching out her neck to drink. The officer dismounted, knelt on one knee, dipping a tin cup into the water and putting it to his lips. Kevit took a quick step behind the officer. With a mighty thrust, he struck his foot onto the man's back giving him a fierce shove into the water. Then, with an agile leap, the Indian sprang into the officer's saddle, dug his heels into the horse's flanks, and gave a shrill yell as he rode off at full speed. Before the guardsman could scramble out of the water and dash after him, Kevit was too far away to be in accurate range of the officer's gun. As he raced the horse toward his home, Kevit's apprehension about his wife's safety filled his thoughts. Not for an instant did he consider his own drastic deed or the consequences of stealing a horse from an officer of the State of Georgia.

It was darkening twilight when he galloped into the yard on the stolen mare. There was no sign of activity around the house. He sprang from the horse and onto the little porch. He pushed against the heavy door. When it did not open, he pounded upon it with his fists. He paused to listen.

A voice inside called, "Go away. Leave us alone." Kevit recognized Fawn's voice. "It's me, your husband," he shouted. The door was unbolted and swung open.

"Thank God, it's you!" exclaimed Fawn in relief. "We saw a party of Georgia soldiers ride by about noon. After that we kept the door bolted. When you rode up, we looked out the window but it was too dark to recognize you. Where did you get that horse?" Kevit laughed, happy to find them safe.

"I took it from a guardsman. I was worried about you; thought someone might harm you. I never should have left you alone."

"You stole that horse?" asked Fawn in amazement.

"Well, yes, I guess I did. I was so anxious to get home. I wasn't thinking clearly."

"Kevit, you must take it back."

"I can't do that. I don't know where to take it, besides..." He broke off, not wanting to tell Fawn how he had attacked the guardsman. He did know, however, that he needed to hide the mare at once. To be caught with the animal bearing the Georgia brand would be a serious crime. The penalty could be prison or death. After relating to Fawn and Essie the details of his trip, Kevit went out to conceal the horse in a dense grove a short distance from the house.

Early the next morning he went out, saddled the mare and rode across the country in the direction of New Echota. His plan was to set the animal free. He dared not go too far; that would mean leaving Fawn and Essie alone again. After a short while he stopped. His conscience pricked him. He wanted to get the animal back to its owner--not so much for the owner's sake, but because he regretted having to turn the horse loose to forage for itself. Even if it were to be all right running wild, some other Indian might attempt to claim the stray animal. It could happen that an innocent person might be caught with it in his possession and be blamed for the crime of stealing it.

At last he was forced to dismiss his wild thoughts. He dismounted, uncinched the saddle and threw it on the ground. Then he stood looking at it. It was a beautiful piece, such fine leather, fine craftmanship. He would love to have such a saddle

42

for himself. He gave it a hard kick with his foot. He hated this business. He took off the bridle, gave the mare a sharp lash with the reins, and with a shout drove her away. He tossed the bridle as far as he could throw. He walked slowly, thoughtfully, angrily back home.

From that time on, Kevit knew he must leave his Cherokee homeland. He had been driven by circumstances to do things he did not want to do. Oh, he could live in constant harassment, even fear. He could fight back against the injustice and oppression. But that could involve loss of something within himself. He had stolen a horse! not out of malicious intent, but out of what he had thought was expedient and necessary. It now seemed to him to be an offense against his better self. Where could such actions lead? He would not allow himself to harbor such festering anger and strife. He longed for the peaceful, tranquil life of which the old folks spoke. There was no longer peace in the Cherokee homeland. The Gospels had been translated into the Cherokee language by his father's friend David Brown. In Kevit's boyish mind a quotation had clung fast, "If a house is divided against itself, that house will not be able to stand." Soaring Hawk had explained to his son that good and evil are at war in every man and in every land. The simple, uncomplicated goodness of his father Kevit held reverently in his memory. How often he had heard his father ask, "Why is the white man, who has had the Bible so long, so unaffected by the lessons it teaches?" Missionaries had brought the gospel of peace, and the Cherokees had welcomed it as little chilren. Now they were now being victimized by their white Christian brothers.

Chapter IV
Stockade Prisoners

It was early in May when Kevit began his preparation to migrate. With his friend Joe White Feather, he began work on building a wagon. He sharpened his axes and put new handles on them. He sold things they could not take and could do without. Fawn dried beef and venison and pickled pork. Kevit worked hard cultivating his corn, beans, pumpkin and squash. Later in the summer his harvest would be placed in the sun to dehydrate. There would be apples, peaches and other fruits, too.

Fawn kept busy at her hand loom making nankeen, cotton cloth. She and Essie made clothes and mended the bedding. They stitched little gowns and moccasins and a complete layette for the new infants to arrive in August and October. Kevit made a cradle of beech wood with a hand-carved leaping pony on the headboard.

On May 28, a group of five army men rode into the yard of the Tanner dwelling. They stopped their horses at the front stoop. Without bothering to dismount, the corporal shouted, "Come out, all you inside. It's the United States Army!"

Fawn and Essie came out the door and stood timidly apprehensive. Kevit left his work behind the house and came around to see what was happening. In solemn declamation, the corporal announced, "By order of General Winfield Scott of the United States Army, all occupants of this property are hereby ordered to vacate and to proceed under supervision of the troops to Fort Buffington. You will be allowed fifteen minutes before you will be obliged to come with us."

"Fifteen minutes!" gasped Fawn. "We were planning to leave in August."

"You will leave now," said the corporal curtly.

"We can't be ready in fifteen minutes," said Kevit.

The corporal gave a nod to one of the soldiers. The man dismounted and prodded Kevit with the barrel of his rifle. "In fifteen minutes, we will join the other Cherokees held by the

45

army out on the highway. Whether you are ready by then or not, Indian, you will go then!"

Fawn cried, "My God, what will we do?"

Essie put her comforting arm around her and said, "Come, we will do what we can."

The two women went into the house and began their frantic activity. Essie spread blankets on the floor and they began to heap things into the middle of them. Into a large canvas which Fawn had begun to make into a wagon cover, they placed cooking utensils and food. Soon the blankets were so full the four corners could not be tied together. Article by article, they furiously evaluated each item to eliminate those things less needed or too burdensome to carry.

Kevit hurriedly gathered his tools. But when he tried to heave them onto his shoulder, he saw that he would have to cut down his load. The reduced bundle of implements he carried to the front of the house, then hastened inside to aid Fawn.

"You have just two minutes more!" called the corporal.

Essie made a hurried trip upstairs to get her clothes and a few personal things. Tearfully, she paused to caress the almost-new shirt she had sewn for Gabe, then turning her face away, she left it hanging on the hook.

Kevit assembled all the baggage on the porch and returned inside to get a little bundle of papers, letters, and momentos and whatever money he had. He placed them into an inside pocket of his vest.

"The time is up. Let's move out," shouted the corporal. The other soldiers dismounted, rifles in hand. They searched the premises, shouting obsenities and banging doors.

Essie grasped the large heavy bag filled with cooking utensils and food. Fawn was in the house frantically pushing the baby cradle to the door. "No, dear, we can't take it," said Kevit.

"Yes, Kevit, yes! We can't leave everything," she sobbed. "Why do they do this to us?"

"I don't know," said Kevit tenderly.

A young soldier burst into the room. "Come on, damn it," he shouted. "The corporal is gettin' mad."

46

On her knees, Fawn clung to the cradle, weeping and wailing. The private nudged her with his rifle.

"She's birthing a baby in five months. She's afraid and upset," explained Kevit.

The young soldier, with a hint of sympathy in his voice, said, "I'm sorry, ma'am. You must go now. You'll have to leave that."

Kevit raised her to her feet and led her to the door. She moaned as she turned for a last look at the room and the little cradle.

"Get those packs and let's go!" urged the corporal harshly.

They picked up the heavy bundles. One bundle of clothes, too hastily tied together, came undone. The young private quickly retied it, but some of the garments fell out on the floor. Fawn struggled to pick up a tiny pair of moccasins, but a stern soldier gave her a shove with his gun. Forlorn and confused, the three set out, with tearful backward glances to their little home, now lost to them forever. The corporal led the procession, followed by Kevit, Fawn, and Essie. They stepped quickly to keep up and stay ahead of the threatening hooves of the army horses behind them.

When the little company reached the main road, they joined a large contingent of troops and Cherokee hostages. As they proceeded northward, a band of white rabble appeared from the south. Fawn, looking back, saw the jubilant raiders turn onto the road to their farm. She knew that all that remained behind would be carted off. She wept once more for her baby's cradle and for the little one to be born in a strange and uncertain land.

Many of the Cherokee people were friends and neighbors to each other, but the doleful situation caused the whole procession to wear a mantle of gloom, accentuated by sobs and moans. Even among friends, there was none able to utter a word of consolation.

The mournful trek to the stockade was wearisome for body and spirit. At frequent intervals other wretched, uprooted families joined the company. Children cried aloud, uncertain about what was happening, frightened by the anguish and distress they saw in their elders. There were a few bitter and vengeful young braves who could find no outlet for their rebellion but to balk and aggravate their captors. Sometimes they sat down on the trail, refusing to continue until the soldiers jabbed them with their bayonets. One youth attempted to escape with a sudden dash toward a wooded ravine. Two army horsemen sprinted in fast pursuit. There were sounds of gunfire. Soon the fugitive returned limping with a bullet wound in the leg. He could continue the journey only with his arm across the shoulder of a comrade. Occasionally, an overburdened traveler stumbled and fell. Often it was necessary to throw off a portion of the baggage in order to keep going. Someone else coming along further back in the train might pick up the discarded treasures.

Most piteous was the plight of the aged whose lives had been well ordered and sedentary. To them the forced march was an unbearable shock. Unable to forsake familiar surroundings and habits and adapt to this new crisis, they were stunned and perplexed. How could the United States Government deal with them so harshly? Surely, the Great White Father in Washington did not know the vast improvements they had made in the Cherokee land. What prosperous farms, what fine cattle, what substantial homes! How could they be expected to forsake such an investment in time and labor, to surrender to the greedy invaders?

Old women wavered and shuffled under heavy burdens. Their faded, watery eyes and dazed countenances reflected their downcast spirits. One elderly woman staggered and fell. Following close after her, Essie dropped her bundle and stepped forward to catch her before she struck the ground. Essie sank down and cradled her head and shoulders in her lap. She quickly untied the scarf from the unconscious woman's throat. Essie pressed her hand over the woman's furrowed cheek. Her leathery skin was cooled with a morbid chill.

Kevit stepped to Essie's side and watched helplessly. "Master Kevit," Essie murmured without raising her eyes to him, "you and Fawn go on. I'll catch up to you." The old woman's son came to attend her. Essie did not heed Kevit's remarks as he moved on with the procession. Nor was she conscious of the

48

action of the huge Cherokee who lifted his mother in his arms and carried her away. Essie had drifted into a melancholy reverie. Once before, years ago, death had nestled in her lap. She was barely ten then.

It was in a dank slave hovel. The last embers were burning out in the charred fireplace. She lay on the little bed cuddled against her sick mother. She shivered under the thin coverlet. When she touched her mother's shoulder, the warmth was drawn from her hand. Essie slipped from the bed. She pressed the covers tightly about her mother's motionless form. The cold earth floor stung her bare feet as she scurried to find wood for the fire. The wood box held only two small sticks. She rushed out the door to where an enormous stack of wood usually stood for the whole plantation to use. Now there was only a barren spot surrounded by traces of drifting snow. She looked desperately for help. The big house was dark and forsaken. Master Wharton was dead, buried two days ago. That morning Essie had watched her father, along with the other slave hands, load old Master's furniture onto wagons.

"We's all goin' t' be sold, sure as shootin'," her father had said, shaking his head. That afternoon men came to take Thad and Chris away. Essie had cried, knowing that her brothers could never again frolic with her and tease her. Mourning the loss of her sons, Essie's mother had taken to her bed. For the past several days she had suffered from a severe cold but had carried on, attempting to conceal her true condition.

"Ever'thing is loaded now," her father had said. "I got t' go on th' wagon t'young Mas'ah Jimmy's house n' unload that furniture. Ah'll see ye all in the maw'nin. Now, sugar chile, take good care o'yer maw. She's got a fierce cold." He bid farewell to his wife and daughter and left. Essie never saw him again.

Why didn't paw see they wasn't no wood, thought Essie. She had not realized that Master Jimmy had thoughtlessly ordered the firewood loaded onto a wagon and hauled to his house.

In desperation she ran back into the cabin. She gasped in horror. Her mother was on the floor entangled in the bed covers.

49

Perhaps in the biting cold she had attempted to rise and put more wood on the fire. Perhaps she had become delirious. When Essie lifted her head onto her lap, the old woman could make no utterance. She was dead!

As Essie sat in the midst of the passing throng of Cherokees, she felt a numbness in her limbs, and the sensation of the heavy lifeless head on her lap still lingered. Slowly she lifted her eyes and saw anew the pathos surrounding her. Then and there she felt they had witnessed her own grief over the death of her black mother. An sense of close kinship to the Cherokee sufferers and sympathy came over her

On a grassy hill, under the watchful eye of a soldier, the dead woman's son dug her grave. As the caravan moved past the little company of mourners, they thought of the ancestoral burial grounds they were leaving behind, left to be forgotten and desecrated.

It was evening when the stockade rose before their sight. The sixteen-foot high walls, built of split logs with sharpened points at the top, stretched before them in vast, abounding dimensions. The massive gates swung open, guarded on either side by mounted army men, rifles in hand with bayonets fixed. Cherokee hearts sank with foreboding and despair as they were herded like cattle into the corral, into the disorder and bustle inside.

There were no partitions for privacy, no cover for protection from rain or summer sun. The incoming prisoners were instructed that they could build their own makeshift shelters. Food, consisting of army rations and salt pork and flour was supplied by the government. At first, water was supplied by a spring, but as the drought of summer came, a large part of the water was supplied in barrels mounted on wagons. Sanitation arrangements were meager. All around wherever the eye could see, Indians were crowded together, enclosed by a high wall and separated from any glimpse of the land they loved.

At first, there was consolation in the knowledge that their imprisonment was temporary. But after the lapse of weary months, some began to fear that their captivity had become permanent. Among the aged and the ill the mistrust became a paranoia. Earlier detachments of captive Cherokees which set out on the westward journey endured such hardships that General Scott suspended the removal of the remaining over 13,000 until autumn. By then, it was hoped, the "sick season" of the cholera epidemic would be over. By mid-July a severe drought came which lasted for about three months.

July passed, August came and with it the completion of Essie's waiting. She lay on her pallet, writhing in spasms of pain, her jaws clamped fast onto a piece of sinew. As her body tensed in labor, her hands grasped a crossbar fastened to two stakes driven into the ground. Fawn soothed her brow with a damp cloth. A rotund Cherokee midwife instructed her to hold fast to the crossbar and raise herself onto her knees in an upright postion for the delivery.

While inside the midwife conducted her ancient ritual of obstetrical art, outside the torrid August sun glared down on the canvas cover. Kevit brought a pail of water, dipped a tree branch into it and sprinkled the tent. A few of the idle curious gathered around. At last, infant cries announced that the ordeal was over, and Fawn came out to say that Essie had brought forth a fine healthy boy.

A few days later the midwife burst into the tent where Essie held her baby. "I heard that baby cry," she said gruffly, "He is hungry." She cupped Essie's breasts in her hands. Her black braids struck against her chubby cheeks as she shook her head. "Humpf! Rotten army food won't make milk to keep your baby alive. You need real food!"

Then gazing at Fawn, who was resting on a pallet, she whispered coarsely, "Fawn, poor girl! To grow little body, the baby must rob mother's body. Fawn needs to have fresh meat. She needs the heart and liver of a deer to make a healthy child. Damn army--it the damn army's fault."

After the granny woman had gone. Essie related to Kevit the midwife's alarming message.

Part Two of Chapter IV

It was the season of the Green Corn Festival, when the corn they had planted would reach fruition. Under happier conditions, they would celebrate this time when Corn Woman gave them harvest fruits for the winter survival. For the past two months there had been little rainfall, a sign, said the old sage who sat outside his lodge smoking his pipe, that the Great Spirit was avenging the injustice done to the rightful dwellers of the land. "Now the government will supply our food," said a young man. "Humpf," grunted the old man. "Salt pork! We grow sick of salt pork." He drew long on his pipe. "We have craving for beef and venison."

"Ben Tukel has offered to buy corn from one of the army officers. Tukel asked for one hundred good ears to give to his friends at the Green Corn Festival," said the young man, wiping the sweat from his brow. Tukel had been the owner of a large plantation with many cattle. His land was about twenty miles east of New Echota, where ten years ago gold had been discovered. Some believed he had buried vessels of gold in his land.

"Tukel can afford to buy corn," said Old Proud Pony. He sat silently smoking and musing. Finally he struck the bowl of his pipe against the palm of his hand to empty it. Feeling the heat of the ashes, he rubbed his hand into the dirt. "If the officer has a kind spirit," he uttered wisely, "perhaps he will let us send forth a hunter to bring deer meat."

"I will gladly volunteer to do that," said the youth eagerly. "I will pursue the deer and not return until I bear him on my shoulder." For a while Old Proud Pony sat looking profoundly wise.

"No, you must not be chosen," he said.

"But I am a skilled hunter. My arrows fly straight," boasted the young brave.

"No," said the old man. "The white man will think you mean to deceive. He will believe you want to escape and hide in the mountains. The army man will not let you go. You are without wife. Kevit Tanner should be sent. He has a wife who grows a baby. He has much reason to come back. Go ask Kevit Tanner to come to me." The young man hurried to Kevit Tanner's lodge to summon him to talk to Old Proud Pony. When Kevit heard the old man's plan, he quickly agreed to leave the fort and hunt for deer. If he succeeded in his quest, he would return with meat to be shared by all those in that area of the stockade. Kevit and Old Proud Pony talked with other men nearby and they agreed to go to the officer of the guards who had seemed friendly to Ben Tukel. They waited until the officer was near the gate all alone. Then they went to him. Old Proud Pony made the appeal. "The expense of feeding the thousands of people in this stockade is big cost. It is not necessary. Cherokee people willing to supply part of their own food by hunting."

The broad shouldered captain sneered, "Of course, you would! You'd go out that gate and ...skedaddle!"

"Skedaddle?" The old man's wrinkled face showed bewilderment.

"Yeah. Gone! Rush to some cave or the mountain wilderness. We'd have to send the cavalry to dig you out."

"I speak the truth. Kevit Tanner has been chosen to go. He will hunt until he brings back deer meat. He is an honorable man; he will return. In his wife grows a new life. He will not forsake his unborn heir."

"I could not desert my wife when she is birthing a child in another moon," explained Kevit.

"Well..." began the captain with a sly smirk, "I would need some payment to guarantee his return. Say...ten dollars."

"Ten dollars!" gasped some of the men. Then the little band of Cherokees withdrew and parleyed together in their native tongue. Finally they returned to Captain Bradshaw. "We pay you ten dollars. Kevit Tanner will be ready to leave here before the sun rises in the east." They gave the officer the ten dollars which they had collected from among themselves.

"I will have a rope over the wall there by that big rock. Your man will have to scale the wall by himself. When he returns, he will tie a white cloth in the chestnut tree beside my office and hide closeby. I will arrange to put him back inside, along with his deer if he downs one," said Captain Bradshaw.

Kevit returned to his lodge. He explained to Fawn what he planned to do. Then he got his bow and arrows, his knife, food, and everything he would need for his early-morning expedition. As he lay on his pallet, sleep did not come to him. He heard the call of the whippoorwill, the screech of the little horned owl, and the bark of the distant coyote. He knew he must succeed. He thought of Fawn's need for food to nourish her growing unborn infant. He must find prey close to the stockade. To carry the fresh meat too far on the hot summer day would make it spoil.

At last he arose, gathered his equipment and crept to the wall. A dog in the camp began to bark just as he climbed to the top of the wall. He placed his deerskin cape over the points of the wall so he could put his weight over it without injury. He pulled the rope up from the inside of the wall, so that in the morning it would not be found and arouse suspicion. He lowered himself on the opposite side. Outside, he took a deep breath, looked furtively about and darted into the woods. Deep into the timber he hurried, taking careful note of his surroundings so that he would have no trouble finding his way back.

When dawn began to break, he searched until he found deer tracks. Silently he followed along, keeping far enough away from the tracks so as not to disturb them or leave his odor. He carefully positioned himself so that the wind would not carry his scent to his prey. He waited. The squirrels in the trees above him ceased their chatter. He remained motionless until they began their noisy activity again. Before long there was the sound of something coming along the trail. Hearing the cracking of a twig, he knew it was a large animal. He readied his bow and arrow. He waited. Then he saw it, a large young buck! The beast proceeded slowly, sniffing the air. Kevit's heart pounded. He dared not miss. The buck threw back his ears and snorted. In a second, he would be gone. Kevit stood up, drew back the bow string and sent the arrow. The buck gave a startled turn of his head, eyes flashing fearfully. With a zip the arrow pierced his heart!

55

Kevit hurried to his prize. Grasping the antlers he dragged the heavy animal onto a little grassy plot. With his sharp knife he skillfully carved into the carcass and removed the entrails. With leather thongs, he tied the two front feet together and the two back feet together. Then he lay down on the grass for a few minutes to relax his tense muscles and calm his overwrought nerves. He had stalked the prey with such determination and felt so heavily the responsibility of his mission that now he rested in jubilant pride. Never had his hunt been so quick and easy! Never had he killed a more handsome buck! Too excited to rest for long, he rose and prepared to carry his booty back to the stockade. His first attempt to heave the carcass to his shoulders nearly threw him off his feet and left him panting. Struggling hard, he lifted it onto a rock ledge. He squatted down next to the ledge and pulled the legs over his shoulders. He was able to keep the dead buck on his back, as he struggled to stand erect. He started out staggering under the animal's weight. "Never has there been a more magnificent buck," he thought. "How proud I will be to have my friends see it. What a blessing the deer meat will be for Fawn!" He uttered his thanks to the spirit of the deer who would give food to his people. With all the exertion he could muster, he tramped back toward the stockade. Once he stumbled and fell down onto one knee, but he did not let the buck fall from his back. As he carried his heavy burden, he tried to identify his surroundings and go back the same way he had come. But now nothing seemed familiar to him. He felt sure he was traveling in the right direction, but what if he were not? He became very weary, but he must go on. Finally, he came to a road. He had not remembered crossing a road early that morning. A feeling of alarm came over him. Still, he assured himself, "I know the stockade is straight ahead of me."

He started to cross the road. At that moment he heard the sound of horse's hooves. Looking down the road he saw a horseman advancing toward him at full speed. Kevit turned to go back among the trees and bushes, to hide until the rider had passed. But he was too slow. He had been seen! The cavalryman followed him into the woods. "Stop," he shouted. "Stop or I'll shoot." Kevit halted, turning to view his pursuer.

His heart sank! There on the steed sat the young blond soldier with the large drooping mustache! The same militiaman from whom Kevit had stolen a horse over two months ago. "Well, well," the officer said with a smirk, "we meet again! You're that rogue who stole my horse. All you redskins are supposed to be in the stockade. It will be my pleasure to put you there," he sneered. "Put that buck on my horse, here behind me," he commanded. "The commissary cook will serve venison tomorrow." Kevit struggled to raise the carcass to the horse's back, but he could not do it until the officer, without dismounting, reached down and gripped the front legs and pulled it up. "Run ahead of me, you thievin' savage," ordered the young officer, "and don't try to get away. I'll shoot to kill!" The soldier's cruel delight in his revenge added to Kevit's dejection.

He had failed his people! Poor Fawn, poor dear Fawn! It was not long until they arrived at the fort. In front of the officers' quarters, an American flag waved gently on its pole. Near the plain wooden building with a narrow porch across the front stood a chestnut tree. Kevit thought of how, if things had been different, he would have tied the white cloth on its branch. "Halt," called the horseman, "we'll go in here. I'm turning you over to the commanding officer. I hope he horsewhips you. But keep your damned mouth shut, you hear?" The officer dismounted and led Kevit up the steps and into the building. He shoved his prisoner ahead of him into a room where an officer sat, his head bowed down as he pored over some papers on his desk. When they had waited momentarily, the officer raised his head to look at them. It was Captain Bradshaw! "Oh, Sergeant Kent, isn't it?" he said in recollection, putting a forefinger to his lips and then pointing to the officer. "You're the man who lost his horse a while back, right? Spooked by a bear, you said. I recall you were thrown into a brook, right? Don't see many bears around anymore. Too much activity, what with the army scouring the countryside and all that. Well, what can I do for you?" Sergeant Kent was a little flustered to have the Indian hear the lie he had reported about the loss of his horse. He had not admitted how he had been humiliated. "I brought in this

57

surly redskin. One o' the stragglers, I guess, or a runaway."
Captain Bradshaw also was a little flustered, not wishing to let it
be known that he had received a bribe to let the Indian out. The
sergeant went on, "He's given me quite a time. I recommend
disciplinary action, sir. Ought to whip a little respect into him,
sir."

"Humm... Gave you trouble, you say?" The captain
scowled. "I'll take care of it, sergeant. Thank you." Glancing
through the doorway he saw the sergeant's horse. "Your horse,
Seargent Kent?" The young man nodded. "And the deer, you
killed it?"

"No, I took it from this red devil. Thought I'd take it to the
commissary."

"Yes, well, I'll take care of it. Put it into that wagon there.
The one there with those water barrels on it," said Captain
Bradshaw. "The army cooks will be glad to get the extra meat."

"Yes, sir," replied the young soldier. "You've done well,
Kent. Don't worry, I'll take care of this prisoner," he said with a
hint of threat in his tone. Captain Bradshaw watched the young
officer transfer the dead buck from his horse onto the wagon and
then ride away. Kevit waited, wondering what would happen to
him. The captain turned to him and asked, "You didn't try to
escape from the sergeant, did you?"

"No, sir," replied Kevit.

"I didn't think so, what with your wife expecting a child
soon." Under his breath he muttered, "Blasted Georgia
Guardsmen, every one o' them wants to be a hero. Pesky as
fleas to the regular army." Then as he glanced toward the door,
he said, "That's some game you downed. Big one." He stroked
his chin, pondering. "I promised your people I'd put you back
into the stockade, and I'm going to do just that." He walked to
the doorway. A teamster was making his way toward the wagon.
"Listen," said Bradshaw, "while I engage that wagoneer in
conversation, you crawl onto the wagon, next to the deer carcass.
Pull the tarpaulin over the barrels so it will hide you. The driver
will move the wagon into the stockade and leave it there. How
you get out without being seen by the army guards is your
problem. Oh," said the captain looking again at the huge buck,

"if anyone asks where you got that buck, tell them it must have jumped over the stockade wall." He laughed heartily. While Bradshaw talked briefly to the driver Kevit crawled onto the wagon and concealed himself under the tarpaulin. Soon he felt the wagon move and jolt along. At the gate the teamster greeted the watchman, who swung the gates open wide to let the wagon through. The team pulled the load of full water barrels to the spot near where a wagon with empty casks stood. The driver halted the draft horses, unhitched them, and rehitched them to the wagon which had been placed there the day before. Then he drove back out of the stockade again. Kevit remained under the tarpaulin while many women came to draw water. The barrels stood on the flat bed of the wagon. Water was conveniently drawn from the spigot at the bottom of each barrel. Kevit lay quietly while the carriers came for their daily water supply. The casks full of cool water, covered by the tarpaulin made a cool place for the fresh deer meat. Still, he knew that he must take the carcass to the women who would prepare it soon. But how? How could he carry it through the stockade unseen? There would not be enough meat for hundreds of people. The prospect of having fresh meat would cause a wild riot among the hungry prisoners. Kevit peeked out from under his cover. The procession of water bearers was deminished now. Then he saw Essie approaching. She was bearing two water pails. Evidently she had left her baby in the care of Fawn. While she drew water from one of the barrels, Kevit whispered, "Essie, it's me, Kevit. I'm hiding under the tarpaulin. I have a buck I shot, but I can't figure out how to get it to our section of the camp without being seen. I can't wait till dark."

"Let me go get help." whispered Essie. "But how can they help," whispered Kevit. "We'll think of a way," said Essie. "While I'm gone you quarter the deer so it will be easy to carry." She hurried away carrying her full buckets. Back at her tent Essie called together Proud Pony and some of the men who knew of the venture. "Kevit has killed a buck," she said. "It is hidden on the water wagon. It would be unwise for him to carry it through the stockade. The guards would be curious and give trouble, and the people would be excited. There is not enough meat for everyone. We must secretly move the carcass." Essie directed that a group of young men should go to the wagon. There they would begin telling stories and jesting. Some would become rowdy and engage in wrestling. This would keep all the women away. While this was going on, from under the tarpaulin Kevit would hand out the quarters of deer carcass. Then four men could each carry a piece, shielded from people's eyes by the surrounding band of friends.

Essie's plan worked. The meat was brought to the women, who began to dress and prepare it. They had begun their preparation of other food for the festival. Out of their limited larder, they would bake delicious breads and simmer savory porridge. Many families had been forced away from their homes at bayonet point, with no opportunity to gather provisions. For others the feasting would deplete the last of their supplies, leaving them to rely hereafter completely on the meager and unpalatable army food. But it would be a time of sharing, a time when all would celebrate. In the vast stockade, confining within its walls several thousand Cherokee people, the few dwelling near Kevit Tanner's lodge were especially favored. The savory scent of cooking venison and the steaming ears of corn furnished by Ben Tukel made it a festive time. Shut up and denied access to the land they loved, they knew the seed they had planted would yield a harvest, not to them, but to strangers. Still, in this time of celebration of the wonderful miracle of reproduction, the earth had given them a son, Essie's brown-skinned boy. They gathered around to view him with wide-eyed fascination and awe. Born as he was in captivity, he shared his fortunes with them, a little brother by association. After the feast, the men sat in a circle around a space as large as their crowded quarters could afford, and there the braves performed their Green Corn Dance to the accompaniment of drums, gourd and turtle-shell rattles, and flutes. The happy festival was too soon ended and the tedious days of waiting returned. The feast had lifted Fawn's spirits and gave her physical strength. Essie's breasts swelled to offer to her son contented bliss.

Chapter V
Gabe--a prisoner

For two days Essie's husband had ridden with the bandits across the Georgia countryside till they came to a secluded plantation nestled in the wooded hills. There they halted. It was a dismal place, poorly kept, and lacking in any signs of prosperity. The outlaw leader, Clem Bassop, was the owner of the property. There the men threw Gabe into a little shed and securely bolted the door on the outside. The victim had struggled and given as much resistance as he could in the face of armed bandits. He glanced about the room and hovered at the door as the men outside talked preparitory to their leaving. From their conversation he surmised that this would now be his home. The other two slaves were to be the property of two of the other outlaws. When all was quiet and apparently all the men had left, Gabe looked more closely about him, scanning the room, testing the sturdiness of the walls with his fists, hoping to find a means of escape. In addition to the door there was only one small opening to the outside--it was hardly a window, only a spot where a narrow plank did not go all the way to the ceiling. All around, the walls were secure, built of thick strong lumber and heavily cross-braced. The floor was solid and rugged. Overhead, the timbers showed no signs of weakness. Gabe leaped up and grasped one of the rafters and swung his feet up to stomp them against the roof boards. Then in exhaustion he dropped to the floor and threw himself hopelessly onto the bed. There was a repugnant stench in the bedding. How long would he be forced to live in such a dour environment? He must find a way to return to Essie and his Indian master. For days Gabe was a forlorn prisoner. He saw no one. He longed for somebody to come and take him from the dismal shed and drive him to labor in the fields. To be goaded to hard labor would be better than the isolated nothingness he was enduring.

Every morning he welcomed the sound of an attendant who came to open a tiny trap door located in the wall at floor level and to shove in a bowl of what was usually insipid gruel or pone and gravy. All Gabe could discern about the man was that his hands were large and black, his impaired speech was a series of unintelligible grunts and nasal mutterings. Any attempt to converse with him was useless. Every day he carried away the chamber pot to empty it and returned it along with a small pitcher of water for drinking. At last--Gabe calculated five days had elapsed--the oaf brought an extra pail of water and a large piece of cloth. He made doltish, muddled sounds which Gabe took to mean "wash" and "clean". After waiting for so long a time to bathe, Gabe was refreshed. Later that day Gabe heard voices. There seemed to be two or more men and a woman outside his door. Finally, he hoped, he was to be released from his prison!

"Unbolt the door, Slobber," the coarse voice of Clem Bassop was ordering, "Keep a tight grip on thet blacksnake. If he try to get away, lay it on 'im hard. Draw blood! He air a right mulish nigger, 'pears like." The brutish giant, Slobber, who daily brought rations to Gabe, was black as asphalt with vile facial features. Most repulsive was his floppy tongue which hung over his lower lip like a piece of fresh liver, dripping saliva. Long ago a previous master had clipped his speech organ as a punishment for his telling lies. His talking was hindered so as to make his utterances like those of one mentally deficient. He was, however, sinisterly clever, capitalizing often on his appearance of stupidity to achieve his own ends. The woman with the two men was a black wench, morosely submissive and indifferent to her plight. She had long ago yielded all hope and all zest for life. Though she was still young--not more than thirty--the youthful beauty, she had once possessed, had faded under a disposition of despair. Still, there was a gentle pleasantness about her. As she stood beside Clem on the small stoop, he scowled at her. "I told ye to wash yerself up. Ye stink from nigger musk--worse'n a rotten fish." "I wash, mas'ah, like you said."

"Then why ye stink so?" he snarled. "This dress, mas'ah. It's dirty. Only got one dress. You don' give me no time to wash it." The gruff boss seized the garment at the neck and gave it a sharp jerk. The sleveless sheath fell to the floor, and she stood before him naked.

When the heavy door was flung open Gabe was almost blinded by the effulgence of sunlight that radiated about the fuzzy outline of the nude black woman. She stood covering her nakedness with her arms. The vision momentarily stunned and entranced Gabe. She was shoved through the opening and the door was slammed shut. He heard the heavy bolt shoved into its latch. "W-Why're you here?" he stuttered moments later. "Mas'ah make me come. It's time I has me a sucker babe, he say." "What you mean by that?" asked Gabe with a dawning suspicion that he knew the answer. "This here a brood farm. Mas'ah grow niggers to sell. Don' you know thet?"

"He means for me...! No! I won't do it. I ain't no studhorse!"

"You sure is now," the woman replied cooly.

"We'll see. What's your name?" "Nelda."

"Nelda, there's a big rag I used to dry myself with, wrap yourself in it. It ain't good you should be standing there naked. Don't be scared. I ain't goin' to hurt you. I'm just tryin' to find out how to get out o' this place. Perhaps you can help me."

The woman crept to the cloth, seized it, and wrapped it around herself. "Ain't no way for to 'scape out o' here, lessen you dies. Th' buck what live in this shed afore, he die two weeks ago. I'm glad he dead. He mean. He sire two o' my chil'ens. I'm glad he dead." She sat on the edge of the bed and began to weep. She refused--or was unable to speak any more. Gabe respected her soft moaning and did not attempt to talk further to her. He sat on the floor and mused over his own plight, thinking of how he must return to Essie.

When night came he slipped the soiled pillow from the slumbering Nelda and placed it on the floor where he had decided to sleep. The next morning Nelda appeared to be still in a sorrowful mood. Neither of them felt like talking.

After Slobber poked two bowls of food and a pitcher of water through the wall and they had eaten, the solemn woman looked steadily at Gabe and asked, "Why you not pesters me like the other bucks does? You sick or sumpin'?"

"I'm married. I belongs to my wife."

"Who say you married? 'Round here ain't nobody married. Clem mix us up an' say who gwin' to mate--only thing, it got to be often, that all. Gotter keep them sucker babes comin'. You Clem's nigger now. Ain't no marryin' to it. All us nigger wenches done watch when you was brung in here. Most looks for'ard to matin' up with yo. Me, I don'. I's made too many sucker babes a'ready. I's sick of it."

"I ain't cravin' to mate up with you, Nelda, even do you want it. Like I done said, I'm married."

"Might jes' as soon forget thet. Now you goin' to have lots of wenches at this here place.

What do marryin' mean anyhow? It not for niggers, jes' white folks. Don't no hound dawg marry no bitches. They jest litters, like us niggers does."

Gabe shook his head. "Dogs ain't got no judgment of what is right and what is wrong. I been oath-pledged to Essie--she's my wife. I made a promise to mate up with nobody except her long's we both live. I promise it in a Christian weddin'."

"You headin' for a heap o' trouble from Mas'ah Clem. I reckon we's goin' to be cooped up here till I shows swellin' in th' belly. Lordy, I don' want to no more. No more!" Her voice broke with emotion. She bowed low, struggling to bring the ragged cloth to her tearful face while, at the same time keeping herself modestly covered. She sobbed bitterly.

Though not understanding her distress, Gabe felt sympathy for her. From his place seated on the floor he moved to sit beside her on the edge of the bed. "What's wrong?" he asked. He started to place his hand on her shoulder, then withdrew, realizing that he must avoid all implication of physical advances. "Why do you cry so much? I ain't goin' hurt you." She drew back and gazed at him with tearful, questioning eyes.

"Why--why you don't rape me? Slap me an' smash me like I's used to. Why you don' go ahead an' get your pleasure. Goin' to have to sometime. Mas'ah Clem ain't goin' to have it no other way."

"I done told you I ain't goin' to do it!" he affirmed sternly. "I want to know what makes you cry like that. I ain't goin' to hit

64

you. Ain't got no cause to. We're going to be friends, if you lets it. Can't have children. Understand? Can't have." Nelda continued to sob and shake with emotion. "Tell me, now, what you moanin' about? Maybe I can help."

"I allus this way when my chil'ens is took from me. I jes' lost my li'l Pug. Sold to a nasty dealer. Poor baby, he cry an' bawl till he gone out o' sight. Most breaks my heart to think 'bout it. I thought he wus mine forever--seein's how he was Mas'sa Clem's chile. How can he do sech a thing? His own boy! Mas'ah say he got human blood. Ain't no good 'cos he got human blood. When he grow up, it make him rebellious--human blood do. Oh, Lordy!" she moaned, "Po Pug! Po Pug."

Gabe was confounded by her words. Gabe, himself, had nearly always been well treated. Till now he had been owned by kind, Christian masters. Gabe recalled painfully, there was a short time when his family had come temporarily under the subjection of a brutal overseer. Gabe remembered how the boss had taken his father from his family and had attempted to mate him with another black woman. Gabe's father had refused to live with the strange woman and had fought his boss-man. Such a command had never been given to the father before and to comply was against his moral conviction. Gabe had watched while the overseer had strung his father up by the heels and had beaten him until the oozing blood covered his nude body. His father did not live long after that. Gabe had been too young to understand the causes of his father's death, but his sorrowing mother had instilled in him the heroism of his virtuous father. How, now, could Gabe do less than to resist as his father had done? "That Clem he ain't my master," said Gabe. "He's a devil. We gotta stand up against him. I plan to fight him all the way. I ain't no animal. Clem, he's a animal, bad one. My wife always said, 'God created of one blood all the nations of the world.' That's what she said, an' she learned it from a preacher. It's in the Bible." Gabe looked with compassion at the poor woman beside him and resolved that he would help her any way he could. After several days went by, Master Clem, Slobber, and another big white fellow came to put leg irons on Gabe. The black prisoner struggled, but the three of them were too much for him. Slobber threw Gabe face down upon the bed. He held the victim's right arm drawn back painfully behind him while Slobber's knee bore down on the small of Gabe's back and left arm. The other men fastened irons onto Gabe's legs. When they were finished, the fettered negro was led outside to chop firewood. From that time onward Gabe was given tasks to do outside. Occasionally a hulking black slave woman came to examine Nelda to find out if she had been "knocked up" yet. When she found no signs of pregnancy, Nelda was required to spend more nights in the shed with Gabe. In the daytime she was taken to scrub clothes at the laundry tubs in the yard. When no act of mating was detected, Slobber spent long hours outside the shed, spying on the couple inside. Day and night he watched and listened at the tiny opening in the wall. Finally he and Clem came to take Gabe out to the whipping post where they severely flogged him. Clem ranted severe cursings and obsenities at the poor slave. He made threats of how he would castrate or use hot irons on Gabe's private parts if he did not perform. Gabe suffered with inscrutable silence, which angered Clem the more. When the beaten slave was thrown into the shed, he fell to the floor, weak and exhausted. Nelda did what she could to bathe and soothe his wounds.

Later at the end of another workday, when Gabe was shoved into the shanty, he found Nelda lying on the bed and weeping. At once he recognized that she too had been scourged. Since she had begun working in the laundry yard, she had donned a Mother Hubbard. "Take off your dress. Let me look at you," ordered Gabe. She raised off the bed. With cries of anguish as the cloth brushed across her raw flesh, she let her dress fall off her shoulders.

"Dear God!" exclaimed Gabe. "How could they do this to you!" He took the pitcher of water and a bit of cloth and attempted to soothe her wounds. "Ole Bess, she run her hand over me an' say I ain't knocked up yet. She tell Mas'ah Clem it my fault I ain't knocked. She say she done hear me say I don' want no more sucker babes," Nelda sobbed.

Her words wrenched Gabe's heart. "Dear God, they had no right to do it! Ain't your fault! I'll make 'em pay for this!"

Still, there was no way he could avenge the master's cruelty. Gabe had sworn to himself and to his Creator that he would die before he would be unfaithful to Essie, but he had not counted on this! God in Heaven, what was he to do? He nursed Nelda's wounds as she had nursed his. He felt tender sympathy for her. In this cage where they had nothing, only despair and longing, how necessary was their tenderness to each other!

Days later when he exanmined her wounds, Nelda turned to him, placed her hand on his shoulder, and said, "I's ready now, Gabe. I reckon it a right thing now. Don't know nothin 'bout love. Ain't never had nobody to love me. I gots a funny feelin' 'bout you, Gabe. Let's don't fight agin' 'em no more." Gabe pushed her away. He had not yet resolved his moral dilemma. His feelings were muddled. Not till he could blot from his mind and heart all feeling and there was left only numbness and emptyness, could he take to Nelda's bed and arms. In the vacant shed and the light of dawn he often hated himself and wept in secret, pleading for Essie's forgiveness. When, months later, he learned that the Cherokees had been driven west, his despair deepened. He had fallen into an intolerable hell!

Chapter VI
On the Trail of Tears

Essie and Fawn stood on a slope of the mountain surveying the area of Rattlesnake Springs. The river wound snake-like across the landscape. Before them rose an assemblage of wagons, men on horseback, and swarms of foot travelers. As far as their eyes could see there was animated, restless activity. Hundreds of teams of horse- and oxen-drawn wagons, hundreds of jittery horses and riders made ready to move. It was October, the time of the migration. As Essie viewed the flurry of activity, her heart went out to those who were forced to bid farewell to sick friends or relatives who could not make the trip and would be left behind. Essie clutched close to her breast her infant son. In all the world of people and things, she held nestled in her arms her only precious possession. She thought of Gabe who was so far from her. Her journey with the Indian people would widen the distance between them. Still she had no choice. She must go, driven as they were driven. How she would have loved to flee, to rush out in search of her man! But for a black slave there was no possibility of traveling. She would be fair game for any rapscallion. Besides, she bore true affection for her Cherokee owners. Her lot was cast with them. She owned no land. No home had ever really been her own. Her attachmemts had never been to things or places. Instead, she had eagerly reached out to take hold of love and friendship. The short months of her life with Gabe seemed to her a wonderful fantasy. She often dwelt upon that fantasy, clinging to it as though it were a very fragile thing. Essie feared that her memory would fade leaving her mind barren even as her life was barren of his presence. She pulled back the corner of the blanket which covered her baby's face and kissed him on the forehead. Here was something of Gabe she held in her arms. It was all she had.

Fawn, standing beside the mulatto slave, turned to look southward toward her homeland. Dark smoke arose on the horizon. She knew that even the temporary shelters, where they had waited for the time of their departure, were going up in leaping flames. Her thoughts were of the beautiful hills, the little farm where she had been so happy. She loved the black soil, the walls of her humble house, the labor which she gave to make it a home. Most of all she loved Kevit's devotion to his farm. Now it was gone! The whole world was insecure and shaken! Somewhere in the hosts of those who were prepared to migrate she had a father and a brother. They had lost all their possessions too. Fawn feared the loss. Still, in her grief, she had Kevit, and she had beneath her breast her unborn child.

Kevit came to announce that he had found a wagon in which they could ride. They must hurry, he said, before someone else took the space. He had tried, in vain, to buy a horse from the profiteering traders who swarmed about the stockade to take advantage of the redman's needs. The animals brought higher prices than Kevit could afford. He would walk beside the wagon which carried Fawn and Essie with her baby. In the same wagon rode a frail old woman suffering from asthma. Baggage, belonging to families who walked or rode horseback, filled the forward part of the wagon. The three women had barely enough room to sit in a half reclining position. Fawn was permitted to ride because of the advanced stage of her pregnancy, Essie because of the frailty of her month-old infant and her need to help Fawn. Other women, with robust children barely able to toddle, were obliged to carry their offspring strapped to their backs.

With solemn tones Chief John Ross offered prayer, a bugle sounded, and the first wagon rolled out behind the cavalry. Most of the Indian people had not had the opportunity to turn their possessions into cash. They had been cruelly dragged from their fields and homes. Now many began their eight hundred-mile journey destitute of heavy coats, blankets or shoes. Six hundred forty-five wagons were to carry the supplies and hay and feed for the horses. There were five thousand horses carrying riders. Most of the thirteen thousand Cherokees walked. They were divided into contingents of about one thousand each. Army soldiers rode along the line and a cavalry unit was to follow each group.

The days inside the wagon were long and wearisome for Fawn and Essie. At evening they climbed out to stretch and move about. Around them, those who walked bivouacked under the open sky. During mild October weather this was not a great discomfort. Soon the dreaded winter would come, and the shortage of blankets and protection would cause extreme hardship.

On the twenty-second of October a black-haired son was born to Fawn. The name given the new-born child was Arley. The birth took place in the wagon, just as several other births had occurred since the caravan left Cherokee country. Midwives scurried here and there as they were summoned. The wagon carrying Fawn pulled out of the line only briefly to allow for the infant to arrive, then hurried to keep up with the procession.

Three weeks later, on a pleasantly warm afternoon, the caravan haulted at a great meadow. It was the same spot where other army-driven exiles had stopped before them. As soon as the wagons stopped, there was an explosion of activity. Men unharnessed the horses, mules and oxen and led them to a crude corral. Others pitched hay over the fences. Women and boys scurried about in search of scraps of wood to fuel bonfires. Men made repairs on wagons, wagon covers and harness. Women washed garments and bedding and hung them on ropes between the wagons, hoping they would be dry by morning. With wet cloths, mothers wiped the dust from their tired, fidgety children. All was done in a cursory fashion in a race to accomplish everything before darkness descended. Cooking was a routine and uninspired chore, the food insipid corn mush, or corn or wheat cakes, and the inevitable salt pork.

As the caravan stopped, Kevit thrust his head through the curtains of the wagon and announced, "I think I saw a pumpkin in a field we just passed. I'm going to run back to get it. We can cook it for supper." Fawn and Essie immediately set about to wash and feed their babies. Fawn spread a blanket on the grass and the little ones were laid upon it. While Essie prepared to warm a pan of water, Fawn sat down to play and coo to them. What a relief it was not to be jostled and swayed in the motion of travel! The autumn air was still, and so delightful was her pleasure with the babies that Fawn was completely oblivious of the bustle and noise around her.

Suddenly, from behind her came a sound so strange and so close to her as to jolt and startle her. Turning, she saw a huge black dog staggering toward her! He snarled and snapped the air, growling and drooling froth!

"Mad dog!" a woman nearby screamed.

The glassy-eyed beast seemed not to notice Fawn as she recoiled in horror. His unsteady, weaving form moved toward the babies on the blanket! With a shriek, Fawn threw herself forward, grasping both infants in her arms. Essie, close by, seized the pail of water hanging over the fire and threw it onto the terrible beast. With a guttural cry the dog fell back, turned away, fearful of the water. Essie grasped an ax fastened to the outside of the wagon bed. She lunged toward the diseased animal. As it turned toward her, she struck a fierce blow onto the mongrel's neck! It staggered sideways and fell, with a gruff rattle, snapping, and struggling to return to its feet. Essie raised the ax, swung it again into the rabid beast's head. With a death tremor, the canine quivered and fell dead.

Essie dropped the ax, raised a trembling hand to her brow. She stood unsteady and exhausted. Then she turned, put her arms around Fawn who stood stunned, holding the babies tight against her breast. "You saved them! Fawn, you saved them both!" exclaimed Essie. "Thank God, you saved them!"

Essie drew back suddenly, a look of horror on her face. On Fawn's upper arm a stream of blood flowed from torn flesh! "No, dear God, no!" Essie cried. She took the babies from Fawn and thrust them into the wagon.

Cries of "Mad dog" had brought crowds of people bearing axes and clubs. "The dog is dead," others shouted with jubilation. "Look," someone cried, "she's been bitten." A hush came over the throng, and the whispered word spread, "Fawn's been bit by the mad dog!"

While others drew away from Fawn in fright, William Ford, the missionary, came forward, called for soap and water, bathed Fawn's wound and bandaged it. Glowing with satisfaction, Kevit arrived carrying a small pumpkin. His prize would cook into a special treat. Before he could announce his good fortune, he sensed trouble. At the rear of the wagon, Essie stood comforting Fawn. His wife appeared stunned.

"What's wrong?" he asked when he saw their worried faces.

"Fawn's been bit by a dog," said Essie.

Just as Essie was beginning to tell about the incident, Joe Blair, a leader among the Cherokee group, and Big Mullen, a medically trained Indian, came to ask questions. "We want to talk to you about the mad dog," said Big Mullen.

"Mad dog?" gasped Kevit.

"If the animal was rabid, it will sure be passed on to anyone it bit," said Big Mullen.

Fawn began to cry.

"Get into the wagon, dear, and rest," said Kevit. "I'll talk to the men." When he had led the men out of hearing distance of the wagon, Kevit asked, "What can we do?"

"Well," said Mullen, "it seems the dog was mad, all right, from the way it looks there and what people have said. It should be buried at once. As for your wife, we could cauterize the wound, but I doubt that it will do any good."

"Cauterize? What's that?" asked Kevit.

"That means we sear the wound with a hot iron to kill the poison. We need to do it at once. Bring a stove poker or a long metal spoon, or somethin' like that. Hurry. Stoke up the fire. I want the iron to be red hot."

Kevit, Essie, and William Ford held Fawn still, while Big Mullen held the hot poker on the wounded arm. The burned flesh smoked and gave off a sickening smell. Fawn screamed in pain. Then William Ford prayed for her recovery.

When it was over, the men talked softly outside the wagon. "Most likely your wife will develop hydrophobia in spite of our cauterization. I'm afraid she'll be lost," said Big Mullen solemnly. "I'm sorry, but there's nothing more I can do. Symptoms will probably develop in a month or six weeks. The bite is worse because it is on the upper arm, and the poison will travel to the brain quicker."

"Oh, my God," sobbed Kevit.

73

"You probably will have to take her out of the train," said Joe Blair. "We can't have her endangering the rest of the group."

During the dreadful days that followed, the wagon bearing Fawn and Essie was held back to the last position of the line, next to the contingent of army horsemen which followed the detachment. A kind of quarantine of the wagon was practiced. The old asthmatic woman, Maggie, who had been riding with them, sought passage on another wagon. Essie, however, firmly refused to leave Fawn's side. The tiny Cherokee infant was not allowed to nurse his mother, for fear he would get the poison from her, instead Essie nursed Fawn's son as well as her own. Although Fawn approved of this--she had, in fact, suggested it herself--still it hurt her not to be able to draw her son to her breast. When baby Arley cried, her breasts filled and swelled painfully. Fawn wondered if this was the beginning of the forfeiture of her motherhood and would end in her surrender of life itself. Kevit demonstrated his love for her as passionately as ever. Sometimes, Fawn, in her doubt and confusion, wondered if his devotion to her was forced and tempered by pathetic sympathy for her. When he could, Kevit brought her and Essie special rations or whatever morsels he could pilfer or forage.

Every few days Joe Blair and Big Mullen came to inquire about Fawn. Sometimes Big Mullen put his hands on Fawn's head and looked deeply into her eyes, asking many questions. Two weeks after Fawn's injury, the two men accosted Kevit on the trail. "The people are afraid," they said. "'Till now we have been able to pacify them, but now we feel Fawn must be taken away. Everyone is afraid of her."

"What's to be afraid of? She's as normal as ever," said Kevit.

"But she won't be for long, I'm afraid," said Big Mullen. "I want to make arrangements for you to take her to an infirmary. There's one in the next town. She'd get good care there."

"I couldn't leave her in a place like that," said Kevit. "What will I do about our baby? He's only a month old. Besides, how much will it cost? We ain't got much money. I refuse to put her in an infirmary," cried Kevit angrily.

Knowing that further discussion would be futile, Joe Blair and Big Mullen turned away silently. They realized in their hearts that they would need to take action, by force if necessary. Later a group of Indian leaders conferred to consider what should be done about the case of Fawn Tanner.

"For the sake of our people we must send her away," said an old chief, "even if her husband puts up a fight."

"Is there any possibility that she could recover?" asked John Buckmaster.

"In my experience," said Big Mullen, "I have never known of a case where a person was bitten by a rabid animal and recovered. An old woman has given me a 'mad stone'. I have yet to take it to Fawn Tanner." He pulled a small stone about twice the size of a walnut from his pocket. "The woman's son found it in the stomach of a deer he killed. But we don't know if the stone has any power or not because it has never been used."

"I think Fawn should be given the stone. Still there is possibility of danger. I have heard that the end comes with great terror," said Ben.

"Not always. Sometimes it develops into what we call dumb rabies. The sick person becomes very quiet and in a kind of stupor. Then again in some cases the person becomes violent and wild. Has to be strapped down. That kind of death is terrible," explained Big Mullen.

"Two of the army fellows asked me about it yesterday," said Joe Blair. "The whole army is upset about having a mad person on the trail. If we need army help, they'll give it. In fact, we can't take the woman anywhere without the army's permission. They will insist on sending an escort to make sure none of us escape."

Big Mullen unfolded a newspaper. "Look here," he said, "here's a notice in this here paper. 'Dr. Maurice Raffet offers expert medical service and nursing care, by day or week. Reasonable rates. Beautiful setting at Shady Lawn Infirmary.'"

"But how can we tear her away from her husband?" asked John Buckmaster.

"We'll have to wait until he's away and his wife's alone."

It was agreed that Fawn should be abducted and delivered over to Dr. Raffet. Four men, along with a delegation of two cavalry men, watched for their opportunity. One evening Kevit Tanner went to help a friend lift a wagon with a broken wheel. The men gathered at Fawn's wagon. "Mrs. Tanner," called Sergeant Dwiggins, "we want to talk with you. We want you to see Dr. Raffet. He ain't far from here."

Fawn put her head through the canvas at the rear of the wagon. Her face was timid and anxious.

"We want Dr. Raffet to treat you. It's for your own good, ma'am. We think you ought t'go now."

"Now? I can't go now," said Fawn. "Kevit ain't here. I can't go without him."

The sergeant's voice grew sterner. "It's all right, ma'am. He can come to you as soon as possible, that is if, you ain't back right away."

Fawn's gaze passed from one man to another, six faces resolute and grave. Sergeant Dwiggins gripped her arm firmly, forcing her to step over the tailgate and down to the ground. Essie followed her out of the vehicle.

Fawn turned to her mulatto companion, threw her arms around her and sobbed, "I don't want to go."

Essie embraced her. "I know, honey," she whispered. "Wish I could go in your place. I wish it was me instead of you."

The men pulled them apart.

"I want to see my baby," cried Fawn. Essie climbed back into the wagon and returned with the Indian infant. The two men holding Fawn released her. They stood by her as she took the baby into her arms. She held the little bundle close to her face and kissed him again and again. The men resumed their hold of her arms. "Take care of my baby, Essie," she wailed tearfully, handing him back to the slave woman. "Promise me, you'll take care of him."

"I promise. You are like a sister to me, honey. I'll love your baby and guard him till you come back," said Essie. It was a solemn commitment. A tear glistened on her brown cheek.

Sergeant Dwiggins decided that he, himself, should accompany two of the Cherokee men on their journey to seek Dr. Raffet. Stunned and submissive, Fawn followed on a tired, spavined old mare. A lead rope was tied to the sergeant's saddle. At times Fawn felt rebelliously reluctant to submit. She contemplated throwing herself from the horse and making a dash to freedom. But where would she go? Were the men really taking her to a doctor who would treat her? Was any help possible? What would her beloved husband do when he found her gone? Perhaps, she speculated, even hopefully, he would accept her absence and realize that this was the best way. The painful, agonizing death she had stoically come to accept would only bring him anguish and sorrow. She prayed that he would never find her. She wept. With the darkness covering all around her she closed her eyes in despair, shutting out all hope for the future.

The migration of thousands of Indians through the land had alarmed all the farmers. They were not sure what the meaning of it was. They kept their rifles loaded and ready. Three times the little band halted at wayside homesteads to inquire directions to Shady Lawn Infirmary. The sound of horses and the sergeant's outcry roused wary householders who cracked a door or raised a window. Directions were gruffly bawled out in curt, meager terms.

It was nearly midnight when they arrived at the large two-storied establishment. A huge sign, barely visible in the light of the waning moon, read: "Shady Lawn Infirmary. Dr. Maurice Raffet, proprietor." Sergeant Dwiggins stepped up on the porch. His hard rapping on the door brought a sturdy housekeeper who held her lamp high and scowled at the visitors. "It's midnight. Dr. Raffet is asleep. "Come back in the morning," said the woman gruffly. She was about to reclose the door.

"We can't do that," said Sergeant Dwiggins. "Wake the doctor. It's an emergency."

"Well...," she growled, arms akimbo, "he ain't goin' to like it. Come on in. Wait here." She withdrew and soon returned, followed by a diminutive man in robe and slippers. He walked with a prissy strut, attempting to uphold his dignity and offset his disheveled attire. He brushed over his hair with his hand, in a self-conscious, exasperated gesture.

"What's this all about?" he asked.

"We have a Cherokee woman outside who needs medical confinement. I am Sergeant Dwiggins. I'm with the army escort that's movin' the Indians into Oklahoma Territory. We want to leave this squaw with you."

"A Indian woman?" he mumbled with repugnance. "What's her problem?"

"She was bit by a mad dog."

"A mad dog!" gasped the doctor. "No. No, I couldn't keep a Cherokee woman here. We have a very fastidious clientele. She wouldn't fit in here."

"But you gotta take her. She can't stay with her people. Surely you can provide for her somehow. The Army will pay you," said Dwiggins.

"Well...maybe I could put her in the attic. How long ago did the dog attack her? I need to know how long she'll need the room," asked the doctor.

"She was bit on the arm about two weeks ago."

"Only two weeks? She could last another month or more. Would require a lot of attention. Very expensive."

"Submit your bill to the adjutant general."

"What if they don't pay?" mumbled Dr. Raffet, cynically. "All that work for nothing."

"Tell you what I'll do," said the sergeant, "I'll give you the horse she's riding, a gentle mare. Horse, saddle and all. You can bill the army too."

The doctor paused, excused himself to step into the next room, where he conferred with the portly housekeeper. Dwiggins slipped over to the door and listened to hear snatches of the conversation: "In the attic..or.locked in the stable...tied and gagged...six weeks, maybe less...could be much less."

When Dr Raffet returned he agreed to accept Fawn as a patient. Officer Dwiggins heaved a sigh of relief as he signed an affidavit declaring the condition of the woman and releasing her to the doctor's custody. Mrs. Crews, the housekeeper, brought a lantern and gave it to Dwiggins. The doctor instructed the sergeant to put the horse in the stable. "She's a gentle mare, you say?" he inquired.

"Gentle as a lamb."

Led by the two Cherokee men, Fawn submissively entered the clinic. She was resigned to her fate. Having been torn from her mountain home, from her husband, from her newborn son, rejected by her race, she was numb and sick of heart, ready to face her certain death.

The insensitive housekeeper led Fawn up two flights of stairs to a little room, scantily furnished. "Go to bed," she ordered. "We'll talk tomorrow. They's water there on the table." She waited only long enough for Fawn to drop into bed. Then she took the lamp, went out the door, locking it behind her.

Sergeant Dwiggins and his Cherokee escort left Shady Lawn Infirmary to return to the caravan. They journeyed in silence, each man pondering over the ordeal he had just experienced. Dwiggins wondered about Dr. Raffet and decided he didn't like him. He was suspicious of the doctor and doubtful of Fawn's future care. "That little swindler will probably put an end to her in a couple of weeks. Probably poison her," he thought. "Well, I guess it's not my affair. Probably a merciful thing for her anyhow." Dwiggins smiled to himself and muttered half aloud, "Gentle as a lamb, that mare's gentle as a lamb. I'd like to see the doctor's face in the morning when he sees that old, spavined nag."

Part Two of Chapter VI

When Kevit returned to the wagon, he found Fawn gone and Essie weeping. "I don't know where they took her," she cried. "To an infirmary, they called it. Six or more men were here. Two of them soldiers. They said she would get treatment. She didn't want to go." "Why did they take her while I was gone? It was a dirty, deceitful trick. Who were the men?" asked Kevit. "I don't know their names. I seen them before, but I don't know their names." "I'm going to find Fawn." He started off then paused to call back, "Are the babies all right?" Essie nodded. "I've got to find her. Poor girl, she's probably scared to death." He ran toward the wagon at the end of the caravan used as the army headquarters. Kevit broke in upon a cluster of officers seated around a fire. "What have you done with my wife? Where is she?" he demanded vehemently.

"Hold on, redman, we don't know nothin' about your squaw," responded a big officer with equal indignation.

"Two officers took her from her wagon. Where is she?" Kevit insisted.

"Wait a minute," said one of the men stepping forward, "this guy's talkin' about that woman what was bit by a mad dog. Yeah, one of our men took her to a doctor. I don't know where they went. Ask some of your own people. They know about it."

Kevit raced about inquiring of everyone he saw. One man confessed that he had been with the men who took Fawn from the wagon, but he didn't know where the men took her. "Three men took her away," he said.

Unable to learn anything from anyone, Kevit was forced to give up his search until morning. He returned to the wagon where Essie and his infant son were sleeping. Wearily he stretched his arms and limbs preparing to curl up in his blanket and crawl under the wagon where he customarily slept. Essie heard the movement of someone outside. She raised from her bed and peeped under the wagon canvas. She watched Kevit stretch and then unbotton and remove his sweaty shirt. She admired his massive chest as it swelled inhailing the cool night air. As his arms flexed, how beautiful he is she thought. He started to grab his blanket, then he turned and strode away toward the trees beyond. How wonderfully the muscles of his hips and buttox moved in his tight fitting pantaloons. He has gone into the bushes to urinate, Essie thought. She could not take her eyes off him as he returned to the wagon. She imagined him curling up in the blanket.

She listened for sounds beneath the wagon. Only silence. Then she heard him emit a long sigh--or was it a sob? Poor Kevit! She must go to him, lie with him and comfort him. She raised herself from her bed not bothering to put on her dress, unaware of the cool, brisk air, she climbed over the tailgate and moved toward him. Kevit too moved toward her. She could smell his flesh and feel his body warmth. Then the sounds of approaching horsemen caused them both to stop short. "It's the men returning after taking Fawn away. I gotta go," he said. He snatched his shirt and ran off. Essie stood watching him go. Her heart poinded. How she longed to enfold him in her arms.

How long had her heart hidden and denied this emotion? Sadly she watched him leave. Kevit crept toward the sound of the horses' hooves as the men drew near to the row of army vehicles. Crouched closeby in the shadow of a wagon, Kevit could hear their hushed voices. Sergeant Dwiggins said to the two Cherokee men, "You better avoid seeing Kevit Tanner. He will be wantin' to know where we took his wife. He may be a mite hostile. You two had better go to the other end of the train where he can't find you."

The men agreed and were about to ride away, when suddenly one of the men paused. In a loud whisper he said, "If Kevit Tanner saw that weasel-eyed doctor, he'd be wild as a cougar. We'll sure stay out of his way." After the two Indians were gone, the sergeant led his horse to a watering tank. Kevit stole close behind the officer. Quickly he sprang upon him, throwing him face down on the ground. Straddling the officer's back, Kevit pinned his arms behind him.

"Where's my wife?" he demanded. Dwiggins twisted and struggled to free himself. He was a broad-shouldered man, but the surprise attack had given Kevit the advantage. The Indian's

82

desperate determination multiplied his strength. "Where is Fawn?" he repeated, as he gave a tight twist to the sergeant's arm.

"We took her to Dr. Raffet's infirmary. But you can't go there. She's in good hands. She'll get good treatment there. You would only spoil her chances to recover. As an officer of the army, I can't let you leave your people. If you try, I'll hunt you down. You stay here!"

"Where is the infirmary," demanded Kevit

"I can't tell you," exclaimed the sergeant.

"Where is she?" he shouted, twisting the arm harder. The raising of their angry voices aroused some of the men sleeping nearby. They hurried to the sergeant's aid. They seized Kevit, and on orders of the sergeant, bound his hands and feet and tied him to a wagon wheel. In the morning, and for three days following, Kevit was forced to walk tied by his hands behind an army wagon.

On the evening of the third day the sergeant said, "I'm going to turn you loose so's you can go to see about your baby son. You're free to travel as before. But I'm warnin' you, don't try to go to your wife. You've had long enough to think about that. Surely you must realize that it would be futile to try. She's adjusted to her fate now. Don't make it harder for her." Kevit made no comment. He rubbed his sore, stinging wrists, then ran to the wagon bearing his son and Essie.

"Oh, Master Kevit, thank the Lord!" exclaimed Essie, "I'm so glad to see you. I know'd they had you tied up back there. Why did they do that to you, Master Kevit?"

"They was tryin' to keep me from going to Fawn. You know they can't stop me from doin' that. I just came now to say goodbye to you and little Arley." Essie held his baby in her arms. He started to take his son from her, but in his haste he simply snuggled his head against the child, his arm held aaround Essie's waist. After he had kissed the infant, he said, "Take good care of my son, Essie." He sought in her eyes the assurance he needed. Struck by the beauty of her face he paused awkwardly, then he kissed Essie on the cheek. Essie felt the warm pressure of his hand around her waist. Not since Gabe had any man touched her like that. A baby hand reached out to stroke her face. Suddenly she had a strange feeling--a motherly sensation--as though the child in her arms were truely hers--yet this was the father! Kevit broke away. "Can you do it, Essie? Take care of two little ones?"

Essie nodded. "We can do just fine, Master Kevit."

"God bless you and little Caleb. When I come back, I'm going to give you your freedom. You'll never have to be a slave any more."

"Thank you, Master Kevit. But it don't matter much, exceptin' if I was free I could sometime hunt for my man Gabe. Don't you worry now about little Arley. I'll treat him same as my own boy. When will you be a'comin' back, Master Kevit?"

"Don't know that. I just hope I can find Fawn. Goodbye." Essie stood beside the wagon. "Lord help you, Master Kevit," she said. Her heart was heavy as she watched him leave. "Poor Master Kevit," she sighed, "Dear Fawn's troubles is more'n he can bear." She bit her lip to fight back her inner anguish. "Ain't nothin' goin' to keep me from carin' for that Indian baby." Kevit had gone. Still her mind held the vision of his strong physique. She realized how often she had thought of Master Kevit as "our man". "Oh, Lord, let him bring Fawn back," she gasped. But oh, if Fawn were lost, what then? Would Kevit really set Essie free? Wouldn't he need her to raise his child? How intently his eyes had fastened on her! Was there a trace of Tom Lovell in that gaze? Or was it only her foolish imagination? Could she live with Kevit to carry out her oath to Fawn and care for baby Arley? To her surprise she found in herself placidly acceptance of that thought. Kevit was not like Tom Lovell. Still he was not like Gabe either, although he was kind and considerate like Gabe. Essie had often watched his loving devotion to Fawn. Would Kevit now transfer his attentions to her. Was there a degree of passion which was less than what she felt for Gabe, but which still might be agreeable to her? Her respect for Kevit could grow into deeper love for him. Strangely, that thought lifted the gloom from her amd brought her consolation. She realized that for now her thoughts were untimely. Guilt gropped her soul as she realized how often she

84

had envied Fawn when her husband had embraced her. She felt she must pray, "Oh, Fawn, you must live for Kevit and baby Arley."

Kevit hurried on going back over the trail which the train of wagons had just traveled. It would be more than three day's journey just to arrive at the area where the Shady Lawn Infirmary was located. Kevit feared that if he were seen, the army would again take him captive, so he made his furtive way behind hedgerows and fences. So long was the procession of wagons, horsemen, and foot travelers that Kevit knew he would be passing them the entire journey. He counted on his Indian folk-knowledge for his survival. In his hurry he had not taken time to collect provisions. Besides, the scarcity was so great among all the Cherokees that any food he might have taken would only deprive Essie and the babies of it. With dauntless determination, Kevit pressed through thickets and briers, forded streams, hid from farmers, fought off dogs, and foraged for food. Sometimes he was forced to eat raw squirrel or rabbit, and by night he attempted to raid one of the army supply wagons. Always, he glanced over his shoulder, fearful that he might be followed by Sergeant Dwiggins or his men. At a wayside store Kevit stopped to ask the directions to Shady Lawn Infirmary. The fearful storekeeper ordered him at gunpoint out of the store. Tossing a couple of coins at the merchant's feet, the Cherokee pleaded, "All I wanted is information about how to get to Shady Lawn Infirmary." The surly storekeeper retorted, "Take the left road at the forks. Now git, and don't come back."

Kevit knew he would need further information, and he hoped that somewhere he would find someone more hospitable. Perhaps a gentle woman would be more sympathetic. When he descried a woman hanging wet clothes on a line, he trudged across a wide field to go to her. She stood with her back to Kevit's approach. He came upon her unnoticed, which was good, Kevit thought, otherwise she would have fled into the house and bolted the door. Just as he was about to greet her, she turned toward him. She screamed, fearing that he was creeping up to attack her.

"Don't be afraid," said Kevit in his most amiable, gentle voice. "I only want information. I'm sorry if I scared you." The farm wife backed away slowly. "I only want to know how to find a place called Shady Lawn Infirmary. You see, my sick wife is there and I want to go to her," said Kevit. The woman stood still.

"Shady Lawn Infirmary!" she exclaimed meaningfully.

"Your wife is in the Shady Lawn Infirmary? My sister was there. Wasn't there but just ten days and she died. I think that doctor kill't her. Took her money and kill't her. Yea, I know where it is. You'd better git there quick or she'll be gone 'fore you git there. Ever'body what goes there dies real quick." The woman eyed him obliquely. "You're Cherokee, ain'tcha? My grandma was Cherokee. Tell you what, when my man comes home, I'll ask him to drive you to that place. Jest wait here for him." The remainder of the afternoon, Kevit spent waiting, seated on the ground his back resting against a giant oak tree. When the farmer arrived his wife explained why the stranger was waiting for him.

"Name's Luke Scarsdale. Sure, I'll take you to Shady Lawn." He pronounced the name with a bitter snarl. Before climbing into the buckboard, he laid his rifle into the wagon bed. Mrs. Scarsdale brought a little basket full of food for them to eat on the way. As they journeyed and ate, they became acquainted. It was about nine miles from Luke's farm to Shady Lawn. They arrived at dusk. "What you planning to do?" asked Luke.

"I'm goin' to the door and demand to see my wife."

"Good luck," said Luke. "I'll wait for you here. Now, watch out for that doctor. He's real trouble." A broad lawn lay between the carriage lane and the house. Kevit leaped from the wagon and ran to the porch and up the steps. He rapped heavily on the door. A matronly housekeeper opened the door. "What do you want?" she asked gruffly.

"I want to see my wife, the Cherokee woman, Fawn."

"You can't do that. She's very sick. It would be dangerous."

"I must see her. Don't try to stop me." Kevit stepped forward. He started to push through the door.

The woman put her arm against the door jam and braced herself, blocking the entrance. "Now hold on, you can't come in here. The patients are all retired for the night. If your wife is awake, I'll have her come to the window. If you'll go into the yard, you can speak to her. Speak in whispers. Don't wake everyone. She'll be at the upstairs window, on that side." Kevit hurried to the lawn beside the house, expectantly gazing up at the window. He was fearful that Fawn had grown worse.

After several minutes, Dr. Raffet came to a window. "The Cherokee woman is not able to come to the window," he said. "She is very ill. Go away. Her time is nearly up. She can't last much longer. She's unable to talk. Go away!"

"No!" moaned Kevit, "she can't be that bad." He shouted, "Fawn, come to the window! I love you! I must see you now!"

"Quiet!" called Dr. Raffet. "You're disturbing the patients. Get away or I'll sic the dogs on you."

Another window was thrown open. A fuzzy-headed old woman appeared, grasping the vertical iron bars at her window. She called out in a coarse voice, "She can't come to the window. She's tied in her bed. She's nearly dead anyway. We're all prisoners here."

Dejected and stung by those words, Kevit screamed, "I'm going to see her. Let me in, doctor, or I'll break the door down." In rage, he started for the front of the house.

"Look out!" shouted Luke Scarsdale from the wagon. A terrible roar! Two large mastiffs bounded across the lawn toward Kevit. Their powerful jaws snarled and snapped. Whack! A rifle shot resounded and echoed against the building. One of the dogs fell dead. Luke, gun in hand, leaped from the wagon and moved toward the second beast. With a mighty thrust the cur sprang at Kevit, his front legs bearing down on the Cherokee's shoulders, his chest against the man's chest, his teeth ripping into Kevit's neck! They fell to the ground!   Afraid to fire at the dog lest he accidently hit Kevit, Luke rushed to the rescue. He swung his rifle with a terrific blow to the mastiff's body. The mighty beast yelped and turned on Luke, who shielded himself with his upraised gun. The powerful jaws ripped into Luke's shoulder, wrestling Luke to the ground.

The young Cherokee struggled to his feet. He staggered to Luke and the ferocious dog. Mustering his strength, Kevit grasped both hind legs of the beast. The mastiff released Luke, thrusting against him with his front legs. He turned to attack Kevit! Holding fast to the animal's hind legs, Kevit moved sideways to dodge the attack. Using the momentum of the beast's thrust, Kevit swung the dog by the legs into the air striking his back hard against the trunk of a tree! With a guttural roar the mongrel fell to the ground. His back was broken! He whimpered. His body twitched and lay helpless.

Kevit fell prostrate to the ground. His last bit of strength was gone.

Luke struggled to his feet assessing his wounds. He moved over to where Kevit lay face down. Kneeling beside the Indian brave, he rolled the limp body over. Crimson blood covered his whole front side. His jugular vein had been punctured. Kevit was dead.

Dazed and exhausted, Luke Scarsdale stood over the form of the dead Indian. What would he do now? He looked about. The infirmary was dark.

As he moved toward it to seek help, Dr. Raffet called out, "Don't come closer! You killed my dogs. I've got my gun on you, and I'll fire to protect myself!"

Luke turned back. Grimly, he contemplated the bloody victim, a sturdy young Cherokee, his throat torn open. "He saved my life," Luke thought, sorrowfully. He sat on the ground, panting and distraught. He could not forsake Kevit, leaving his body for the despicable Dr. Raffet to bury. "He deserves a proper burial by his own people," he thought. Luke gripped the corpse under the arms, dragged it to the buckboard and loaded it into the bed. Sadly, Luke returned to his farm.

Part Three of Chapter VI

On a late November morning a cold wind swept from the North as Luke Scarsdale took Kevit's body south toward the trail of the Cherokee Indians. Long before he could see the caravan, an updraft of dust swept high into the sky. The rumble of wagons, din of hooves, the lowing of cattle, and the shouts of weary drivers were heard, too, before he reached the hill overlooking the trail. Then at the first sight of it, he halted and sat surveying the awe-inspiring sight. As far as his eyes could see, to the east and to the west, a broad migration moved before him. Amid all the tumult, a myriad of weary travelers huddled against the wind, some astride tired, laggard mules or horses, others, burdened with baggage, trudged along on foot. Some had bare feet or feet wrapped in rags, their blankets or wraps clasped tightly around them. Luke pulled his wagon close to the moving caravan. Time and again he called to the passersby. No one heeded his cry.

Finally, he dismounted and physically accosted two diffident braves. "Come see what I have in my wagon," he pleaded. As the two appalled Cherokees viewed the bloody corpse, Luke said, "He was my friend." He recounted how he had met Kevit, how they had had gone to visit Kevit's wife, and how they had fought against the killer dogs. "He saved my life. I want this brave man buried by his own people. Did you know him?" asked Luke. The two men shook their heads solemnly. "A slave woman is keepin' his baby son somewhere far ahead of this part of the train." The two Indians agreed to bury Kevit's body, even though their families and friends would move on ahead. "If you can," said Luke, "send word to the man's people. They may be seventy-five or a hundred miles ahead of here." Luke drove home assuring himself that he had done all he could. The despairing sight of the Cherokee people had touched him profoundly. He felt brooding concern for the tiny papoose whose father had died so gallantly and would now be buried in an unmarked Illinois grave.

Outside, the sound of hymn-singing pervaded the camp. In the wagon Essie knelt, pensively hovering over the little form of the Indian infant. The canvas wagon cover flapped with a gentle clapping sound. "Your daddy is comin' back soon," she whispered. She counted the days since Kevit had gone away. Why had he been gone so long? she wondered. Suddenly a premonition of Fawn's fate came over her. "Dear Fawn is dead, I feel it!" she moaned with a compelling conviction. She grasped the Cherokee baby in her arms. Her slender body swayed convulsively as she pressed her tear-dampened cheek against little Arley's. Then she tenderly laid the tiny one down. "Don't you fret none, little angel. Your daddy be here soon." Turning to her own little brown child she moaned, "Ain't no way we're goin' to see your paw again. Again? Why, this little tyke ain't never ever seen his paw! Wonder where your poor paw is. We sure do need that man now," she sighed. "Thank the Lord he don't know what trouble we're in! Oh Lordy, he hisself could be in a worse fix than we are. Lord help us! Don't be sad, my little darkie. We goin' to find your daddy someday. Lord help us, we sure will."

When the babes were safely asleep, Essie climbed down onto the ground. It was dusk on a Saturday evening. A throng of Cherokee captives, attracted by singing and a cheery blazing bonfire, gathered into a shallow valley below the trail. The next day would be a day of worship and prayer, for they refused to travel on the Lord's day. Rumor had spread that day that because of the extreme number of cases of sickness the cavalcade was to remain camped on this site for several days. Doctor Stanley had ordered it, the rumor reported. There had been a light falling mist during the day as little mounds of earth had been heaped over shallow graves bearing six coffinless bodies, victims of cold, hunger, and disease. That evening the cold of the day had moderated somewhat with the wind subsiding. It was a natural inclination of the oppressed people to worship and pray, presenting their petitions to the Great Spirit.

The Baptist preacher, William Ford, led them as they sang: My heavenly home is bright and fair; Nor pain nor death can enter there; It's glittering towers the sun outshine, That heavenly mansion shall be mine. I'm going home, I'm going home, I'm going home, to die no more, To die no more, to die no more, I'm going home, to die no more. My Father's house is built on high, Far, far above the starry sky; When from this earthly prison free, That heavenly mansion mine shall be. I'm going home, I'm going home,... Essie leaned against the wheel of the Conestoga, and softly her vibrant contralto voice joined the ethereal hymn that rose from the valley: "I'm going home, to die no more." The music stopped, and William Ford gave a short message of consolation and encouragement. As the singing began again, Ford walked among the people comforting, blessing them.

As he came to the edge of the crowd, he spied Essie and came to her. "Essie," he said, "I've been wanting to speak to you. Sorry to have to bring you sad news. Word came to me today about Kevit Tanner. Essie, he's dead. He was killed by a vicious dog while trying to see his wife. I'm sorry. God Bless and keep you, Essie."

The mulatto slumped forward groaning. "Not Kevit, too. Not Kevit."

She covered her face with her hands and wept. "Is Fawn --d-dead?" she asked.

"I don't know," said Ford, "I only heard about Kevit from a missionary who helped to bury him. Essie, I know how you've been taking care of two babies. Isn't there some other woman who could take the Tanner baby?"

"Ain't no one I know what could wet-nurse him. He can't take solid food yet. Besides, I gave my word that I'd take care of him myself."

"God bless and help you, Essie. I wish there was some way I could help."

"Thank you, reverend, but I'll get along all right." She straightened herself erect, speaking with a firm, resolute tone. "I'd better go to the little ones now. The night air is getting cold. I'd better cuddle them to keep them warm."

"Oh," said Ford, "many of the old people in the wagons are being forced to walk to make space for the sick. I pray you will not have to walk and carry two babies."

"They ain't heavy. I'll do all right," assured Essie. "Good night, reverend."

The next day Essie began to make canvas bags to hold the infants whenever she should have to carry them. Before the caravan had begun its westward trek, the army had issued each person a blanket. Essie, in a sad act of great resignation, forfeited the blankets of Kevit and Fawn to two shivering, sick widows in the wagon ahead of hers. To her it was a token of final farewell to the two people she had dearly loved.

Maggie, the old woman who had left the wagon fearing to travel with Fawn, now lost the spot where she had been riding and returned to take her place with Essie. Puffing and gasping she struggled to climb into the front of the wagon.

From the driver's seat Nick Choates called impatiently, "Hurry up there, old woman. We ain't got all day." Finally he leaped from his perch to the ground, jostled the aged squaw to the rear of the wagon and gave her a rough boost over the tail gate. She fell in a heap before Essie.

The mulatto helped Maggie straighten herself to a sitting position. "That brute, he ain't got a kind feeling for nobody," said Essie. "Are you all right, Maggie?" The old Cherokee woman coughed and wheezed, and nodded. "I'm glad you're back," said Essie as she pulled a blanket around the trembling crone. "That big yahoo, I distrust him." Essie thought of how Choates glared at her whenever he saw her out of the wagon or, for that matter, when seated in the driver's seat he often parted the canvas to peer into the Conestoga. In his dark eyes she recognized a lascivious glare such as she had seen in Thomas Lovell's softer blue ones. Both leered sensually at her, but whereas Lovell's charming devil-may-care attitude made his lust seem natural, almost wholesome, Choates' surly expression conveyed perverse, obstinate lechery which seemed demented and evil. Essie feared him. Now with Maggie as a constant companion, even though she was old and sickly, Essie felt herself not alone. Women of the caravan had observed how hired white drivers and young soldiers attempted to lure young maidens into the woods. Wise females dared not venture to the woods privies unaccompanied by other female companions.

Near Cotter, Arkansas, whiskey peddlers came to sell gallons of overpriced liquor to the distraught Cherokees. One frigid evening, hordes of reveling braves, warmed and stimulated by spirits, roamed about the encampment. Raucous carousing, shouting, and laughter disturbed the travel-weary and ill exiles. Essie lay restlessly on her side with her knees drawn up to form an angle into which the infants were nestled. She felt the penetrating cold on her back. She heard the soft, gentle breathing of the little ones and the flapping of the canvas against the ribs of the wagon. Far down the camp the sounds of the revelers was heard. It grew louder and louder until the men were outside Essie's wagon. For the most part, the prattle of the men was unintelligible. Essie wished they would move away.

Then she heard one distinguishable, familiar voice. It was Nick Choates, the wagoneer. She listened intently to his coarse voice, able sometimes to catch a word or phrase. Her curiosity was piqued by certain words: "nigger," "slave trader," "good prices."

Essie raised herself from her bed and sat upright, her ear inclined toward the voices. Her heart palpitated fiercely while she pieced together the fragments of conversation. As she understood it, the drunken scoundrels were talking about a slave trader who had approached the camp seeking to buy Cherokee-owned Negroes.

Then she clearly heard Nick Choates say in a thick-tongued whisper, "Why, right in this here wagon is a nigger wench what ain't owned by nobody. She'd never be missed. An' good lookin' like she is, she'd fetch a pretty price from some southern gentleman wantin' to keep a little mistress on the sly." While speaking confidentially to some comrade, Choates had moved close to the wagon, and in his drunkenness he had not realized how loudly he had spoken.

Essie's distraught brain could comprehend nothing further, nor could she expel the menacing thought from her head. The rest of the night and the next day the devastating threat would not leave her head. Would Nick Choates dare to abduct her and sell her down the river? Kevit had promised to set her free, but now her master was dead. Even in the desperate distress and hardship of the journey, she had enjoyed one gratifying condition--she had only now realized it-- she had been a free woman. There had been no master. Still, her fate and future was bound up with the Cherokee exiles. God forbid that she should be spirited away, sold to another master, forced into another kind of life. At times she tried to resolve her fears. She assured herself that Choates' remarks were nothing more than idle talk of a drunken sot who would not remember them in the morning. Most of all, Essie's concern was for little Arley. What would become of him? No slave trader would dare to buy a Cherokee child. She could not leave him behind! She would not forsake the son of dear Fawn!

At the end of the day, while Essie struggled with her bewildering vexation, two men met in a little tavern near the Cherokee camp. One of them was a short, stocky man, garishly dressed in a gray frock coat flung open ostentatiously to reveal his lavishly clad figure. He strutted about like a pouter pigeon. He greeted a coarse rustic fellow with the broad, loose swagger of a mule skinner. "M'name's Nick Choates," said the giant teamster. "I cum to trade with ye." He gave a furtive glance about the room and lowered his voice confidentially. "I got a beautiful nigger wench ter sell." The trader's fat face flushed with interest. He brushed chubby fingers across his waxed, smartly-trimmed mustache, a gesture sure to impress his fellows with a lavish desplay of rings.

He grasped Nick Choates by the elbow and ushered him to a secluded table. He called for a bottle of rye whiskey and glasses. The two men conferred in low tones. "You will agree, when you see this mulatto," said Choates, "she's worth top price. She's got a finely-molded shape and the bearing of a duchess and the strength and stamina of a racing filly."

"That may be," said Erlich, "still it's a murky business, no legal bill o' sale and all that. I don't take no risks without monetary satisfaction." He dangled the heavy gold chain that swagged across his garishly embroidered vest. "I sure don't relish no ruckus with the army nor riled-up redskins." He poured two glasses of whiskey and shoved one of them to Choates.

94

"Ain't no call for concern there. I told ye, she ain't nobody's property. She don't get out o' the wagon to neighbor much. She's too busy nursin' two younguns. 'Sides some is desertin' the train all the time. Most o' the others is glad of it. Ever'one what deserts or dies leaves more food for them that's left. Folks'll figure she just pulled out." Choates ejected a cud of tobacco into the spittoon and downed the shot of whiskey.

"Maybe so. Still they's that redskin tot. How old's he? You dassen't fetch him."

"He's a couple months old or so. Don't fret about it. They's a old squaw in with 'im. She kin look after 'im. Tomorrow when I gets paid I'm tradin' for a nag. On the next night, that's Thursday, I'll fetch her to ye, and the black kid too."

Erlich cleared his throat and drawled, "Wa-all, then I'll be a'countin' on yer takin' care o' it.

I'll meet ye at the forks jest down the road a piece from here. Eight o'clock Thursday night. If ye ain't there by eight, I'll be gone." With a chubby fist Erlich gave a rap on the table, the sound of his heavy rings giving finality to his words, like a gavel to a judge's verdict. He arose from his chair and strutted toward the door. "Remember," he said, "I'm buyin' this merchandise an' I don't know where it come from. Understand? We kin dicker over the price when we gets her in the light where I kin look 'er over."

"Aw right," agreed Choates, a little dubious that he would get a fair deal from such a smooth trader.

The next morning William Ford came to greet Essie. "I just wanted to know that you are all right," he said. "I know how hard it must be for you since Kevit's death. I've been praying that the Lord will give you strength. I brought you this little wedge of cheese and some hardtack that I inveigled from the army quartermaster." Essie thanked him. For an instant Essie had thought to relate to the good minister what she had heard and how it had disturbed her. Then the thought came to her like a heavenly revelation: the cheese and the hardtack were sent by the Lord and delivered by his very servant! With it came the answer to her prayers, the message she had sought. The unspoken, implied message: TO FLEE!

Chapter VII
Essie's Escape

That afternoon Essie planned her escape. She gathered things together that she must take: small cooking utensils, a small hatchet, sharp knife, a couple of tin plates, spoons, forks and whatever food she could secure, clothing, blankets , cloths for baby diapers, matches and string.

Maggie, who watched Essie with languid interest, finally asked, "What you doin', Essie?"

"Just arranging my things," Essie said lightly. "I'm going to give my place here to someone sick. I'm able to walk." Essie enumerated in her mind the list of things she would need. Oh, yes, she thought there was a packet of papers belonging to Kevit. Whatever they might be, they now belonged to Arley. She must take them, too...and the little Bible in the Cherokee language. Essie planned to leave in the middle of the night. She would travel north into Missouri, she decided. The division of the Cherokee immigrants, of which she was a part, was the second one to leave Rattlesnake Springs. Eleven more sections were to follow. While the first two traveled south after crossing the Mississippi River, going into Arkansas, those which followed journeyed across Missouri as far as Springfield before turning south. Perhaps, Essie reasoned, she would go north and join the other Cherokees. Gabe would search for her someday among the Indian people.

Essie rested uneasily that night. Attempting to sleep lightly, lest she should slumber past the hour when she wanted to start out. She heard Maggie wheezing in deep sleep. All around, the camp was quiet save for the sound of a barking dog answering a distant howling coyote. When she peered out of the wagon, she saw no signs of activity. No army sentry was in sight. Around her waist she tied two duffle-cloth pouches into which she quietly packed the supplies she had selected. She slipped the Cherokee baby into a casnvas bag and bound it onto her back. Another bag holding her black child, she strapped onto her chest.

With her heavy load, she struggled from the wagon and stealthily crept between the wagons into the clearing beyond.

The waning moon gave scant light in the unfamiliar terrain where she forged onward, determined to get as far away as she could before daybreak. The rugged land, with its hills and ravines, reminded Essie of the rocky country of the Cherokee nation in Georgia. The sound of the rustling leaves and broken twigs under her feet seemed magnified in the stillness of the night. A distant coyote howled forlornly and gave her an alarming sense of the vastness of the wilderness about her. Barren branches and vines brushed against her, and sometimes their tentacles held fast to her skirts. Suddenly the flapping of a startled screech owl rising from a scrub oak terrrified her. She uttered an astonished shriek.

If only she could find a road where walking would be easier and the profusion of brush would not croud against her. At times a forlorn and desoloate mood came over her. How, she wondered, could she endure for long in that strange, dark, perilous country? But in the exigency of her flight, doubts and fears were soon crowded out of her mind, and her endurance was augmented to supernatural limits. She looked wildly about her, searching for she knew not what. When she noticed a cottage a quarter of a mile away her thoughts vacillated from a desire to run to it for refuge to a terror that somehow it might betray her flight.

As the sun's first rays gilded the western mountain crags with saffron radiance, Essie sat on a boulder to rest. Although she craved food, she resolved to wait until her appetite became more ravenous. She watched the dawn's fog move through the valley and thin into filmy streamers. She shivered in the cold. Later she heeded the soft whimpers of her babies and stopped to nurse them. She ate a portion of the cheese and a few bites of the hardtack. She savored every nibble with ceremony, thanking the good Lord for the manna He had provided in the wilderness.

At the same time Essie was eating her cheese and hardtack, Choates was discovering Essie's disappearance. He had taken his place on the driver's seat unaweare that Maggie was the only passenger. The cavalcade had begun to embark, each wagon pulling out in turn, wagoneers shouting for the passengers to get on board, yelling at their teams and cracking their whips. The campsite was rough and rocky, and when Choates snapped his whip and bawled at the team, "Getee up," then, "Gee," and, "Haw," the snorting, screaming beasts struggled and strained, plunging to the right and to the left. The wagon rocked back and forth but would not roll over the large rock blocking one of the wheels. Crack! A trace chain broke, clanging to the ground. The horses stumbled forward. "Whoa!" cried Choates, and he leaped from his seat to check the harness. He went to the back of the wagon where he had stored a few tools and pieces of chain. Then he discovered Essie's absence!

"Where'd she go?" he demanded of Maggie.

"She said she walk, not ride no more," said the old woman.

Choates turned away from the wagon, cursing umder his breath. In a frenzy he raced through the throng of travelers, searching for Essie's slender figure. Twice he crept from behind to seize a blanket-concealed figure, and then with apologies, released a startled Indian girl. After a vain search of more than half an hour, he gave up. What had happened? Had Essie somehow learned of his scheme?

Giving solemn promises that he would return it in good condition, he rented a horse from a young brave. He then realized that there would be little chance of capturing the fugitive without blood hounds. He sprang on the nag and raced to the slave trader. Fortunately, Ehrlich owned a pair of well-bred hounds which he planned to transport, along with the blacks he acquired, to the New Orleans market. Ehrlich mounted a steed and joined Choates in the hunt. Back at the site where Choates' wagon still remained stranded, the dogs got Essie's scent from the pad on which she had slept. The hounds took off in hot pursuit, their ears flapping against their black muzzles.

After her meager breakfast Essie resumed her flight feeling refreshed. Soon, however, the strenuous hours of travel again exhausted her. She was seeking a place of refuge when she stumbled onto a narrow road, and her way was easier. But just as she was rejoicing over it, she heard the terrizing yowl of pursuing hounds. Her heart sank. Often she had heard that sound, and she knew the fear it struck in runaway slaves. Now she was the hunted! She began to run. The baying grew louder, closer and closer!

Then she heard a small buggy approaching behind her. The driver was a slender pioneer woman who drew her mare to a halt beside Essie and gazed at her inquisitively. "What you carryin'?" inquired the white woman.

Essie paused, dubiously observing the woman. "My babies," she replied breathlessly.

"Two babies? You got two babies?"

"Yes, Ma'am."

"How far you aimin' to tote 'em?"

Essie spoke in a tremulous tone, "Sorry, no time to talk. Hear them dogs. They's after me." She resumed her journey with vigor.

"Wait up there. You kain't outrun them dogs. You look plumb tuckered out. Get in here with me," called the woman gesturing to the seat beside her.

Essie hesitated. Why should this soul be so kind? she wondered. but the intensifying voices of the hounds impelled her to action. She climbed into the buggy, struggling with her cumberous burden, and with a deep sigh settled into the seat. As the carriage plunged forward, Essie clung to the dashboard, holding her aching back erect. She dared not rest herself against the cushioned back of the seat lest she crush her weight against the infant behind her.

The rural matron looked askance at Essie. "Be ye a runaway slave?"

"Not exactly," said Essie nerviously, "I've been a slave. My owners is dead. A bad man wanted to steal me and sell me to a slave peddler, so I ran away."

The woman took the buggy whip from its socket and snapped it above the mare. "Come from Connecticut. Can't abide by slave holdin'," she said with a firm set of her sinewy jaw.

"Thank the Lord," mumbled Essie.

As the brown pony stepped sprightly along, the mistress plied Essie with questions about her escape and her infants. "Two babies!" she exclaimed. "I had five. But two nurslings at one time! Whew! And traveling on the road with "em!" She wagged her head solemnly. "Say them dogs is gettin' closer. Let's turn here." She gave a quick snap of the reins. "Hounds don't scent a prey in a carriage so good. This here road has got a heap o' crossroads and turn-offs. We'll keep them dogs befuddled," she said with a glint in her dark eyes.

"I'm sure beholden to you, ma'am," said Essie sincerely. "Sorry, I've been so taken up with my troubles, I ain't never asked your name."

"The name's Daisy Acton. I live hard by here." She guided the buggy onto another side road, continuing her circuitous route until the howling of the hounds could be heard no more. "We done it! We lost 'em," she exclaimed with delight. "Now we kin go home."

At the Acton farm, Daisy introduced Essie to her husband Tim. "I figure we kin put this poor soul up for the night. She's been trailed by a pack of bloodhounds and a crafty slave traider. Lord help 'er, she's totin' two babies! I thought she kin sleep upstairs."

"Whatever you think, Daisy," saod Tim.

It was a simple pioneer home, the main core built of logs to which had been added at separate intervals three weatherboard additions. Daisy set the supper table with fried potatoes, sausage, and corn muffins. Afterwards she set out a bowl of dried apple slices for munching. To Essie it was a lavish feast. Her acceptance as a guest was unconditional, with no hint of condescension. Essie told them of the arduous journey and suffering of the Cherokees and how she became the guardian of a Cherokee boy. "I will return to Georgia to join my man there soon's I get so I can," said Essie.

Daisy and Tim exchanged doubtful glances, but as they sensed Essie's resoluteness, their skepticism was replaced by hope for Essie's dream. "Land sakes, woman, how you expectin' to do that," asked Daisy.

"Don't rightly know, ma'am. Just know I'm going to do it."

Daisy heated a kettle of water so that Essie could wash her little tikes. The rural woman watched the bathing with intense interest, recalling the days when she had scrubbed her own five youngsters. "My babies is all growed up and moved out," she said wistfully. There was a hint of incredulity in her voice as she asked, "You aimin' to fetch up both them young-uns together, a Indian and a-a-yer own child? Some folks don't have no use fer redskins. Me, myself, I ain't had no dealin's with 'em, so I wouldn't want to spend a opinion on 'em." She gazed at the two squirming forms. "Land sakes, cute ain't they!"

Never was a bed more luxurious, thought Essie in the morning as she swung her feet onto the cold floor and sat on the edge of the bed. The mattress of corn shucks rustled as she moved. There was even a little crib held over from the time the household had infants of its own. When she descended the narrow stairs carrying her babies she found Daisy acton preparing a breakfast of sausage, grits and gravy. Tim brought in a pail half full of milk. He grumbled that the cow was going dry. Still Daisy insisted that Essie drink a large glass full. "You need this so's you kin pass it on to them boys."

Later Daisy sacked up enough corn meal to make four or five meals. "Ye kin make mush cakes. It may keep ye from starvin. We ain't got much bacon, but I kin give ye a little piece. We ain't aimin' to butcher 'til next week."

Daisy gave instructions about how to find the best route north. With sympathetic concern she warned, "This country ain't no fit place for a young woman like yourself to be on the road alone, what with onery thugs and outlaws ever'wheres. They's right smart o' proslavery folks, too. Better be careful, child."

"Poor soul," muttered the good farm woman to herself as she stood at the door watching Essie plod down the road.

Following Daisy's advice, Essie often scurried off the highway and hid in the thickets whenever she saw anyone approaching. She walked all day and slept that night in a little school house which had retained a little heat from its use that day. The following evening, after a long days journey and a frantic search for a place to sleep, she found a huge straw stack.

She burrowed deep into the straw, nursed her babies and went to sleep. The next frosty morning when she crawled out of the straw, she found a cow lying against the stack, sheltered from the wind. Essie gave her a kick and twisted her tail until the old cow struggled to her feet. When Essie got out her little cooking pan in hopes of getting a little milk, the haughty beast walked disdainfully away. On the spot where the earth had been warmed, Essie laid her babies and sat down to change them. She worried about their being bound up in their pouches and not being able to exercise, so whenever she could she gave them a chance to kick and wiggle about.

That day a farmer in a wagon came up behind her and offered her a ride. Since he had two young girls riding in the bed of the wagon, she accepted the offer and climbed in and sat with the two children. She enjoyed a restful ride for about five miles before the man came to a side road leading to his home. There he stopped and let Essie out. The rest of the day she walked. When evening came she could find no shelter. At last she found a wagon trail leading from the road. She followed it thinking that a house would surely be nearby. But when the trail finally became overgrown with brush she lost her way. A storm appeared to be developing. She must find shelter soon.

In the dark she stumbled across a field, struggling against the shrieking wind. The cold stung her face and cut sharply against her weary limbs. But snug against her breast and at her back the pervasive warmth of her babies kindled her. She clutched the tattered blanket around her head and shoulders and turned her face from the wind. Suddenly she tripped over something and plunged headlong, catching her weight by thrusting her hands against the stubbled earth. She felt a sharp pain in her back. She straightened herself up on one arm. Bringing a hand to her cradle sack, she was relieved that the child had not been crushed against the ground. She struggled to her feet, trying to regain her balance before she pressed on. There was a movement in the sack at her breast and a little whimpering. Not daring to uncover the child's head and bare him to the wind, she whispered, "Don't cry baby. Don't cry."

"Hungry--they must be hungry," she thought. "No shelter--no place to tend my babies. Oh, Lord, help me!" she gasped. She looked about unable to discern anything in the black night. It no longer mattered which direction she traveled. After tumbling over a fallen tree branch, she limped cautiously on a painful ankle, stepping carefully over rocks and brush. Searching for some shelter from the wind--perhaps a ravine--she moved toward a clump of cedars. As she entered among the trees, the wind made an opening in the clouds and a sliver of the moon showed through, so that the momentary light revealed some kind of structure in the dim distance. With a gasp of relief, she struggled towards it. The weight of the children, unbearably heavy now, pulled at her shoulders. "Please help me, Lord," she prayed.

She came to an old shed. There was no sign of life, only bare weathered boards, a sagging door, slightly ajar, and a tiny window covered over with rough boards. Essie pushed against the door, fearful of the darkness.

She steeled herself and forced her steps into the blackness. In the room, she thrust her hand into the bag at her waist, searching for a match. She struck the match against the inside of the door and cupped the flame with her hands. In the flickering light she saw some broken chairs, a large cracked kettle and assorted rubble. Perhaps it had been a kind of storage shed. The match burned her fingers and fell to the floor. She searched for another one, lit it, and held it to a scrap of paper. Holding the paper torch she recognized the iron kettle as a suitable place to build a fire. She laid the burning piece of paper into it and gathered some rubble--leaves, fragments of wood, anything combustible. Soon she had a little bonfire whose flames leaped above the rim of the kettle. The smoke rose to the ceiling and moved out through the cracks in the walls. Now she could see clearly about the room. Remains of an old couch stood at one end. "Praise the Lord, she whispered, we can sleep here."

Part Two of Chapter VII

During her flight, whenever Essie came to a village she skirted around it when possible, keeping out of sight. There seemed to always be inquisitive busybodies around. As the days went by she grew weary of her fugitive life. She had not realized that her slavery had given her such stability and protection. Besides becoming tired and frightened, she felt terribly alone. In her marriage, she had adored her husband. Now she was a vagabond, with no one but the two babies she carried. Of course, she loved them, but how she craved companionship! She needed the conversation, fellowship and love of people who could respond to her. To the infants she was their very life-giver. That gave her fulfillment, but still, her existence needed more than that. Worst of all, she found it necessary to be suspicious of everyone she saw, to eye people as being capable of doing her harm. This was a new plight for her, one that she did not like.

On the fifth day of her flight, as she was nearing a settlement just north of the Missouri-Arkansas border, she became aware of a man following her on horseback. Attempts to elude her pursuer failed. Why was he pursuing her? Was he a slave bounty hunter?

As she approached the little town, she decided she must not appear to be a fugitive. She must walk through its streets. To be sure, she could not hope to expect help from anyone. She had no special right to protection. The white man who now pursued her on foot, if he wanted to make trouble, his testimony would be the only word that would count. Before the law, her word would not count for anything. As she walked, the few people about the streets fastened their eyes on her. She gauged her walking gait. She must not walk too casual as to make herself look like an idle vagrant, not too hurried as to appear desperate or too urgent.

Essie sometimes stopped as though there were something in a window or open door that had caught her interest. She would give a casual glance back to see her follower walking behind her. He was a chubby, middle-aged man. When she stopped, he stopped. He paused to light a cigar which protruded from one side of his unshaven jaw. He grimaced with partly closed eyes and a wrinkled nose, as though the cigar were strong and distasteful. Fearing that her follower was drawing closer behind her, Essie entered a general store. She stood looking about, she must think of some item of merchandise that, when she asked for it, the storekeeper would not have it in stock. She heard the proprietor giving instructions to the young black delivery boy.

"You understand," he was saying, "those things go to the Kastendiek home. Are you sure you know the way? It's the next house past the Foster plantation. Now, Wilford, please be careful with that big flat carton," he said with emphatic pleading. "It's a mirror ordered special for Mrs. Kastendiek."

While the boy began to load the boxes into the wagon, the storekeeper turned to Essie. He eyed her with a wrinkled, quizzical face, and gave no greeting or inquiry about what she wanted to purchase.

"Oh, sir, I am sorry to bother you," said Essie. "I just would like to inquire, sir. I am wanting to get to the Foster plantation. I am not sure where it is. Is there a livery stabel around here where I might hire a driver to take me there? I've traveled a long way. I need to hurry on my way. You see, I'm a nurse and a teacher.

The mulatto's voice and manner had a certain refinement which impressed the merchant. Her unkempt clothing and the loaded pouches and haversacks made her a mystery to him. He wanted to ask her about them. He suspected that there was an infant in at least one of them. Essie repeated, "I do need so much to hurry."

The Foster's were important landowners. The shopkeeper was desirous of helping them. He could not suspect that Essie's only knowledge of them was that she had heard his reference to the Foster name.

"No livery stable in town, but my boy there is on his way out past the Foster place. You're welcome to ride with him if you don't think the ride would be too rough. You be a new governess for the Foster children, eh?"

"Oh, thank you kindly sir. I'm really in such a hurry." Essie was pleased that she had led him to make assumptions favorable to her purpose. But she did not want to affirm his guesswork with outright lies. She hurried out the door. The man who had been following her stood within earshot as she said, "Young man, I am so grateful to be able to ride with you to the Foster plantation. It's so important to me." She struggled into the front seat of the wagon. The black boy drove away. Essie smiled to herself as she turned back to see the man who had followed her, was entering the store. "Now let the shopkeeper tell the rascal I'm a new governess," she thought.

The delivery boy stopped at the carriage lane leading to the Foster house. Essie got out of the wagon and started up the lane. As soon as the wagon had passed on, she stopped. Looking about she saw several slave shanties. She would wait. In a short while it would be dark, then she would go to seek aid from the black folks there. An old black couple took her in, fed her and offered her a bed for the night. "Where's you all goin'?" asked the old man during the course of their conversation. "Looks to me like you is lost."

"I sure enough am," said Essie. "I'm headed north but I don't think I can make it much farther. I thought I'd go up toward Springfield. I heard some of the Cherokee people are moving through up there."

"Don' know 'bout thet," said the old man. "I thought one time I'd go north. Try t' get t' thet free territory. But I was too skert t' try it. Now days they's the undergroun' railroad an' I's still too skert, too skert an' too old." The old darkie scratched his grey beard and rested his chin in his hand with his elbow on the armrest of his home-fashioned rocker.

"Paw's too old an' I'm too stoved up for travelin'. But say, paw, that under groun' railroad might could help this gal."

"Yep, that could be. Missy, they's white folks willin' t' help po' black folks. Now let me tell you how you kin get on thet undergroun' road..." He gave directions about where to go to find the house of an abolitionist who operated not far from that very plantation. "Don' you go tell no body I done told you 'bout it," warned the old man as Essie set out the next morning.

The abolitionist farmer took Essie, along with a black boy about thirteen, to the next underground station. They journeyed at night on horseback. They slept in the daytime the second night they stopped at a place north of Highlandville. From there

107

another farmer was to move the fugitives during the next night. It was severely cold and rainy. Their hiding place was in a kind of root cellar which opened up inside a barn. Essie and the boy slept during the daytime. That evening the farm wife came with hot food. "My husband won't be a'goin t'night. He took up with a bad cold. I put him t' bed with a mustard plaster. I reckon you'll jest have t'wait till he gets over this here spell o' sickness." The following evening, the woman returned to say that the farmer was still "ailin".

After spending two nights and a day in seclusion, Essie was very tired and anxious to be going on. When the sun came out the next morning, Essie thanked the woman for her kindness. She bid farewell to the youth and started out on her way. Springfield, she was told was not far away.

By evening Essie was tired and exhausted. She sat down on a large rock beside the road. Before her lay the river. Its cold black water rippled and churned with swirling eddies. The bleak autumn trees cast their reflection in the water. On the opposite shore a large buck deer and two does stepped into the water to drink. A crow called plaintively from high in a sycamore. The late afternoon sun hung just above the steep hills across the water. There was no visible way to get across the swollen stream to the opposite shore, so Essie decided to wait until morning before trying to cross.

She rose, walked wearily along the river road, scanning the landscape for a barn or other shelter in which to spend the night. Finally, there appeared a large, well-kept, two-story house, its white walls reddened by the evening sun. behind the house was a large barn. She crept toward it, veering away from the house, and keeping under cover of the horseweed and sumac when she could. No farmer was in view; she heard no barking dog. As she was feeling relieved and pleased with her progress, several geese sounded her arrival with loud honking and hissing. She moved quickly across the clearing to the barn door. A big old gander flogged her with his wings, and with his beak he pinched her leg, twisting the flesh with a turn of his head. Kicking at the old gander to keep him outside, Essie squeezed through the barn door. It was a divided Dutch door, and she fastened the lower section of it and was about to close the upper part when she glanced toward the house. She thought she glimpsed the form of someone at the window. Was it a standing child there or an adult sitting? She closed the door quickly, wondering whether she had been seen.

A mound of hay in the barn made a soft bed for the weary travelers. She nursed her babies and soon felt safe and comfortable. After a restful night, Essie was awakened by the sound of someone at the barn door. She had latched the door on the inside. The person outside could not enter until he broke loose the hook. Before she could get to her feet and go to the door, a large man broke through and came to stand over the trespassers. He was handsome man about forty years old. His hands were smooth and soft, as the hands of a professional man. His eyes were keen as he looked down on the reclining mulatto woman and the two sleeping infants. "Why are you in my barn?" he asked sternly.

Essie sat up, smoothing her skirts. "We just wanted a place to sleep. We traveled a long way."

"Are you runaways?"

"No, sir, we ain't. Ain't nobody after us. We don't have no one in the world."

"Then why are you traveling? Where are you going?"

"It's a long story," Essie sighed. "All we wanted was a place to sleep. I shoulda' asked permission, but I was scared you'd say no. I was too tired to take that chance. Thanks for your barn, mister. We'll be goin' now." As she spoke one of the babies began to cry loudly. Essie picked him up and began to rock him back and forth.

"What's the matter with him? Is he sick," asked the man with a gentle softening of his tone.

"Just hungry."

"Are they twins?" he asked.

"No they ain't twins," said Essie.

"But they look about the same size. Are you the mother of both of them?"

"No, this one's mine. That one's folks is dead. I promised his mamma I'd take care of him."

The confused man rubbed the back of his neck with the palm of his hand. "Well," he said,"when you're ready to leave, stop by the house. We'll give you food for the babies."

After the man had gone, Essie diapered her babies and did what she could to make herself presentable. She walked timidly toward the house. Even before she reached the porch, the door opened, and a woman in a large wooden wheelchair sat in the doorway. "Come in," invited the woman, backing her chair out of the entrance. "I saw you being attacked by the old gander as you went into the barn last night. I hope you weren't hurt. My husband would have been out to see you then, but he was away and didn't get home until late last night."

Essie entered shyly. "Sit down there," said the woman pleasantly. "Oh, you can put the babies in that big armchair if you like. I want to look at them." She rolled her chair to the front of the big chair, taking obvious delight as the little ones stretched, yawned, and exercised. The woman was a frail person. Her face and hands seemed incredibly soft and supple, her complexion a beautiful glowing pink. Her hair was soft, turning grey, pulled loosely into a bun on the back, held in place with a tortoise-shell comb. Her eyes were grey and quite expressive.

It was a big airy kitchen, with a massive cast-iron woodstove, a large, ornate oak table with matching chairs. On one wall hung a vast assortment of pans and utensils. The big man had donned an apron and stood at the stove, cooking bacon. The scent from the skillet filled the room and gave Essie a ravenous appetite. Heaven must surely smell like this, she thought.

After a few moments of silence except for the sound of frying bacon and sometimes the gentle chuckling of the hostess who delighted in watching the babies, the invalid woman said, "Forgive me. I don't have many visitors. My name is Mary Stanton. My husband is Benjamin." The man at the stove turned and nodded at Essie. "Ben does most of the cooking since my illness."

"M'name is Essie, and their names is Caleb and Arley."

At first ill at ease, Essie soon felt an affinity for the kind, gentle woman, helplessly confined to her wheelchair. The kitchen was a place pleasantly familiar to her, a place quite similar to the one at Fern Haven Plantation. Essie watched as Benjamin Stanton worked at the stove.

"Can I wash my hands there?" asked Essie pointing to a washbowl and pitcher on the stand table.

"Of course, you may," said Mrs. Stanton.

Essie rolled up her sleeves and washed her hands and arms up to the elbows. Then going to the stove, she said, "Now, Mister Ben, I was once a cook for one of the most prominent families in all the area of Decatur, Georgia. I don't want to be too presumin', but if you'll let me, I'll take over the cookin' of this here breakfast. I'll have biscuits an' gravy, eggs n' grits ready in no time at all."

The big man moved back, astonished, yet pleased to give up a job in which he was a novice and for which he held no fondness.

"Where will you take breakfast?" asked Essie. "Here or in another room?"

"In the dining room," said Mrs. Stanton. "I'll get out the linen and silverware."

It was a sumptuous breakfast and a treat to the householders. It was also a special pleasure for Essie to use her culinary art, after being deprived of the opportunity so long. After she served the two and waited upon them attentively, Essie fixed breakfast for herself and the babies. Mrs. Stanton watched and sometimes helped in her limited way. "Many thanks to you folks," said Essie, "We ain't had anything so good since we left Georgia."

Mary Stanton watched Essie and her babies with rapt amusement and intense concern. So delighted was she with the two boys that she insisted that she be allowed to feed them their porridge. She laughed when she was spattered with food.

When the breakfast was finished, Mary could withhold her curiosity no longer, "I just can't imagine how you can travel with the young children. Where are you going, Essie?"

Essie sighed and smiled. She recognized the sincere, friendly interest of her hostess. "I don't rightly know, Mrs. Stanton."

"Where do you come from? Can't you go back home?" asked the good housewife.

"Ain't got no home, ma'am. Did have a home back in Georgia."

"You came from Georgia? On foot?" gasped Mary. "Why, honey, that's six or seven hundred miles, isn't it?"

"I rode most all the way in a cover't wagon. Don't know how far it was. You see, I belonged to a Cherokee family. They was forced to move west by the army. That child there, the one with skin the color of a honey-ginger cookie, he belonged to them Cherokee folks. When his mamma was a-dyin', I promised her I'd care for him and raise him like he was mine. Poor tyke, his ma and pa is both dead."

Mary gazed at the little papoose with warm compassion. "But weren't there relatives to take the child?" she asked.

"Don't know if they is or where they is. The Cherokee baby – his name's Arley – Arley needed a woman to nurse him. Too tinsey to take solid food when his maw died. I had to feed him same as my own baby."

"But why are you traveling? What are you running from?"

"You know how the Cherokee people is bein' forced to move to Oklahoma? I was goin' with this big travelin' passel of folks. One night I heerd some men talkin'. They was plannin' to take me and Caleb and sell us to slave traders. Arley would have been left without nobody to care for him. I had to run away so's to keep my promise to Arley's ma."

"Oh, Essie!" Mary Stanton caught her breath and slumped back into her chair, overawed by the dilemma which the slave woman had faced.

"You've been kind and understandin', ma'am. I'd like to ask one more favor of you. My chil'ens ain't had no bath in so long, I'm afeared their little hides is goin' to break out in sores. I was wonderin', you got a tub I could wash 'em in? If it's no trouble, that is."

"Land sakes, yes, honey. There's a tub hanging right out there on the back porch. And there's water right there at the sink. Add hot water from the stove to it." She wheeled off and returned with a large soft cloth for drying.

While Essie was bathing Arley and Caleb, Mary Stanton had gone from the room. When she returned, Arley, dried and dressed, was sitting on the floor playing with a wooden spoon. Essie was taking Caleb out of the tub. Mary spread the cloth towel on her lap to receive him. "Give him here to me," she said. As she dried the little brown body, she told Essie that she had had a talk with her husband. "Ben and I have decided to invite you to make your home here. We want to hire you to cook and help keep house. There wouldn't be much salary, but there would be lodging and good food." She held the little Arley up high in her arms and bounced his bare feet on her lap. "Look at this poor child," said Mrs. Stanton. "He's thin as a yearling doe after a winter blizzard."

"You're mighty kind, ma'am," said Essie with a pleasant smile. "But I ain't never hired myself out before. Always been just a slave worker. I wouldn't know how to act. Guess we can just pretend you bought me, 'til I get used to it."

"Ben and I don't approve of owning slaves, Essie, but I guess pretending won't hurt, just for a little while, but we will insist on paying a small salary. Of course, you know you are free to go away any time you like."

"Thank you, ma'am, but I plan to leave and go back to Georgia soon as I can get m'self together and my young'uns is rested and able."

Mary Stanton handed baby Caleb to his mother. "I'll go tell Ben, that you plan to stay a while," she said as she rolled out of the room.

Mr. Stanton came to talk with Essie. "We'd be very pleased if you'd decide to stay with us permanently. For a long time I have sought someone to stay with Mrs. Stanton and help her. Occasionally we have had a neighbor woman come in, but it will be good to have someone here all the time. Sometimes my work takes me away from home for long intervals. Come, let me show you your quarters."

He led Essie, carrying a baby on each of her arms, from the kitchen, through the hall, and up a stairway. Upstairs was a comfortable room, well-furnished, with cheery dormer windows overlooking the front yard and the Finley River.

So it was that Essie and her babies came to live with Judge Benjamin Stanton and his wife Mary. The grateful Essie worked

113

diligently, serving Mrs. Stanton, cleaning house, and caring for her two sons. The end of each day found her happily exhausted and too busy to plan for her return to Georgia.

Chapter VIII
Essie's Two Sons

After Essie was about a year in her new home, she was approached, one evening, by Mary Stanton. "I've been thinking for some time, Essie, you have such a heavy burden here caring for me and your sons. We need you so much. I--I was wondering--" she hesitated, choosing her words carefully. "Ben's nephew and his wife have for a long time wanted a second son. You've met Simon and Grace; you know how kind and loving they are. I wanted to ask--now, dear, don't be offended--I just wondered, would you consider letting them take Arley? Wait now, it's only a suggestion. But it saddens me to see you get so tired."

Essie stood speechless, startled by such a new, preposterous idea.

"Oh, Essie, I have hurt you!" said Mary. "Forgive me. I just wanted to make things easier for you. Let's forget all about it."

But the seed had been planted, and Essie could not dismiss the thought. At first wounded and piqued by the idea, later she began to weigh the advantages. Simon Collier was an admirable man. A farmer who provided well for his family. In a few years, Arley would be able to work on the farm, and it would be good for him. Arley needed a father. Simon's son Bill would be a good companion for Arley, but, of course, Caleb and Arley were like brothers. How could they ever be separated? And how, oh how, could she give up the baby she had taken from the arms of poor Fawn? Still, the Colliers lived only five miles away. She could see him often. She would not be giving him up completely. Essie could not force herself to make a decision, not now anyhow. The idea remained in the recesses of her mind. She acknowledged that some white people had taken black children to raise and, she supposed, even Indian children, but when, if ever, had black folks adopted a white or Indian child? In this world, white folks just naturally have better chances than black folks. Tears came to her eyes as she thought that she, herself, might be a handicap to Arley. After all, she was only a slave, a chattel possession. Still Essie set the decision aside.

Sometimes Essie and her boys went with Judge and Mrs. Stanton to visit the Collier family. Essie watched her boys at play with Simon's boy Bill. What marvelous fun they had!

One day Essie sat in the yard under a spreading oak tree, mending one of the judge's shirts. The boys sat on the ground nearby. Arley was five, nearly six, and Caleb a couple of months older. They had caught a couple of walkingsticks and, using some of Essie's thread, had made little harnesses for the insects. Amused by their antics, Essie dropped her stitching and stood over them, watching.

"My pony ain't movin'. Get-e-up, Prince," said Arley, giving the little walkingstick a push with his finger. "Move now!" he said impatiently. The slender insect stood stubbornly immovable. No amount of coaxing or nudging would induce him to walk. Suddenly, Arley seized a board, which was used as a bridge in their playing. He raised it into the air and slammed it down on the obstinate insect, smashing it flat.

Essie was amazed at Arley's sudden reaction. "Why did you do that?" she questioned.

"'Cause he wouldn't do right."

"I don't think he knew what you wanted him to do," said Essie.

"He wasn't no good. Jest a old walkingstick."

"But you didn't have to kill him. He was one of God's creatures. God made him just like He made you and Caleb. We shouldn't kill things when it ain't necessary. It's not kind."

"Why did God make him?" asked Arley.

"I don't know why, but I'm sure He had a reason. We are all important to God."

Arley raised his wide eyes heavenward. "I'm sorry, God, I smashed yer bug. Was it much trouble t'make?"

That evening, as Essie led her boys to their bed, Arley asked, "Mamma, am I as 'portant as a walkingstick?"

"Oh, Arley," said Essie, "you're much more important than a walkingstick."

"Am I as 'portant as Caleb?"

"All God's people are important, Arley. Very important."

"People say Judge Stanton is very im-portant. When he tells you to do sum'pin, you do it. Is he more im-portant than you, Mamma?"

"Arley, it's just that he's the master, and I'm the-- servant."

"When I grow up, can I be the master, so's when I say sum'pin, people has t'mind me? They won't jest stand there like a old walkingstick."

"That's enough now, Arley. You boys say your prayers and go t'sleep."

They climbed up and knelt on their bed and whispered their prayers. Before they plunged under the covers, Essie bent over, cuddled, and kissed their tousled heads. She pressed the light quilt snuggly around their shoulders. Pensively, she stood watching their contented smiles fade into quiescent slumber. How incredibly piercing had been the questions the little Cherokee had uttered. Such puerile questions to perplex her and fill her with contemplation! They are so alike, she mused as she gazed at their prostrate forms, yet so different. "Merciful God," she murmured as she stroked Arley's warm forehead, "help me to know how to raise this one, this one of the Cherokee people." Her own black son's future she could easily conjecture. He would have the same limitations, the same shackles which had bound her own life. His life could be little more than a servant. He would be a good, faithful servant, she hoped. But Arley-- Arley would not be likewise encumbered, not unless he became so bound to her and Caleb that the world would treat him as black. The thought seared her soul, brought tears to her eyes. It meant that she must relax her attachment on him. How could she do it? Her love for him led her to determine that Arley should have every advantage, every opportunity the white society would permit him to assume. He must go to school, even though Caleb couldn't.

Essie did not, nor could she, then or ever, give Arley over to Simon and Grace Collier. Still she permitted, even encouraged, Arley to go to visit them. When he returned to tell her what marvelous fun he had had during his visit, Essie shared his joy. Bill Collier, who was two years older than Arley, became the

Cherokee lad's idol. As time went by Arley spent as much time at the Collier farm as he did at the Stanton house. Simon and Grace were pleased to have him come as often as he liked and fondly looked upon him as the second son they could not have.

Most upset by this arrangement was Caleb. "Why is Arley going over to Bill's house today?" Caleb would ask, "I wanted him t' play with me."

"Because Arley is learnin' how t' be a farmer and he has got t'work over there. You have your work here," Essie would reply and then add, "Anyways, Judge Stanton wants you t'spade the garden patch today," or, "The judge wants you t' clean the horse stalls today. You got important work t'do."

Nevertheless, Essie said Caleb and Arley were brothers, and it was easy for the two boys to accept that.

It was mid-September. Essie was folding and packing Arley's clothes into a carpetbag. "Now, Arley, I'm sending you over to the Collier place so's you can go t' school with Bill. The school house is just a short piece from Bill's house. It ain't a far piece t'walk. You'll stay with them over there while school keeps. That'll be four months." Essie put her arms around the little Indian and pressed him tight against her. "Lordy, I'm goin' t'miss you, child!" Grasping his cheeks in her hands and looking lovingly into his eyes, she said, "You mind now and obey Simon and Grace. Do good in school so's you can be a big man when you grow up."

"Why can't I go t' school with Arley?" whined Caleb.

"Fer land sakes, child, you done forgot you are black. Ain't no black children 'lowed in school." Tears flowed down his bulbous cheeks, his head bowed in disappointment. "Oh, don't you fret none! I'm going t'teach you t'read. I was learned in Georgia, secret like, and I never let on. Fawn Tanner, rest her soul, she helped me t'read Cherokee. We don't want no trouble with white folks so's we got t'play thick-headed. Make 'em think they's the only smart ones." She forced a little laugh as though it were a delightful prank to play on the white race. Although she was sorely touched by Caleb's chagrin, in her wisdom, she knew that she must teach her son early the

118

inexorable laws governing her race. Squatting beside Caleb and putting her arms around him, she consoled him saying, "Arley will be coming home t'see us some of the days when they ain't no school--providin' his farm chores is kotched up." Placing her hand on the Indian lad's shoulder and reinforcing her admonition with a solemn shaking of her finger, she said, "Now Arley, you be cer'tin t'earn your keep by helpin' Mister Simon."

"I will, Ma," said Arley.

Mr. Horatio Dent stepped out of the door of the tiny unpainted frame schoolhouse and gave his hand bell a violent shake. Reluctantly, the youngsters left off their play and moved toward the classroom. Seven boys and ten girls scrambled into the room. Among them was little Arley, frightened and dreading his unknown fate. He carried a little slate and a small cloth sack holding an apple, a couple of biscuits, and a piece of dried beef. For assurance, he clung to Billy Collier's hand.

Along the two sides of the room were worn benches, and before them were ten battered, knife-scarred tables with sloping tops, each serving as work desks for two students. Light came from four windows, two on each side of the room. A pot-bellied stove stood in the room's center. When the weather was mild the door was allowed to stand open to let in extra light.

After summoning the children with the bell, Mr. Dent went to his desk at the front of the room and sat down. He paid little heed to the children's entrance. At last he rose from his chair, looked hard at the round-up of squirming juveniles of varying ages, and gave the command, "Sit down on the benches. Permanent seating will be assigned later." His voice was thin and shrill, but his mien was that of a newly commissioned army sergeant. The response was a scramble for the best seats. Mr. Dent scowled. A hushed silence fell over the room.

"As some of you know," the schoolmaster began, "last year's teacher gave up his position here because, as he said, some of you were --er-mischievous." The tall lanky fellow strode before the classroom in a loose-jointed shuffle. "I will expect you all to obey respectfully and to work hard." A hornet buzzed close to his nose. It was fall, and as the day warmed the insects began to emerge. Some of the bolder boys snickered to see the teacher glower at the annoyance. He went to the window and threw it open. "I run a strict classroom, and anything that disturbs me will be thrown out the window." With these words he stepped back into the center of the room. He gave a little leap swinging his arm high into the air, and with a swift stroke, he hit a hornet's nest fastened to a beam overhead, flinging it with one continuous motion through the open window. He slammed the window shut. The children gasped in astonishment. Outside, the windowpane became darkened with hornets.

"Mr. Dent, some of them hornets is inside the room!" stuttered one of the boys.

"So they are," remarked the teacher, gazing calmly about the room.

"Kin we get out o' here?" asked one of the braver youths.

"And go out there where all the hornets are? Just sit quiet. It's time we began work," said Mr. Dent.

"I'm scared. Can't I go home, please?" said one of the older girls cowering away from a buzzing insect.

"School will be out at the usual time," said Mr. Dent, and he proceeded with the lesson, amid the hum of hornets and the gasping, dodging of fearful students. Any boy, disrupting the lesson with the banging of a book to crush one of the preditors, was apt to get a stern, ominous glare from the schoolmaster.

"Ouch! I been stung!" cried Arley, pointing to the back of his hand and expressing his suffering by the tone of his outcry.

"Go to the water pail and pour a dipper of water over it," said Mr. Dent with indifference. "And try not to disturb the class."

Muddled, the beginning scholar looked about, uncertain where to find the water bucket. Bill rose to help his little protege, but sank back into his seat when Mr. Dent gave him a squelching stare. By the time the day had ended two other children had been stung, and all had learned the serious demands of an education and the unpredictable, unyielding nature of their taskmaster.

As the days progressed, Mr. Dent ruled with incredible ease, often with his limp frame slumped in his chair with his long stockingless legs stretched from his too-short trousers extending out beyond the confines of the area under his desk. An unruly child, summoned to the desk to be scathingly reprimanded, fidgeted and squirmed and often stumbled over the schoolmaster's feet. Such an incident gave Mr. Dent distinct pleasure.

On the third day of school, at lunch time, the children sat in a circle under a tree in front of the building. As was his custom, Horatio Dent reclined under a sapling apart from the pupils. The students were opening their lunch pails or sacks, and Arley opened his little cloth pouch. He pulled out a patch of black hair! Bewildered and flustered, he glanced around to see if anyone was watching.

"It's a human scalp!" screamed one of the large boys, springing to his feet and pointing at Arley.

Feeling the shock of the furry patch to his touch, Arley threw it down.

"A man's scalp! The Indian's got a head scalp in his lunch sack!" shouted Biff Wilson in mock horror.

The larger boys roared with laughter and jeered. For a moment Arley was too startled and repulsed by the patch of black hair to move. Bewildered, he stared at it. Then slowly he reached down, picked it up and turned it over. "This ain't a man's scalp," he said with restored confidence and mounting anger. "This here's a piece o' bear's hide. Who put this in my lunch sack?"

"Say, he's right!" said Biff in pretended seriousness. "You can't fool a Indian about scalps. They's taken too many o' 'em."

There was another peal of laughter. One of the older girls, Freda Harner, came and stood between Arley and his tormentors. "You bullies go on and leave Arley alone. I reckon you think yer sumpin' pickin' on the least kid in school."

The three youths turned away. "We was jest funnin'. Injuns has got no business bein' with white folks nohow."

Mr. Dent, chewing on a rib bone, had watched the whole proceeding with amusement. He had no inclination to intercede.

Arley's older foster brother, Bill, was at first confused by what was going on, but when he understood the prank, he thought it best not to interfere. He did not want to make it appear that Arley was unable to cope with the situation by himself. As they walked home that afternoon, Bill remarked, "You did all right not to be more upset. It made me fighting mad. We'll get even somehow." Bill would have liked to give the three bullies a good thrashing. He gave Arley a reassuring pat on the back.

When school was out on Friday afternoon Arley hurried home to Essie. That morning he had made a plea to Simon Collier to be excused from his week-end chores, and Simon, realizing the boy's first week at school had been a crushing experience, had indulgently consented.

Securely resting on Essie's lap with his arms clasped around her neck, Arley poured out his burdened heart. "Some o' the boys allers hecter me. They don't like me 'cause I'm a Indian."

"You ain't no ordinary Indian, chile. You are MY Cherokee brave. You ain't got no cause to cow down t'nobody," Essie assured him.

"But they's lots bigger than me."

"They ain't whupped you, did they?"

"They just pesters me with their talk most. Allus funnin' me. They call me Scalper." Then he told Essie about the piece of bear skin in his lunch sack and how "the older boys is given to laugh at ever' li'l slip up I make."

"Don't the teacher fault them feisty bullies?"

"He don't care none. He don't care a'tall."

"Oh, baby, I got me half a mind t'go over there and give 'em all a sound threshin'."

"No, Mamma, don't do that! They'd plum whoop me out o' school for sure. I can stand their funnin'. Just knowin' you stand by me helps. I love you, Mamma Essie!"

Essie kissed him on the forehead and said, "Just remember, honey child, we ain't plannin' t' stay in this country. Caleb's got a daddy back in Georgia, and, 'course, he will be your daddy, too. Soon as we're able we'll get to travelin'."

It was an unusually warm day for late September. After the school day was over, Biff Wilson and his two friends, Rudy and

Lon, decided to take a dip in the creek. Though other boys wanted to swim too, they knew that there could be no pleasure in it while the bigger boys were there.

"They like t' 'of drownded me onc't," remarked Tim Overby.

"Me, too," said Ned.

"It's kinda cold fer swimmin' anyways," remarked Arley.

"Listen," said Bill, "this'd be a good time t'get even with them bullies. Let's go down there and tie their clothes in knots."

The four boys crept through the thickets to the swimming hole. Quietly they spied upon the nude bathers. When the rollicking swimmers disappeared out of sight, Bill slipped out of hiding and gathered up all the boys' clothes.

"Jest tying their clothes ain't good enough fer 'em," said Tim. "Let's put their stuff up in a tree."

"Yeah," said Ned, "once me and my cousin found a grape vine growing way up in a little hickory tree. We pulled on the vine 'til we pulled the top of the tree over. Maybe we could do that!"

The boys searched through the woods until they found a tree which could be pulled over so that they could reach the crown of it. Holding fast to the top of the tree, they removed the grape vine. Three of the boys held the top down low while the fourth boy tied clothes onto it. When the first tree was laden with all it would hold, they let go of it. Shirts, trousers, and shoes swung high into the air. A second tree was pulled down and filled with garments. Happily the four boys viewed their handiwork. The clothing was almost hidden from view. They slipped away to their homes.

The swimmers climbed out of the water and up the bank. They searched for their clothes, exploring all over the area. Shivering in the autumn breeze, they were flustered and very angry. Not until one of them stumbled and fell back onto the ground did any of them discover their missing clothes. "There they are!" he shouted. But after repeated attempts to bring their things down by throwing rocks, and after trying to climb the trees and scratching the skin of their nude bodies only to find that the limbs were too small to hold their weight, they decided that they needed an ax to fell the trees. At last, they waited until dark and slipped to their homes.

The four younger boys, who had so enthusiastically engaged in the prank and were too absorbed in the fun to contemplate the after effects, were, the next morning, fearful of facing the three bullies at school. "We're in for it now," said Bill to Arley. "They're sure to know who hid their clothes."

When Arley and Bill came down the path toward the school, they found Tim and Ned crouching behind a fallen tree, afraid to go into the playground. "We heard Biff and Rudy askin' about us," said Ned. "They're after us all right. What we goin' t'do?"

"Let's wait here 'til Mr. Dent rings the bell, then we can go in after the others is all inside. They can't do anything after school starts."

During the day's session, whenever Mr. Dent turned his back, the three bullies shook their fists and made threatening grimaces at the younger boys, who, thus intimidated, dreaded to think about their fate when school was dismissed. "Stay in the building and leave when Mr. Dent does. We can walk with him most o' the way," whispered Bill.

So when school was out, the four boys remained behind under the guise of seeking answers to questions about the English lesson. Mr. Dent gave hasty replies and made his way out the door. The four youths followed him. Down the path a call came from out of nowhere, "Go on ahead, teacher. Leave them boys behind. We got business with 'em!" The voice was that of Biff Wilson.

Mr. Dent quickened his pace. The boys attempted to keep up with him. There came a whooping yell! A missile zinged toward them! It struck Arley on the shoulder at the base of his neck, squashing as it hit. "Ugh! A rotten egg!" exclaimed Arley.

"I got the Injun!" shouted a distant urchin. There was a raucous laugh.

Suddenly the attackers rushed at their adversaries, eggs flying. At first the youths backed away attempting to keep the eggs in sight so they could dodge them. Finally they turned and ran, pelted by the stinking splatters. At the schoolyard the attackers ran out of ammunition. With catcalls and shouts of ridicule, they left their stenchy victims. The boys felt defiled, nauseated, repulsive even to each other. First one, then all four of them began to rub themselves with autumn leaves or to roll about in the dry grass like skunk-sprayed hounds.

"Look," said Bill holding up an egg, "They dropped this in the leaves an' it ain't busted. I wisht they'd come back. I'd like to let them have this'un."

"I hate that Mr. Dent. He coulda' saved us, but he didn't even care. I'd like to let him have that egg, right on top o' the head," said Ned.

"Yeah," said Bill thoughtfully, "he deserves this egg. But I wouldn't dare! Wait a minute--" Bill had an idea. He removed his shoe and took off a worn-out stocking with holes in the heel and toe. "I need a piece of wire. Where can I get a little piece of wire?"

After a few moments of thought, Arley said, "There's a piece of wire on the outhouse door that we hook over that nail on the inside. I'll get it."

Bill tore the foot off his stocking and threw the rest away. He put the egg into the ragged foot of the stocking and twisted the bit of wire around the gathered opening. "Now let's go put this egg where Dent will get it," said Bill, as he led the boys into the schoolroom. He took the bell off the teacher's desk and threaded the wire through the ring on which the clapper hung, so that when the wire was securely twisted in place, the egg hung inside the bell. All was done carefully so as not to break the eggshell. The others watched with delight. Then Bill returned the bell to its customary place on the desk.

The next morning Bill, Arley, Tim, and Ned stood near, but cautiously not too near, to the stoop where Mr. Dent would ring the school bell. They endured without retort the older boys' ridicule and boastful references to the egg battle. At last, Horatio Dent, stepped out on the stoop, the bell held in his right hand at his side. He stood for an instant looking out over the playground. Then with the dignity and deliberation of a general saluting his troops, he raised the bell into the air and gave it a fierce shake. Holding the bell by the handle he rang it toward the youngsters. There was an orange-yellow spray from the bell and it would have showered away from the schoolmaster had it not been for a little breeze which carried the putrid fluid back to spray the bell ringer. No method of application could have been more sparingly effective!

Dent was completely stunned. He glared at his clothes and then into the bell. Then with mounting vengeance, he threw the bell with all his might. The older boys laughed to see the loss of composure in their teacher and his strange actions. The younger boys were frightened and paralyzed by the terrible anger in Mr. Dent's scrawny face. The hard muscles were drawn in tension. His eyes flashed rage. If only their prank had not been quite so effective!

The teacher stomped back into the room. As the students filed in, he stood stern and rigid, his arms folded across his chest and in his hand the heavy wooden paddle. With timid apprehension and alarm, the children took their places. Mr. Dent's piercing eyes scanned the room. For a moment his gaze fell on little Arley.

Arley trembled. "He wants to punish me. He hates me 'cause I'm Indian," he thought. He wanted to run out the door and flee into the arms of Essie. Mr. Dent cleared his throat with a loud "hrumpf". Arley winced, slid low into his seat. Bill reached out to clasp the small lad's hand.

"There will be no school today," said the schoolmaster. "Everyone is dismissed except Biff, Rudy, and Lon." There was a gasp from the young boys who had expected to hear their own names.

When all had gone except those whom he had named, Mr. Dent whipped the three boys without mercy. Their pleas of innocence had no avail. The schoolmaster was unconvinced. He had seen them throwing eggs, and he was in no mood to listen.

Horatio Dent never fully recovered from the humiliation he had suffered. His inherent overbearing authority in the classroom had never before been challenged, and he had gloated over his ability to dominate the students. The embarrassment of being splattered with rotten egg left a lingering stench in his nostrils. It was an unthinkable shock to his self esteem. He drew even tighter on the control reins of the classroom and considered every child a maverick to be subdued. Often he lashed out at an individual child with caustic sarcasm. It was his excessive verbal tantrums which were at fault. For the most part, the trauma which a child felt from the teacher's paddle was transitory. But the barbs from Mr. Dent's tongue struck deep and stung sharply. Such was the lingering indelible imprint on little "Scalper."

The response to the schoolmaster's bitterness was that the more aggressive boys, filled with rancor, became bolder and more defiant. Arley often bore the brunt of more and more cruel pranks of the larger boys. The little Cherokee tried to be a stoic, "brave little Indian" as Essie had so often admonished him to be. But underneath, his soul often fumed with anger, and he wondered whether his frustrated meekness was what Cherokees were really like.

It was a relief to Arley and Mr. Dent when, a few months after the rotten egg affair, Biff Wilson quit school. Two years later, before the school term was quite completed, Mr. Dent slammed the schoolhouse door and never returned. Where he had gone or why could only be speculated. Behind he left malignant psychological scars.

Part Two of Chapter VIII

In the brotherly affection existing between Caleb and Arley, perhaps no occasions brought them closer together than their excursions on the river. With adroitness the two youths guided their little row boat about the stream, often searching out the best fishing grounds, sometimes thrilling to a bounding ride over the rapids, frequently tying their little craft to a tree, shedding their clothes and boisterously frolicking in the water, and time and again they beached their boat on a sandy reef and lie in the sun while they revealed their innermost thoughts and feelings. One day, when they were both sixteen, they returned from fishing. to the big Stanton residence to find three scrubby horses tied to the hitching rail. Whose were they? they wondered. As they drew nearer, they saw a dark-bearded fellow come out of the house and go towards the barn. His furtive manner, his unkempt attire, and his obnoxious swagger further aroused their curiosity. Why was this man stealing toward the barn? Certain that he meant to do no good, the lads slipped to the back side of the barn, entering it through an open door. They had been gigging fish. Caleb carried a couple of good-sized catfish which he carefully laid aside. Arley carried his heavy long-shafted gig. Inside, the two youths separated, moving silently toward the front of the barn, Arley on one side of the center passaageway and Caleb on the other. Two horses were shut up in their stalls, but Caleb crawled through the dividing cross rails, giving rise to only a slight whinnying from the caged animals. The intruder had entered the barn and stood beside the door looking about and listening. Caleb crept forward into the cubicle next to the stranger. His heart sank in fright as he heard the gruff command, "Come out o' there!" Caleb stood upright and took a step into the center runway. "Get yer hands up," ordered the intruder, pointing a long-barrelled pistol. The stranger backed up against the wall, a little timidly, as though he were inexperienced in this sort of banditry. "Don't try anything or I'll kill you," he threatened. "We want them horses." Arley, still undetected, had not moved so close to the intruder. Cautiously he peeked out to survey the situation. Suddenly he stood up and, with a terrorizing whoop, hurled the heavy gig its sharp prongs pierced through the man's wrist and sank deep into a plank of the barn wall! The outlaw gave a loud shriek of pain, dropping the pistol from his helpless hand. Caleb sprang forward to pick up the weapon. A little astonished by their own success, the boys stood fairly tuckered and flustered for a moment. Then Caleb rushed to Arley, threw his arms around him and said, "Good throw, brother!" "Don't forget," said Arley, "there were three horses. There must be two more gunmen in the house." The captive outlaw writhed and moaned with pain, his arm pinned fast against the barn wall. "The way he's carryin' on, they're bound to come out here to see what's wrong.' The three men had forced their entry into the Stanton house, surprising the occupants. Judge Stanton, his wife, and Essie were held at gunpoint. The leader, whom the other two called Grover, was a rough, crude man with long graying hair and a large crooked nose. He had ordered the younger member, who was his brother Jake, to seek fresh horses. The other one, Charlie, was commanded to ransack the house for money and valuables. Mrs. Stanton, cowering in her wheelchair, clung to Judge Stanton on one side and to Essie on the other. Both outlaws and hostages heard the piercing cry which emanated from the barn. "Go see what's the matter with Jake," said Grover "Probably a horse stepped on his foot," he sneered. Charlie hurried out the back door toward the barn, unaware that the youths were watching him through knotholes in the barn wall. "Here he comes," whispered Arley. "Get down." They hid behind the partition. The man came through the door, cautiously looking all about. He turned toward Jake, who moaned in agony. "What happened?' he asked. Before Jake could answer, Caleb sprang out of his hiding place, putting the pistol to the bandit's back. "Put your hands up," he cried. Arley came to remove Charlie's gun from its holster. "There's a rope over there," said Caleb. "Tie him up." Arley bound him tightly, lashing him to a post. Then the two young men slipped toward the house. They attempted to spy through the windows but could see nothing. In the dining room, where the hostages were being held, the window panes were stained glass. Arley tossed a tiny pebble against the glass. "What was that?" asked the startled outlaw. "Just a bird flew agin' a window somewheres," said Essie. "Naw, it was right here clos't." There was a squeaking sound in the kitchen as Arley entered there. "Sounded like a door. That you Charlie?" asked Grover. "Lan' sakes," said Essie, "this ol' house is full o' squeaks and noises. Scares me lots o' times. Ah's jest prays and prays, so skert Ah is." She feigned the role of a superstitious Negro. "Lord a'mighty, Ah's skert right now. Lord, hear this poor nigger." She rolled her eyes heavenward and took off in a monotone of vocal utterances. "Shut up, nigger! Stop that gibberish," shouted the gunman. He called again to the kitchen, "That you, Charlie?" "It's de Holy Spirit what makes me talk in tongues," said Essie. "Ah can't stop!" But to Arley and Caleb her message was clear. Essie had reckoned that her boys had made the noises. In the Cherokee language, she gave a sing-song recitation describing the situation, telling them where the hostages were being held and giving instructions how best to surprise the bandit. She also feared that the boys would do something foolish. She noticed how quickly Grover's hand had moved to the knife at his belt when he became startled. She gave warning that he was probably expert at knife throwing. Pointing his gun toward the kitchen, the outlaw moved to behind Essie. With his knife point against her back, he growled, "Now shut up, damn ye, or I'll run this knife through ye!" Again he called out, "Charlie, Jake, you there?" Suddenly Essie shouted in Cherokee, "Now attack!" Arley, in the kitchen, threw a sack of flour into the open doorway. Crack! The bandit's pistol shot exploded the sack into a cloud of white dust. Essie dropped to the floor, too quickly for the knife to be used against her. The frightened gunman faced the kitchen. Caleb entered the room from the front of the house. "Drop that gun," demanded Caleb, "or you're a dead man!" The villain spun around and fired at Caleb. Crack! Crack! Crack! Grover crumpled to the floor. Arley and Caleb had both hit their target. The intruder's shot went wild. The bandit was dead! While the boys guarded the captives in the barn, Judge Stanton rode off to summon the sheriff. The victory was cause for celebration. Judge Stanton was lavish with his compliments of

131

Essie and her boys. "Your actions were ingenious. Frankly, I thought we would be fortunate if we got off alive and unhurt. I fully expected to lose the silverware, money, horses, and heaven knows what! How can I ever repay you and the boys?" "Master Stanton," said Essie, "you already know what's most on my heart--to go back t' Georgia and find my man. For all these years I been frustrated and foiled in my setting out to go. First, the boys was too young. Then they was too poorly, what with measles, pneumonia, and all. Then Misses Mary took sick. Always somethin' is stoppin' me. Master Stanton, seems it just ain't meant for me to go. Now my sons done proved they's growed up. I'm goin' t' go!" The judge gazed at her sympatheticlly. "Essie, it will be hard for us to let you go. You've meant so much to us. But we understand. Only, Essie, I don't see how you can go by yourselves. It just wouldn't be safe for you to travel alone. Women of color can't travel across the country. Even if you took the boys, as young as they are, you'd have trouble. A slave can't travel without a master along." "Master Stanton, I don't like to ask such a big favor of you, but, maybe, could you take us to Georgia?" "Oh, Essie, I'll do what I can. We'll see." Mrs. Stanton gave Essie's hand a fond squeeze. "Essie, you've been a godsend to us. We love you, dear." Caleb and Arley, too, were exhilarated by the flush of victory. Impulsively, they embraced Essie and each other. "Whee!" they exclaimed, exchanging pats on their backs. They recounted to each other the incredible adventure, as though trying to convince themselves that they had really acted so heroically. Caleb and Arley were brothers forever. Essie took a bucket of water to the dining room and knelt down on the floor. With a shudder, she began to sponge up the blood. "So much hurt in the world!" she mumbled. She thought of the evil men who had carried Gabe away. Were those men like the outlaw whose blood she now swabbed up? Could it be that Gabe had been pushed into a corner where he had to protect himself as Caleb had done? "I hope no bad man has done killed him." She shook her head sadly. "I wish you could see your son, Gabe. I got me two boys, Gabe. Two wonderful boys!" Essie sat motionless, the wet scrub rag losely clasped in her hand. "Poor Mas'er Kevit, he sure would be proud o' his boy now," she mused. She rose to her feet, brushed a tear away with her sleeve and moved into the kitchen. Soon, she told herself, she would seek her husband. However, less than a month later, Mary Stanton suffered another stroke similar to the one which had put her in the wheelchair. This time she was put to bed. Her future condition was uncertain. Over and over again, while Essie kept her vigil at Mary's bed, she poured out her heart's longing: "Oh Gabe, dearest husband, if you only knew how I would gladly plod through thorns, over craggy mountains, across deserts or swamps to be with you--but--oh, Gabe,--to release Mary's hand now-- Gabe, that I can not. Dearest, I know this about you, as you must surely know about me,--that if it were possible, you would be searching for me, and I for you. I am held here a captive of love and duty. I pray to God above that someday we both can cast off the shackles that bind us --that we may rush into each other's arms. But for now, Lord, lay your healing hand on Mistress Mary."

Chapter IX
The Brood Farm's Ending

The sixteen years Gabe had spent at the brood farm had numbed his spirit. He now thought of Essie only as an elusive dream, an ethereal experience he had once known. For long periods he dwelt upon her memory, attempting to rehearse every shred of her recollection. He visualized her movements, listened for her voice, dreamed of her soft touch. And he wept, knowing that, in spite of all, his recall of her was weakening. In his torment, he sometimes wished she would vanish entirely from his miserable existence. How torturous to the damned are the rapturous pleasures of the past! Was hell like this? Little by little he despaired of ever finding her again. So desecrated was his survival that Essie's glowing spirit brought to his mind painful shame. How unclean he was! Among the wenches for the plantation, Nelda was Gabe's favorite. She had given birth to her sixteenth child, and now she was past child bearing age. She lived in constant dred of being sold or being disposed of otherwise. Five of her offspring had been sired by Gabe. Now she had only her infant son, Paul, a gift of God at the time when she had thought her barren years had begun. Soon, she knew, Clem would wrench the child from her, and Paul would be sold as all the rest had been. She would rather die than give him up. Glancing up from her washtubs in the yard, Nelda often sought out Gabe to watch him at his work. When he was occupied with tasks close to her, she studied him closely. She saw him pause to see the black children at their play. What were his thoughts? Was he able to recognize which of those were his, his own flesh and blood? She imagined that she could tell. They were the sturdiest, most beautiful of them all. She saw the sadness which was written on Gabe's face. She longed to fill the void which brought on that sadness, for he was the only man for whom she had ever held any affection. Gabe had not been at the brood farm long until his carpenter skill had been discovered, so often his work was on buildings in the nucleus of the plantation. He was never fully trusted by Clem. Consequently Gabe was never without a shackle on one of his ankles. When one leg became sore and infected, the chain was moved to the other one. Slobber was never far away and kept a sharp eye on the defiant slave. One day Gabe was assigned to build a rude shelter near the spot where the laundry was being done. When the work was finished the women would have a cover for the inclement winter days and would be able to hang Master Clem's clothes there to dry. As he worked some of the slave children came to watch. Several of the older boys, perhaps eight or ten years old, took loose boards from the construction area and used them in play, building a place of their own. Struggling with a long board they accidently entangled it in the line of garments which the women had just washed and hung to dry. The rope broke and all the clothes fell to the ground. At once Slobber appeared cracking his scorge and uttering loud, ghastly sounds. He startled and frightened the children, attempting to flee his wrath, backed into the entanglement of clothing and ropes, tumbling over each other. Slobber flailed his whip across the sprawling bodies. Twice the thong struck. The children shrieked and bawled. The blacksnake lashed through the air again. Gabe moved behind Slobber and caught it in his gloved hand. Slobber spun around. "Au-ugg," he roared and raised his massive fist to send Gabe reeling. Gabe recovered and came toward Slobber. With a mighty blow Gabe struck the slave driver's belly. Again the monster pounded Gabe and sent him staggering. The fettered slave rushed back at Slobber with his powerful fists. The first blow struck Slobber on the side of the head; the second followed with a quick, deadly battering to the giant's jaw. The force of Gabe's jab bore the impact of his entire stiffened torso. The colossal brute gave a savage yell, sputtering blood from his slashed, dangling tongue. Momentarily stunned, he staggered back. Behind him was a huge iron caldron filled with clothes which Nelda was boiling. He felt the scorching rim of the kettle against his buttocks. Still dazed, he turned facing the attack which seemed to come from behind. With all her might, Nelda seized his head with both her hands and thrust it under the boiling water. With the paddle she had used in stirring the clothes, she struck him with a blow to the back of his head. She held the paddle stick against his head until her strength gave out and her painfully scalded hands could hold it no longer. The monstrous body, of its own weight, slumped back pulling the hideous scalded head out of the kettle. Slobber lay lifelessly sprawled on the ground. A crowd of slaves had gathered. Their cries of awe and wonder arose at the struggle and defeat of the terrible Slobber. The clamor of excitement brought Clem running, determined to learn the cause of such an uproar. The Negroes' cries of victory over the demise of the hated slave driver hushed as Clem bowed over the huge corpse. Detest for the slave owner was no less intense than that which they held for Slobber. Black faces which gloated over Slobber's death now changed and assumed hateful sneers. They would have jeered loudly if they had dared. They watched in apprehension and dread of Clem's reaction. "What happened?" he screamed. "He dead. Who done it?" The horrified Negroes were too scared to answer. Surveying the crowd menacingly, Clem's eyes fell upon Nelda's red, tortured hands. "What ye done? It yer fault, ain't it?" Gabe moved toward Nelda, but the chain which held him fettered to a post held him back, short of reaching her. "Ye kilt him, 'pears like. Come here, let me see yer hands. They's been skalt, ain't they?" All around, the black folks wanted to defend Nelda but none dared. Then a woman who had been gutting and filleting fish at a bench nearby moved to the front of the crowd. "She never done nothin', Mas'ah Clem, suh. Nelda she try t' pull him out when he fall into the kettle. He done trip an' fall." Clem reached out to grasp the fish cleaner's arm.

"Now ye tell the truth. Never stumbled, did he? Don' make no sense, him fallin'. Don' lie ter me! What thet wench done?" "Mas'ah, yo hurtin' me arm," the woman cried. Clem pulled her closer. Behind her, in her free hand, she held her fish-filleting knife. With a fierce swing of her arm she sank the knife into Clem's back, piercing his heart. With a shriek of pain and a death gurgle Clem slumped across the body of his dead henchman. Almost immediately pandemonium and chaos broke forth on the farm. An explosion of joy and celebration! Shackles were unlocked. Slaves romped and danced about. Food and liquor supplies were raided and squandered. With jubilation all work was suspended, all, that is, except the task of digging two graves, the most joyous activity of all. When the wild confusion began to subside, Gabe began to consider his future.

At last, he was free to seek Essie. But how? Where? A few of the other slaves disappeared, running--hoping to find their way to other plantations where they had friends or relatives, where they had known more gentle masters. Gabe knew that the Cherokee people had gone. Somewhere in the distant West they had settled. He had heard the reports. Could he go there? While he had been miserably enslaved, he had for years promised himself that he would. Now he must decide. Could he do it? Should he try? To travel disguised as a free man of color would be difficult. His ankles bore the scars of the shackles. Everywhere in the slave territory strangers would be suspicious. Finally he whispered to Nelda, "I'm goin'. I sure 'nuff goin'. Ain't nothin' gonna stop me." He searched the plantation for supplies he might take with him. In the morning he would start out. The sun rose bright, and Gabe was filled with a buoyant spirit, ready to start out. Then came Nelda. Her countenance was solemn, even melancholy. Dressed in her loose Mother Hubbard she crept timidly close, seeming almost apologetic for being there. At her side, clinging to her skirt, was a little pickaninny. He pulled at her hem, and with an imploring appeal he begged her to pick him up into her arms. She looked down at him lovingly, knowing that he could not understand how excruciating was the pain of her burned hands. "Gabe," she said, "I wanted yo ter say goodbye ter Paul. Won't never remember it. He nearly a year ol' now. But I wants ter tell him some day, he oncet saw his paw." Gabe stood still, stunned by her words. He had seen the child before, but only momentarily, at a distance. At once the piercing thought came to him--the knowledge that he was, indeed, a father. His relationship with the farm's wenches had been so impersonal, so lacking in true love and compassion, that he had purposely benumbed his soul. He had shut up his heart, imprisoned it, even as his body had been imprisoned. He had forced himself to believe that what he had been compelled to do as a copulating stud had no real meaning or significance. Suddenly, the tiny black form clinging to his mother's skirts was evidence of something which he had preferred not to think about. Then and there came a revival of the compassionate spirit he had once possessed. He was no longer an animal! With tears in his eyes he stooped down and scooped up the little one in his arms. He hugged and kissed the child. And he wept. What was Gabe to do? His blissful first love had been for Essie. She tugged him with unrelenting power. He hugged and kissed the baby over and over before he could set him down to return to cling to his mother. He stepped close to Nelda, put his arms around her and kissed her on the cheek. "Goodbye," he said, "Goodbye, my son. Goodbye, Paul- -my--son." He heaved a deep sigh. "I'll come back someday. God be with you always. You understand--I must go." And he hurried off. He never looked back. His heart was heavy. Only sheer dogged determination impelled him. Gabe traveled westward. He had no idea of the route he must take nor how far he must journey to find Essie. First he would seek out the old forsaken Cherokee country and from there--he did not know. Suddenly there appeared before him a band of mounted Georgia militia men. "That there's one o' 'em. He's one o' 'em what's escaped from Clem Bassop's plantation." The speaker was a civilian riding with the soldiers. "Grab him!" Gabe was taken prisoner. With his hands tied behind him he was driven back to the plantation. Clem's brother-in-law had somehow discovered the trouble at the breeding farm. He had appealed to the law officers. His wife and the other sisters of Clem were due to inherit the property, if indeed there had been a massacre. There ensued an investigation into the deaths of Slobber and Clem Bassop. Witnesses were questioned. There was such a diversity of stories from the frightened slaves that not much could be determined. The most prevalent tale was that the owner had gotten into a quarrel with his overseer and they had killed each other. The bodies were exhumed. But no conclusive evidence was reached, and no one was brought to trial. In the end, all the slaves were divided up among the three sisters of Clem Bassop. Gabe was taken to one of the plantations and Nelda and her son were taken to another. On very rare occasions they were able to see each other but were never allowed to visit. The new plantations were regular cotton producing farms. The new masters were more generous and less cruel. Twice Gabe tried to run away, but he was caught and severely beaten. His existence was like that of the millions of slaves of the South.

Chapter X
Caleb and Arley

Caleb, now seventeen, paced aimlessly across the room.

"Caleb, what is it? What's troublin' you?" asked Essie, looking up from her needlework. Caleb sank down onto a footstool before her chair. He looked intently into her concerned face. "It's--it's Arley," he said hesitatingly. "I can't understand him."

"What's he done?"

"He's different. It's that paper--that paper that says--well--that you belong to his father. You don't belong to Kevit Tanner do you, Ma? He's dead. You can't be Mr. Tanner's, can you?--his-slave? Arley's got that paper. What's it mean, Mamma?"

"You know that, Caleb. I done told you lots of times. I was bought by Kevit Tanner. All my people was slaves. You know that. That ole paper I gave to Arley because it belonged to his daddy."

"But Arley sez that what was his daddy's is his now. Are you his property, Mamma?"

Essie laughed a little. "I reckon I am. The law sez that when parents die, their children get their things. Funny, ain't it? I always thought Arley was my boy, just like you, but I guess I'm sure his property."

"That's what Arley sez."

Essie smiled. "What would that boy want with an old woman like me? 'Sides, he don't need no paper. He knows I belong to him. And I always thought he belonged to me! Been mine since he was a baby."

"You allways said Arley and me was brothers. We ain't brothers no more, Mamma."

"What you mean, son?" Essie looked at him with intense seriousness.

"Arley sez he owns me too. Sez I gotta do things he sez."

"Has he asked you to do things bad, things you don't want to do?"

Caleb looked at his fumbling hands. "Well, no. He ain't asked for much. It's the way he acts, most. He acts like he's better than me. Lots of white folks think they's better than us. Is Indians better than us too, Ma?"

"Land sakes no, child. You just gotta understand folks. They's all struggling to get on top." She paused thoughtfully. "When I was a girl back on the plantation, I used to watch the chickens. One big ole red hen would peck every other chicken in the flock, and none dared to peck her back. Then they was another hen who could peck all the other chickens except that first hen. She was the number two hen. Then they was the number three hen. She could peck all the other chickens but them first two. An' so it went. All the hens could peck somebody. All but one poor little ole hen at the bottom of the list. She couldn't peck nobody. I felt sorry for that little hen. Sometimes I cried about her. One day I caught her and decided to make her my pet. I put her in a box and fed her special. I talked to her and petted her--kept her a long time. Then one day she escaped out of the box and was back with the other hens. I watched her a long while, and then I seen she was peckin' two of the other hens and they didn't fight back. I didn't feel sorry for her no more."

"We ain't chickens, Ma."

"Sometimes we are, Caleb. Some people just got to lord it over other people."

"Why would Arley want to lord it over me, Mamma?"

"It ain't that he wants to lord it over you. He ain't thinkin' of you. He's thinkin' of hisself. Poor Arley, he don't know who he is. He thinks he's the lowest chicken, and he's lookin for somebody to peck. All to once, he's found he's got something most people ain't got. He owns two slaves. Poor Arley. He don't know who his folks is. He don't know he's one of them great Cherokee people. Lawdy, I loved his mamma--like my own sister she was. I was proud to be working for her. Arley sure ain't got no cause to feel inferior.

Caleb was sadly perplexed. "But we are slaves, Ma! Just slaves! I thought we was like other folks. We ain't. Arley is puttin' hisself over us. Arley and me ain't brothers. Why you say, 'Poor Arley?' Ain't he better Than me?"

"If Arley tries to make hisself better than you, it's 'cause he ain't sure of hisself. Big people don't need to act big. It's little people what's gotta act big. Poor Arley feels little and unimportant, that's why he's tryin' to make you inferior."

"Am I inferior, Mamma?"

Essie put her arms around him. "No, my son, you ain't inferior. You ain't inferior until you think you are inferior." Essie stood gazing thoughtfully at Caleb. "You know, maybe it's good that we are slaves of Arley. Now I think maybe he's grow'd up enough to be a master who can travel and take us with him. Yes, I think he can really do it if he wants to. We gotta make him willin' to take us to find your paw." She smiled with contentment in her speculation.

"But my paw ain't nothin to Arley."

"Oh, Caleb, Arley belongs to us. I know your father. He will take Arley as his son. And when you get right down to it, yer paw is Arley's property same as us."

It was early April. On the Collier farm Simon and the boys were busy plowing and harrowing the earth for the spring planting. After a long hard day's work, they sat at the table loaded with Grace's country cooking.

"Tomorrow," said Simon as he heaped spoonsful of boiled potatoes onto his plate, "we will work in the north bottom field."

"Have you forgotten?" said Grace, "You promised Maude Howser that you would work for her tomorrow. I plan to go over there to help her with her garden planting. Some of the women of the church are coming to cook for the hands who will be working in Maude's fields."

"That's right. I had forgotten. Tomorrow, boys, we will work for Widow Howser."

"Oh, did I tell you? Maude said her niece is coming from St. Louis t'live with her. I'm glad. Maude needs companionship. Still, two women living alone, I don't see how they can make it," said Grace. "And from the way Maude spoke of her, I gather that her niece isn't much more than a child."

The Howser eighty-acre farm bordered Simon's land. Paul Howser had died of pneumonia in February. The neighbors were rallying to Maude's aid to repair fences and cultivate and do spring planting.

A week later, Maude's niece Evangeline came by stage coach to Hershfield's store and in a hired hack to the Howser farm. She was a pretty blond of fifteen, just out of the academy for young ladies. She had been sent to southwest Missouri by her father to make her home with her deceased mother's sister.

"I saw the new girl over at the Howser place," remarked Bill one evening at the supper table. "I was riding by and she stopped me. She sez she's got a colt what needs broke. Could I help her? she sez. I reckon I can; can't I, paw?"

"I think you can when we get some free time," said Simon.

"I can help too," said Arley. "I got a special way with horses."

"No need," said Bill. "I think I can still gentle a colt by myself."

A few days later, Arley remarked to Bill, "I rode by the Howser farm and seen you workin' that colt, but you wasn't spendin' much time with it. 'Peers you was mostly talkin' with Evangeline. You sweet on her or somethin'?"

"Aw, hush, Arley. You didn't jest ride by. You stopped and gawked. You got no business spyin' 'round. I ain't doin' nothin' but tryin' to be neighborly. Besides, she saw you! She sez, 'Who is that dark boy there watchin' us?' 'That's my brother, sorta',' sez I. 'He lives with us at our place most of the time.' 'Why doesn't he come over to be friends and help, instead of staying out there looking.'"

Arley took these remarks of Evangeline to be an invitation of a sort, so that at the earliest opportunity, while Bill was busy helping his father, Arley rode over to the Howser farm.

"I'm Arley Tanner. I live next door. I come to help gentle that colt, if I can."

"Glad to meet you, Arley. Bill told me about you. Thanks for coming to help, but I don't know whether you should. Bill

144

won't let anybody do anything with that horse but himself--not even me," said Evangeline.

"That's 'cause he's afraid you might get hurt, what with the colt not fully broke yet. Now me, it would be good for me to ride him. He needs to get used to different riders. What you call him?"

"I call him Buttercup. He's blond, you know."

"Yeh, I know. Blond and beautiful like..." Arley broke off.

"Like what, Arley?"

Arley hesitated, trying to muster his courage. "Like--you," he said with embarrassment.

Evangeline laughed uproariously. "That's the first time I was ever compared to a horse!"

"I meant it for a compliment," stuttered Arley. "It's a compliment 'cause I love horses."

Evangeline continued laughing until the frustrated Arley pleaded, "Can I go see Buttercup now?"

"Of course," said Evangeline.

In the saddle, Arley put the handsome palomino colt through his paces with skill and precision. The youth's shining black hair rebounding to the rhythm of the steed. He sat majestically, confidently in control of the animal's every movement. Evangeline, watching from the top rail of the corral fence, was captivated by Arley's superb skill and his severe Indian features. When he withdrew his foot from the stirrup and swung his leg over the horse's back, slipping so agilely to the ground, the smooth and graceful motion was that of a dancer. Leading the palomino by the reins to the young spectator on the fence, he assumed a stature and strength which the city girl had not seen before.

"You ride very well," she said, wishing to compensate for the embarrassment she had caused him in the conversation earlier.

"He's a beautiful animal and very intelligent," said Arley. "Thank you for letting me ride him." Again, he wanted to say that the horse's mistress was beautiful too, but he did not have the nerve. Instead, he said, "I gotta go now. Maybe I can come see Buttercup again sometime." And he swung into the saddle of his bay mare and galloped away.

The next day Bill upbraided Arley, "You went over to the Howser farm and rode Evangeline's colt, didn't you? Why didn't you ask me first? I was getting that horse where he was doing just fine. It's not good t'change teachers in early training."

"It didn't hurt the colt none. He rode very well. I'd say he handled beautiful," said Arley.

"That's what Evangeline said. What I'm sore about is that you did it without askin' me. You went over there to show off didn't you?"

"No, I didn't. I just wanted to see the palomino. You don't see many of them 'round here. Where'd she get him?"

"Evangeline's father travels. He sent it to her from Texas," said Bill.

"Well, I'm sorry I didn't talk to you before I went. You done a good job in trainin' him."

146

Part Two of Chapter X

One March day Grace Collier sent Arley to Hershfield's General Store to buy a few yards of domestic, a spool of thread, and a few other items. For the nearly four mile trip to the settlement, Arley rode the bay mare, taking with him a couple of gunnysacks filled with turnips and sweet potatoes to be traded off to Mr. Hershfield. Upon arrival, he found a freight wagon backed up to the dock. The teamster was rolling barrels of sugar, salt and coffee from the wagon into the warehouse. As Arley looped the reins around the hitching rail, the lead mule of the draft team kicked up his heels to repel a horsefly. The other mules bolted nervously, jerking the wagon. The teamster was overbalanced. As he pitched forward his foot fell into the crack between the wagon bed and the platform. He caught himself by clinging to a barrel which rolled and lodged in the crack. Arley heard his outcry and rushed to his aid. First, Arley blocked the back wheels with large rocks which he found close by. Then he helped the teamster out of the crevice. When his leg dropped down, it had scraped against the angle-iron edge of the platform, severely damaging the skin and muscle.

"Lucky thing for you," said Arley, "that the wagon didn't move no more. If it had, both you and the barrel might a' fell through to the ground. You coulda' been under the barrel and hurt bad."

"The brakes didn't hold and I forgot t'block the wheels," moaned the limping teamster, his face twisted in anguish.

Mr. Hershfield came out of the store. When he saw the man's leg he said, "Jim, ye'd better get to a doctor. Ye ain't goin' t'be able to unload this stuff. Take my rig and get over to Doc Fisher."

"I'll unload them barrels," volunteered Arley.

From this beginning, Arley developed a friendship with Mr. Hershfield and the drayman Jim Thompson. Sometimes Arley helped move merchandise for the elderly shopkeeper and sometimes he ran errands and made deliveries.

Essie received the news of Arley's employment with pride. Now, Arley," she said, "work hard and tend to business. You know we're going to need money to get to Georgia. We'll put your wages in the bank."

The half-mile-wide glade was bright in the early June sun. At the western side, a high rocky cliff cast its reflection in a shadowy pool fed by a little brook wending its way among creek stones and boulders which in ages past had tumbled from above. In time the water had undercut the bluff and sculptured the random masses of dolomite into rugged shapes with holes and fissures. At the eastern edge of the glade thickets of red cedars bore ice-blue berries and were interspersed with scrubby oaks and hickories. The sound of horses' hooves and the rustle of movement through the foliage startled a Cooper's hawk, who took off with noisy flapping wings into the sky.

Two riders burst through the thicket and halted just beyond the timbers. "Here it is. This is the spot I was telling you about," said Arley.

"It's beautiful," remarked Evangeline.

Before them lay a tapestried field of purple coneflowers, yellow tickseed flowers, fragrant verbenas, and purple phlox. Here and there were patches of little bluestem grass.

"Over here is where Bill and me went swimmin'." Arley's horse took off at a gallop.

The young woman followed on her cantering palomino, gliding over the glades with skill and ease. The poised rider moved with expertise and grace, her blond hair flowing on the breeze. Her sprightly laugh had the intonation of a shepherd's pipe. As she approached Arley on the edge of the pool, she remarked, "You always race your poor horse like a pursued highwayman. It must be the Cherokee in you."

He ran to her and extended his hand as she dismounted. "Do you not like the Cherokee in me?" His tone was light but his purpose was solemn, and he hung intently on her reply.

"Yes, I do," she replied. Arley welcomed her response with a squeeze of her hand. "To tell the truth, I find many of your Cherokee traits rather attractive," she said with a broad smile.

148

"Let's sit here by the water," suggested Arley, leading her to a large flat stone. His spirit was elated and his confidence bolstered by her remark. "Evangeline, you are the most beautiful girl I ever seen. Your way o' doin' things and your way o' talkin' is real pretty. It must be 'cause you're from St. Louis."

"Thank you, Arley." She spoke quietly, a little uneasy to be so lavishly complimented.

For several moments Arley floundered, unable to find words to express his feelings. "I got me a job at Mr. Hershfield's store," he remarked brightly, with relief that he had finally found a casual remark as a place to start.

"Yes, I know," said Evangeline. "Mr. Hershfield sez I work good and am good at ciphering. He leaves me alone to keep the store lots o' times."

"That's splendid. I'm sure he knows how dependable you are. He has confidence in you," remarked Evangeline. Although she sincerely recognized in him great capability and intelligence, she had often observed how necessary it was to him to be reassured. Her remarks were unfeigned.

"Now that I have work, I..I was... Do you think...," he stammered seriously. "I...I want you t'marry with me, Evangeline. Will you?" The young woman threw her head back and gave a little laugh, an expression not of amusement but of uncertainty.

Arley mistook her response as mocking him. He was chagrined.

"Oh, Arley, I'm not taking what you say lightly. Thank you for asking. You must surely know I am very fond of you. But what you don't know is that yesterday Bill asked me to marry him. Two proposals in two days! That can overwhelm a girl." She smiled at him tenderly, trying to ease his hurt feelings.

"W..What did you say t'him?" he asked apprehensively.

"I couldn't give him any answer. I don't know what to say." She shook her head a little, her mind confused. "The three of us have had so many good times together. How could I choose between you? Maybe I'm in love with you both."

Her reply put Arley in a quandary. For the remainder of the afternoon his mind was full of comparisons of himself with Bill.

Bill had a much more secure future. His father had offered to give him land and to help him build a little house whenever he should decide to marry. Bill had told it all to Arley, not boastfully but matter of factly. Arley had been happy for him. Still, now it seemed to give Bill an enviable superior advantage. Most of all, Arley could not put aside the fact that Bill's was not an Indian. Bill's family was really his own. Simon and Grace Collier had accepted Arley like a son, but he could not expect equal treatment with Bill. An orphan boy gets everybody's sympathy and kindness, but he always remains a little apart. "I got Essie and Caleb. They're my family," he thought. Further doubts crept in. When he was with his black family, how often strangers had scrutinized him. Why did he have to be "different"? Who were the Cherokees, anyway?

Evangeline, too, was distracted as she and Arley explored the glades and the pool with its overhanging bluff. Her thoughts turned from Bill to Arley and from Arley to Bill.

One morning, when Mr. Hershfield had business away from his store, he left Arley in charge of the place. A pernickety, pinched-faced woman came in to buy molasses, salt and other staples. "I'm Mrs. Pickett. Where is Mr. Hershfield?" she asked laconically, reluctant to trade with the merchant's errand boy. "You're that redskin stripling that got into a scuffle at school with my Loren, ain'tcha? Who was sending you to our school?" She spoke condescendingly.

Arley replied briefly with courtesy, disregarding her snobbery. "I'm stayin' with Simon Collier and his family."

"Humph," the woman grunted and proceeded to order her supplies. Arley filled the order compliantly. "Here, let me sack my own crackers," the fastidious woman demanded, crowding her way to the barrel.

At that moment Essie came through the door, and Arley went to greet her. "Ma Essie, I'm mighty proud t'see you. You sure look all-fired pretty," said Arley giving her a little embrace.

At the cracker barrel, Mrs. Pickett eyed the strong, slender woman obliquely, curious to know why the young Cherokee shopkeeper should be so cordial to the mulatto with complexion a shade darker than his own. The vexatious customer could not withdraw her gaze from Essie. The smooth satin plane of Essie's jaw passed across the faint crimson blush of her cheek to the golden brown temples and brow to the wavy embossed black hair. Her nose was slightly Negroid, her lips the color of roses in an antique tapestry.

Mrs. Pickett, resented an intrusion which diverted the clerk's attention away from herself, spoke curtly, "Now will you finish my order? I'm in a hurry." She carried a woven basket on her arm, and after all her supplies were stacked on the counter, the ciphering done and duly checked under her sharp eye, she pulled out a block of something wrapped in oily paper. "This is fresh-churned butter." She leaned over the counter and spoke softly to Arley. "I want to exchange it for some of the store-bought butter o' your'n."

"Why? I don't understand why?" asked Arley.

"Well," she said, flushed, "We was about to pour the cream into the churn when a rat fell into the bucket. Oh, he wasn't in there but a minute. Didn't hurt it a bit. But I jest can't stomach it, knowin' what happened. Somebody else, that don't know, can use it, and it ain't goin' t'bother them none."

Arley hesitated, "I don't know if I oughta do that."

"See here, boy, Mr. Hershfield would do it fer me."

She shoved the package toward Arley. "Now, fetch me the butter."

"The butter is kept in the cooler in the back room," he said and disappeared.

Mrs. Pickett muttered to herself, "Why Mr. Hershfield would leave his place to such riffraff, I can't figure." Again she looked disdainfully at Essie who sauntered about the store with confidence adding grace and adornment to the simple, rough home-spun garment she wore.

"I thought I knowed about most o' the niggers in these parts. Whose girl are you?" asked Mrs. Pickett with a glower.

"I work for Judge Stanton," said Essie.

"Oh?" said the woman curiously, "I thought the Stantons wus ag'in slave holdin'."

Essie did not reply.

Arley came back into the room and handed Mrs. Pickett the package of butter. "I'm sure you'll feel better about this butter," he said.

As Mrs. Pickett moved to another part of the store, Essie whispered to Arley in the Cherokee tongue, "Do you really think Mr. Hershfield would have exchanged that butter?"

"I don't know, but I sure wouldn't." "But..." Arley smiled. "Oh, I just took the butter and reshaped it and wrapped it again in fresh paper," he whispered.

While Mrs. Pickett was finishing her shopping and paying the bill, five horsemen rode up to the front of the store, dismounted and came in. They were Indians. Two of them wore hats decorated with eagle feathers. Three men bound their heads with brightly colored turbans. Their clothing was a assortment of tunics, shoulder blankets, coats, and deer skin vests and leggings. The men and their garments bore the disheveled, dusty appearance of having been long on the road. They stopped just inside the door, gazed slowly about the store until their eyes rested inscrutably on Arley, who returned their stare. Mrs. Pickett froze on her spot, her expression was alarm and fear.

Recognizing them as Cherokees, Essie watched with keen interest to see how Arley would react.

"Asiyu," said one of the youths in Cherokee greeting.

"Asiyu," replied Arley.

The expressions of the strangers mellowed and they were intrigued, recognizing that they had met a kinsman. "Where is the store owner?" asked one of the men, speaking in Cherokee.

"The owner is not here. I am in charge," said Arley, also speaking in Cherokee.

The young men burst into laughter. They dispersed at once into every corner of the store, handling the merchandise, creating a general disorder. Some of them put small items into their pockets.

"If you want t'buy anything, I'll be glad t'wait on you," said Arley. "Don't scramble the merchandise." He cringed at the sound of something breaking at one corner of the room.

One man went up to Essie, grasped her arm and spun her around. "Look what we have here," he called out. "Pretty ain't she, for a nigger, that is."

Mrs. Pickett screamed in terror and rushed out the door leaving most of her supplies behind on the counter.

Arley, who up to that time was rattled and confused about what to do, seized a meat cleaver and poised himself ready to defend Essie.

Essie pulled herself free of her aggressor and confronted the man with the arresting impact of her eyes, dark fierce gems in ivory spheres. She spoke in Cherokee, "What kind of men are you? You speak the language of the Cherokee but act uncivilized? I shared with the true Cherokee people the hardship and suffering on the trail where we cried. Your fathers were brave and honorable men. Can it be that you are a generation of chicken snakes? This young man is the grandson of Chief Soaring Hawk, and I done raised him as my son. I stand by him proudly, but it is sad to stand against our own people. Get out o' here!"

A sobering hush came over the men. One of them came to Arley. "I am ashamed. I will do no harm against a brother." For a few tense moments Arley and the penitent stranger stood facing the other men. Then the four turned one by one and left the store.

"My name is Grey Wolf," said the young brave. "We drove cattle to Springfield and sold them. Now we are going home. We did not honor our people this day. I did not choose my friends wisely. I desire friendship and seek your pardon."

Arley extended his hand and smiled amicably.

"My name is Arley. I shall value your friendship," he said.

"I want to buy food--meal, beans, bacon..." said Grey Wolf. After he had paid for his purchases, he said, "I hope our trails will meet again ."

"Asiyu," said Arley and Essie.

After Mrs. Pickett fled from the store, she proceeded down the street in her buckboard wagon. Before she had gone far, she espied Mr. Hershfield passing along the boardwalk. She pulled her horse to a hitching rail and called him over to her wagon.

"Mr. Hershfield, you better git back t'yer store. That redskin boy you left in charge is in trouble. A band o' onery Cherokee thugs come in and is wreckin' the store. They's upsettin' things and puttin' stuff in their pockets. I don't know if they's friends o' yer boy or not, but I 'spect they are. I left most o' my staples on the counter, so scared I was. If you keep thet boy in yer store, I don't aim t'shop there no more. If yer agoin' t' yer store now, I'd thank you t' bring out my stuff I done paid for. I had to leave and run fer my life out o' there."

Mr. Hershfield accepted her invitation to ride with her back to his place of business. After he carried Mrs. Pickett's purchased things to her wagon, he returned to talk to Arley. By then Essie had made a few purchases and had gone.

"Tell me what happened," asked the storekeeper.

After Arley had finished his account, Mr. Hershfield said woefully, "Jest look at this place! Couldn't you a'done somethin'? After all, they wus yer people, wusn't they?"

"No, they wasn't my people. Sure, they was Cherokees, but I never seen them before. And they was five o' them."

"Thet lamp they busted costs four dollars, an' I figure they must o' stole six, maybe eight knives of that rack over there, and...and no tellin' what else."

"If you think it was my fault, take it out o' my pay."

"I don't know if it wus or if it wusn't yer fault, but yer pay fer a whole month wouldn't give me back all what I lost." Mr. Hershfield was becoming more and more vexed.

"Well, take it out o' my earnin's," urged Arley in resignation.

"I ain't wantin' ter do thet...Still..." He hesitated, giving Arley a long, staid glare. "If...If you wasn't a Cherokee yerself maybe they wouldn't a'been so treacherous an' thievin'. Leastwise, Mrs Pickett sez she don't aim to come in the store no more if ye'r here."

Arley was dejected. Mr. Hershfield had been his friend, and Arley had been proud to work for him. "Ain't nothin' left for me exceptin' t'quit workin' for you, Mr. Hershfield. I done the best I could, but I quit!"

154

"I'm sorry, but they don't seem nothin' else ter do. Don't want to see ye go, but it looks like yu'll have to."

The unhappy Indian youth left Mr. Hershfield's store, mounted his horse and rode down the village street. His thoughts were about the Cherokee scoundrels who had ransacked the store. They had been so brazen and insolent. It was strange, though, they had entered the building diffidently, modestly. When they had learned that the establishment was in Arley's charge, only then did they break forth in their pillage. Why? Why should the Indian youths, who would have been quite restrained had Mr. Hershfield been there, suddenly feel they take advantage of the storekeeper because he was a Cherokee? Deep chagrin swept over him. He stared at the brown hands loosely holding the reins. His Cherokee trait was indelibly stained upon them. Idly, he stroked his hand along the horse's shoulder, and then turning his hand over, he subliminally rubbed the back of his hand against the horse's hide, as though his subconscious mind was attempting to expunge the Cherokee stigma from it. His horse trudged along the vacant, cobbled street. The sharp, crisp clop of hooves added to Arley's lonely, bleak depression. The rhythmic sound of his horse found response in a rude shop with its wide-plank doors swung open. The clang of a blacksmith's hammer invaded Arley's reverie. He saw the flaming forge and the brawny smithy in his greasy leather apron. Near the iron-worker stood the Cherokee Grey Wolf. who had stood by him against the four rowdies who raided the store. Arley turned his horse to the front of the shop. He dismounted.

"Asiyu, Grey Wolf. Thank you again for your friendly help today. I was afraid your friends might give me more trouble than I could handle."

"They ain't exactly my friends. They gone and left me. I don't care none. I can go home alone soon as my horse gets shoed."

"Tell me about your people and your home land," said Arley. "I'm Cherokee, but I ain't never lived with Cherokee people. My ma and paw died 'afore I was a year ole."

"Don't know what t'tell. Our people is poor. The gover'ment at Washington done made us poor and give us poor land. Old folks tells about good land they left back East."

The two youths talked until the shoe was formed and fitted on the mustang. Grey Wolf led his horse, and the two men stepped from the shop out into the open.

Arley looked up at the sky. "It's gettin' late. You can't go far 'afore dark. Which way you goin'?"

"South," replied Grey Wolf pointing down the road.

"I live down that way. I'll just ride with you a piece." Together the young men traveled from the village. Grey Wolf, wearing a turban of red and black, a red and yellow plaid shirt, and fringed buckskin vest and leggings, rode a colorful brown and white mustang. In contrast, Arley, in dull-hued shirt and pants, sat on a nondescript bay horse. Yet there appeared a close resemblance between the two. Arley noticed this similarity, and he fixed his eyes steadily on his companion. He compared the thrush-brown color of their skin. He brushed his hand over his shiny black hair and realized it was similar to Grey Wolf's even to the shoulder length of it. He calculated his own body size against the stranger. They were the same height and muscular build, he thought. Never before had he met a man so like himself. In fact, he had been so isolated as to have never had contact with many Cherokee people. Arley imitated his new friend's erect carriage in the saddle and his easy riding skill. Slowly he realized that now, for the first time within his memory he felt pride in being a Cherokee. All at once he felt he had met an ally, someone who must surely have feelings like his own. This metamorphosis of his mind puzzled him a little. Was Grey Wolf ever ashamed of his Cherokee heritage? Arley studied his proud handsome face, his high-held head with his colored turban, the necklace of bear teeth, beads, and silver nuggets around his neck, the bright yarn and feathers interwoven in the horse's mane. All these were signs which proclaimed boldly, without embarrassment: "Cherokee redman."

As they journeyed silently, Grey Wolf became aware of Arley's scrutiny. He returned the look, studying Arley thoughtfully.

When their eyes met he remarked, "I wonder, that nigger woman in the store, she say she was on Trail of Tears with my people, that she growed you up."

"Yes," said Arley, "she's the only maw I knowed."

"How was it happen? You here, not in Indian territory?"

"Essie took me away from the wagon train. I was a baby. She ran away from danger."

"I understand," asserted Grey Wolf. "Sometimes in war Cherokees steal Osage babies or Pawnee babies. Sometimes them tribes take Cherokee children. Woman steal you from your Cherokee people." He nodded his head perceptively.

The outlandish statement struck Arley like a blow to the belly. Never before had such an implication come to him. He caught his breath, and there seemed to be a violent pressure on his chest. Essie--the thought was devastating--abducted him away from his people. He had always known it, but always it had seemed a benevolent act. It had never occurred to him that there was also an overwhelming tragic aspect to it. No, he affirmed, Essie would never do anything malicious! Still, here he was in southern Missouri. For whatever the reason, he had been taken away, deprived of his right to live with his people.

Arley did not undertake to explain to his new friend the true details of the past. Silently they traveled until they were near the Stanton homestead. "Grey Wolf," he said, "it's gettin' along about sundown. I'd sure admire t'have you turn into my place for the night. You'd be mighty welcome."

Arley smiled broadly. He hoped to show Grey Wolf how fortunate he was to have Essie and Caleb. He had no doubt that the Judge and Mrs. Stanton would accept Grey Wolf with gracious hospitality. The Indian accepted Arley's invitation.

The next morning Essie prepared breakfast at the kitchen table for her family and the Cherokee guest. Mrs. Stanton had taken her meal in her room. Judge Stanton was holding court out of town. Arley had barely started on his plate of sausage, eggs, and grits when he sprang from his chair. He was exuberant with the idea that had taken possession of him. "Ma," he exclaimed, bursting upon her as she stooped to remove a pan of biscuits from the oven, "Grey Wolf has asked me t'go with him to the

Cherokee country. Otherwise he will have t'travel by hisself."
Essie fairly threw the hot pan on the stove top, then pushed it
with her cloth-wrapped hand to a cool section of the stove. She
straightened herself and turned gazing at her son.

"Is that what you want?"

"I think this would be a good time, Ma. Since I just lost my
job with Mr. Hershfield, I ain't got nothin' else t'do. Please, Ma,
you always told me how wonderful the Cherokee people are. All
I know about is them four hoodlums in the store yesterday and
Grey Wolf here. I want t'know if most Indians is like them or
him." He lowered his voice on the tail end of his remarks and
gave a slight nod toward the young Indian busily devouring
biscuits and sorghum".

Essie stood thoughtfully considering the request. The
evening before she had enjoyed talking with Grey Wolf in the
Indian language. She liked the young visitor. She had
welcomed the chance for Arley to use his speaking in the tongue
of his parents. She had a strange notion that when she taught
Cherokee things to Arley, it was like making an offering to Kevit
and Fawn, sort of like putting flowers on the graves of those she
had loved. "It won't be easy for me to let you go. How long you
aimin' t'be gone?"

"I don't know. Don't know how far away it is." Essie took
him into her arms. Arley squirmed a little with embarrassment.

"You're all growed up, taller'n me, and I couldn't keep you
here if you got a mind t 'go. But, Arley, you know how much I
have wanted to go to Georgia to find your pa." She had for some
time now spoken of Gabe as though he was the Cherokee lad's
father.

"We'll go, Mamma, I promise. Just a little while later,
Mamma. But first I want t' see the Cherokee people." She
cocked her head and looked tenderly into his eyes. How could
she deny her son this chance to go see his own people?

"Of course you can go if you think you should. But you
must come back very soon," she said in a firm tone. She paused
thoughtfully. How are things for the Cherokee people? she
wondered. Had the hardships they had suffered changed them?
Sometimes trouble makes people bitter, turns them into mean,

158

stupefied creatures. The thought that Arley might be disappointed and disillusioned bothered Essie. She put a fresh pan of biscuits before the boys and left the room. After breakfast Arley went to pack his saddle bags with things necessary for the trip. Grey Wolf followed him.

Caleb had sat quietly during the discussion at the breakfast table. Afterwards he went upstairs to his mother's room. He knew he would find her sitting in her rocker by the window. She always went there when she needed to reflect on a weighty problem. Caleb sat on a little stool in front of her, took her hand and said, "Don't worry about Arley, Mamma. He'll be all right. I wish't he wouldn't go though. He ain't been home much lately. Mamma, you're the bestest friend I got. If I ain't got Arley, I ain't got nobody but you."

"Oh, Caleb, honey, I know how you feel." She held both of his hands in hers. "Sometimes I feel like we're just two black ravens in a world o'white doves. Them doves ain't fightin' against us. They's just flutterin' about tendin' their own business and payin' us no mind. We ain't birds in a cage with wire bars and all. Our cage is that we're neglected, shut out, and outlawed in things. But we're goin' t' Georgia. Goin' to find your Daddy. Keep thinkin' 'bout that, son." To her, the joy of that thought transcended all unpleasantries. "Oh, Caleb, you can't know how much it hurt me 'cause you was never allowed to go to school."

"It's all right, Mamma. You learned me to read," he said to hearten her. "I can read as good as Arley, and both of us can read in English or in Cherokee. One night Arley and me was readin' from the Bible. I read in Cherokee and then Arley read the same part in English. It was fun. But some o' the words we couldn't understand in either lingo. Arley said we need a dictionary. I wish't I knowed how to use a dictionary, Mamma. Judge Stanton's got one. I saw it on that shelf with them books in the study."

"If we had one and I knowed how to use it, I'd learn you, son." She spoke absently; her thoughts had returned to Arley. "You know, we really ought to be glad about Arley. He's got people of his own kind. That ought to make him feel good to be with them for a while."

"What if he don't never come back t'us?"

Essie smiled assuredly, "He will, Caleb, he will." Secretly she had some fears about that too. She passed her comforting hand over his head and looked into his dark eyes.

She diverted his thoughts with a consoling whisper, "Maybe Judge Stanton will show you how to use the dictionary."

"Wouldn't that be against the law?" Essie smiled and gave a sly shrug. She knew that in Missouri, as it had been in Georgia, it was illegal for anyone to teach slaves to read. But in her present situation she often became oblivious of her servitude. On a few occasions when the judge had caught her reading, he had pretended not to notice.

A call came from the stairwell. "Ma, Caleb, we're ready to go." Essie and Caleb hurried down the steps. The boys had tied their horses to a hitching post at the front of the house and were making their farewells on the front veranda.

Mary Stanton was rolled out so that she could express her motherly concern for "one of her boys" who was leaving her household for a while. "Come here, Arley, I insist that I be given a big goodbye hug," she said. Arley bent down to her. "Don't forget you were less than a year old when you came into my house. This will always be your home. Here, let me give you this little gift." The invalid woman thrust her hand into her apron pocket. "This belonged to my father. I saved it all these years figuring to give it to my own son, but I guess you and Caleb are as near to sons as I'll ever have." She pressed a gold-handled pocket knife into his hand. "May God go with you, boy."

"Thank you, Mis'es Mary, I'll keep it always to remind me how real kind you been."

Arley went to Essie and gave her a tight squeeze. "I'll miss you, Mamma," he said looking into her eyes. "I'll miss you a heap. I--I-", he dared not say more. He wanted to reassure her that he would return soon, but his voice was choked with emotion.

160

Essie clung to him. "I promised your real mamma that I would care for you and raise you 'til you was full growed, but I done it for more than that. I done it 'cause I loved you, Arley. I always will. Take care of yourself and don't be away too long."

Caleb stepped forward and stood silently before Arley. Neither boy could find adequate words. Ill at ease, Caleb brushed the back of his hand across his throat where a tightening sensation seized him. Arley moved to him, and they locked their arms around each other. Tacitly, they broke apart, and Arley skipped briskly down the steps.

"Wait, Arley, I want t'go with you," called Caleb impetuously. Arley paused. His heart sprang with a jubilant surge. He turned back, grinning. Caleb added slowly, "Aw, I can't go. I won't go and leave Mamma. She might need me." In his heart, he feared leaving home and traveling to a place where he would be surrounded by Cherokee people. To him, Grey Wolf had seemed somewhat alien. Of course, Caleb understood his Cherokee talk. He understood when Grey Wolf had unwittingly remarked, in Cherokee, that in his homeland most all the "niggers" were slaves. Arley had blushed, Essie smiled indulgently, and Caleb felt again the ignominy of being black. "I'll be back in about three months, I reckon. Goodbye," called Arley.

The Cherokee youths sprang upon their horses, but before the nervous animals were spurred away, Essie ran down the steps crying, "Wait, Arley!" She rushed to the side of her son's horse. "I don't know how to tell it, but Arley, dear, could you ask around and try to find word about my husband Gabe? I know it's a silly, foolish hope, but if Gabe was to get free so's he could, he would try to find me and our old master, you know, your father. But Gabe don't know..." Essie's voice broke with emotion. Arley bent down from his saddle and took her hand. Essie dried her eyes with her apron. "He don't know where I am."

"I'll try, Mamma. I'll ask if anybody knows about him." Essie turned away, again wiping her eyes. With a sigh she mumbled to herself, "After all these years, I reckon they ain't no hope." Arley was gone. He would not soon be able to escort her

161

to Georgia. Her dream of union with her husband was again postponed. She had foregone the fulfillment of her own yearning to allow Arley to follow his.

Chapter XI
Caleb's New Perception of Slavery

In the front yard Caleb glanced up from his work in a flower bed. The rumble of an approaching carriage had captured his attention. It was a rented hack, a surrey such as seldom came into the vicinity of the Judge's home. Not many visitors came either, not since Mary Stanton's disability. Ever since Judge Stanton had announced that an important visitor from St. Louis was soon to arrive, the Stanton household had been in a tizzy.

Caleb dusted his hands by clapping them together in an up and down action. He brushed off his trousers. Essie had given him explicit instructions about how to welcome the guests. He stood watching the carriage come to a halt. In the front seat, a livery stable coachman sat alone. Behind him an august, little gentleman sat beside a short, plump, fastidiously-dressed woman. While the driver stepped down to the ground and went to remove the valises from the rear of the vehicle, the two passengers bent low to look under the roof of the surrey up at the tall white house. Slowly the gentleman descended from the carriage. He wore a grey pinstriped suit, a large ruby-colored cravat, and a tall grey silk hat. He held out his hand to have it grasped by his wife's chubby hand with its sparkling rings and dangling pearl bracelet. She stepped down with feminine grace and gave her frothy skirt a flip. Her multicolored pastel dress was embellished with ruffles and flounces.

Caleb stood in awe. Never had he seen such elegant clothes. When the gentleman made a beckoning motion toward Caleb, the youth ventured forth.

"Our driver states that this is the home of Benjamin Stanton. Are we right about that?"

"Yes, sir, that be right," answered Caleb. Then remembering Essie's instructions, he bowed low saying, "Welcome to the Stanton place. The judge and Missis Mary has been lookin' for you. They'll be glad to know you have arrived. May I help with your luggage?"

"The driver has set our things on the porch. Perhaps you would kindly move them inside."

Caleb opened the door, invited the couple into the house, leading them into the parlor. "I'll summon Judge Stanton."

Before Caleb could leave, Benjamin Stanton entered the room. "David and Estell," he exclaimed, "after all these years! How good it is to see you again. We were delighted to get your letter accepting our invitation. We want your stay to be pleasant."

"I hope we won't be too much bother," said David Caldwell.

"Not at all. Our housekeeper is marvelously capable and a wonderful cook. Her name is Essie and this is her son Caleb." He gestured toward the youth who stood with a valise in each hand. "Caleb, put their things in the east bedroom and tell Mrs. Stanton our guests are here." Then turning to the visitors he said, "Please be seated. How was your trip?"

"Exhausting," sighed the plump woman as she sank into a chair.

"I hope you will find here a rest from busy city life. David, I am anxious to learn about Westcook and Caldwell."

"It's Westcook and Preston now. I withdrew from the firm last fall," said David, "I decided to devote all my time to my campaign for the United States Senate."

"I am sure you have much support among your many friends in St. Louis."

"Yes," said David, "we came here by way of Jefferson City. It's my friends in the legislature whom we have been seeking to win to our side. I hope you can use your influence there."

"You know that I will," said Benjamin. "I often think about how helpful you were to me when I apprenticed with Westcook and Caldwell. I thank you for that. And, Estell, I remember the lavish receptions at your home." Judge Stanton glanced toward the door. "Oh, here is Mary."

David Caldwell went to pay his respects. "Dear Mary, it is a pleasure to see you again. We were saddened to learn of your malady, but seeing you now looking so vibrant and charming, we are reassured." He bent down to kiss her hand.

164

"It has been twenty-eight or thirty years since we have seen you. Our welcome is of a thirty-year vintage, cordial and heartfelt," said Mary. "Benjamin, I'm sure our guests are travel-weary and would like to rest and freshen up. We will have plenty of time to visit later. Dinner will be at seven."

The banquet table was a display of glistening white linen, centered with glowing candles on sparkling silver stands, with florid English china and fragile goblets, all tastefully arranged by Essie. With Caleb's help she had prepared Southern cuisine and served it with finesse. The hosts beamed, and the guests paid lavish compliments. As the diners rose from the table, Judge Stanton remarked, "Now if you ladies will excuse us, David and I will enjoy our cigars in the study." So while the women visited in the parlor, the two men relaxed in the chamber surrounded by shelves of books, treasures and momentos.

Sinking into a leather-cushioned armchair, David remarked with a sigh of satisfaction, "That was one of the most delectable meals I have ever had the pleasure to enjoy. Your girl Essie is indeed a jewel. What a price she would bring in the St. Louis market."

"Heaven forbid that Essie should ever be subjected to such an indignity. I recall most vividly the slave auctions just east of the courthouse. I purposely avoided the building's east entrance," reflected Judge Stanton.

"Things haven't changed much there, except that the market is much busier than ever," said the St. Louisian.

"Yes, I'm sure it is. One of my neighbors journeyed to St. Louis for field slaves. He was very wroth, when he got home, to find he had been duped. Within a week the black dye began to fade from the hair of two of the men. Of course, they had been coached to falsify their ages and were much older than they had said. The neighbor came to me for legal advice. I had to explain that there was nothing I could do about a fraudulent transaction which took place so far away."

"I must say, Benjamin, knowing your abhorrence of slavery, I was greatly surprised to find two household darkies in your home. I supposed you may have had a change of heart," remarked the urbane attorney.

165

"Not at all," said the judge. "Essie fled to us from the South. Her owners had died, and she feared being shanghaied by slave-traders. She is not here against her will."

As he spoke, Caleb, who had just served coffee to the women in the parlor, passed by the open door of the study. When he heard Essie's name spoken, he stopped to listen behind the door in the shadows of the hall.

"I don't have to tell you the serious consequences of offenses against the Fugitive Slave Law. I suppose there are not many violations of the law here in southern Missouri, but federal commissioners based in St. Louis dash all about seeking to recover runaways. If the slaves, mainly those trying to get to Illinois, are returned, the commissioners are paid handsomely. Forgive me, Benjamin. Of course, you know all that! I just wouldn't want you to put yourself in jeopardy. Surely the woman's former owners had heirs who have a claim to her."

Benjamin laughed lightly, appreciating his friend's concern. "It is a most bizarre situation, I'm sure you will agree. Essie was the property of a Cherokee man and his wife who both died in Arkansas during the Cherokee removal to Indian Territory. As she fled from some men who planned to capture her, she carried the infant son of her Indian owner. So actually the slave was transporting her slave-holder during her escape."

"Astonishing!" exclaimed David, "Incredible!

"And to add to the unique story of this courageous woman, I want you to know that she carried the Cherokee infant along with Caleb, her own son, both of them only a few months old. One morning I found her and the babies in my barn where they had spent the night."

Caleb, behind the open door, attempted to peek through the crack. A piece of statuary in his line of vision forced him to crouch in order to glimpse the judge. Caleb was filled gratification and abounding love for his mother.

David Caldwell asked, "And what happened to the Cherokee offspring?" he asked.

"He's gone to Oklahoma. He left only a few days ago. He will return in a few weeks. The boys, as well as their mother, have become very dear to us."

"Have you never received any public censure because of the racial combination in your home?"

"None."

"If it ever came to a test, have you any legal proof to substantiate such a fabulous tale?" The visiting attorney pointed with his cigar, wagging it toward Benjamin for emphasis. Both men knew that in court a Negro's testimony would be disqualified.

"Yes, I have proof. When the Cherokee youth--his name is Arley-- reached seventeen, Essie presented him with a few keepsakes of his parents, among them was a bill of sale showing that she had been the property of Arley's father. The boy recognized the importance of the paper and gave it to me for safe-keeping."

"Then," concluded Caldwell, "the adopted son is legally the owner of his mother. A most singular circumstance. I must say, Benjamin, that you have furnished a safe haven here. Anyone with a less prestigious standing in the community could not have done it."

In the hall Caleb shifted his position. His weary legs became cramped in the crouched position needed to give him the best view through the crevice of the door. When he attempted to sit on the floor, the cramp in his leg caused him to fall with a thud! His heart leaped with fear of being discovered. But at that moment Caldwell cleared his throat and turned the conversation to a new subject.

"The whole of St. Louis is in a tumult over the court's decision in the Dred Scott case."

"Let's see," reflected the judge, "that's the case of the slave taken by his owner into Illinois and then to free territory-- Wisconsin, I believe--then taken back to MIssouri. Yes, I remember, Dred Scott claimed to be a legally free man because he had lived in free territory."

"The Supreme Court's decision appeared in the papers shortly before we left St. Louis," said David Caldwell. "I doubt that the full disclosure of the news has reached here as yet, nor the significance of the case realized. But in St. Louis it has stirred up quite a hornet's nest."

"No, we have had no details," said the judge.

"As to be expected, Scott was declared to be still a slave. That would have caused no great stir, but in the obiter dicta the majority of the judges gave the opinion that Congress had no constitutional right to exclude slavery in the territories."

"That doesn't surprise me," said Benjamin, "since the majority of the justices are Democrats from slave states. But, Congress has prohibited slavery in most of the territories."

"Yes," said David Caldwell, "It promises to be a bitter contest. For now, it appears to be a major victory for the pro-slave faction. The argument was that by outlawing slavery in the territories, Congress has deprived slave owners of their property without due process of law. Chief Justice Taney gave his opinion that Negroes could never become United States citizens because the founders of the Republic did not intend for them to."

"Preposterous!" exclaimed Benjamin.

"Taney declared that at the time the Republic was formed, Negroes were--to use his exact words-- 'were beings of an inferior order and altogether unfit to associate with the white race.'"

"I can't believe that the fathers of the Republic held any such attitude," interjected Benjamin.

"Nor can I. Most northerners are highly incensed by Taney's remarks. Worst of all, many people have misunderstood the comments and misapply those harsh words to be Taney's opinion of the present day condition. What the Justice meant was that at the time of the writing of the Constitution the black race had--I believe his words were-- 'had no rights which white men were bound to respect.'"

"I refuse to believe that the men of our early history were so bigoted," stated the judge firmly.

In the hall Caleb broke out in a nervous sweat, sickened by what he had heard. The color of his skin had often been a source of embarrassment. He had been led to believe that white was better. He had always accepted that. But the callous remarks, "beings or an inferior order" and "unfit to associate with the white race" struck him hard. He arose from the floor, not quietly but clumsily and with some commotion. He scurried away.

168

Benjamin Stanton heard the disturbance, stepped to the door, and peered into the darkened hall. "Caleb," he called, "come here." He had seen nothing, but the sounds he had heard were definitely Caleb's. His call brought no reply. Caleb had fled to his room, too hurt to answer his master's voice.

Caleb did not sleep that night. He tossed about in his bed, his mind filled with the most despairing thoughts. Over and over his bitter past experiences paraded before him. Degrading slurs and vulgar monikers rang in his ears, words and actions intended "to put a nigger in his place." And repeatedly, again and again, came the St. Louis attorney's remarks, "...beings of an inferior order and altogether unfit to associate with the white race..," "had no rights which white men were bound to respect." While Caldwell's words were less coarse than those stinging slurs the black youth had so often endured, it was the very cultivated language of those remarks that troubled Caleb. Of course, Caleb did not grasp the full significance of Taney's remarks, but he felt that somehow he was grossly threatened and maligned by words which were all the more evil because he did not fully understand them. Who was Taney anyhow? And what is the Supreme Court? The judge and his guest had given such serious credence to the damning remarks.

During his lifetime, Caleb was the recipient of such tender love and understanding and had enjoyed a large degree of sanctuary in the Stanton household. He was vulnerable when confronted with the outside world. In trouble, Essie was his refuge.

The next morning Essie exclaimed, "'...unfit to associate with the white race!' Hogwash! I done scrubbed and cleaned and cooked for white folks. Some was nice and some mean as devils. What a body is don't come from his skin but out of his heart. The color of their skin ain't got nothin' to do with it."

"Mamma, it ain't white people that the man was talkin' about. Sure, white folks is some good and some bad. But all colored folks is inferior to the worst white folks. That's what the man sez."

169

"Well, I was fitting 'nough when there was work to do," said Essie with an indifferent shrug. Her years of experience had convinced her that it was useless to war against the inevitable.

"Mamma, what are we going to do?"

"Why, son, there's no call for us to do anything. We just go ahead doing the best we can, treating everyone like we would like to be treated. You know I've always told you that all people are the same. The good Lord made us all of the same blood. If others don't recognize how we ought to all be equal, they're the ones that need to change."

Caleb was perturbed by her apparent insensitivity. He did not realize that Essie knew that resistance to the prejudice was a vain struggle. Essie did not dare to say anything which might encourage him to take up a lost cause whereby he might be injured. How often in this white man's world she had cautioned him to "remember your place." At the same time, she prayed that her words would neither stifle his self-esteem nor fill him with venomous hate. She plied him with encouragement and compliments and hoped that she could steer him along the narrow, rocky path of black survival.

Part Two of Chapter XI

"Mamma," said Caleb, "yesterday when I was on my way home from the meetin' over at Stultz's barn, I was kinda singin' a song, one of them spirituals we sing over there. I was moseyin' along feelin' real good when all to once I heerd, 'Sisst', comin' from a clump o' sumac. Then I heerd a gal's voice whisper, 'Hey, boy, you there. You been to the gospel meetin'?' I stopped short and looked an' seen this here black gal about my age--maybe a little bit younger. She was hidin' in the brush. "'Yeah,' I sez, 'I jest come from there.'.

"Wish't I could go! We kin hear them beautiful songs. What you all singin' 'bout?' she ask't, still whisperin'. "About the Lord,' I sez. "'Don't know nothin' 'bout the Lord,' sez she. 'Tell me 'bout him.' Then she looked around real skert like and sez, 'I gotta get back to work now. Somebody a-comin'.' "Then I heard a whip crack and a man scream. When I moved up a little I seen a black man on a horse usin' a long bull whip on the naked back of a field hand. He was a kinda old man with grey hair, and he just stand there and didn't scream no more. Just that first lash o' th' whip made him scream. After that he just made a pained expression and looked hate out o' his eyes. I was so stunned I couldn't move. I ain't never seen such a beatin'. "The nigger on the horse, th' super'tendent, I reckon, he swore at the man and sez, 'I seen that wench and I seen you follerin' her.'

"Then all to once't he saw me, and he turned his horse to come after me. I run but he whizzed that whip and struck me acros't the back. 'Ye son o' bitch,' he yelled, 'takin' my workers from their work, wuz you? I'll show you!' "I run acros't the road and into a thicket. He started t'foller me but then he turned back crackin' his whip an' cussin."

"He struck you with the whip?" asked Essie with concern.

"I wasn't goin' to tell you, Mamma, not til my back healed up. I knowed I'd have to tell you sometime, cause that whip tore my shirt, that new one you just made."

"Let me see your back," ordered Essie, unbuttoning and removing his shirt. A dark red slash extended across his back.

Essie hurried to get warm water for bathing the wound. "Mamma, it was Sunday 'bout noon an' they were workin' in the fields at that McShane place. Mamma, I just gotta find out if he whipped that gal. She ask't me 'bout the Lord. I want to go back and tell her 'bout Jesus."

"Oh, Caleb, I don't think you better," said Essie and then she added, "Not lessen you're real, real careful." For days following, Caleb deliberated how he could contact the slave girl. He dared not appear again near the field where the workers were, so he thought it best to locate her near the slave shacks. He hid in the shrubbery at the edge of the lawn of the big McShane house. Near sundown an elderly house servant came from the dwelling and went into the garden to cut roses to decorate the master's table. Caleb crept cautiously toward him. Finally the black fellow spied the youth. From behind a lilac bush Caleb made a gesture to silence the old Negro. "I want to see a girl who works in the fields," muttered Caleb. "I'm scared of the overseer. He won't let me see her during work time."

"No, he wouldn't," said the old man softly. "He's a nasty one, Bart is. Watches ever'one alwus, day n' night. You can't see her.

But wait, which one you wantin' t'see? Are she skinny or fat?"

"She was skinny, just a little thing. Not more'n fifteen years old. Maybe Bart whipped her a couple o' days ago," said Caleb.

"She a relation o' your'n? That why you want to see her?" asked the old darkie.

"No, no relation. She ask't me questions about the meetin's at Stultz's barn."

"We ain't 'lowed to go there. Massah McShane ain't got no bent toward religion, an' don't take kindly to them that preaches it to black folks. Oh, massah ain't no hard man. Leaves ever'thing to Bart. Don't think he knows how beasty Bart is." A rose thorn pricked his gnarled finger and he put it to his mouth with an expression on his wrinkled face which aptly showed his pain and his repugnance for the overseer. "Don't cross ol' Bart, boy

"All I want is t'see that gal--uhh--what's 'er name?" "Sarah." "I just want to talk to Sarah." "Don't know how you kin do that. I tell you where she lives. See that row o' shacks next to th' creek. Her maw's house is th' next to the last one, that one covered by Virginia creeper." He pointed with his knotty finger.

Then he turned to Caleb with a sly smile. "Say, you aimin' to call on her with a mind to court her?" "Naw. Don't know her yet. I'm mighty obliged to you for your information." "Got to skiddoo back," said the servant abruptly and scuttled off toward the big house. That night as soon as darkness came, Caleb crept along the creek gully toward the shanty that had been pointed out as the one where Sarah lived. It was a moderately dark night. He slipped from the creek bed to the rear of the cabin and then around to the door where he tapped lightly. Inside the hushed occupants waited cautiously to see if the sound would be repeated. In response to the second rapping, the door was cracked open and three faces peered out into the blackness. A middle-aged black woman stammered, "What you want?" Her tone was not irate, only softly wary. "I come t'see Sarah," said Caleb.

"You ain't one of our people, is you?" asked the woman, holding the door only slightly ajar.

"No, ma'am, I live down at Judge Stanton's place. I just came to help you, friendly like," said Caleb awkwardly.

"You're the one I seed comin' frum Stultz's barn, ain't cha?" interjected the girl peering through the door from behind her mother. "Yes," said Caleb, "and I come to answer your questions."

"Come in," invited the woman. "Can't jaw in the doorway. Bart might ketch us." Caleb stepped into the room. The only light was that which the fireplace made. The delicate child was in her nightgown, and her equally frail brother was in his underwear. Obviously they had already been put to bed. They stood curiously eyeing Caleb, unembarrassed to be seen in their nightclothes. It was a squalid room with one bed bearing a rough straw tick. There was another straw tick on the floor. A

173

rough table stood in the center with two crude benches. A more humble room Caleb could not imagine.

Suddenly he realized that they were waiting for him to say something.

"I just came 'cause Sarah ask't me about the doin's at Stultz's barn. It's a church meetin'. We all sing songs and talk about Jesus. Brother Shannon is our leader. I want t' give you an invite, iffen you could come." The three gaunt figures made no verbal response or gesture. Caleb waited selfconsciously. When no one spoke he continued, "I know yer overseer's strict. Did he punish you for talkin' to me the other day, Sarah?" Her forlorn face brightened at the sound of her name.

Then her smile faded and she replied solemnly, "Yassah, he sure did." "He's a bad'un, bad as they cum, thet Bart is," said the woman with a sympathetic pat on her daughter's cheek. "I reckon we can't never go t' them meetin's." "Wish't we could," said the girl wistfully. "I likes t' sing. Don't know only one song."

"I could teach you some songs right here," volunteered Caleb.

"That'd be nice, real nice," said the mother. "I al'us wanted my chilens to get learnin'. Lawsee, they sure don't get none from me." Then her smile vanished from her weathered face, and she cautioned solemnly, "But we all can't sing no louder'n a whisper. We don't want no trouble." Caleb sat on the bench at the table and the two children took the bench opposite him while their mother hovered over them. Occasionally the woman shuffled toward the door as though she had heard something or was expecting something. The young man repeated a spiritual over and over while the three followed along in subdued plaintive voices. When he finally decided to go, they had rehearsed three songs.

"You all come back agin, Caleb. We sure does thank you for them songs," said the woman who had given her name as Myrtle. "I will, Myrtle," replied Caleb. "Mind now, you keep a sharp eye out for that Bart," she warned as she held the door open for Caleb. As he hurried away Caleb sang softly to himself. It had been a rewarding evening for him

The next day Sarah could hardly keep quiet as she worked. Sometimes lilting melodies escaped from her lips, ever so gently. A male laborer working beside her stopped still, listening, and then asked, "Where you all gettin' that singin' from?" "Jes' seems to come to me," said Sarah evasively. Time and again Caleb returned to the slave shack until he had taught all the songs he had learned at Stultz's barn.

In the fields, as she worked Sarah was not able to keep secret the source of her songs. "That sounds mighty like one o' them songs we scarce kin hear from Stultz's barn. When you go there, child?" asked one of the women suspiciously.

"Ain't never went there," replied Sarah. There came a time when the inquisitive slaves would no longer take the girl's evasive answers, and she was forced to reveal her secret. To gain assurances that they would not tell Bart, she invited some of them to the nightly singing sessions. Before long nearly every slave on the plantation had learned the spirituals. Those who had not been to hear them from Caleb learned them from others. Keeping Bart from catching them proved to be an exciting game. They devised diversions to keep the overseer busily occupied away from the slave quarters. Sometimes they turned the pigs loose or caused other mischief. While Bart was suspicious that something was afoot, he was unable to detect what it was. Working in the fields the slaves seemed happier than before. The reason for their uplifted spirits could not be hid for long.

Once when one of the laborers began a soft involuntary singing of one of the spirituals, gradually one by one the whole crew joined in a spontaneous outbreak of singing. Bart was filled with consternation and bewilderment. He stomped his feet and shouted threats and obsenities until the singing stopped. Across the field a second gang took up the song, knowing it would draw the angry boss away from their fellow laborers. Bart sprang onto his horse, uncoiled the whip and cracked it as he galloped off. As he neared the offending group, the singing stopped abruptly. In his frustration the incensed foreman lashed his whip across the back of the nearest toiler. He bawled a tirade of threats and insults 'til he was forced to pause to catch his breath. Then the sound of distant singing by the other group sent him racing back to them. Again the singing stopped. Bart, his brow streaked with sweaty kinky hair and the blood vessels in his temples and neck dilated fully, slid from his horse near exhaustion. His snarling lips could only sputter warnings about what he would do if the slaves slacked off in their work.

From that time on there was nothing he could do to stop the Negro singing. However, when the crew was assigned to extreme physical toil, such as digging irrigation ditches or moving cotton bales, the rhythm of singing inspired their swinging motion into a frenzied, heated activity which tired the workers to near exhaustion. At such times Bart took sinister delight in seeing their tired, struggling bodies. Knowing that it was their spiritual singing that drove them so hard, sometimes he mercilessly set a faster rhythm by pounding a wood plank against a hard surface. Caleb's night time visits to the slave quarters continued even after he had taught Sarah, her mother and brother all the songs he knew. When he thought about it, the little shanty seemed a dismal place with its dank dirt floor and the reeking stale odor of cooking. But he was drawn to the friendly cabin where he felt a great measure of self-confidence and fulfillment. There he was able to help the unlearned and oppressed people of his race. "Caleb," said Sarah, "You ain't bound to no massah like we is. Yet you is black as us. Why that? Why is some folks got so much and some ain't got nothin'. I reckon the Lawd don't like all folks the same. That's His business I 'spect. But you, Caleb, why you sech a pet of the Almighty? What you do He likes you so much an' let yo live so good?"

"It ain't that way, Sarah," explained Caleb.

"The Lord loves ever'body the same. This world jest ain't no fair place, especially for black folks. The Lord is th' boss in heaven. Down here the devil done took over, but he ain't here permanent. He's goin' to get ousted some day." "How you know that?" asked Sarah. "It's in the Bible. You don't own one, do you?" "No, don't got one. Can't read noway," confessed Sarah. On his next visit Caleb brought a Bible to them and assumed the task of teaching them to read. In the evening at the supper table, Caleb said to Essie, "They don't have nothin'.

There treated so bad. They work ever' minute they're awake. No time to have fun. 'Least now they can sing, if that Bart don't find a way to stop 'em." Essie stopped eating and lowered her hands to her lap, listening without commenting. Caleb's words about the McShane slaves distressed her. Their fortunes would never change, and Caleb, she feared, would be forever distressed for them. Finally, Essie determined that she should visit the slave family. She thought that, perhaps, in some way she could help Myrtle and her two children. On two different evenings she slipped with Caleb to the little slave hut. On some occasions she sent dishes of food or pieces of handiwork she had stitched. Recalling her own childhood hardships, she found in her heart sympathy for Sarah. Essie began to speculate that when the time came for her to leave Missouri, perhaps the Judge could purchase Sarah so that the girl could help care for Mary Stanton. How else, she thought, could she leave?

Caleb had wanted to talk to Judge Stanton about his conversation with David Caldwell, but the disturbed youth did not want to confess that he had been eavesdropping. Knowing that Caldwell was a lawyer and that most of the books in the judge's study were about law, the youth began to browse among them. Sometimes he pulled out volumes, selecting them indiscriminately or choosing those with brightly colored bindings. Leafing through the pages he attempted to read passages. Usually he found his perusing uninteresting and the text incomprehensible. Seldom did he find a nugget of information that meant anything to him. Once he had forgotten to return a book to the shelf. When the judge came into the room and found it open on the table, he paused in bewilderment, wondering about it. On another occasion the judge himself left a legal volume open on a small stand and had not returned to pick it up for two days. When he was ready to resume reading where he had left off, he found the volume turned to a different page. His eyes fell upon the words which subtitled a section of the text: "Legal Limitations of Persons of Color in the Missouri Judicial System."

Curious about it, he questioned Essie about whether she had been in the study, perhaps to dust in there. She apologized for having been too busy to clean the room and promised that she would most certainly get to it soon. Ben Stanton was puzzled. Sometimes he carefully arranged books on the table and made note of the titles and the order in which they were stacked. Later when he returned to them there was no doubt that several of them had been moved about. Could the actorn behind the mystery be Caleb?

The judge was determined to find out without directly quizzing Caleb. He took a piece of paper and wrote: "I must not forget to instruct Caleb to clean the buggy and curry and groom a horse for my trip to Gallaway Tuesday. I will drive Captain since Flip has received some ugly scratches. Important case. Want to make a good appearance." He put the note inside an easy to read book and left it on the table. On Tuesday the judge went to the stable to discover Captain all clean and brushed and the buggy scrubbed and polished. Caleb was there to help him with the harness. "Oh, Caleb, I had written a note to remind myself not to forget to tell you that I would be going to Gallaway today. Even then, I forgot to read my note, so I forgot to tell you. But I see you have the buggy all cleaned and ready. Thank you, Caleb."

"Yes, sir," said Caleb with a flustered look, "I 'lowed it was about time to give it a good washin'." From that time on Ben Stanton discreetly encouraged Caleb's interst in books. Simple and interesting copies were selected and left on the library table. Sometimes the judge scribbled notes and inserted them within the pages, such as: "Everyone ought to know how laws are made," or "Why elections are important," "A young student of law ought to study this," or "This is important information about contracts." For weeks he guided a course of study for Caleb Logically, the judge had reasoned out his legal position.

Technically he himself was not teaching the boy. Soon, however, the judge was too involved, too curious about Caleb's progress to continue such devious procedures. Yet the big man did not directly talk to Caleb. He had a plan. Before his journey to Forsyth, Judge Stanton remarked to the young Negro, "Travel to these distant courthouses is becoming very tiresome for me. Caleb, would you like to go with me as my driver?"

"I'd be mighty pleased to, Mas'er Stanton," replied Caleb with obvious pleasure. Thus began the young man's practical education in jurisprudence. As a servant of the judge he was privileged to stay near the judicial bench. There he developed an absorbing interest in the legal disputation. When they traveled the judge gradually became more and more open to discuss the cases with his chauffeur. The jurist was pleased with his Caleb's insight, his ready grasp of the law, and his youthful passion for justice.

Caleb continued his clandestine visits to the McShane plantation. At dusk, he crept from the road into the bed of the creek, then followed along beside the gently flowing stream for about half a mile to the spot behind the cabin of Sarah, her mother, and brother. He peeked from behind a bush to see if anyone would see him. One dark cloudy night Caleb surveyed the sky and thought to himself that rain would come soon. Just as he raised up from behind the clump, ready to scurry around to the front of the cabin, a startling flash of lightning illuminated the slave quarters, the big house, and fields. A reverberating thunder crash! He gave a little outcry, dashed to the shack seeking cover from the impending downpour. He beat desperately on the rude door. "It's me, Caleb," he shouted, abandoning caution. He was given admittance just as the sporadic peppering on the cabin roof swelled into a clamorous din. A steady leak through the roof dripped onto a tin plate on the table and spattered sparkling droplets in the amber light of the fireplace. Myrtle brought a pan to catch the drip. She wiped the spattered bench with her apron, offering Caleb a seat. Talking was difficult because of the sound of the storm. Sarah drew close to Caleb and gestured to indicate the dress she was wearing. "The two dresses you brung me jes' fits me," she said.

"You look very nice," remarked Caleb. "Essie is making you another one besides." "

She is real good to me. But another dress! This here one is the only one I dar'st wear. Bart looks at me so. I gets scared. I run home t'put on my old one. He gets suspicions where I got a new dress." Caleb gazed at her, thinking to himself how much prettier she was than when he first saw her.

Suddenly there was a frantic pounding on the door.

"Mercy me," Myrtle muttered with a start, "Who that in this storm?" She unbolted the door.

A frightened old Negro burst into the room.

"Quick," he exclaimed, "Bart's coming!" There were exclamations of alarm. Then came a futile agitated movement with the intent of hiding Caleb. The bare shack lacked a place of concealment.

"I got to make a run for home," said Caleb desperately. He flung the door open and dashed into the deluge. The old Negro scurried off too, hoping not to let Bart catch him. The three occupants stood stunned with fear. Bart on his horse sped past the open door splashing water into the room. "Poor Caleb," gasped Sarah. Caleb sprinted along the bank of the swollen creek, fleeing for dear life. Behind him he heard the splashing feet, the snorting, blowing nostrils of Bart's horse. Bart shouted threats and profanities. Closer and closer he came. Suddenly Caleb plunged into the dark raging stream. The water slashed about his chest. He was quickly swept down stream! As he grappled up the rocky bank, he heard the pursuing horseman come to the opposite shore. Caleb struggled out of the ravine. The sound of the horse plunging into the stream filled him with terror. He was all but caught! In the darkness he raced across the field, not daring to look back or pause to listen. The horse gave a terrifying scream as it struggled up the bank! Caleb dashed wildly over the spongy ground, his heart pounding frantically. His legs began to ache. Still he exerted himself harder. On and on he raced. There was no place to hide or take refuge on the open fields. Surely he would be caught! The rain blurred his sight. Wet clothing bound his weary body.

Reaching the edge of the field he felt he could not go further. The road lay just ahead of him. He made a desperate surge to cross the drainage ditch and onto the clay road. His fatigued limbs stumbled over a clump of grass and he fell headlong into the quagmire. Expecting to feel the sting of Bart's whip across his back, he raised his head shielding his face. He saw nothing and felt only his cool, drenched clothing. Where was his pursuer? Surely Bart was playing a game, like a cat plays with a mouse. Caleb arose, struggled to the roadway and began his sprint homeward. Feeling certain that Bart had not given up his tenacious pursuit, Caleb viewed every clump of trees or bushes with expectation of being pounced upon. He did not stop until he reached the Stanton place, flung open the kitchen door, closed it, and he collapsed against the door. Judge Stanton heard the door shut and Caleb's gasping and panting. He came into the kitchen.

"Where have you been?" he demanded.

"To the McShane place." The judge looked at him coldly. "Caleb," he said, "I have been looking for you all afternoon. Where were you?" The master's tone was unusually severe. "This afternoon I was in the west pasture," replied Caleb, still breathing hard. "I split some rails to rebuild the fence there. It was in bad shape. I worked a long time on it. Nigh to sundown I picked a couple o' apples to eat. Since I was so clost, I jest went to see my friends at the McShane quarters."

"That's just what I want to talk to you about," said the judge sternly. "Kerry McShane came to see me this morning. He is quite upset over your visits with his slaves. Claims you are subverting their morale. His overseer is furious about it." Caleb stood stiffly waiting to be reprimanded. A puddle of water formed at his feet. The judge said, "Go change into dry clothes and come to me in my study." When Caleb returned and stood before the judge's desk, he felt like one accused in the court room. Essie came and watched.

The judge cleared his throat. "This morning I promised McShane that you would not cross into his property again. Of course, you didn't know that. McShane has instructed his overseer to capture you. He said he plans to hold you until he can turn you over to the sheriff but that he can not be responsible for what Bart might do to you. McShane said that if I can't control you and keep you away from his place he will bring suit to gain ownership over you." Essie gasped and moved to Caleb, placing her hand on his shoulder.

The chagrined youth inclined his head. "Could he do that?" "I don't know," said Judge Stanton. "I didn't explain to him that you are not my slave, but I did not tell him you are Arley's possession." The judge rose from his chair and stepped around the desk, facing Caleb. "I don't think McShane has any legal grounds to gain ownership of you but I don't want it to come to a trial. Promise me that you will stay away from his plantation." The judge spoke out of sincere concern for Caleb. Caleb gave his promise.

Essie looked intently at Caleb, "Did anyone besides the slaves see you tonight?"

"Yes, Bart chased me. I don't understand how I got away."

"Well," said the judge, "The laws are made to protect the slaveholder's property rights. There's nothing to do now but wait and see."

The next day Caleb secluded himself in the house puttering around helping his mother. He had been sternly warned. Judge Stanton came in shortly after noon.

"Caleb, Essie," he called, "a strange tragedy has taken place over at McShane's. They pulled Bart out of the creek this morning. It seems he was riding his horse in the storm. He was crossing the stream. They think the horse stumbled, broke a leg, fell back into the water pinning Bart under the animal's body. Bart couldn't raise his head above the water and he drowned. The horse drowned too. Strange! People wonder why Bart was out riding on such a night."

Chapter XII
Arley's Visit with the Cherokees

Under the Western sky two Cherokee Indians rolled up in their blankets and gazed up at the starry heavens. "Tomorrow we will be entering the Cherokee Nation," said Grey Wolf.

"It was not a long journey and was fun. But now I feel scared a little. I've never been among Indian people before. I was when I was a tiny baby, I guess," remarked Arley, in Cherokee. "Will Indians receive me with favor?"

"Yes, you are Cherokee. You are welcome. My father will welcome you like a son. You come to my house. Welcome," said Grey Wolf. He was pleased to be going home. Arley had given companionship and made the journey safer. The four other Cherokee men had joined with Grey Wolf to drive cattle to Springfield. The cattle were sold there. In his money belt Grey Wolf carried his proceeds from the sale. When the others deserted Grey Wolf, he knew that all alone there was a possibility that he might be robbed on his way home. Once on their journey the two young men had glimpsed those former companions on the road ahead of them. In drunken revelry they were passing a bottle among themselves. Arley and Grey Wolf turned off the road and rested, not wishing to make contact with the riffraff.

It was a brisk late September day. As the horses trudged lazily along, the youths began to see the houses of the Cherokee Nation, on scattered farms with chickens and livestock. Often times children, whose brown-skinned bodies were nearly naked, played outside the log or pole houses. Occasionally a woman was carrying firewood on her back.

"We will soon be to my house," said Grey Wolf. In the familiar surroundings he recounted the names of many owners of the farms.

"Of course," Grey Wolf explained, "people living at these places do not own the land. All the land is owned by the Cherokee Nation. Houses, barns, and improvements of the land, these things are owned by the farmers." They passed by a

183

particularly beautiful estate. "This here place is called Honey Creek, and that house over there is where Stand Watie lives. He is a big leader of Cherokee people, a friend of my father."

Grey Wolf's home was less pretentious, still it revealed the considerable prosperity of its owner. A large sitting room served as a place for conversing with visitors. Grey Wolf's father had just returned from Arkansas where he visited Cherokee people living there. He welcomed Arley warmly. He was pleased to become acquainted with the young man from Missouri.

In the days that followed, Grey Wolf and Arley enjoyed riding their horses over the rough terrain amd out into the prairies. At night they bivouacked on the prairie, and during the daytime they waited, knowing that the buffalo would soon be moving from the northern plains. Their patience was soon rewarded. They killed a fine young bull which they skinned, cut up, and roasted part of. The rest of the meat they carried home, along with the hide.

Walter Adair, Grey Wolf's father, had just learned that Stand Watie had returned home from a visit to Texas and that now would be a good time to pay him a visit. While in Arkansas, Adair had gone to Fayetteville to pay his respects to Susan Ridge, widow of Major Ridge. The widow had given him a message to relay to Stand Watie, who was the nephew of her deceased husband. The three men--Walter Adair had insisted upon taking Grey Wolf and their Missouri guest with him--rode their horses up to the front of the large log dwelling. Several slaves were busily working in the yard and gardens. A black woman ushered them into a huge room where guests were received. A great fireplace was built of rocks, some of which weighed several hundred pounds. Before the hearth were spread large bear skins where Indian leaders often met to discuss the future of the Nation. The walls were decorated with animal hides, woven blankets and mats, and trophies crafted with feathers and other decorations.

Stand Watie was a broad shouldered, stocky man. His dark shoulder-length hair framed his broad face. Heavy black eyebrows shaded his deep brown penetrating eyes. "Welcome, my good friend Adair, and Grey Wolf, you I know, but who is

184

this young man?" He had shaken hands with each in order as he spoke.

"This is our guest, Arley Tanner, visiting here from Missouri. My son met Arley near Springfield," said Adair.

"Welcome back home to the Cherokee Nation," said Watie, assuming he had once lived in the Cherokee land.

Arley had responded to his greeting by smiling and nodding cordially. He felt shy in the presence of one whom he recognized as a prestigious Indian. "I didn't come back to the Cherokee Nation. This is my first time to see the Cherokee Nation."

The heavy brow of Stand Watie arched. "My cousin John Rollin Ridge lived on a farm near Springfield about eight years ago. He may have been acquainted with your family. Could this be so?"

"My father and mother died on the trail where Cherokees cried. I don't know any Cherokee people," said Arley.

"But you speak Cherokee?"

"I was taught by my black mamma," said Arley. He related how Essie had fled from the Cherokee trail and had raised him. He explained that she had told him about his parents and that his grandfather had been Soaring Hawk.

The two older Indians were much impressed. "I knew Soaring Hawk well," said Walter Adair. "How embarrassing that his grandson should be relegated to adoption by a Negro! Young man, I offer to keep you as a son in my own home."

Arley was flabbergasted. "I...I could never leave Essie and Caleb," he stammered. "Caleb is Essie's son, he's my brother."

"But how do you live?" asked Stand Watie. "The black race is poor. They're slaves, almost all of them without exception. As a son of Adair you would have all the advantages of a Cherokee."

"But I can't leave them. They are my family," repeated Arley.

"Then bring them here," said Adair. "They can live with my other slaves. If the woman belongs to the Cherokees she can't object to that, no right to object. They aren't free niggers are they?"

185

"Well, no," said Arley, "but..."

"You own them, don't you?"

"Yes, but..."

"I see no reason why you would not be able to bring them here," said Adair, and he ended the subject with a comment, "You can think about it and perhaps we can talk about it later."

Stand Watie bid them to be seated.

Arley was speechless in the face of such a strange, perplexing situation. He felt a new pride in the respect and eminence they had shown him, savoring the full knowledge that he was a Cherokee--a slave-holding Cherokee. Arley fell into a long reverie about Caleb and his mother. Forsaking them would be impossible.

When Arley recovered his thoughts and again gave heed to the conversation going on around him, Walter Adair had given Stand Watie the letter given to him by Watie's aunt Susan Ridge. It was a letter she had received from her son John Rollin Ridge, who was a fugitive wanted for murder. He had fled to Springfield and then had gone to California. Now he proposed returning to the Cherokee Nation. "Rollin has written me previously and I have responded that I favor his proposal to establish a newspaper, but as yet I am not financially able to undertake such an enterprise."

"Would Rollin be able to come back to the Nation?" asked Adair. At the age of twenty-two, John Rollin Ridge had quarrelled with David Kell. Rumor had it that Kell had been sent to provoke a quarrel with the purpose of killing young Ridge, but instead it was Kell that had been killed. David Kell had been a follower of John Ross who was the leader of the majority party which opposed the the Treaty Party, those who had signed the treaty of 1835 which brought on the loss of Cherokee land in the East and led to the "Trail of Tears." The John Ross faction fiercely hated the Treaty Party. Stand Watie was the leader of the Treaty Party. The Cherokee Nation had nearly been plunged into civil war.

Learning about the bitter strife within the Nation, Arley was shocked and disappointed to learn that his people were so

186

contentious. He had journeyed to the land of the Cherokee people in hope of finding peace for his own troubled soul.

Before he left the home of Stand Watie, Arley remembered his promise to Essie. He told Adair and Watie that his father had owned three black male slaves who had been stolen from him. "One of those slaves was the husband of my black mamma, Essie. This happened before I was born, back east on my father's farm," said Arley. "My black mamma believes that if her slave husband--his name is Gabe Forbes--were ever to escape from those that kidnapped him, he would come to the Cherokee Nation looking for her. She still grieves for him. I promised her I would ask around in the Cherokee villages." The men denied having any knowledge of him or ever having seen him.

Whereever he went Arley made inquiries about Gabe Forbes, but to no avail.

Arley and Grey Wolf set traps for beaver, fox, raccoon, otter, and mink. They dressed the skins and stored them in a dry ventilated outbuilding. To Arley those experiences were new and fascinating, and Grey Wolf was very patient in teaching him those skills. After over two months, Arley became anxious to return to Missouri. As he prepared to leave, Grey Wolf brought a beautiful young filly from the stable. "You have big bundles of skins from our trapped animals. I give you this young mare, three years old, to help carry them."

"You are very generous. Even though I may never become a son adopted into your father's house, still I want to be your brother," said Arley with a warm handshake.

"I would like for you to stay here always," said Grey Wolf.

Chapter XIII
Arley's Business Venture

Arley battled the wintry winds back to Missouri. At last on the familiar road toward the Stanton house, he paused at the junction of the lane leading to Evangeline's house. He longed to stop and visit with her. He thought of how joyous a reunion with her would be after the more than two months absence. He envisioned her soft blond hair, her lithe body, her flouncy movements. He imagined the soft warm touch of her hand in his. "Later," he promised himself, "I'll return to her right after I have seen Mamma Essie. Yes, I must see Essie and Caleb first and clean myself up in fresh clothes, then I can join with Evangeline for a long, long visit." He was anxious to see Bill Collier also. "Good old Bill! He's my brother too, him and Caleb and Grey Wolf." All was well in a bright friendly world. The warm afternoon sun on his shoulders was a euphoric blessing.

He arrived at the Stanton place. Caleb and Essie gave him excited embraces. Their babble of questions sought a complete account from the homecoming Cherokee. "Grey Wolf gave me a pony, I led it home laden with fur pelts. I want to give you what you want of them. Use them as you please."

Essie asked the question which had been uppermost in her heart. She hoped against reason, knowing before she asked it what the disappointing answer would surely be. "Did you ask," she spoke with a plaintive note in her gentle voice, "Did you ask if anyone has seen a black man named Gabe Forbes?"

"Yes, Mamma, I asked. No one had seen him. I found men who knew my grandfather, Soaring Hawk, and some even remembered my father, but nobody remembered Gabe Forbes. I'm sorry, Mamma."

She gave a little nod and bowed her head like a mourner at the graveside of a vanishing memory. In a few moments she rose silently from her chair and climbed the stairs to her room. Her two sons exchanged knowing glances. They knew she would be in her rocking chair, dreaming of the past and shedding a few tears over joys she had once had with Gabe. The two young men visited until late at night. Finally they went upstairs, they were filled with brotherly affection. They paused at the door of their mother's room. Whether Essie had fallen asleep in her rocker or whether she was still dreaming they did not know. They trod softly off to bed.

The next morning Essie had recovered from her melancholy. She came down stairs to find Arley preparing to go visit the Colliers. "Wait," she said, "sit down, I want to talk with you." The young man took a chair impatiently waiting for her message. "I spent a sleepless night thinking about our trip to Georgia to seek your father." Arley had become accustomed and accepted her speaking of her husband as though Gabe was his father. "We are not doing much to get ready to go. I was thinking about how we could earn money for the trip. Then I thought of all those beautiful furs. Arley, we can go into the fur trading business! The Cherokee people can help you and I can help too. I want you to follow my instructions. We've got to get the money we need."

Arley listened as she outlined her plan. At his first opportunity he withdrew, pleading that they would talk more about it later. Off he went to see Bill and Simon and Grace Collier. He presented them with several furs which were cured until the hides were soft and supple, the fur luxuriant and glossy. "How beautiful they are," exclaimed Grace Collier. "I'll make me a muff, hat, and scarf."

Excitedly Arley announced, "I have decided to go into the fur trading business. My friends at the Cherokee Nation will help with the trapping. 'Cause I'm a Cherokee, the Indian agents will grant me trading rights. I can bring the pelts to Springfield, take them to St. Louis, or ship them by steamboat on the White River."

"That sounds great," said Bill. "I can help too after the crops is in in the fall. There's still beaver, fox, otter, and maybe some mink in these parts." Arley was pleased with Bill's offer.

"I figure to go over to see Evangeline now. Ain't seen her yet."

"If you can wait 'til I get some hay down for the cows, I'll be goin' with you," remarked Bill.

"No," said Arley impatiently, "I better go on. Got t'get back home before too long." He preferred to see Evangeline alone. With a quick word of goodbye he rode off. When he arrived at the Howser farm, he saw Evangeline strolling toward the stable. The golden morning sun gilded her hair with a shimmering aura. Her ivory skin seemed to glow in the enchanting December light. Missouri never appeared more beautiful to Arley. An unusual warm spell that early morning had transformed the night's hoarfrost into drops of emerald dew which sparkled on every stubble and every needle of cedar and pine. He slipped silently to the maiden's side. "Where to, this bright morning, dear Evangeline?"

"To feed Buttercup," she replied, and then, "Oh, Arley, you're back! I'd begun to think you'd never come back." She threw her arms around him.

Arley was speechless as he gazed into her radiant face. He had dreamed of this moment.

"How was your journey?"

"Pleasant. I'm beginning a new business. Fur trading with the Cherokees. I brought you a present, over there behind my saddle." He hurried to his horse and brought a bundle of pelts. He unrolled them on the ground at her feet.

She stooped down to examine them, putting a soft fur to her face. "How lovely!" she exclaimed.

"The Cherokees will sell me more, and I'll take them to the markets. I know there'll be big profits in this." Arley smiled contentedly.

Evangeline was happy to see him so confident and optimistic. "That will be wonderful for you, Arley."

"Wonderful for us, you mean. Now very soon we can be married. I can provide for you now, Evangeline."

"Oh, Arley..." She faltered awkwardly. "Of course, you didn't know. I...Bill...Bill and I are promised to each other."

Arley fell back dumbfounded, his heart foiled in its fantasy of bliss. Then he turned abruptly and went to his horse, sprang into the saddle and galloped away. He rode hard. When his winded steed loped onto the glade, his flight ended. His spirit was numb to his surroundings. Unguided, his horse wandered to the pool and stretched its neck to drink. Arley saw the boulder where he had sat with Evangeline. He had reached out for her hand. She had grasped it meaningfully. For an instant he wished to turn back to that happier time. With the full realization of his loss, a tear rolled down his cheek.

The splashing brook tumbled cold and unsympathetic over rocks hard and unyielding. Across the glade the dried coneflowers, drooping faded phlox and other wildflowers were grey and brittle. Arley felt the gloom of the lonely place. He wanted to run away. But to where? To the Cherokee Nation? Yes, perhaps there. He was a Cherokee, anywhere else, an alien. It was his skin that Evangeline had rejected. He was sure of it now. Ever since long ago when he had entered Mr. Horatio Dent's school he had felt rejection. Until now he had protested, strove and fought against it. Now he understood; he was simply misplaced, a misfit. He belonged with his own people.

Back at the Stanton place, he regained a little of his feeling of worth. Essie was gentle and kind. She attempted to understand her Cherokee son. But Arley shielded his feelings from her, and she could not fathom the depth of his hurt. Caleb endeavored to be a brother, but Arley was offish and moody. Benjamin and Mary Stanton were kind and considerate but not closely affectionate. They all understood how Evangeline's engagement had disappointed him. But Arley would soon get over it they told themselves.

Essie revived her plans for Arley. While his attention was listless, she hoped that he would soon recover his heartbreak and forget Evangeline, and enter into the business venture she had planned for him. She felt sympathy for Arley, but secretly she was glad that infatuation with Evangeline would not now stand in the way of his going with her to Georgia.

A few days later Arley left for the Cherokee territory. He told his family that he would return soon with bundles of skins. He dedicated himself wholly to his new business. He ran his trap lines. He heaped his pack horses high with pelts and rode with urgency from the Cherokee Nation to Springfield and back again and again. He became a shrewd bargainer. Springfield bankers recognized him as a rising young business man. Many leaders among the Cherokees, Arley observed, were men of wealth. Their prominence extended across racial lines; many were cordially accepted in white circles. Some had married white women.

On the day Bill and Evangeline were married, Arley was in Perryville, Cherokee Nation. He sent regrets. He had gone to Old Fort Wayne to negotiate for pelts with the Arkansas Indians.

When he returned home a few weeks later, Essie handed him a piece of paper as she said, "Billy Collier brought this note for you, Arley."

He unfolded the note. It read: "Arley, I have missed you very much. I have bundles of pelts for you. Evangeline misses you too. We want you to come to supper with us on Sunday. Please come if you can. Bill."

"Bill wants me to come to supper on Sunday," Arley remarked to Essie.

"You should go, Arley. You've been slighting them. I think you have vexed them by making yourself so scarce. You must go, Arley. Bill thinks you're riled up against him 'cause he stole Evangeline. Oh, and you must see their little cabin. Bill and his paw finished it two months ago."

For a moment Arley deliberated the invitation. He fought down the jealousy in his heart. Bill and Evangeline...and a new home! "Well, yes, I reckon I ought to go," he said slowly. He knew it would not be easy.

Bill and Evangeline welcomed Arley cordially. Bill wanted to erase any animosity, if such may have existed, between them. He could only guess what the loss of Evangeline must have meant to Arley, and his sympathy for Arley had caused him much distress. He wanted to prove his affection and even compensate for Arley's loss. Evangeline, too, was happy to relieve the anguish in her own soul. She had not wanted to lose Arley as a dear friend. Most of all she felt she must let him know she had acted with her heart--the cruelest blow of all to Arley. His Cherokee blood had nothing to do with it.

Arley was friendly in a perfunctory way. He was grateful for Bill's support in the fur business. Together they planned to build a shed to store pelts. Bill said, "With a warehouse we can accumulate a bigger stock of merchandise so's we can take much larger shipments to St. Louis. If I make the trip with you we can avoid any mishap, hijacking, robbery, and such." Bill offered to furnish land for the building.

Together they constructed a log warehouse. Time and again they filled it with pelts and transported them to the St. Louis markets. Their profits grew. As a third party in the venture Essie, on the side lines, was wisely coaching and prodding.

"If we could transport the furs to New Orleans we could increase our profit. Down there we could sell directly for the European market," said Bill. In March, Bill made a trip to Forsyth to inquire about shipping on the White River. The B.J. Carter steamboat was docked there. The water level was too low to allow boats avoid snares and shoals. Her captain was waiting for the spring rains when the river would rise. Then the vessel would start out for Batesville, Arkansas.

"Our storage shed is filled. Now is the time to ship to New Orleans," said Bill as they sat in Evangeline's kitchen. He took a long draft from his coffee cup. "Captain Overmeyer sez he would unload our cargo at Batesville. There we could wait for another southbound steamboat."

Arley was a little wary of transporting their merchandise so far. Once when he was on his way to St.Louis, three men had waylaid him and took his two pack horses. They taunted him as an Indian who had "no right dealing with Christian white people." The thugs boasted that if the army could not restrict the "savages" to their own territory it was up to them to teach the "barbarians" to stay where they belong. Arley was wounded by their slurs, but he outsmarted them by stealing into their camp by night and while they were asleep, making off with his pack horses. He had told Bill of the hijacking but he had been too chagrined to relate the details of how he had been verbally insulted and humiliated.

Bill had, himself, sometimes been chided for his association with his Indian partner.

"If you want," Bill offered, "I'll take the responsibility for conveying the merchandise to the market. I've always wanted t'see New Orleans." He shot a side glance to Evangeline who stood solemnly pouring Arley a cup of coffee. Bill knew how upset she had been whenever he left her alone to make the trips to St. Louis with Arley. She had warned that she would surely not survive without him. This time Arley would be left behind. "Will you see to it that Evangeline is kept in firewood and do the heavy chores for her while I'm gone?" he asked.

"Yes, of course," Arley replied.

Later, when Arley explained the plan to Essie, she was skeptical. She had not planned for the operation to become so big. They had already accumulated enough cash for their journey to the East. She was anxious to go. This new venture would entail expending considerable money for transportation. Against her protests, the boys had insisted. They assured her that huge profits were within their grasp. It was therefore arranged. The shipment was prepared to go out as soon as the river's water level had risen. Bill made ready for the journey.

A cargo of cotton, which had been stored since last summer, furs, and wool were loaded onto the B.J. Carter. Seven passengers came aboard. The twin paddle wheels began their sloshing, churning the river, leaving a foamy wake. Those who had come down to the wharf to watch the departure turned away, and only Arley remained. Bill at the steamer's rail waved a last goodbye and watched Arley grow smaller, to a miniature blur. The little village at the mouth of Swan Creek was overwhelmed by the enormous bluffs which surrounded it, The mountain cliffs seemed to rise higher and higher at the river's edge. Out of rocky crevices the tenacious trees and shrubs began to display the first signs of spring. In places where the mountains gave way to bottom land there was an array of redbud trees and white-blooming serviceberry. Occasionally there was a flutter of blue where bluebirds or blue jays reveled in the spring day. Blue heron stood statue-like on the shore or in the shallow water's edge. Deer and elk in the meadows raised their heads to gaze at the supernatural monstrosity as it passed.

When he tired of the panarama, Bill turned his attention to the intricacies of the steamer. He climbed into the pilot house to observe the navigator at work. The host of the pilot's lookout was less than cordial and made it known that passengers were not permitted there and, most of all were not to talk to the steersman. The pilot could not resist, however, boasting of his knowledge of the river and demonstrating his navigational skill. He pointed out where the snares were and how by his orders one or both paddle wheels were disengaged to effect a tricky maneuver through a risky passage. Sometimes a second man came to wield the helm, while the pilot kept a watchful eye on the river and gave orders to his steersman. He could discern from the sound of the escapement pipe whether there was too much or too little steam pressure. The pilot was puffed up with self-importance. Bill could not become his close friend.

On the other hand, two of the firemen--of which there were four--were pleased to visit with the passenger. As they stoked the boilers they were subjected to searing blasts from the open doors of the fireboxes and then exposed to the chilling dampness of the river air while they carried firewood across the slippery wet deck. At the end of their twelve-hour shift the two men came out coughing and exhausted. They joined Bill on the deck.

"The pilot is a grouchy son o'bitch," growled one of them. "They ain't no pleasin' him. He calls fer more steam at the same time the engineer sez we don't darst fire up no hotter. Them two is goin' to end up in a fisticuffs sometime."

The second fireman agreed and added, "The captain is plumb dilatory. He goes dawdling around an' don't even know what is goin' on."

That there was some discontent, even discord, among the crew did not strike Bill as being unusual or of any particular significance. Men confined for weeks together on the limited space of the steamboat were bound to have frayed nerves.

Besides the crew and Bill, there were six other passengers aboard. A man and his wife were on their way to Vicksburg after having visited the woman's sister in Springfield. The poor woman was terrified by the roaring of the draft that emulated in the two black chimneys and by the ear-splitting blasts of steam from the escapement pipes. She shivered at the cold, dark water that rippled past the sides of the boat. Consequently, she kept to the shelter of her tiny cubicle and prayed that the journey would be quick and without mishap. Her poor husband dared not leave her side and spent his time soothing and reassuring her. The four other passengers, veteran riverboat travelers, spent their time in their cabin where they idled away their time by gambling at cards.

Bill, therefore, was alone on the deck most of the time, watching the scenery or dozing in the fresh river air. In a seven-hour battle the vessel maneuvered through Elbow Shoals at the Arkansas border. Bill's firemen friends assured him that the greatest obstacle of the voyage had been conquered. The steamer made brief stops at Dubuque, Talbert's Ferry, and Calico Rock and was drawing near its destination at Batesville, over three hundred miles from Forsyth. All the crew were eager to reach the port, where most of them lived and where they could spend a few days resting. Like a weary dray horse musters strength to speed to the pleasant pastures of home, the J.B. Carter strained and groaned to reach full power, the boilers forced to the limit

Bill sat with the back of his chair leaned against the pilot house. He felt the steady vibration of the deck and heard the low pulse of the engines in the hull directly below him. The fresh river air and the continuous chugging sound soon lulled his senses and his eyes closed in sleep. How long he had slept he never knew, but he was awakened by a spray of hot mist that stuck his face. His eyes popped. He saw a jet of boiling water forced from the main pipe line just aft of the chimney. Steam vapor filled the air! There was a thunderous roar! Bill was suddenly lifted high into the air! A cloud of steam enveloped him obscuring all from his sight. All earth and heaven seemed to have vaporized in one catastropic blast of sound and motion! He experienced intense pain in his lower extremities. He felt himself falling, plunging into the cold water! From the depths he struggled to the surface. Debris splashing into the water made staccato sounds all around him! A large beam struck flat onto the water with a resounding plop. The force of its movement and the splash of cool water cleared away the steam so that for an instant he would see the floating timber before him. He struggled toward it but his legs had no sensation or control. He would have to move by his arms alone. Paddling furiously he reached for the wooden beam and put his arms over it. "My legs," he thought, "I can't feel my legs!" Struggling to hold tight to the floating timber he felt faint. The last of the debris, some of which was thrown skyward some two or three hundred feet, was still plunging back downward. A board struck Bill on the head and he lost consciousness. The J.B. Carter was forever gone!

Chapter XIV
Caleb Goes to Jail

After the death of Bart, Kerry McShane hired another overseer. He was a huge, burly, white man named Otto Fluger. Although he came to McShane with the best of references, the Irish planter was skeptical of Fluger's stand on the disciplining of slave hands. "Don't use no scourge on ary nigger," said the applicant. "Ain't never had no call to, sir." He squared his shoulders and stood with his massive arms folded across his broad chest.

As McShane studied the man, he was reminded of the Clydesdales he had seen pulling enormous draft wagons back in Ireland. Such a hulk of a man! Such broad strong hands! He was indeed impressive. Still there was something about his eyes and mouth that seemed gentle. "Some o' our darkies is used to the lash," said McShane. "Don't seem t'understand nothin' else. Missouri ain't like things is down south. Much harder here to make a place pay here. I expect my niggers t'earn their keep and then some."

"Don't be worryin' 'bout that, sir. They'll work hard for me. You'll see," said Fluger.

"Well, I'll be givin' ye a chanc't to prove that. But mind now, if the work don't hold up, ye'll be out o' a job."

Otto Fluger went to work. At first the slave hands were unsettled. They were relieved to have Bart gone. There should have been cause for rejoicing, but such a mysterious death had struck them with awe, and the most they dared do was to whisper that "he got what he had comin' t'him." They viewed the new giant foreman with uncertainty, fearing to behave in any but the most servile way. It took weeks for them to realize that they could now enjoy freedoms which they had never known before. Fluger did not scowl when they sang at their work, nor did he prowl among the slave shanties when they gathered to sing and dance. Soon they were to discover that boss Fluger did not police them after dark, and a few dared to slip away to Stultz's barn. It was a ramshackle old structure which farmer Stultz no longer used because of his advanced age and crippling arthritis. Roughsawn boards which were ripped up from the floor of the hay loft were placed on sections of logs to serve as benches. The cobwebs were kept swept down as far as a rag on a pole would reach to make it a place of respectability, a place for fellowship and gospel meetings. Blacks came donned in their finest apparel.

One meeting night Brother Shannon was "bad sick" and the congregation was without a leader. Someone on a bench in the rear shouted, "Let Bro'er Caleb do the exhortin'". All around the room there echoed the call for Caleb to take the pulpit. Reluctantly Caleb left his seat on the bench beside Essie and stepped up onto the platform. He glanced about at the waves of black faces and became nervous and self-conscious. His restless hands fumbled about, went into his pockets and out again. When he finally found his tongue he spoke in a small faltering voice, "What you all want me to talk about?"

"Heav'n!" came the cry. "Tell us 'bout heav'n!" There were sporadic outbursts of "Praise the Lawd" and "Amen."

Caleb stepped behind the crude pulpit, gripped it tightly with both hands. He bowed his head and whispered, "Heaven! Heaven help me." As he began, his voice was shrill and trembling. Slowly he began to tell what he had read in the scriptures. When that ran out he began to expand upon the Word with visionary inspiration that seemed to rival that of John the Revelator. He described the marriage feast of the Lamb and interjected it with recipes right out of Essie's cookbook. In his easy vernacular and his earthy speculation of the glorious hereafter he stirred his listeners lifting them above their earthly anguish. They shouted and groaned.

Suddenly the clamor hushed. A flutter of apprehension swept across the room. Caleb scanned the crowd. He saw Essie's concern and alarm. Out of the reach of the light from the flickering grease lamps stood Kerry McShane. Beside him in the shadows was someone else. Squinting his eyes Caleb was able to recognize the county sheriff. The two white faces, both with greying beards, appeared like silent apparitions. Caleb was in mute confusion. He saw some of McShane's slaves slip from their benches and pass into the shadows to escape into the night. Caleb thought of Judge Stanton's warning of McShane's anger against him. What was McShane up to? Since the night of Bart's death, Caleb had not trespassed onto McShane land. Now the services at the old barn lured McShane's Negroes off the plantation.

Caleb took a big gulp of air and began again. "Heaven ain't open to ever'one. Money can't buy a place there. Prestige and power ain't goin' to get you there. Whoever is servant here on earth is goin' to be greatest up there." Courage returned to Caleb as he spoke directly to the two white faces he saw in the shadows. The audience warmed up again to shout "Amen" and "Praise de Lawd." "They ain't no way through the pearly gates 'lessen you go with Jesus. Less you repent and let Jesus wash away your sins you can't get in there. Sin is anger, hatred, and jealousy against your neighbor. Your neighbor is your master if you are a slave, and a slave is neighbor to his master. No man covered with the black sins of lyin', cheatin' and stealin' can walk them streets o' gold."

The sheriff had started to take a step forward, but McShane put his arm in front of him to hold him back. The planter seemed to be listening. Finally he gave the sheriff a little nod. Slowly, the officer walked the straw strewn path up to Caleb. A hush fell over the congregation. "Come with me," he said. The Negro youth made one last appeal as he departed, "Repent!" he called over his shoulder. "Repent, else you'll perish like the scribes and pharisees." The Sheriff escorted him from the barn.

On the second floor of the brick jailhouse was a bare room. An army cot with a chamber pot under it, a wash stand with a water pitcher and wash bowl, and a rickety chair were the only furnishings. The window was protected with steel bars. Caleb slept little that night. He thought of his mother and he thought about Judge Stanton who would be expecting him to drive him to court the next day. Would he himself be brought into court? for what reason? He knew very well that the testimony of a black man would have no persuasion and be disavowed in court. What was to become of him?

In the morning Kerry McShane came to be admitted into the prisoner's room. "I come to press charges agin' you, Caleb Forbes, for subverting my niggers. You done been teachin' them to read. Thet's agin' the law," he said.

"I just wanted them to be able to read the Bible. Can't see any wrong in that. I didn't give them any abolitionist papers to read," said Caleb.

"I reckon thet's true," admitted McShane, "but still, ye broke the law. I lost my overseer on yer account. Don't know exactly what part ye had in him bein' kill't."

"Didn't have no part in that. I was tryin' to escape from him."

"But you was on my land," said McShane with a scowl. "I got meself another overseer, but I ain't sure he can handle the job. The niggers ain't skert of him. Leastways not skert enough, seems to me."

"Slaves don't have to be scared to be good workers. And they don't have to be beat neither."

"Thet's what my new boss sez. I doubt thet's true. Anyways, can't have ye interferin' with my workers."

"Ain't done nothin' to interfere," said Caleb.

The slave holder stroked his grey-bearded chin and leered menacingly. "Ye has interfered! My boss man come to me this morning, sez the niggers is all upset, women cryin', men too grieved to work, all 'cause ye been arrested. It ain't right ye should have such a hold o'er my property. I won't have it." He arose from his chair and started to leave. Then he paused and turned back to Caleb. "I ain't no religious man. What's repentance? My niggers is all tryin' to repent." The man's face held a mystified expression.

"Repentance is a'turnin' away from doin' wrong, a changin' your life to doin' good. It's bein' born again."

"I reckon I done thet," said McShane. "My maw had me baptized by the priest when I wus a baby."

"'It ain't somethin' somebody can do for you, Mas'er McShane. You gotta' do it for yourself."

McShane raised his hand as though he was thrusting the idea away from him. He had heard enough. He called to be escorted from the room.

It was Kerry McShane's birthday. He had eaten his dinner alone. Since his wife had died, he was a lonely man, finding little pleasure in life beyond the pleasure of eating. The table had been replenished with the most delectable dainties. He stood up and rubbed his belly. He clapped his hands together. "Cook! Cook Delphena!" he called. "Come here." In waddled a plump colored woman bowing deeply. "Your dinner was quite satisfying, Delphena. But them wild strawberries was plum laripin. Where in tarnation did you get 'em?"

"Toby fetched 'em. Don't know where they was picked. He jest give 'em to me. Sez, these is for mas'ah." The pudgy woman twisted her apron uncomfortably, as though she had expected to be reprimanded. "Send him to me," said McShane.

In a few minutes Toby came. The old man approached the master with trepidation. "Here I is, mas'ah," he said shyly. He was stooped as though he were perpetually in an attitude of obeisance. His frail form was clothed in a tattered jacket and butternut jeans.

"Toby, tell me, I et wild strawberries tonight. Cook said you brought 'em in. Where'd ye get 'em?"

"Mas'ah, don' be angry at me. I picked 'em in the woods west o' the plantation. They wasn't on yer land, mas'ah."

"Why, Toby, why'd ye bring 'em for me?"

"I done it 'cause 'tis yer birt'day. I know I weren't 'sposed ter get off plantation land. Don't thresh me, mas'ah."

"Toby, I et them berries and liked 'em." McShane smiled slyly. "I want you to fetch another mess o' them strawberries "

"Oh, yes, mas'ah," said Toby, his fears relieved, "I'll do that. I bring lots o' berries."

On the afternoon of the next day Caleb was released from the upstairs jail room. It was wholly unexpected by the black youth and he was puzzled by it. Judge Stanton was there waiting for him in the room downstairs.

203

"Thank you, Master Stanton," said Caleb, "for gettin' me out. I reckon I been a heap of trouble to you."

"No," said the judge, "I had nothing to do with it. Essie told me about what happened. We were very worried when you didn't come home that first night. By the second night we understood that the sheriff was still holding you. I suspected McShane had something to do with it, but he refused to see me. I couldn't find out the details. Then this morning Sheriff Bolger came to me and said McShane had dropped the charges. McShane said he had made a mistake and there would be no charges against you. He wouldn't say any more than that. It was all very mysterious."

"I don't understand it neither," said Caleb.

As they rode home in the carriage, Caleb told the judge all that had happened.

As Judge Stanton and Caleb neared home they met a band of six men on horseback. Arley was among them. Curious to know what the commotion was, Caleb pulled his horse to a stop. Arley came to the buggy's side, while the other men rode on toward the McShane plantation.

"One of the McShane slaves is missing," said Arley. "He was spotted up north of here, long way off from the McShane place. I'm goin' with the posse to bring him back."

"Who is the runaway?" asked Judge Stanton.

"An old man named Toby."

"Toby wouldn't run away," said Caleb. "There must be some mistake. He wouldn't do such a thing."

"Well, we're goin' after him," said Arley.

"Don't go, Arley. It's a mistake. If Toby was to be a runaway, there's good reason for it. Don't go. He's a old man. Those posse men could do somethin' desperate. Toby could get hurt."

"We can't jest let runaways go. We got to stop 'em," said Arley.

"Then let them do it. Why should you help?"

"'Cause I want to," said Arley, and he spurred his horse to overtake the men.

204

Caleb was disturbed. He had wanted to get a promise from Arley that he would protect Toby from harm by the other men. Caleb's sympathy was for Toby, a docile, good-natured man. Arley had ridden off so blithely. He had taken the pursuit as a sport to be enjoyed. Caleb was angry.

Late that evening Arley returned. Caleb was still upset and infuriated, anxious to know whether Toby had been recovered. In response to Caleb's angry tone, Arley was reticent and sullen. His only remark was that the runaway had been taken back to the McShane plantation.

The next day Caleb broke his resolve not ever to trespass on McShane's property again. He felt he must know the details of the slave's escape and recapture. He learned from the other Negroes that Toby was sick in bed.

At Toby's bedside, Caleb learned the truth. Toby had gone to pick wild strawberries. When he went to the spot where he had found them before there weren't any. He searched farther and farther until he became disoriented and lost. When the posse men found Toby they had forced him to trot the long distance back. The old man's plea that he had not intended to run away was not heeded.

Caleb faced Arley with accusations. While Arley recognized in his heart that the posse was unduly harsh on the elderly slave, he could not accept being criticized by Caleb. Bitter words arose between the two. In a huff Arley left the Stanton home and went to stay in the shed he and Bill had built.

Chapter XV
Arley Courts Evangeline

The kitchen was warm with the smell of fresh-baked bread. Evangeline sat at the table looking at the golden brown loaves. Her hand rested on the handle of the butter churn. She yearned for Bill to be there to join her, to share slices of the soft light bread. He loved the fresh crunchy crust. Nine days had passed since he had gone, nine lonely days. The butter had come. Such a lot of butter, she mused. It would not be too much if only Bill were there. Perhaps she could send part of it to Judge Stanton's household. She sat quietly with her rambling thoughts. The cow was giving such a large amount of milk now. Milking her was such a tiresome chore. Funny, she didn't mind milking when Bill was at home, but so many tasks seemed hard and futile when he was gone.

There was a knock at the door. That would be Arley, she thought. She brushed a wisp of blond hair from her face, rose and went to let him in. She returned to her chair remarking, "You're just in time to have a piece of fresh-baked bread." Wearily she moved again out of her chair and to the cupboard. She brought a bread knife and a crock for the butter. Then she noticed how dark it was getting and she went for a candle. She ignited a scrap of paper at the fireplace and touched it to the candle.

Arley took a seat at the table. Her kitchen seemed such a pleasant place, so restful, a place to eat and visit. Evangeline sliced the bread, removed the top off the churn, jabbed a knife into it, and spread butter on the slices of warm bread. With a smile, Arley accepted a slice. With the exception of a few trivial remarks they were quiet. Arley took the knife and sliced himself another piece of bread. "I started down to Forsyth today," he said. "I wanted to find news about the J.B. Carter. I went about eight miles when I came across a runaway slave. He looked tired and scared, I knowed he was a runaway." Arley thought of old Toby whom he had helped the posse recapture and take to the McShane plantation. This runaway was old and frail like

Toby. Caleb had been right. Arley wished now that he had not been a part of the posse. "I felt a mite sorry for him. Wanted t' give him a couple o' biscuits out o' my saddlebag, but he was so scared he jest run off. I reckon he thought I was tryin' to catch him. I goes on my way. In a little while I come to four men with bloodhounds. They sez, 'Did ye run across a nigger up the road there?' I didn't say nothin'. I jest made out like I was puzzled by the question. 'Did you see a runaway nigger?' They asked agin. I couldn't decide what to say. I just spurred my horse and rode off."

"I'm glad you didn't help them," said Evangeline.

"I don't know. There are more and more of them tryin' to escape. I reckon it's 'cause so many folks is willin' to help them. That encourages them to try. Southerners is gettin' mighty riled up about it. Some folks sez that that's goin' to bring on a war."

"But you haven't said what you found out in Forsyth," said Evangeline impatiently.

"I didn't go. After I left the slave chasers, I got curious. I turned around and followed after them. 'Afore long they passed me going south. They had the old nigger. His hands was tied together. He hadn't oughtta tried to get away. He was somebody's property."

"I'm sorry he didn't get away," said Evangeline.

"I'll go to Forsyth in the morning." He rose from his chair to leave. "You've plenty of firewood on the porch. I'll stop in when I get back. Good night, Evangeline."

She moved to the door with him. "Good night, Arley. Be sure to come by. I'm anxious to know what you find out in Forsyth."

He moved out into the darkness. In his mind he carried her image, her wistful eyes, her melancholy expression. Was her life happy? Really happy? Bill had been gone only nine days. Surely she could endure nine days of his absence. Was she content with Bill even before he left? Was it Arley's jealous imagination that brought such questions to mind?

In the morning Arley went to Forsyth. Arriving there in the afternoon, he strolled along the board walk stopping at a blacksmith shop and a general store. His inquiries about the J.B.

Carter steamboat were met with no news report. He moved along the street seeking more people to question. Suddenly, there was a blast of a steamboat whistle. Men, boys, and dogs scurried toward the dock. "There she comes!" was the shout that arose from the crowd. Around the bend of the White River she sailed from behind a high rocky bluff toward the dock at the mouth of Swan Creek. The beautiful glistening water monster sputtered and belched. It was a thrilling sight to Arley. Could this be the J.B. Carter? Nine days was too soon to expect to see Bill return, unless he was able to sell the furs at Batesville. He would seek to get a handsome price there. Failing that, he would transfer his cargo to a larger steamboat and continue his trip toward New Orleans. All Arley could hope for this early was some word about the progress of the J.B. Carter. He could discern the lettering now. The approaching vessel bore the name: Dauntless. With no visible machinery, the great stern wheel churned the water awesomely. She glided to the dock. Briskly the ropes were secured, the engines shut down, and the gangplank lowered. The captain disembarked pompously down the plank.

Arley approached him, "Pardon me, captain, I am anxious to know if you could give me any news about the J.B. Carter. Perhaps you passed her?"

"Indeed I did," said the captain. "I passed her, I did, what there was left of her."

"What? What do you mean? Was something wrong with her?"

"Wrong with her? She's gone! Don't know what happened for sure. She went onto a shoal, I reckon. When she couldn't back off, I figure they fired her up--probably blocked off the safety valve--fired her up 'til she blowed. The crew was blown to kingdom come. What little was left caught afire, I reckon. I heered they wasn't no survivors."

"No survivors?" Arley exclaimed in disbelief.

"That's what I heered. Course I don't know nothin' exceptin' I seen the wreckage along the shore. I expect she was loaded down beyond her capacity. Don't see how there coulda' been survivors. Them that survived the explosion was killed by the fire or was drown'd," reported the captain.

The crew members of the Dauntless confirmed that the wreckage they had seen was that of the J.B. Carter. Arley spent a sorrowful night in a small Forsyth hotel. He arose early the next morning for the sad trek home.

Bill Collier was dead! How could he ever tell Evangeline! There seemed to be no way to soften the tragic news. He considered postponing his visit to her and thus avoid telling her. She would be devastated. Still, he had told her of his intentions to make the journey to Forsyth. Now it he was obligated to take her the report.

Before going in to Evangeline, Arley stopped in the yard to relieve his anxiety by splitting a few sections of logs. He swung the ax as though he was wielding blows against fate. As he carried an armload of wood to stack on the porch, Evangeline cmerged. "I've been wondering what you learned in Forsyth," she said.

Stacking the wood, he struggled for words. "Evangeline,...let's go inside. There's something... I... need to tell you." They went into the kitchen and sat at the table. Arley hesitated. "Evangeline," he began, "I have bad news. The J.B. Carter had...a wreck."

The young woman sat silently, her lip trembled. "A wreck?" she asked softly, not seeming to understand the word.

"Yes, I don't know exactly what happened. I talked to the captain and crew of a boat that passed the wreckage. It was all hearsay. The men just said they seen the ruins of the J.B. Carter as they sailed by it, not far from Batesville."

Evangeline gasped. "What about Bill?"

"There is no word about Bill." Arley placed his hand on her's resting on the table. "The men I talked to seemed to think all were lost."

"Dear God," she muttered. She turned away and covered her face as she burst into tears.

Essie's first knowledge of the steamboat wreck came a few hours later when she rode over to the storage shed to take Arley some fresh-baked cakes. For days she had worried about the rift between her two sons. Now the blow of Bill's loss overshdowed that concern. Her heart sank in grief and disappointment. Bill Collier was gone! Their investment in furs and transportation fees, gone! Saddened though she was over Bill's death, still she could not keep from wondering how long now would she have to wait before she could go to Georgia.

As she went back home, she was also worried about Arley. She had vehemently urged him to return to the Stanton place. He had cooled, she observed, in his resentment of Caleb. Why was he insisting on staying in the warehouse? Then the realization came to her. Arley wanted to stay close to Evangeline. "Dear Lord," she thought "how can I now get Arley to take me to Gabe? How can anything withstand against a young man's infatuation for a girl?"

Every day Arley went back to see Evangeline. Though words could not console them, gradually their grief wore away. Evangeline busied herself about the farm. She began again to cook and bake bread. To be sure, when she heard the sound of horse's hooves she stepped to the window with new hope that Bill was returning home. Inevitably the approaching one was Arley, and in her loneliness she was glad to welcome him. Three months passed.

One evening Arley came, split and stacked a little firewood, then seeing a blanket hanging to dry on the clothes line, he threw it over his shoulder and took it inside the cabin. "It looks like a storm acomin' up. Your blanket will get wet," he told Evangeline. He draped the blanket over the back of a chair.

"Oh, yes, I forgot it. Thank you, Arley. I've got supper all ready. I set a plate out for you, Arley."

They finished the meal and were sitting at the table in a feeling of warmth and satisfaction. Arley said, "Evangeline, you been grievin' long enough. Are you aimin' to keep yerself penned up forever here in the house? Come with me Saturday to the doin's at Foster's. There'll be music an' games. It's time you begun to enjoy yerself."

"Oh, Arley, I just couldn't. I wouldn't feel right. I'd be thinkin' of Bill all the time." She rose from her chair and went to the wooden sink. She set out the dishpan. Arley went to the

211

fireplace to get the teakettle and pour the water into the pan. As he came behind her, she gave her eyes a quick brush with her apron. He was so touched by her grief that he set the teakettle down and took her into his arms. She rested her face against his shoulder.

"I thought maybe by now you might sometimes be thinkin' of me," said Arley tenderly.

"I do, Arley, I do. Sometimes it makes me feel guilty, like I'm disloyal to Bill."

"I understand. I miss him too. You've been loyal and faithful, but don't punish yerself. Remember, I love you too. My love is kinda like a fettered mustang that longs to bolt across the wild, green mountain country but his legs is hobbled." He paused with a shy smile. Evangeline responded by placing her hand on his. Arley continued, "Last month I killed a deer. Remember? I brought you a leg of venison. When I brought it to you I asked for some ears of corn. You looked kinda puzzled about it. That was a special token to me. Long ago when a Cherokee girl was gettin' married she carried ears of corn and the Cherokee boy carried a leg of venison. In the weddin' ceremony they exchanged their tokens. It meant they would look after and care for each other. When you gave me those ears of corn I made out in my mind like we was married. I pledged myself to you. Don't laugh, Evangeline, I wanted so much for it to be so."

"Oh, I couldn't laugh, Arley." She looked tenderly into his face. He took her into his arms and kissed her passionately. She turned her face away. "I can't," she whispered. "It's wrong. I still feel married to Bill."

Arley relaxed his embrace. Thrown across the chair was the blanket he had brought in from the clothes line. It was fresh and dry. He picked up the blanket and held it up. "Here hold this end of the blanket," he said. "This is a symbol of your marriage to Bill." He took the blanket in his hands and gave it a fierce jerk ripping it down the middle. "By Cherokee custom, that marriage is now dissolved."

Evangeline gasped. She stared at the torn half blanket in her hand.

"It's over, my love," he said as he put his comforting arms around her. He picked her up in his arms and carried her off into the bedroom.

Outside there was the din of heavy falling rain.

Part Two of Chapter XV

Early the next morning Arley slipped from Evangeline's home. He had written a note to her and left it on the kitchen table. It read: "Dearest Evangeline, I woke up this morning filled with remorse. Not that I do not love you and want you, but that I am afraid I took advantage of your gentle nature and forced my affections upon you. Forgive me, dear. I can understand your holding back and keeping your love in store for Bill. Three times I went to Forsyth and have asked about Bill. The answer's always the same. There ain't no word of any survivors of the J.B. Carter. Because I can't bear seeing you so unsettled in your heart and mind, I'm going to go down the White River and search out the wreckage of the steamboat. Then perhaps we can both put an end to our grief for poor Bill, and you can give your love to me with no strings attached. Till I return, all my love, Arley" First, Arley went to tell Essie and Caleb of his intentions to be gone for an extended time and to bid them goodbye. He wanted also to pick up a few of his clothes and to ask Caleb to keep an eye on Evangeline. For over three months now Arley had been living in the storage shed. Essie had made numerous trips to beg him to return home. She feared an intimacy between her son and Evangeline was about to develop. Things were not going at all according to her plan. Arley seemed disinterested at that time in taking her to Georgia. Arley left Essie and Caleb with the admonition that they should not worry about him. How long the journey and investigation would take, he was unable to say. Of course, he would be anxious to return in order to make known his findings to Evangeline. He journeyed southward on horseback over the rough mountain trail to the little town on the White River. He had often made the trip coming north from Harrison with packs of pelts gained from the Arkansas Cherokees. Now as he traveled he thought of the time when he had left Bill on the J.B. Carter. The furs had been loaded onto the steamship, and he had made the journey back north with the empty wagon. With excitement, Bill had bid him farewell and had left with such high hopes for a prosperous trading venture.

As the troubled young man neared Forsyth, he did not know how soon there would be a steamboat ready to leave, but he would bide his time until he could gain passage to Batesville, taking the same route Bill had taken.

It was late afternoon when he arrived in Forsyth. He learned at the wharf that a steamboat would be ready to leave in the morning. Arley was pleased with his good fortune. He would eat dinner, spend the night in the local hotel, and be ready to sail in the morning. It was still daylight when he ordered food at a small tavern. Choosing a seat next to a window, he could watch the people passing by on the wooden sidewalk. Down the street was a small livery stable, and he had already made arrangements to board his horse there until he came back from Batesville. He had barely bagun to eat, when through the window he saw a figure of a man who seemed very familiar to him. There were two men walking together, one huge older man and a younger one with a bad limp. Both of them wore beards and had the look of being backwoodsmen. It was the younger of the two men who captured Arley's attention. As he stared out the window he was dumbfounded by the impression that the man had a striking likeness to Bill Collier! The man who held Arley's gaze was thinner than Bill and dragged his left foot. Of course, too, his brown beard detracted from the impression that it was the cleanshaven Bill Collier. The men crossed the street and passed along just outside the window where Arley sat. Arley was flabbergasted! Could it really be? At close range, the similarity was unbelievable! Arley was hypnotized by the sight. For so long a time he had hoped and had clung to the idea that somehow Bill was still alive. At last, he had thought his time of grieving had drained from him any expectation that he would ever see Bill again. Bill was dead! Arley knew it! He felt it down into the very depths of his being. He had resigned himself to it. Now, Bill's ghost had appeared. It was some sort of punishment for his night with Evangeline! The fork trembled in his hand. His food lodged in his throat. Arley turned in his chair to look toward the tavern's entrance. The two men were entering the door! So unstrung by the vision was he, that he had the impulse to rise from his chair and flee from the room, but he

216

could not move! The two men looked about the room selecting a table. Then all at once they turned in Arley's direction. There was a delighted, happy smile on the young bearded face. He spoke to his companion and hurried to where Arley sat. "Arley, oh, Arley! What a welcome sight!" The voice was Bill's. They embraced, as Arley half rose from his chair. Arley was stunned. It was more than he had allowed himself to imagine. Bill rattled on, "You should have seen your face, Arley! You didn't recognize me, did you? Honest now, have I changed that much? Do you like the beard?"

Finally, Arley was able to say, "Bill, it's been over three months. I thought I'd never see you again!"

"Yes," said Bill, "three long, painful months." "We heard about the steamboat explosion and thought you were killed." At last, Arley realized that his response had not been a heartfelt greeting.

"Bill, you can't imagine how happy I am to see you alive," he said and meant it. "Where have you been? Why didn't you let us know about yourself?"

"We'll tell you all about that, but first, how is Evangeline?"

"She's fine. She was worried to death about you and when she got news that all the people on board the steamship were lost, she was beside herself in sorrow. Why didn't you send her word?"

"Arley, I couldn't. I owe my life to my new friend here. This here's Claus Hassler. On two different days Claus waited for river boats to pass the place where the J. B. Carter wrecked but there was no way he could get attention of a crew to send a message."

The big mountaineer held out his calloused hand to Arley.

"I heerd lots about ye from Bill," he said. "Sure proud to make your acquaintance."

"Claus, tell Arley how you saved my life," said Bill.

The three men sat down at the gingham covered table.

The huge man cleared his throat with a roar. "It weren't much on my part. I was huntin' for turkeys down by the river. I was just about to head my nag back towards home when I heerd a steamboat on the river. I allus like to watch them boats, so I

217

stop. Just as she come up even with me, she gave out a big hissing sound and then 'bang'! She blowed to smithereens. Parts of thet boat was flying ever'where. I seen Bill here shot up, musta' been fifteen feet into the air. Pieces of that outfit began to rip through the trees all 'round me. My danged horse got scared an' reared into the air. Woulda' bolted off, except thet a piece of boiler iron from that ship was hurled about two hundred yards an' struck my old nag right in th' neck. Well, ye kin believe it or not, that iron piece cut my nag's head clean off from her body slick as a whistle. I was thrown to th' groun'. When I got onter my feet, I seen this here fellow hanging onter a big timber in th' water. Well, th' current was carrin' him near the shore. I jumped in and fished him out. He was stunned by the accident and was plumb conked out. I carried him, musta' been, two miles to my cabin and took care of him."

Bill stood by with an amused, excited smile, then took up the story.

"When I come to I was in Claus' cabin. My legs was crippled. Couldn't move them, even a little bit. Claus took care of me, what time he wasn't huntin' or scroungin' around for food. We was stranded in the woods in Claus' little cabin, 'bout twenty miles from Batesville. He didn't have no horse. There wasn't no post office nor nothin'. About twice a year he used to go to town for supplies. But he didn't dare to leave me, 'cause I couldn't take care of myself. In about ten weeks I could begin to get my legs to move. And Claus said he thought I could get along by myself. So he goes to hunt up a couple of horses so's we could go to Batesville. He was gone two days and come back with a couple of scroungy nags. Then a little later we set out for Batesville. I tell you, without Claus, I'd never a' made it. We got onto a boat and arrived here yesterday."

"That's fantastic!" exclaimed Arley.

"I'm sorry we lost all our shipment of pelts. They mighta got to New Orleans, floatin' down th' river, but I wasn't there to collect any money for 'em. Sorry the trip wasn't profitable, Arley."

"That couldn't be helped."

"Now, since you'er here, maybe Claus can go back home. You can go with me home. I can't wait to see Evangeline. Tell me again, did she miss me? Is she all right?"

"Of course, she missed you. She's fine. But, Bill, I can't go back with you." Arley floundered for words, "I must go on to Fort Smith. I'm expected there by Tuesday." It was a lie. Arley could not bring himself to go with Bill and be there when he greeted Evangeline. It was too distressing even to think about. It would be anguish worse than death. How could he ever face Evangeline again? "Oh, Bill," he said with shamefaced stammering, "I...I'm so sorry to have to let you down this way. But I can't go back now. I...I"

"It's all right," said Bill. His agreeable attitude added to Arley's shame. If only he weren't so damned agreeable! "I'm glad I found you here. A day later and you woulda' been gone, and I might not have seen you for another month or longer. Thank you, my brother, for looking after Evangeline while I was gone."

"When I left, I asked Caleb to see to her till I get back. He promised he would," said Arley.

Claus spoke up, "I'll be goin' on to your home, young man. After tendin' ye for three months, I ain't hankerin' to see nothin' happen to ye now." "I'll be beholden t' you, Claus," said Arley. "Me and Bill is brothers." Arley put his arm across Bill's shoulder. His affection was genuine. Yet, his soul torn. The next day Arley and Bill made their farewells. Arley set out on the road toward Harrison. He had no particular desination. But since he had told Bill he was on his way to Fort Smith, that course was as good as any. Arley, this time, stayed away from home longer than he had ever been before. He wandered aimlessly among the Cherokee people, trading when he could, when he could working for days in various locations. Eventually he made his home in the Cherokee Nation.

The rift between the anti-slavery North and the pro-slavery South helped to heighten the conflict of the Ross-Watie feud. Chief John Ross strongly favored the Union but hoped to steer the Cherokee Nation into a policy of neutrality. . The richer mixed-blood Cherokees supported succession, many of them owning slaves. Alarmed by the election of Lincoln in 1860, many of them were ready to take whatever measures necessary to protect slavery. Ironically Stand Watie, their leader, a full blood Cherokee, led the aggressively active faction against the John Ross loyalists. After the State of Arkansas called a convention for the purpose of seceding from the Union, Arkansas state authorities seized the arsenal at Little Rock. General Ben McCulloch became head of three regiments from Arkansas, Texas and Louisiana, to which were added Indian regiments. Their goal was to secure the frontiers. Rumors spread that abolitionist Senator James H. Lane was raising troops in Kansas to be used against Missouri, Arkansas and Indian territory. Lane's notoriety as a murderer, robber, and plunderer brought fear to the Cherokees. Many of the young, energetic Cherokees crossed the Arkansas border and joined with the forces of General McCulloch.

Chapter XVI
War, Horrible War!

In his chambers in the Greene County courthouse, Judge Benjamin Stanton relaxed in his chair, his feet propped up on an open drawer protruding from his desk. Before him he held a copy of the Springfield Advertiser. The bold headline read "South Carolina Secedes." The judge pondered the new development. The text of South Carolina's resolution did not use the word secession. Instead it stated that the purpose was "to dissolve the Union between the State of South Carolina and the other states united with her under the compact entitled the Constitution of the United Sates of America." The ordinance whereby the state had ratified the Constitution in 1788 was now "repealed".

"Humpf," mumbled the judge to himself, "Legal jargon! It's secession all right. And it means war!" He pitched the newspaper aside and sighed. War was only a matter of time, he thought. The judge loved the Union. He feared war.

While Stanton was meditating, Caleb entered the room. "Master Stanton, the grand jury has just indicted Mr. C.S. Brodhamer for cruelty to his slave," reported Caleb.

The judge sighed, rising to his feet. "Let's go home," he said wearily.

As the two men rode, they discussed the possibility of war. How could Missouri remain unaffected if armed conflict began? "I wish Arley would come back home," remarked Caleb. "It ain't good that he should be gone when things are so unsettled."

The judge nodded in reply. "He's not ready to settle down just yet. I too wish he would return since the future seems so uncertcain."

"He's been gone more'n seven months now. Don't he know how we worry about him? Leastways, he could write."

The unsettled conditions and tensions of the nation bore heavily on the judge's sensitive invalid wife. She became neurotic, requiring constant attention. Essie's suggested that judge Stanton inquire of Mr. McShane about getting Sarah to help. While the slave owner refused to sell the slave child, he was willing to hire her out. The poor girl was relieved to leave the field work and quite willing to enter the luxurious home as a nurse and housekeeper.

As the judge had predicted, within six weeks after the secession of South Carolina, six other states had severed their relations with the Union. On April 14,1861 Confederate ships bombarded Fort Sumter. War had begun!

Early in May, the Confederates began negotations with the Cherokee Nation to induce it into an alliance. Missouri's Confederate Governor Jackson, a pro-secessionist, appointed commissioners to visit and secure Cherokee services.

Secessionists from Missouri went to Arkansas to solicit aid. Arkansas was doing what she could to concentrate troops near the Missouri border. Governor Jackson helped form the secessionist "State Guards." In Springfield Unionist details, known as "Home Guards" were formed to patrol streets. Roads into town were carefully watched.

While these clouds of war and unrest greatly disturbed Essie, she was most distressed because now any possibility of travel to seek her husband was once again out of the question.

Also, all else was overshadowed by more personal circumstances involving individuals she loved. She had watched with tender concern the progress of Evangeline, who was pregnant. Mary and Benjamin Stanton made frequent visits to see nephew Bill and his wife Evangeline, and Essie accompied them. Since the invalid Mary Stanton had never borne a child, it fell upon Essie to give counsel and active help to Evangeline.

On a night in early April the baby had came, a healthy boy, and the Stantons were anxious to go to see the new arrival. The Judge carried Mary and placed her in the carriage. Essie went along to look after Mary, securely wrapped with a heavy carriage robe against the chilly spring air.

Ecstatic with pride, Bill Collier ushered them into the bedroom where Evangeline lay, the tiny infant at her side. Evangeline's Aunt Maude was there to help the new mother. In a hubbub of excitement, they gathered around the bedside. For a few minutes the judge was induced to hold the baby. Then aunt

Maude, with a desire to discuss the birth and to engage in "women's talk," shooed Bill and Benjamin out of the room. Yearning to cuddle the new infant in her arms, Essie took the tiny bundle from Judge Stanton. She smiled. How naturally her own arms snuggled the tiny form to her breast! Her mother feelings welled up. She pressed down the soft blanket around the tiny face, cooing gently to him.

Then, just as a sudden gale, with unexpected fury, thrusts open a cottage door, a chill came over Essie's heart. The little one in her arms was baby Arley! There was no mistaking it! It was not Bill Collier's child! It was Arley's! Dismay and sickening horror came over her. Passing the infant to Aunt Maude and steadying herself on the chair's armrests, Essie sank into a rocker. She clasped her hand over her mouth in alarm. Her wild eyes passed from one person to the other. Did they know what she knew? Apparently not! Their demeanor was bright and happy. They smiled and gushed attention on Evangeline and her tiny son. Essie sat in anguish, terrorized by innocent remarks: "How tan his skin is," "What black hair he has." When would they realize the shocking truth?

Filled with thoughts she could not express, Essie rode home in silence. During the months to follow, her withdrawal was noticed by Judge Stanton and his wife, but it was attributed to the threat of war and her concern for Arley who had been absent from home so long.

On June 24, 1861, Springfield citizens living in the eastern part of town looked out on the St. Louis road and saw a column of soldiers moving leisurely along. They were mainly St. Louis men of German heritage led by Major Sigel. A few days later, Captain T.W. Sweeney came with fifteen hundred of the St. Louis Home Guard. Still later, General Nathaniel Lyon with two thousand troops joined the Union forces in Springfield. From Springfield, a number of Union expeditions were launched to other locations where the secessionist forces were encountered, sometimes victoriously and sometimes in defeat.

To challenge the occupation of Springfield by Federal troops, General Ben McCulloch with men from Texas, Arkansas, and Louisiana, proceeded toward the city. They were soon joined by the larger Confederate force of General Sterling Price, commander of the Missouri State Guard. The rebel army moved, to near the Greene County line. Ten miles southwest of Springfield they set up camp on both sides of the Wilson's creek.

The massing of troups was frightful! People of Greene and nearby counties began to learn the meaning of war, horrible war! Serene fields became military camps. Homes became officer's headquarters and hospitals. Ill-disciplined soldiers of both North and South ravaged the countryside, killing livestock, plundering gardens and smoke-houses, "pressing" countless articles of property to their use. Peaceful plow horses were harnessed to cannon carriages. The rumble of army wagons and caissons disturbed the populace at all hours of the night. Terrified out of their wits, many fled or planned to vacate their homes, moving north or south according to their political sympathies.

In Elk Valley, Judge Stanton's place, set apart from the little town of Ozark, was somewhat removed from the activities which plagued so many other citizens. The judge carefully hid the grave situation from his wife, lest it worsen her neurotic condition. When business matters took him away, he counted on Essie and Sarah to safely attend her.

In early August, barricades were set up at the entrances to Springfield. People were permitted to enter but not allowed to leave the city. The judicial processes of the circuit court came to a standstill. Yet, claims and counter claims multiplied. The county court-houses were packed with prisoners. Troubled by the breakdown of civil government, Judge Stanton went to the headquarters of General Lyon. Outside, Caleb waited in the carriage while the judge was in conference with the chief Union general.

General Lyon said, "I appreciate your concern, Judge Stanton. The civil government is, under these war conditions, suspended in favor of martial law. I would like, however, that you establish yourself, along with my military disciplinary board, to help settle civil disputes. I will commission you with military authority."

The judge hesitated. "My home is in Christian County," he said. "I would be most happy to serve, sir, provided my servant be given authority to enter and exit from the city at will. I must have daily word from home about the health and safety of my invalid wife."

"If you can assure me that the man is loyal, I will grant him a pass as a military courier," said General Lyon.

"I know of no person more loyal and dependable," assured the judge. "Did I tell you, sir, that the youth is a black? He has been under my roof, living with me as a servant since early childhood. I guarantee his patriotism to the Union."

"Very well, then," said the General. He proceeded to draw up the papers.

In his new military assignment Judge Stanton stayed at a boarding house in Springfield. Each day Caleb journeyed on horseback to visit Essie and Mary Stanton. Often when he found the road patrolled by Confederate soldiers, he detoured across the open country.

The tensions of the war grew more ominous daily. Generals of both armies deliberated whether to attack or to withdraw. While McCulloch knew his secessionist forces were superior in number to Lyon's, he knew also that Lyon ought to be, and probably would be, reinforced soon. Therefore, logic dictated that the Confederates should attack the enemy before reinforcements came. General Price, impatient with McCulloch's indecision, threatened to resume independent command and advance his troups against Lyon, alone if necessary. It was agreed that the Confederate troops should attack at 9 o'clock p.m. on August 9. However, when after dark, it began to rain and a heavy storm threatened, McCulloch feared that some of the Missouri troops would find their ammunition wet and unserviceable. It was feared also that in the severe darkness, marching columns might become lost or confused. Just as some of the troops were preparing to move, McCulloch countermanded his marching order. The men lay down to sleep, prepared to move at a later time.

Meanwhile, Lyon reasoned that fighting defensively in the streets of Springfield, where women and children were, was unthinkable. On the open country surrounding the city the enormous Confederate cavalry would gain quick victory. His only chance was to strike first. So at the time when the Confederates had planned to attack, they were to be surprised by an unexpected Union offensive.

On that Friday afternoon, outside the courthouse, Caleb was waiting for Judge Stanton. It was uncertain to Caleb whether the judge would be wanting to travel to his home for the weekend or not. Late in the afternoon Caleb began to detect a flurry of activity among the officers' adjutants. Some communication was being sent to all the subordinate commanders.

Looking very grave and concerned, Judge Stanton came out of the court building. "It will be necessary for me to stay the night in Springfield," he said. "I would like for you to be on hand, if I should need you. We'll find you sleeping quarters at my boarding house." The two men rode to the livery stable, left their horses, and walked the short distance to the large two-story house where the judge had living quarters. The air was tense and evening was still. Yet there was a foreboding undercurrent. The Home Guards had been on active duty for days. Now a company of the guard congregated outside the bank where wagons were stationed. Inside, workers, busy behind closed blinds, were preparing a vast amount of money ready for shipment, should adverse circumstances require it. At about 6 P.M. the movement of troops began.

The matron at the boarding house listened grimly as the judge remarked that his black servant would be sleeping on the couch in his room that night. For his supper, she would prepare Caleb a plate of food and serve it on the back porch.

Later, in his room, the judge took a walnut case from a dresser drawer and placed it on a table. Inside were two dueling pistols. "I want you to carry one of these," he said. "If anything should happen to me, you are to defend Mrs. Stanton and Essie with your life."

"Oh, Master Stanton, what is it? What's goin' to happen?" asked Caleb.

"The Union Army will attack the enemy in the morning. Our forces are greatly outnumbered. The guard is staying behind to protect the city. Let's pray that we may have a victory tomorrow."

Shortly after daybreak the first firing began. The Federals had made their surprise attack. Thirty minutes later, the continuous booming sounded plainly in Springfield some ten miles away. Anxiously the people listened, the tension almost unbearable. Ambulance wagons were readied, and proceeded toward the action. By 10 o'clock in the forenoon the wounded Federals began to straggle into the city. Lyon's men were pressing the enemy at all points. The courthouse and the sheriff's residence were set up as hospitals. Soon, the Methodist church and the Bailey House were likewise filled with the wounded. Shattered men were brought in ambulances, carriages, butchers' wagons, express wagons, and every other sort of vehicle.

Caleb helped transport and care for the injured. He carried water, tore sheets to be used as bandages, and washed the wounds. He listened to the wailing and shrieks of the suffering.

"We gave them a good go of it," boasted a young soldier. "We struck 'em at a black-jack hill west of Ray's farm. Time and again we drove 'em back. For hours we fought like the devil. Oh, God, it was awful!" The youth winced with the pain of his shattered arm.

A lanky farmer lying in the next bed said, "I was there with you on that bloody hill, buddy." Caleb moved to him with a pan of cold water to wash his blood splattered face. "That's my best friend's blood there in my beard. Some o' his brains is spattered there too!" He gasped and shuddered in horror. Caleb sponged his bloody leathery face and coarse matted black beard.

The gaunt farmer groaned. He was thinking of the horror of the battle and of his comrade whose head had been exploded by a shell. "Poor Eddie," he cried, "poor Eddie!" And he covered his face with his hands, while the tears ran down his forearms.

Caleb moved on among the writhing men on the cots. A huge rowdy fellow called out profane denouncements of the rebel army and cursed his shattered ankle. "We had 'em bottled up!" he shouted. "We cut off their retreat on the Fayetteville road. Then, 'Here comes the Iowans!' we yelled, 'Lyon has whupped 'em!' Our color-bearers signaled 'em to come on. We wus ready to hug our arms 'round 'em. Then they opened fire on us with shells, shrapnel, canister, ever' damned thing! They wasn't Iowans, they was goddamned Louisiana rebels, in grey outfits just like the Iowans." He wiped the sweat from his ruddy face. "Them jabbering St. Louis Germans was skert out o' their wits. 'They're firing on us! They make mistake!' they cried. Oh, God, what a mess! We scurried about. It was too late to level our guns. All we could do was stampede like hell. General Sigel threatened and bullied, but it weren't no use. He couldn't coax us to stay and fight. The general run just the same as the rest of us."

Most of the Germans fled south into Christian County. They threw away guns, cartridge boxes, everything which would impede their flight. The Confederate cavalry pounced upon them whenever they could. Had the war been carried to the Stanton place? Caleb wondered. Were Mamma and Missis Mary frightened or in danger?

A youth, not more than seventeen, cried out in delirious, incoherent utterances, "Made m' blood curdle! Screamed a war whoop... Savage redskins... I got two o' 'em! Look out!!" He cowered in terror. "Look out...for the bloody tomahawk!" He sank back in exhaustion.

Indians! Were they Cherokee? Caleb was alarmed and tormented. Could it be that Arley was in the battle? Had he joined his friends in the Southern cause? Leaving the wounded behind, Caleb went outside to meet the wagons coming from the battlefield.

Suddenly as a tornado passes over the land and disappears, the battle ended. The exhausted Federals retreated to Springfield. Nathaniel Lyon, their General-in-Chief, was dead, as were several other officers. Left behind were the wounded and dead, strewn all about the countryside, their faces waxy white, eyes frozen in glassy stares, faces shattered, heads torn apart. In pleasant shady nooks, under the blazing sun's glare, in the riddled corn field, dead bodies were everywhere. The water of Wilson's Creek frothed with the blood. Among the dead, wounded men crawled, delirious with agony and pain. Some lay

228

prone, too weak to move, their bowels shot through. Others were destined to perish with a tiny bullet hole small as a blueberry. Groaning, shrieking, muttering prayers and violent cursing, imploring help, begging for water, wounded were everywhere, struggling, exerting to cling to life, or quietly languishing, surrendering, ready to be relieved in death. Amid the pathos, rose the frantic cry. "Arley! Arley!" Caleb stumbled among the corpses. Now and then he stopped to place his canteen to the lips of a crying soldier. Now he stopped to turn over the dead body of some black haired, perhaps Cherokee, victim. Still, vainly searching, he called, "Arley! Oh, Arley!"

The Federals and the Confederates lay together, side by side, midst the blood-stained sod and wild flowers. And somewhere perhaps--the vision haunted Caleb--perhaps, somewhere, his bloody rifle still gripped in his clenched fist, lay Arley. Poor, impetuous, tormented, malcontent Cherokee brother, to whom the world had shown too little kindness and compassion.

Dusk came before Caleb gave up his desperate search. Staggering with exhaustion, weary and despondent in spirit, he wandered back into the city.

Part Two of Chapter XVI

Even after the Federals had retreated from the scene, it was not clear to the Confederates how the battle had gone. Whether the retreating army would turn back to attack again was not certain. McCulloch's men made ready for just such a redoubt. The confederate cavalry with 6,000 fresh, well-rested horses might have cut off and captured the Unionists on the high prairies west of Springfield, but the Confederates were too confused and disorganized to pursue. General Sturgis, commanding the remains of Lyon's corps, entered the city, and took time to rest briefly. The town square became packed with cannon carriages, army wagons, farm wagons, buggies, horses, mules, and cattle. Hundreds of frightened men, women, and children added to the confusion and hysteria. At midnight, the train of wagons three miles long set out on the road to Rolla, Missouri, followed by refugees in carriages, wagons, and buggies, on horseback and on foot. With the fleeing townspeople went wagons carrying $2,000,000 in money and stores. The Union had given up the city.

About eleven o'clock that Sunday morning, the first Confederate corps came to the outskirts of the city. They made no attempt to pursue the defeated army. Sadly, defeated, the judge and Caleb fled from the city. Troubled by the news that Cherokees had taken part in the battle and worried about the welfare of Mary Stanton and Essie, they raced their horses toward Ozark. They watched, cautiously, for enemy stragglers who might challenge them. Sigel's defeated German troops had fled south into Christian County.

At the Stanton residence Essie heard the sounds of cannon. Her curiosity and concern for Caleb and Judge Stanton mounted. Leaving Mary Stanton in the care of Sarah, Essie saddled a horse. So eager was she to investigate that she gave no thought that she would, in all probability, not be able to locate either of the two men. She raced across the verdant countryside, hoping simply to know something of the terrible conflict. Her heart pounded as she thought of the danger, the bloody struggle which must surely be transpiring. She would not go far, just close enough to learn from someone what was happening.

Suddenly the cannon were silent, the rifles hushed. What was happening? Now she could see men ahead of her plodding across the fields. She halted her horse and called to the war-weary soldiers fleeing from the battlefield, "How did the battle go? Who won?"

Stunned soldiers made no effort to respond. Then her eyes fastened on a lone man dressed in a bright tunic. She called him in Cherokee. He raised his eyes and acknowledged her words with a little nod of his head. "Give water," he mumbled in Cherokee.

Essie had no water to give, but she had just crossed a little stream. "Water is over there," she said. Had Arley been in the battle? She raced forward. Soldiers retreating from the scene ignored the mulatto horsewoman. Somewhere, perhaps, she would find her Cherokee son. Suddenly, she saw Arley limping across a field! She dashed toward him. She sprang from her horse and to his side. They embraced. A bullet had pierced Arley's thigh. He had bandaged it to prevent blood loss. With Essie's help he struggled onto the horse, and together they rode double to the Stanton place.

While Essie examined and washed her son's wound, she listened to his troubled spirit. "Oh, Mamma, I'm so glad to be home. I've just been through hell. It was horrible! I was so scared. A miserable coward that's what I am." He covered his face with his hands. "Men were falling all around me. Cherokee war-whoops rang in my ears. What screams! I fired my rifle aimless like. I couldn't make myself kill anyone. I was such a miserable, useless soldier. Wounded men ever'where! What butchery! One of my friends took his knife and tore the scalp from a fallen Northerner. Ugh! I was so sick. I wanted to die. When I felt the pain in my leg, I was glad. I remember thinking now maybe I'll die."

"Try not to think of it," soothed Essie.

"Mamma, I'm a coward, a spineless, yellow coward."

"No, you're not. You just ain't been raised up to take part in such cruelty. Besides, I bet most of the others were just as

232

scared as you." Suddenly there was a clatter of horses coming on the carriageway in front of the house. "What's that?" asked Essie.

Arley rose to his feet and hobbled to the window, peering through the curtains. "It's Confederates, about eight of 'em."

"Lord, help us. They've come to raid us! They'll probably take everything. I just brought in a ham from the smokehouse. Take it to them. Maybe that will satisfy them, and they'll go away." She hurried to the kitchen and returned carrying a large ham which she gave to Arley. "Now go out and plead with them to leave us," she said. "Poor Sarah has done fled out the back door and probably home by now."

"Bring Misses Mary and come out on the porch," Arley said as he limped to the door. He faced the soldiers boldly. "Don't get off your horses. You're not coming inside here. I just came from the battle where I fought with General McCulloch and Stand Watie. I got a bullet through my leg. This here black woman is my slave and this poor woman in the wheelchair is my Aunt Mary. Ain't nobody else here. If you plan to do them harm, you'll have to kill me first, and me a Confederate same as you yerselves. Now take this here ham and get. I'll kill the first man who sets foot on this porch!" Arley had set the ham onto the newel post of the porch railing. He removed his pistol from his holster and held it firmly pointed at the soldiers. One of the men dismounted long enough to seize the ham and lift it up to a comrade. Then he sprang back onto his horse. The men, with scarcely a word, turned their horses and rode away.

Essie smiled. "That wasn't the action of a yellow coward," she said proudly.

When Judge Stanton and Caleb returned home safely, so glorious was the reunion that the tragic dissolution of the nation and the terrible hostilities were nearly forgotten.

General McCulloch occupied the city of Springfield. Scouting parties went out to forage, and "press" horses and mules into the army's service. Fortunately, the harvest that year was more abundant than ever before known. There was plenty for both the Confederate army and the citizens, too.

The Stanton place was not in the vicinity where the raids were made. Judge Stanton remained secluded in his home, knowing that if he were to be seen, some southern sympathizer would denounce him.

After about three weeks of rest and recovery, and recruitment of fresh men, General Price's army was ready to leave. Price resolved to move north where secessionist farmers were terrorized by Kansas jayhawkers along the Missouri-Kansas border.

A large number of General McCulloch's "wild and woolly" Arkansas troops, whose term of service had expired, demanded to be sent home. A day or two after Price withdrew from Greene County, the forces of McCulloch withdrew also, going to Cassville, and thence to Fayetteville, Arkansas.

Later Fremont's Union army came into the county. As might be expected in a large army, there some lawless characters, among whom were Jim Lane's men. Larceny was common; Negroes were carried off; a few houses were burned.

The dwellers of the Stanton household remained secluded. The judge left the house only occasionally.

Arley explained to his family the aspirations and fears of the Cherokee people. His participation in the battle had been a result of a feeling that he was subject to white man's prejudice. It was a declaration of his Cherokee identity. Sometimes Caleb became vexed over Arley's references to the Cherokee Nation's dedication to slavery. At home, Arley found love and compassion. There he had no need for defensive pretense.

Arley did not go to visit Evangeline and Bill. He avoided all conversation about them. Essie knew that she would, sooner or later, need to discuss Evangeline's baby with him.

Mary Stanton was first to reveal to Arley that a child had been born. "I want to go tomorrow to see our new grand nephew. Arley, have you seen him?" she asked.

Arley stuttered, "You mean, a baby...born...to Evangeline?" He blushed, coughed and grinned selfconsciously. "Evangeline has a baby?" Had he been gone that long?

Later Essie followed Arley to the horse stalls. There, while Arley curried his horse, Essie asked questions. "Arley," she said, "will you go to see Evangeline's baby?"

"Mamma, you know how I have always felt about Evangeline. I'm glad she has a baby, I reckon, but I don't want to talk about it." He began vigorously brushing the horse's flank.

"I've got to talk about it, son." She paused. "Arley, the baby that Evangeline had...he isn't...well, Bill isn't the father..."

The brush in Arley's right hand rested motionless against the animal's loin. Her words had shaken him severely. What did she mean? His left hand clutched the horse's withers. He steadied himself with his forehead against the beast's rib cage.

Essie continued, "I've seen the child, Arley. That child is yours, isn't it?"

Arley did not move. His body tensed.

"Evangeline's baby is yours, isn't it?"

Arley swung around and threw his arms around his mother. "I don't know that! You saw him. I didn't," he sobbed. "Why do you say that?"

"The baby looks like you. He's Cherokee, Arley. I know it."

"Oh, Mamma, I---loved---her. You don't---don't understand what---what it's like--loving someone you can't have."

Essie's voice was sympathetic. "Yes, Arley, I know," she said slowly. "For twenty-three years I have known."

"I thought Bill had died! I wouldn't betray Bill! You know that."

Holding her son in her arms, she bowed her head against his shoulder. She had no more words, only sorrow, agony, and compassion.

Arley never went to see the baby. He tortured himself by staying away. It was torture he felt he justly deserved. A more confident man might have done otherwise. He could never bring himself to contend against Bill for Evangeline's affection. Pray God Bill would never know! Sometimes his anguish was on Evangeline's behalf. Was she suffering as he was? Had he forced her to live with deceit and heartache? Was he a wedge of contention between Evangeline and her husband?

Essie did not scold nor lecture her son. She had given him an example of extraordinary faithfulness to her own husband. She understood the tensions and loneliness that can build up in a young life. Sometimes her wandering thoughts went back to the time when she was a young slave at Fern Haven Plantation. She was naively childlike then. She thought of the dashing, charming Tom Lovell, master of Fern Haven. What a scoundrel he was! How he had schemed to entrap her! She smiled--she could not hate her old master. Likewise, she could not love Arley less than she had always loved. Essie fondly remembered also the Cherokee farmer Kevit who was the Arley's father. She thought of how devoted he had been to Fawn. When Fawn had been doomed to die, she hoped to become Kevit's wife and to raise the infant Arley. It was a cherished dream for her life which vanished with Kevit's death! How devastated she had been. Her secret dream was never to be told to Arley or anyone else. More clearly than ever Essie had resolved that her destiny was with Gabe, nothing short of that would do.

Chapter XVII
The Jayhawkers

Bill Collier slid his horse to a furious halt at the Stanton place, leaped from the saddle and dashed up the steps. He pounded sharply on the front door. Essie answered with the salutation, "Why, Bill Collier, you look all flustered. Is something wrong?"

"Is Uncle Ben here? Is he hurt?"

"Master Ben ain't here. He ain't hurt that I know about."

"I jest passed his wrecked buggy on the side of the roadway. The front axle and a wheel was broke. There was a big boulder on the road. I guess it rolled down the bluff and hit the buggy just as Uncle Benjamin was riding by," said Bill.

Mary Stanton wheeled into the entrance hall. "What's that about Benjamin?"

"Seems like he's had a accident, Aunt Mary. His buggy is all cracked up about a mile down the road. If he was in it when it happened I don't see how he kept from gettin' hurt. If he ain't here I wonder where he is."

"Caleb was with him," interjected Essie.

"I'm goin' to look for him," said Bill.

"I'll go with you," said Essie. She scurried off to saddle a horse.

At the scene of the accident Bill and Essie inspected the wreckage. They handled the broken wheel with its shattered spokes. They examined the buggy shafts. The harness had been unsnapped. The horse had been unhitched, but where was it? And where were Benjamin and Caleb? Essie and Bill searched inside the buggy and the ground around it, looking for signs that would solve the mystery. They gazed about for neighbors who may have seen the accident or for a house where the two passengers may have gone for help.

"Could it be that they were unhurt and have gone on to some business appointment with the help of some passerby?" speculated Bill.

"Course that could have happened," said Essie, "still I doubt it. If Master Ben went on to take care of business, he would have sent Caleb to let us know so we wouldn't be worried."

Just as they were about to leave the scene, Arley rode up on his bay horse. "I went home jest now and Misses Mary told me about Master Benjamin. Did you find out what happened?"

"No, we haven't. It's still a mystery," answered Bill. "I'm just about to go search all around for signs."

"I'm goin' with you," said Arley.

"Reckon I better go back home just in case they go there and need help," remarked Essie. "Anyways Misses Mary needs someone to stay with her."

The two young men searched diligently all around the neighborhood. They found nothing to give them any clues about the missing people. They had searched a circle of nearly five miles in radius when suddenly Arley raised his hand and they both came to a halt. "Look there," called Arley, " see that broken branch." He pointed to a little snapped twig dangling from a sapling. "It could be Caleb is leaving us a signal that he went along this way." Arley dismounted and studied the earth. It was a scarcely used path. "Some horses just went over this trail. Look, over there is another broken branch."

They followed the series of hanging broken twigs until they came to a clearing. In the center of a field stood an old ramshackle shed. Three horses were tethered nearby. One of them was Judge Stanton's carriage mare. "I betcha that there's some men holdin' the judge and Caleb in that there shack," said Arley.

"If they are, we'd better be careful. They're armed, that's for sure," warned Bill.

"Hide our horses over in that little gulch, back of that clump of trees," said Arley. "I'm goin' to sneak 'round in back to see if they's a window there. You keep watch. If they come out you give a bird call so I can hide."

Arley crept toward the cabin. Every snapping twig under his feet seemed loud. He crouched close to the building under the window. He raised up to look into the room. Inside he glimpsed

238

the back of Caleb's head. He dropped back down quickly lest he be seen. From the shed he crept back into the brush and timber. Then he moved to Bill who stood near the outlaws' horses. "They're in there," whispered Arley. "I could'nt to see how many men there was."

"How can we lure 'em away so we can untie the judge and Caleb?" asked Bill.

"Get over there and be ready to dash into the shanty," said Arley. He cut loose the reins from the trees where the horses were tied. Then he moved to the rear of the animals and took off his shirt. Suddenly he burst forth in front of the horses frantically waving the shirt. The spooked horses neighed and reared into the air. They took off in a gallop. The door of the shack swung open with a bang, and two men sprang out. They raced after their horses. Arley and Bill dashed into the shed. Arley cut the ropes binding the judge and Caleb and said, "Go quick! Our two horses are waiting for you in that gulch over yonder back of them trees. Take them and ride like hell." The released victims fled, not taking time to explain the reason for their captivity.

"Come on, let's get away from here!" said Bill. The two raced into the woods as hard as they could go. Arley was slowed in his flight by the gunshot wound he had received in the thigh. When exhaustion forced them to pause and catch their breath, they listened fearfully for the two outlaws who might be pursuing them. "If we only had firearms we'd stand a better chance," panted Bill. Before long, they were sure the outlaws were trailing after them on their recovered mounts. They scanned the scene looking for some steep mountain passageway where a horse could not go or a place to hide. As they scurried up a little hill the sound of hoofbeats seemed louder and closer. A weatherbeaten two story house stood at the summit. "It's the old Toberman place," said Bill. "Let's go inside." The house looked empty. Rumor had it that the Toberman family, being southern sympathizers, had fled to Arkansas. Perhaps someone had been left behind, someone who would help them. Arley and Bill entered the house. It was completely empty except for a few pieces of rickety furniture. Their footsteps, their voices, even

239

their gasps for breath had a strange hollow sound in the vacant halls. They heard the outlaws arriving outside! They were filled with terror.

One of the men called, "Go around to the back and don't let 'em get away." Arley and Bill looked about the rooms for a hiding place. Not finding any, they slipped quietly up the stairs to the second floor. They could see from the central hall that the two small rooms offered them no place to hide. They heard the scoundrels walking through the rooms downstairs. "Better search upstairs," they heard one of them say. Their hearts pounded hard. They were trapped!

Bill tiptoed to a dormer window. He raised the loose-fitting window and looked out. "Come on," he said, and he crawled through onto the roof. Arley followed him and closed the window after himself. They drew back under the eaves of the dormer.

The sound of a man's footsteps as he came up the stairs and into the room beneath them brought panic to their hearts. He went to the window! Arley and Bill scarcely breathed. They heard the man turn and leave the window. "They ain't up here," he called and noisily descended the stairs. From the rooftop Arley and Bill could see the outlaws' horses. Hopefully, they waited for the men to mount and ride away. But they did not leave. Apparently they had given up the chase and were resting.

"We'll just have to wait it out," said Bill. Late afternoon came, still the men did not leave. When it was almost dark, the clatter of horses hooves resounded from the north. The branches of a giant post oak offered a screen through which the young men could peek down on the men below. Eight horsemen rode up to the house. Some of them wore Union uniforms. As they dismounted, their jocular prattle and laughter reverberated against the walls of the empty building. "They're comin' inside. Who are they? Where'd they come from?" whispered Bill. "They don't act like Union soldiers."

"I s'pect we'll have to stay here all night. This must be their headquarters. What if they don't leave tomorrow? We could die of thirst up here," remarked Arley.

"They'll probably discover us before then," said Bill. It was dark. He stood up on the sloping roof stretching his unsteady legs. He almost lost his balance and caught himself with a heavy foot stomping on the shingles.

"Ssh... They'll hear you. Someone has come up to the room," whispered Arley. The night chill was beginning to penetrate their weary flesh. "What they doin'?" asked Arley leaning his ear against the wall of the dormer.

"Sounds like they're playin' cards," said Bill. "That's card talk, and I hear coins clinkin'."

"We're sunk," sighed Arley, "this could go on for days." They lay back onto the roof looking up at the starry sky. The shingles still held the sun's warmth and felt good to their backs. Sleep overtook them.

How long they were asleep they didn't know, but they were awakened by loud voices from the room below. An angry quarrel was taking place. A weatherboard of the dormer was broken loose and sagged down from the outside wall. At the same spot a chink in the plaster inside the old house let a tiny ray of light come out. Arley raised himself to his knees and peeped into the crevice. Flickering candles lit the room. Men were gathered around a box serving as a table. It was scattered over with cards and coins. Two of the group sprang to their feet and were snarling at each other.

"Damn it, Joe, you couldn't a' had another ace," the short stocky man shouted.

"Ye goddamn runt, you say I'm cheatin'? Why, I oughta break your damned neck," growled Joe.

Arley turned back to Bill and whispered, "They're havin' a squabble. About to come to blows."

When he looked again through the crevice, a tall slim man was standing between them, holding them apart. "Cut it out, you two," he said sternly. "I ain't aimin' to allow wranglin' amongst ourselves. Long as you'uns are my men you'll do as I say. This here game's over. Me an' Carl is goin' down stairs to get in that game down there. Ye two hotheads kin stay up here. Maybe if ye get some sleep ye won't be so cantankerous."

"You aimin' that I should sleep in th' same room with that skunk?" blustered the big red-headed fellow.

The tall boss of the outfit replied firmly, "This here is the room I assigned to ye, so shut up. Now I don't wanta' hear of no trouble, so I'm askin' ye both to give me yer guns. That way ye won't kill each other." He and his companion left the room leaving the big red-head and the short stocky one to sulk and snarl at each other. They seemed to have great respect for the leader who intimidated them with a sort of military discipline.

Arley whispered, "They're a part of the militia, I reckon."

Each of the two antagonists took an area of the room on either side of the window. They spread out their bedrolls. The big redhead took off his pants, which were heavy with the booty he had won in the card game. He rolled up his trousers and placed them beside his pallet. Then he decided to go outside to urinate. With the same intention, the stocky ruffian followed along. Arley had watched them through the crack in the wall. The house's second floor was now vacated. Carefully Arley moved to the window, slid the pane up and crawled into the room. Alert all the while, he unrolled the big man's jeans and took out the leather pouch full of gold and silver coins. He rolled the garment back up and placed it where it had been before. Clutching the money bag, Arley crept back through the window and onto the roof again, carefully closing the window after himself.

Bill watched in amazement. "What th' heck you doin'?"

"I got that big fellow's money pouch."

"What you plan to do with it?" asked Bill.

"I thought we might bribe one of them to help us get away."

"You can't do that. Soon's they wake up in the mornin' ever'one in the house is goin' to know that guy lost his money. If they find us with it, they'll hang us for sure."

"Yeah, I guess you're right," admitted Arley. "I'll put it back."

Just then they heard the two outlaws returning up the stairs. Arley chuckled as he peeped at the big fellow in his misshapen underdrawers. "You know," Arley whispered, "I got it figured out these men is Kansas jayhawkers that goes about robbin' an'

242

terrorizin' people. When they first pulled up to this place I heerd one o' 'em mention Jim Lane. The judge called him a outlaw captain--s'posed to be a Union soldier. He ain't much for keepin' discipline amongst his border ruffians an' outlaws. They drive a herd of livestock they've stole. Even carry furniture, farm tools an' stuff. They say there's a train of niggers that follows him. That Jim Lane is a Senator from Kansas. The judge sez he's a powerful source of embarrassment to the Federal gover'ment."

"I wish you could put the money back. We're sure to be in bad trouble," said Bill. "I wish you coulda swiped us some drinkin' water instead. I think I'm goina' die of thirst. Hungry too."

The two fugitives lay side by side glumly contemplating their fate. The shake shingles were rough and irregular. Their muscles began to ache. Sleep came in short intervals. When the first faint light of morning came, Arley awoke. His shoulder rested uncomfortably on the pouch of coins. "The men in the room would be sound asleep," he thought. "I gotta put the money bag back." He moved quietly to the window and carefully raised it. He could hear the deep breathing of the two men. He put his foot through the window. A board squeaked as he put his weight on it. The huge redheaded man gave a loud sonorous snort. Arley's heart stopped for an instant then raced frantically. He stood paralyzed, one foot still behind him on the roof. The big fellow rolled over turning his face toward the wall. Arley waited in his cramped, awkward position. Again the huge man moved! He threw his arm from his side up to above his head. Arley gripped the money bag tightly. Being too fearful to move toward the uneasy sleeper, he considered laying the purse down. He turned to look at the stocky fellow who was slumbering placidly on the opposite side of the room. His trousers lay in a heap beside his pallet. Arley pulled his foot through the window and stood on both unsteady legs. He could reach the short chubby man's pants with just one step. Slowly he moved, bent down, took hold of the belt of the pants and raised them gently a few inches from the floor! He slipped the pouch into a pocket. There was a slight clinking of the coins.

He looked back toward the bigger man, who gave a snort and turned his face toward Arley! With agonizing stealth he withdrew to the window and climbed back onto the roof. He inched the window down and moved back to where his companion was sleeping. Bill opened his eyes. "What you doin' now?" he asked in a coarse whisper.

"I just put the money bag back."

"Good," said Bill. They both rested back against the roof and dozed off to sleep again. When the dawn had fully come they were awakened again by loud voices in the room. The two men were quarreling vehemently.

The voice of the huge man shouted, "I found my money in yer pocket. I missed it when I went to put my pants on, and it was in yer pocket!"

The short pudgy man stammered, "Joe, I never took your money. How can you say I did? Lessen...lessen you're just lookin' for a excuse to pick a fight with me. I was asleep. I never seen you take that money outta my pants pocket. You're a liar to say you did."

The big man growled, "Listen, ye little bastard, I woke up first an' couldn't find my money 'cause ye took it."

"I ain't no thief, I ain't." He backed toward the door leading into the hall.

The giant fellow pressed threateningly toward him. "Ha!" he sneered, "Them's yer pants ain't they? That's where I found m' money, right there in yer pants."

"That's a lie! A damned lie!"

"Bah! Ye blasted thief..." he roared. He drew back his right fist. The chubby man dodged a powerful blow. At the same time he seized the giant's left arm and gave it a backward shove. The forward thrust of the assailant's right hand and the backward push of his left arm spun him around. The shorter man threw his thick shoulder against the chest of the larger attacker who fell backward tumbling down the stairs. The huge man howled. The ruckus drew the attention of the other men who came and stood over him in shock.

After the injured man was rolled onto a pallet on the floor, the boss of the gang gave his instructions. "This ain't no cause for us not to go ahead with our plans. Lem, I don't know what went on betwixt you an' Joe, but now bein's Joe's hurt, ye can stay an' take care of him."

"That ain't right, Harry. Why should I be the one? I was attack't for no reason."

The gang leader scowled and reaffirmed his decision, "Ye stay here! And, Al, ye can stay too, just to make sure Lem don't do Joe no more harm. That means there are seven of us to go after Judge Stanton. When we're done with that job we'll send back for you guys here. Al, if Joe gets to feelin' better ye come join us."

"How can we do that?" asked Al. "Joe can't ride, not lessen it's in a wagon, an' we ain't got no wagon. I think he's hurt bad, Harry."

"All right," said the boss. "We'll send a wagon to get ye. But watch yerselves. Them two rubes that got away yesterday might come back armed. They might bring a posse."

"We'll be real careful," said Al.

Watching as best they could without being seen, the two men on the roof listened to the seven men chat together as they prepared to leave. When Judge Stanton's name was mentioned, Bill and Arley were greatly upset. How could they stop the raid or give warning to the intended victim?

When the judge and Caleb were released from captivity they had raced back to their home. Their thoughts during their flight were filled with anxiety for Mary Stanton and Essie. They were relieved to see the house still standing and to find the two women safe inside. Immediately, Benjamin Stanton prepared to ward off an attack, if there should be one. He cleaned and loaded his firearms. Caleb and Essie and even Mary Stanton were provided with guns and assigned positions at the windows in case of a siege.

"They may not come," said the judge, "but we've got to be ready if they do." He had told the women how they had waylaid him and Caleb in the buggy on the highway. Eight or ten men had rolled the boulder in front of the buggy. They had made dire threats which they would carry out if the judge did not meet their demands. Two of their gang had been arrested and were being held on robbery and assault charges. The case was to come under Judge Stanton's jurisdiction. The outlaws were trying to force the judge to arrange the release of the accused criminals held in the Greene County jail. He explained that the raiders were jayhawkers. They were terrorizing western Missouri by attacking home owners and robbing them. Most of the men were abolitionists from Kansas. They were a part of the army of Captain Jim Lane.

When the outlaws neared the Stanton residence the sound of many horses alarmed the judge. Mary Stanton became paralyzed with fear. "It sounds like there are more of them than we can handle," said Benjamin. "Caleb, you had better go for help. Go outside, but wait to make sure that it's really a gang come to pillage. Then run to get help."

Caleb realized he would not have time to harness a horse. The outlaws rode to the front of the house. It was clear to Caleb that they meant no good. He hurried on foot to the nearest place where he could obtain help, the McShane farm. Caleb knew that the slaves there would give their help if they could. But what chance would they have if they were armed only with shovels and hoes? They would need real weapons. He would have to go to the big house and appeal to Kerry McShane.

"Master Stanton is in trouble," said Caleb breathlessly. "His house is surrounded by jayhawkers. I'm afraid they'll burn the house down and take Master Stanton or kill him!"

McShane viewed Caleb skeptically. "What you expect me to do?"

"Go help him! For the Lord's sake, go help him," pled Caleb.

"What can I do? There's only me and Otto Fluger. That's all that's here, excepting the nigger crew." He thought seriously. "No, we'd better stay here to protect our own property."

"Mister McShane, if they burn the judge out, they'll be after you next. That's for sure. Give your best slaves guns and let's go. We've got to hurry!" McShane hesitated. "Get the guns I'll call Otto. There's no time to waste!" Caleb rushed out the door and into the field where he saw Otto. The slave

246

superintendent was dubious. When he deliberated, Caleb made his appeal to the slaves. "Come on," he implored, "Come up to the big house. Master McShane is expecting you." Otto was resentful of the Caleb's assumption of authority, but he felt that McShane must surely have given his approval. They trooped to the big house.

McShane stood on the veranda. He was overwhelmed with the way the situation had gotten out of hand. He held a pistol in his hand and two rifles were on the bench beside him. He gave Otto a rifle.

"That all the guns you got?" asked Caleb. Then he called out the names of the most dependable slaves. "All of them need weapons too," he said. Otto took the cue. He stepped to the door and held it open for McShane to reenter the house. The reluctant slaveholder went in and returned with two more pistols and another rifle.

"Let's go," cried Caleb, and he led the way with rousing words of encouragement. As they went, Otto Fluger began to catch the spirit of the expedition, and Caleb judiciously gave way to let him take over as the leader. As they neared the Stanton place they could hear sporadic gunfire. One by one they passed amunitions around until all the guns were loaded. While Caleb and Otto had culled the Negro workers to the most dependable and courageous individuals, still many men had no weapons except what tools they had hastily grabbed.

Otto whispered final instructions and gave orders as to where the crew should be stationed. They heard shots from the house. The judge was still in control of his home. When all his men were ready, Otto called out, "Listen, you thugs, give it up. You can't take this house nor the judge neither. We've got you outnumbered. It's suicide for you if you continue. Get your horses and clear out o' the county or we'll wipe you out." The raiders had taken positions to protect themselves from gunfire from the house, now they were vulnerable from behind. One of the gang fired a shot toward Otto's voice. A pistol crack and the raider fell dead.

The leader of the desperados caught glimpses of his opponents. "Why, they's all black men," he shouted in amazement. He raised his voice and shouted, "Ye black wretches, we're abolitionists! Join with us! Turn yer guns on them white bastards what's kept ye down. Join up with us, and we'll take ye to Kansas and freedom!"

There was a tense pause. Slaveholder McShane was in muddled confusion and anxiety. "No!" he shouted to his Negroes, "Ye can't do thet. Listen t' me, ye niggers. You're mine. Ye was born on my place or else I bought ye. Ye can't leave me!" His voice had a pathetic whine.

"I ain't goin' to join with those thievin' outlaws," affirmed Caleb loudly. "They're the thugs that kidnapped me and Judge Stanton."

The boss of the raiders considered his position. There were many men, mostly slaves. "Are all your men armed?" he asked.

"All our men have weapons," shouted Otto. He had warned the slaves to keep their farm tools out of sight.

"Are ye guaranteein' us a safe get-a-way?" he called.

"Yes," replied Otto, "if you go an' keep on goin'."

"Come on, men, let's go," called Harry. The jayhawkers fled to their horses and rode away.

Judge Stanton came out on the porch to thank his neighbors. Caleb went inside to see Essie. In a few minutes he returned. "Where's Mamma?" he asked. "I couldn't find her in the house."

"Oh, dear God!" exclaimed Benjamin, "I let them get away and they had Essie. When they had us surrounded and there seemed to be no hope, before I could stop her, Essie went out into the yard waving a white flag. She was pleading to them for mercy. She did it for Mary's sake. Essie was afraid the excitement would kill her. They grabbed Essie, tied her up, and hauled her off in a wagon--my wagon they stole from the barn. If Essie hadn't done what she did the raid would have been over before your help came. She gave us extra time."

On the rooftop Arley detached a shaft of steel from the lightning rod at the gable end of the house. He planned to use it as a spear against a squirrel that sometimes scampered across the roof. The scent of bacon that rose from the chimney with the smoke and heat from the breakfast cooking below had given them enormous appetites. Arley and Bill had visions of roasted squirrel on a spit placed across the waves of heat rising from the chimney. But the men in the house allowed the fire to die out after they had their breakfast, and the squirrel followed some innate instinct of his own and never returned.

Bill and Arley lay together on the roof looking at the cloudless sky. "I haven't seen you to talk with since I came back from the wreck of the steamboat," said Bill. "That's been over ten months. Funny, it took something like this to bring us together."

"I didn't mean for it to be that way, Bill. I caught a bullet in my leg. I couldn't get over to your place."

"I know," said Bill. He reached over and clasped Arley's hand. "Ain't nothin' ever goin' to come between us."

Arley could not reply. Already, there was a barrier between them. Apparently Bill did not know. The barrier was Arley's guilt. He had betrayed his best friend! With every thought of Bill there were thoughts of Evangeline--and her baby. At times he longed to see his son. He felt he must talk about it to Bill. Dear God, how he wanted to! But how could he hurt his dear friend that much? Was it possible Bill did not know? Essie had seen through it at once. She had recognized the truth. Sometimes Arley hated himself.

Sometimes his envy seemed to be destroying him. Once when Bill stood at the edge of the roof, Arley had an overpowering urge to push him off. Evangeline and the infant would be his! No one would know. But no! Essie would know! Arley turned back away from where Bill stood and threw himself down onto the roof. He wept. How he hated himself. What kind of beast could have such thoughts?

Bill came to him with sincere compassion. He raised Arley up and put his arms around him. "What is it?" he asked. Arley was unable to reply. Bill held him tenderly.

Finally, when Arley's troubled spirit came under control, he said, "I guess the tension is getting the best of me. Hunger and thirst." He had lied. His life seemed a lie! Then he said with the sincerest truth, "I fear for your safety, Bill. I wish you were home with Evangeline and your baby."

Bill said, "Don't worry. We'll soon be out of this fix."

Once, Arley peeped into the room and saw a coffee cup left on the box there. In desperation, he risked being caught as he entered the window and snatched the cup. He gingerly carried the half cup of coffee to the roof. "Look what I have for you," he said and gave it to Bill. Bill took an eager swallow and handed the cup back to Arley.

"No, I had my share when I first picked it up in the room." It was a lie, but Arley felt better having said it.

In the middle of the morning they heard a wagon coming down the road toward the house. As it came closer and turned into the carriageway Arley remarked, "That's Judge Stanton's buckboard!" The two outlaws came out of the house to meet the wagon. As it rumbled still closer, Arley gasped, "Mamma Essie's tied up in the bed of the wagon!"

The driver bounded down from his seat. "Come on, let's get Joe into the wagon," he said. The three men went into the house. Several minutes later they returned. They did not go to the wagon, instead they went to a grassy spot. One of them carried a rusty shovel. He began to dig in the sod.

"What're they doin'?" asked Bill. Soon the answer was obvious. The shape of the hole was that of a grave. The spade was crude and worn, one that had been left behind by the former homesteaders. Each of the outlaws took his turn at gouging into the rocky clay. It was a hard task and took a long while to complete. If only those men had selected a grave spot out of view of the wagon, thought Arley and Bill, the wagon could have been filched away. But while they watched Essie struggling in vain against her rope restraints, their eyes also regarded the jayhaweker's guns. How could they save Essie?

The three men went into the house and came out carrying Joe's huge corpse. One of them brought a blanket slung over his shoulder. He spread the blanket on the sod. They rolled the sprawling body onto it. Taking the corners of the blanket they lowered the hulk into the cavity. Then the edges of the blanket were flung down into the grave to cover the deceased. They began the job of refilling the hole. Before all the dirt was replaced, the wagon driver was deserted by the other two who went to saddle their horses. As the last shovel of dirt was in place and the back of the spade smoothed and slapped the mound of earth, the two horsemen rode up and sat on their horses for a few minutes. The third man leaned on his shovel. They contemplated the grave and thought about the grisly business.

Then the two riders, anxious to leave the tragic scene, made a quick departure, exclaiming as they rode off, "We'll meet you at Yancey's corners."

While the grave was being covered, Arley and Bill had come down the steps and had watched from the first floor window. With the two horsemen gone, their best and last chance to free Essie had come. "When I stop the horse," instructed Arley, "you jump on the back of the buckboard and attack the driver from behind."

The wagon started on its way, and there was no further time to plan. They took off after it. As best he could on his leg that had been injured. Arley raced across the yard to cut off the horse just before he made the turn onto the highway. He planned to leap upon the back of the animal and bring it to a sudden halt. He had done the same trick many times with his own saddle horse. The disgruntled driver, in a bad humor because he had been deserted by the other two, drove off at full speed. He was surprised by Arley's attack coming from the right side and to the front of his horse. He was making the turn onto the main road. Gnashing his teeth, he gave the reins a pull to the right just as the young Cherokee was getting his stride to leap into the air. The driver had guided the horse, intending for the animal to trample the attacker. Instead, the wagon shaft struck Arley in the abdomen piercing into his body and breaking off. In sudden agony, Arley clutched the reins and the horse's mane. His paralyzed body hung limp while his grip held firm until the beast dragged him to a stop. Then Arley released his hold and fell to the dust. The splintered section of the shaft protruded from his bleeding belly.

Bill had not been aware of what had happened. As the vehicle slowed he had leaped upon the wagon. While the driver was busy controlling the horse, from behind Bill seized the man's pistol from its holster. He raised the weapon into the air and struck it down on the driver's head. Then he turned to untie Essie. Crouched in the bed of the wagon Bill did not see what had happened to Arley. But when he stood up and turned around he was able to see his companion on the ground. "Good Lord, Arley!" he screamed. He sprang over the side of the wagon to the young Cherokee. Arley was lying on his back, the splintery wood extending about six inches out of his abdomen. He writhed painfully, making ghastly, guttural sounds.

Essie, at first, sat up and tried to rub relief into her sore wrists. She stood to her feet and looked about. At the sight of Arley she shrieked and trembled. She struggled out of the wagon bed. At Arley's side she kneeled. She took his hand and held it to her cheek while she sobbed. Her son stirred feebly and opened his eyes. "Is Mamma Essie all right?" he whispered.

"Yes, Arley," replied Bill softly. "We saved her." Then Arley lapsed into unconsciousness.

Bill and Essie lifted him into the wagon. Bill examined the broken shaft and found it had been broken beyond the attachment of the harness. When he dumped the injured driver out Bill could still drive the wagon. Essie held the head of her Cherokee son in her lap as the wagon rolled slowly over the rough road. Gently she caressed his face.

Caleb was sent flying to summon Dr. Cartmell. The physician removed the shaft of wood and pack the wound with gauze. He offered little hope. Night and day Essie stayed at the bedside. Arley did not improve. The doctor came daily. On the third day the patient rallied a little, and hopes rose. "I want to see Bill," he whispered, "Send for Bill." His companion was keeping a concerned vigil nearby. When he stepped to the bedside Arley smiled faintly. "Thank you, Bill. Thank you for ever'thing. You are a true...brother. Thank you." Tears rolled down his bronze cheeks. "I'd never want to hurt you, Bill. I'm sorry." He spoke in feeble broken sentences. "Got to tell...Oh, God!...Got to tell you.. Little Jeremy is my...son. Don't blame...Evangeline... my fault...Forgive me...Bill...Forgive. I...loved Evangeline. I thought ...you..had died...on the river. I mourned... for...you, Bill. I...was...so lonely. Forgive. I'm glad...Jeremy...will have....you ,.for father. Take good...care of...him. Forgive, Bill... Don't hate...me. For God's sake...don't hate..." His voice trailed off into a struggle for breath. With moist eyes he looked imploringly at the white man who had been a brother to him.

Bill bent over the invalid and gave him an affectionate hug. "Me? Hate you? Brother, I could never hate you. I know about Jeremy. I've always known. It's all right. I understand and love you, brother." Not wishing to further tire him, Bill turned sadly away.

"Mamma," Arley whispered. Essie moved to his bedside. "Mamma, dear Mamma." He raised his hand to give her a trembling caress of her light brown face. "I...love you,...Mamma. I'm your...son, ain't I, Mamma." It was not a question but an affirmation. All he sought in reply was her reassuring smile. "No one ever... had a... right to make a slave... of you. Might just as well make ...slaves of angels," he said with rallied strength. "I ... kept ...your ownership ... papers ... 'cause sometimes ...I felt maybe ...I wasn't really... yours. That's all. I want to be... yours ... your son. Don't leave me, Mamma."

"Oh, Arley, that could never, never happen. You will always belong to me. Always." She bent down to kiss his cheek. For a few minutes they were silent, their hands clasped together. Essie's thought went back to the time of her flight from the Cherokee trail, how she carried two tiny babies, one on her back and one at her breast.

As though he knew his end was near and he wanted everyone beside him, he asked, "Caleb, where's Caleb?"

His black brother stepped forward and kneeled at the bedside opposite Essie. "I'm here, Arley, I'm here." The clasp of Caleb's hand in Arley's was warm and firm. Arley smiled faintly and whispered, "Jesus is waiting for me." He closed his eyes. He was gone.

Sadly, Caleb drove to Ozark to select a coffin for his Indian brother. Essie tenderly washed his body and clothed him in his best garments. For a day his bier was displayed in the Stanton parlor. Men were hired by Judge Stanton to dig a grave in the family cemetery east of the house. A few friends came, most of whom had learned the news of his death from Mr. Hershfield, proprietor of the general store.

Standing by his coffin, Essie viewed Arley's body with tear-dimmed eyes. He seemed to her so small. Her hands, always so dedicated to his welfare and comfort, could not now find repose. She caressed the polished pine of the box which held him. She smoothed the wrinkles of his shirt and the fringe of his deerskin jacket. Judge Stanton placed his hand on Essie's shoulder.

"He called me to him just a few hours before his passing," said the judge. "He wanted assurance from me that you would be well cared for after he was gone. He said all that he had should be yours, Essie. He has a small bank account. Then, very solemnly, he asked me to bring to him the title of ownership which his father had received when he purchased you as his slave. I, of course, assumed that he wanted to make a declaration for the legal manumission of you and Caleb. Instead, he took the paper in his hand, ever so tenderly, like it was a sacred relic. He smiled and gazed hard into my face. 'When I die,' he whispered, 'put this paper in the coffin with me. Lay it right over my heart. I want all heaven to know that Mamma Essie and me belong together.'"

The judge held the paper in his hand. He shared Essie's sorrow as he looked into her face. Essie slipped the title of ownership from the judge's fingers and placed it into Arley's hand. Along with the paper would be buried a part of her heart. Now, she thought, I must forever hereafter share him more completely with dear Fawn. Her association with the Cherokee people had finally come to a grievous end. The words which she had spoken to her sons so many, many times filled her heart: "God hath of one blood created all the nations of the earth."

At Arley's grave, Caleb built a huge monument out of rough Ozark stones. He gathered and heaped them together until his body ached. Throughout later years he would often go to the grave to rest and meditate. But the ache in his heart never fully healed.

Essie, too, often went to sit on the rude bench at the graveside. She felt that this consecrated spot was not only the resting place of her son, but it also symbolized the graves of all

254

those who had touched her life. Sometimes she poured out her heart in conversation with dear Fawn. Often she mourned for her mother and father. Where were her brothers? she cried in despair. But most of all she grieved for her husband and the happy life he had given her so long ago. Sometimes she talked to him as though he, too, was interred beneath the stones which marked Arley's grave. "Gabe," she cried, "I'm comin' to you!" Then she pondered whether her longing would ever be fulfilled in this world, or would it be in the next life. "Wait for me, Gabe," she mourned.

With Arley's death had vanished the hope that he could take her to Georgia. She had been glad to acknowledge herself to be his slave. As her master she could have safely traveled with him as soon as the terrible war was over. "Sometime, God help me, I'm comin' to you, Gabe," she sobbed.

Chapter XVIII
War's End and Emancipation

In March, 1862, the little town of Ozark was quiet. The every-day activities were not much altered by the course of the war. Sometimes the merchandising establishments temporarily locked their doors. The post office closed when the mail could not be safely delivered. The blacksmith, the flour mill, and the saw mill halted their operations for weeks at a time. But all in all, the small community struggled along. People did the best they could during those adverse times, always alert to the dangers, ready to flee into the backwoods should the occasion demand it. Valuables and food provisions often were hidden underground in barrels. Livestock and wagons were stationed back in the timber when soldiers or bushwhackers appeared. Through it all, it was a deadly game of wits in which the Ozark people were pretty well able to hold their own. The Stanton household made its own adjustments. Nestled on a relatively isolated trail, it was able to escape many of the threats common to most homes. After the battle of Wilson's Creek and the conquering Confederates left the city, Springfield undertook to return to normal. The churches, some of which had been used as arsenals or hospitals, attempted to resume regular worship services. The post office was reopened and began to receive mail. There was talk of opening the schools. To be sure, defense and safety were still foremost on the public mind. In March, 1862, plans were made for the organization of a regiment of the State Militia for Southwestern Missouri. Judge Stanton, who had received the commission of captain from General Lyon, took great interest in the new military corps. However, his army title was more honorary than functional. Judge Stanton attempted to return to hold court normally in the counties south of Springfield and Greene county.

At the same time, the glorious Union victory at Pea Ridge, Arkansas, appeared to put Southwest Missouri safely under Northern control.

Even while the area remained in Federal control, conditions were not altogether peaceful and safe. During the war it was not the Confederate guerillas and bushwhackers alone that were raiding, plundering, killing, and burning throughout Southwest Missouri. Bands of Federal raiders and jayhawkers rode throughout the country, pouncing upon unwary Confederate sympathizers. Sometimes men were called out of their beds and slain in view of their terror-stricken families. Then the torch was put to their homes. Federal troops occupying Greene and the surrounding counties shot, with military precision and coldness, offending murderers, robbers, assassins, and army deserters.

Following the reelection of Lincoln in November, 1864, the end of the war came five months later. Then the assassination of Lincoln. Most Missourians mourned, although a few cantankerous Confederate sympathizers expressed satisfaction and pleasure.

During these troublesome years, Caleb usually journeyed with the judge to the cities where court could be held. They took firearms with them and kept carefully alert to any threats of danger. Caleb took an active interest in all the legal matters, and Judge Stanton willingly taught the black youth.

Caleb continued to attend the worship services at the old barn. To the slaves who gathered there, Caleb was the bearer of news concerning the war. Sometimes the sounds of gunfire terrorized the poor blacks. On a few occasions violence touched their lives, but it was primarily a white man's war, and it was usually the slave master or his family that was struck with misfortune or tragedy. Then came the end of the war. And the Thirteenth Amendment! The Emancipation Proclamation had been issued in 1863 had proclaimed slaves free in rebellious territory under Federal troops. Now slaves of Missouri were free at last! Wild jubilation rang from the rafters of the old barn sanctuary. Such celebration as the county had never known stirred the humble black souls. They sang and shouted and danced in ecstasy. All day and all night they reveled. Some resolved that they would stay on there forever. No more toil! No more cowing to the white man's bidding. They would take life easy and bask in their new freedom!

Then came the cool light of dawn. Exhausted by the festivity, little by little the black folks moved out of the building. Suddenly the frenzy of the occasion vanished in the sharpness of reality. Tired and hungry, they realized with dismay that their warm beds, chairs, fatback, corncakes, sorghum, and tobacco, however rude and meager, were all a part of the plantation. What did freedom mean?

Some of the free Negroes took off, seeking brighter prospects in the uncertain fields which lay beyond. New vistas and frontiers beckoned now to liberated dreamers and fantasizers. Others clung to the land with tenacious dread. For them, freedom would have to incubate, to nurture, and grow slowly into their conscious thinking. Caleb began to counsel his black friends. He cautioned the foolhardy, gave confidence to the fearful and perplexed. He became a mediator between them and their former owners. The old masters came to recognize Caleb's good judgment and many kind and gentle farmers were able to work out good relationships with the black freedmen.

Kerry McShane found it difficult to relinquish his hold over his slave workers. Who would pay him for his economic loss? Fortunately, because of Caleb's influence, McShane had already granted certain privileges to his Negroes. Otto Fluger had been a wise and just foreman. Now Caleb was able to arbitrate greater freedom, modestly fair wages, and a feeling of Christian goodwill between the previous master and the now free workers. Of course some black folks preferred to leave the old homestead. Sarah, discontent with work in the fields, expressed her desire to become a housekeeper in a private home. Caleb, fearing that she was about to go to Springfield or some distant place where he would never see her again, persuaded the judge to employ her permanently to assist Essie in the Stanton home.

In the Stone County courthouse at Galena, Judge Stanton spoke to two backwoods lawyers. "I would like to confer with you two gentlemen at the conclusion of this case," he said. The two had risen to their places of esteem through popular acceptance by their fellows. Oscar Travis excelled in moonlight 'coon hunting and had the best pack of hounds in the county. Andy Parsons, legal kibitzer among those who occupied the benches on the courthouse lawn, was also champion horseshoe pitcher of all those who played on the grounds there. Such admirable skills had gained for each of them the exalted position of legal counselor. Of course, there were certain legal formalities which were fulfilled. A license was granted to a candidate only after he had satisfactorily answered questions put to him by a judge and two attorneys. In the cases of Oscar Travis and Andy Parsons, Judge Homer Slipfield had asked each candidate, "Are you a judge of good whiskey?" When an affirmative reply was given, a second more difficult test question was asked. "Do you have the price of four drinks?" Having properly answered the second question, the candidate was asked to demonstrate the veracity of his statement. The judge, the lawyers, and the applicant for a license marched to the local saloon where the final requirements were fulfilled, and the license was granted.

When these two lawyers, invited by Judge Stanton, came to his chambers, the judge asked them to be seated. "Caleb Forbes has gone on an errand for me and will be back soon. In the meantime we can discuss the reason I have asked you to come here. It is my plan to submit Caleb as a candidate for a license of a legal solicitor. By the law, a judge and two attorneys are to examine an applicant to determime his qualifications for the license."

"Ye mean, jedge, yer askin' us to help ye make th' nigger a ...a lawyer?" asked Oscar Travis.

"Yes, that's it," said the judge amiably. "I hope you are not one of those people who think that the black people should not be given fair advantage." Judge had foreseen that predjudice might be an obstacle. He also knew that the two he had chosen were too unlearned to ask sensible questions, yet would be reluctant to display their ignorance. "I'm sure you remember when you, yourselves, were applying for your own licenses. You probably remember some of the difficult questions each of you had to answer." The judge had heard the rumor of how they had been examined. He had not sought a way to make the examination easy for Caleb. He knew that Caleb could pass any test. His fear was that prejudice against the black race would not give the young man a fair chance. "Let me ask that each of you ask Caleb three questions."

At that time Caleb entered the room. The young man had received only a vague hint from Judge Stanton that he was to be tested. Calmly, he took a seat facing his inquisitors. The two men squirmed in their chairs. Sweat popped out on their brows, their faces contorted in anguish.

"Oh, come, men, I'm sure you can think of something, perhaps a question about torts." The judge knew that neither of them could distinguish between a tort and a breakfast roll. "Perhaps you want to ask a question about change of venue."

Embarrassment of the two lawyers was more than they could bear. They began to whisper to each other. "Why can't we ask thet we go t'Oakley's saloon, like we done?" asked one.

"We can't do thet, stupid, ye know thet temperance speaker, William Ross was here. Rube Oakley got religion an' dumped ever' barrel o' his whiskey into the street an' set fire t'it. Think o' something else."

"You think o' something."

Judge Stanton pretended not to heed their dilemma. Finally, one of the men rose from his seat. "Jedge Stanton, we done thunk o' all th' hard questions we kin, but we'ns thinks it would be a waste o' time t' ask 'em seein's as how th' black fellow has been workin' fer ye. If ye allow he kin be a lawyer, thet's good enough fer us. We give him our recommend."

"Gentlemen, that's mighty kind of you!" exclaimed the judge. "I'm proud of your vote of confidence in my judgment. We'll sign up the papers."

Caleb's new title did not change much the way he lived and worked. White people were reluctant to hire a Negro lawyer. Besides, they had no money to pay for an attorney. In a few instances Caleb gave legal advice. Once he even took a case to court. To his disappointment the all white jury could not put aside their racial prejudice and Caleb's client lost the case. Judge Stanton was very disturbed by Caleb's discouragement. Perhaps, he thought, I made a mistake in encouraging him so much.

One day Judge Stanton came to Caleb to show him a newspaper announcement. Federal jobs open to both black and white workers were available in the reconstruction of the war-torn South. "If you like, I will help you to apply for one of these positions," he said. "Of course, it would necessitate your leaving home and going where the government wants to send you."

Caleb talked it over with Essie. They both agreed that it was an opportunity which Caleb should take. Letters were written to the War Department in Washington. Recommendations were sought from prominent friends of the judge.

Finally, the long-awaited reply came. Caleb's hands trembled as he read the return address on the envelope: Freedmen's Bureau, War Department, Washington, D.C. He tore open the letter. "You are requested to come to Washington for an interview," it read. Of course, there was more, but that was what caught the young man's attention. Could he go? He had never been away from home before. What would it be like to leave Essie and Benjamin and Mary Stanton? And then there was Sarah. He had grown used to her being a member of the household. The young house servant had grown into a beautiful woman with confidence and poise which she had acquired from being in the presence of Essie. All of them encouraged Caleb and urged him to seize the opportunity. "Write and tell them you are coming at once," they said.

Where in the South will he go? thought Essie. Oh, if only he could go to Georgia! And if he would by chance happen to meet Gabe. What if... She caught herself. It's been over twenty-seven years! TWENTY-SEVEN YEARS! Still, Gabe is Caleb's father. Surely the boy would want to find and know his father. Oh, no need to go over it now with Caleb. He already had heard everything. She had told him often enough. Besides, what remote chance was there that he would be sent to Georgia? "I want him to go into his new career fully dedicated to the work he has to do," she resolved. "In his present excitement, no need to trouble him further. But, Oh," Essie's soul cried out, "I can't relinquish the hope! Someday! God grant that SOMEDAY..." She put her hands to her face and hurried to her rocker upstairs.

262

Part Two of Chapter XVIII

In Washington, Caleb wanted to spend considerable time looking at the government buildings, but he did not feel free to use his time that way. He knew that soon all his money would be spent. So when the hansom cab brought him to the War Department offices on Pennsylvania Avenue, he could look to the east at the White House, and felt that he would have to be content with that. The War Department building was a three-story brick structure with a huge portico of marble pillars. It was quite old, dating back to the time of President Monroe. Before it were a number of large, grand trees, the oldest and finest in the city. As Caleb gazed at the huge trees and the vast Corinthian columns of the building, he felt very small and insignificant. Timidly he entered the gloomy halls. Several soldiers stood guard. An officer seated at a desk asked gruffly, "Who did you want to see?"

"Where will I find..." In confusion and trepidation, Caleb had forgotten the name. He nervously unfolded the letter and referred to it. "Where will I find ...General Oliver Otis Howard?"

"Right there where his sign is on the door." He spoke as though his time had been enormously infringed upon. The gold-leaf lettering read "General Oliver O. Howard, Director of Freedmen's Bureau."

The brass door knob was as cold as the soldier's voice had been, and the heavy door resisted his shove in a most inhospitable way. Inside, the office was impersonal and austere. There was a musty smell of office ledgers, stale tobacco, and oil lamps. Several people sat on benches which lined three sides of the room. At the fourth side, a male clerk was seated on a high stool behind a long, four-foot tall counter. By this time the letter which Caleb held was fairly crumpled, and not trusting his voice to be without a quiver, he handed it to the clerk.

"Oh, yes, Mr. Forbes," said the clerk after scanning the letter, "I'll tell the general you're here. I'm sure he can see you soon. Just have a seat there."

With so many waiting besides himself, Caleb assumed the wait would be lengthy. But in a short while, the secretary called Caleb's name and ushered him into the inner office. General Howard stood behind an enormous mahogany desk. "Come in, Mr. Forbes," he said cordially. "I'm glad you came so promptly." He walked around his desk and offered Caleb his left hand. The young Negro hesitated then realized that the general had lost an arm in the war. They shook hands. "It is not my custom," said the general, "to interview personally every man whom this department gives employment. Ordinarily, the State Commissioner would choose his own subordinates. But since you are requesting service in a specific district, I felt it best to talk to you first." The general sat down, took a file folder from his desk and opened it before him. With a broad smile, he gestured toward a chair. Caleb seated himself.

"I thank you, sir, for your consideration." Caleb's confidence was being restored.

Glancing at the open folder, General Howard continued, "I have received correspondence on your behalf from Senator Caldwell of Missouri. On the basis of your legal training under Judge Stanton, with whom the Senator is well acquainted, Senator Caldwell highly recommends you." The general studied the papers before him.

"Senator Caldwell!" thought Caleb. "The judge had spared no effort in soliciting assistance!"

"It also says here that you were a military courier for Captain Stanton at the time of the Battle of Wilson's Creek."

"Yes, but..." Caleb had started to clarify that his title was insignificant and his contribution to the battle was minimal.

The general continued, ignoring Caleb's feeble interruption. "I read in Frank Leslie's newspaper about General Lyon's death in that battle to save Missouri for the Union. A very heroic thing, his effort there! Tell me, young man, since the battle was lost and the enemy was so numerically superior, how was it that the entire Union forces were not completely annihilated?"

"Some say the army of McCulloch had suffered such losses as to render them unwilling to pursue the Federal forces.

However, I believe that the general had 'the slows,' the same as our General McClellan."

The General Howard chuckled, delighted with Caleb's reply. Lincoln, whom the general greatly admired, had characterized McClellan as having "the slows."

"I am not particularly interested in recalling the war years. Thank God, they are over. Now it is our problem to reconstruct the Union. The purpose of this department is to protect the former slaves of the South. Some of the states have legislated Black Codes which are subjecting the Negroes to a condition which amounts to a kind of slavery, such as they endured before the war. This must not be. There is a need to help these freedmen find work under equitable conditions. This bureau is dedicated to aiding them in the building of cottages and schools. Do you think you would be interested in this kind of work?"

"Oh, indeed I would," said Caleb enthusiastically.

"Yes, I believe you would. I have here a letter from a Mr. Kerry McShane. He has recommended you on the basis of what you have done to insure good relations between him and his liberated black people. It was this letter which most impressed me, young man." The general sat thoughtfully studying Caleb, his hand gently rubbing the shoulder from which hung an empty sleeve, as though perhaps there was some ache there. "Tell me," he remarked, "you state in your letter that you would like to be employed in northwestern Georgia. Why have you designated that area?"

Caleb's heart leaped! He had not told Essie that he had written this request. He had not wanted to raise her hopes in such a faint possibility, but now the general was bringing up the subject! "Because I was born in Georgia," he replied. " My father was stolen by raiders before I was born. I have never seen him. My mother mourns for him still. I thought I might possibly locate him."

"There are many of the black race who were separated from their families when they were sold under the slavery system. Now many freedmen are searching, hoping to find their loved ones. Too bad! Too bad!" Such sympathy and concern had led the newspapers often to refer to the general as the "Christian soldier." He was touched by Caleb's remarks. "Yes," he said, "I think you could do an admirable job in the Freedmen's Bureau. And I think we can use you in that geographic area. If you have followed the war campaigns, you know that Georgia has suffered tragically from the war. It was my onerous duty to have been with Sherman during his destructive march to Savannah. When you see the havoc wrought there, I hope you will remember that it was our purpose to end the war with the loss of as few lives as possible. The destruction of property seemed the most expeditious way to do that. I will write a letter to the Georgia State Commissioner asking him to put you into the job of regional commissioner. Your legal training gives you special qualification. I will have the clerk write a letter which you can carry and which will identify you to the state commissioner. You may wait in the outer office until you are given the letter."

"I thank you, sir, for your time and generosity. I shall do my utmost to serve you and my country well."

"Oh, one thing more," said the general. "I recommend that you travel by steamer to Savannah and then by railroad to the capital at Milledgeville. I believe the Central Railroad from Savannah to Macon is now reconstructed. Beyond that, I am not certain. But I am sure you will find transportation to the capital. Good luck, Mr. Forbes. May God go with you." He stood up and shook hands as he bid farewell.

Caleb was ecstatic over the visit. As soon as he recieved the letter of identification, he hurried to make arrangements for the journey.

While Caleb had written to Essie as soon as he reached Washington, it was not until he reached Savannah that he found time to write again:

Dear Mother,

I arrived in Savannah, Georgia, last evening at about seven o'clock. Since the coastal steamer which brought me did not leave the harbor until sometime in the morning, I decided to spend the night on board. I went

266

to the railroad depot early this morning and booked passage on the train to leave here at 8:00. While I am waiting here I am writing this letter to you. I know you must be surprised to learn that I am in Georgia, the state where you once lived and where I was born.

The station is a beehive of activity. Everyone seems to be rushing here and there. Most of them are United States soldiers or ex-secesh soldiers. Some of those in rebel uniforms are mere boys. All in all, it is a most depressing sight. The evidence of war is everywhere. One youth--sixteen years old, perhaps younger--sat next to me. He was missing his right arm and two fingers of his left hand. His face was without expression and he appeared to be dazed by the horrors of the war. I saw one woman come into the station looking wildly about. Then a man, in a rebel uniform, hobbled on crutches to her. His left leg had been amputated above the knee. The couple embraced each other lovingly, the man's crutch falling to the floor. Emaciated and worn by the war, the soldier held to the woman convulsively. Tears streamed from their eyes. Then they attempted to pick up the crutch. She could not release her hold of him lest he fall. I caught sight of their dilemma and rushed to recover the stick for them. Some of the veterans have terribly disfigured faces. One man, with a bandage over his head, had, no doubt, lost one eye. A loose cloth hung over the left side and center of his face, but when he exhaled his breath blew the loose cloth revealing a ghastly cavity where once his nose had been. Mother, I can't go on writing about it! It is too awful. What a waste war is!

There are many Negroes in the station too. Most are carrying a bundle of some kind--probably all their earthly possessions. Some are reticent and selfconscious; others are aggressive and insolent. There are also business men from the North. Their natty clothing and brisk manner makes them easily

267

distinguishable from the somber-faced southerners, whose clothes are outmoded and threadbare.

I will take the train to the capital. There I will call on the Commissioner for the Freedmen's Bureau for the State of Georgia. Of course, I am a little ill at ease about being interviewed by an important United States agent, a Mr. Brownlow. However, General Howard was so gracious that he relieved my unsure feelings from the start. I hope I will have an equally satisfactory interview with Mr. Brownlow.

I will write you again when I get permanently located.

Give my best regards to Master Benjamin and Missis Mary, and, of course, Sarah, too. I miss you all very much.

Your devoted son,
Caleb

The journey on the railroad was slow and tiresome. The cars were crowded with people, mostly soldiers. Freight cars were loaded with government supplies and equipment. Once, there was an extended delay because three cars were smashed together. As Caleb looked through the car window, he was amazed by the extent of the destruction of property along the route. Wooden bridges and trestles, which had been burned or bombed, were rebuilt or in the process of reconstruction. Sometimes wrecked cars or engines, too damaged for future use, lay rusting in the ditches beside the line. Also there were bent and twisted sections of iron rails. Sometimes the track rails were wrapped around trees.

At Milledgeville, Mr. Brownlow was formal and business-like in his interview with the young Negro who was to become a new district commissioner. Caleb was to take charge of the office in Atlanta which supervised agents in some forty different towns. Many of these workers were lieutenants from volunteer forces of the army. It was their duty to examine, and approve or disapprove, all contracts between the Negroes and the planters.

They were to arbitrate all cases of grievance or complaint between whites and Negroes or among the Negroes themselves.

Caleb, following the State Commissioner's instructions, first went to make himself known to the headquarters of the Commander of the Army of Occupation in Atlanta. By this time, the Missouri youth had realized that he must take on a facade of confidence and authority. A meek, unassuming demeanor would not do. He must demand and expect the esteem due his office. It was a role which he played, at first, with some inward timidity, but as time went by, he soumetimes found himself fearlessly confronting, ordering, or reprimanding high-level army officers. His zeal for the work, his passion that justice be done gave him courage and vigor.

In his search to find information which would help him locate his father, Caleb was unsuccessful. He had scanned all the records in most of the district offices where he had gone to inspect and supervise. He had hoped that somewhere in the journals or files there might be the mention of the name Gabe Forbes. But, alas, it was not so. He wrote to his mother letters telling how hopeless and discouraging his efforts were.

Back in Missouri, Essie opened each of his letters with trembling hands, and after perusing them, she laid them aside, lonely and melancholy. At last, her anxiety and disappointment was more than she could bear. She determined that she must go to Georgia and there satisfy her desire to know. Nothing less than that would satiate her longing. Sarah had become so adept in caring for Mistress Stanton that Essie had no misgivings about leaving. Both Benjamin and Mary urged Essie to make the trip, for they had known the years of yearning that Essie had endured. Essie withdrew from the bank the savings that Arley had left her. It would be an arduous journey, but not as wretched as she had taken with the Cherokee people.

By stage coach, by riverboat, and by railroad, she journeyed to Atlanta. Every mile of the way she imagined herself to be a step closer to Gabe. When she stepped from the train at the railroad station, she was amazed at how invigorated and serene she felt. Already she sensed that she was succeeding on her quest. This was Georgia! she exclaimed to herself. How glad she was to be here, so near to Gabe. She carried her valise through the streets. It was a city full of rubble, despair, and defeat, but not for Essie,whose heart was light with hope. It was early afternoon. She had spent the night on the train, yet, how rested she was! First she would go to the Freedmen's Bureau. Everyone she asked knew where the office was. She hurried along. Soon she would see Caleb.

It was a frame building, not very impressive in its structure, but the sign was large: Freedmen's Bureau--United States of America. A small gathering of mostly black folks stood in front. Inside another assemblage of people waited for the clerks to hear their grievances. Essie slipped through the door, curious about what was going on. Three clerks stood behind a little fenced-in area. One of them, Essie assumed, was an ex-Union soldier. To him, a black man exclaimed, in a loud insolent voice, "I's come to claim my forty acres."

The ex-soldier rolled his eyes in exasperation. He stepped up on a small box where he was easily visible to the whole room. "Listen, ya'all," he announced, "we've answered this question so many times we're blue in the face. If you came here expectin' to be given forty acres, you might just as lief go home. There ain't no forty acres to be given away, an' what's more, there probably never will be. Ain't no mules to give away neither. There jes' ain't no truth to the rumor you been a-hearin'." There was grumbling of complaint and groans of disappointment.

Essie pressed closer to see what was going on.

A distressed black man had accosted another agent, "My ole Mas'er Cole say I gotta work for him. He say I done stole his chicken, an since I done thet, I gotta work for him. Less I does work, he say he gwine t' tan my hide . I sez I's a free man now an I don' gotta work for him no mo'."

"Did you steal a chicken?" asked the agent.

"Law, no! I jes' took one o' them chickens like I allus done. They jes' runs wild ever'wheres."

The agent had once been a plantation overseer. He understood the problem. "Hear me plain now, darkie. Once yo'all belonged to this here white man." The agent gestured toward a sullen-faced white planter, "Now yo're free. When

270

yo'all was a slave, there wasn't no harm in puttin' mass'er's chicken into mass'er's nigger. But now that yo're free', the chickens ain't." The black fellow looked puzzled and hurt. "D'you understand? You can't have no chickens 'less yo'all pays for 'em."

"Might jest as well talk ter a billy goat," grumbled the planter. "Tell him he's got ter work to pay for the fat hen he stole. Blasted niggers! I wus allus good to em. Give'em a good home. Didn't use the bull whip scarcely none a'tall. They's the most ongratefullust creeturs on earth. Now they won't work an' is tryin' to steal me blind. Snatchin' m'pigs, chickens, garden stuff, an' most ever'thing. Mister, I tell you, 'tain't right. M'niggers wus took from me an' no payment for 'em. Jest ain't constitutional!" The planter raged on.

"Hold on here a minute," snapped the clerk, putting both his palms up before him. He turned to the black man. "Nigger, yo'all got thirty cents?"

"Yassuh."

"Put it down here onto the counter." The old darkie searched out his change. Holdin' it carefully in the palm of his hand, he blew the lint from it and slapped it down on the counter. "Here yo'are, Mr. Cole, here's the price o' yo' chicken," said the agent . This here darkie ain't workin' for yo' this time." Then turning to the black fellow the agent shook his finger as he said, "Nex' time, it's a days' hard labor yo'll be payin' Mr. Cole." The planter and the black man both left the building, grumbling as they went and eyeing each other with resentment.

An irate southerner, once a political office-holder, was ranting to another agent because the Republican Party, carpetbaggers, the army, and the Freedmen's Bureau were displacing the bona fide, pure and rightful governors of the South.

Essie became tired of waiting, but there seemed to be no opportunity to get the attention of any of the three clerks. She had just decided that she would have to submit to a long wait, simply to inquire about where she might find her son. But just as the southern aristocrat was becoming loud and belligerent, Caleb came through a door leading to an inner office. The exasperated agent turned and said to Caleb, " Sir, this man is a former southern politician. He is discontent over the regulations forced upon the South."

"Yes," replied Caleb, "his complaint rang loudly into my office." He went to the portly man and said, "Sir, I understand that you are not pleased with the situation here in the South, but we are following the laws of the Congress of the United States and are not in any position to alter things to satisfy former officials of the Confederacy. I suggest you..." Just then his eyes caught sight of Essie. "...I suggest you write a petition to Mr. Jefferson Davis. You will find him confined at Fortress Monroe." It was terse, biting sarcasm, not in keeping with Caleb's gentle nature. He had no desire for further discussion and broke away from everthing to go to Essie. He led her into his office and asked not to be disturbed.

The reunion between the mother and son was affectionate. Before long they were planning how they could search for Gabe Forbes. Caleb had already sifted through many of the Bureau records. He had kept a sharp eye on all the men who came into the offices. Of course, he was greatly handicapped by not ever having seen his father. Often he made an announcement that he was looking for a man named Gabe Forbes, but no one volunteered any information. Perhaps now, they thought, there was much greater hope for success.

Such was not the case, however, and after two weeks went by, they were forced to admit that they were no closer to finding Gabe than they had been at the beginning. Essie was very discouraged and weary. Her only pleasure came from observing Caleb at his work. His mastery of the position seemed complete. She watched him with great pride.

Weeks later she decided that a little relief from her search would be desirable. She would go to Fern Haven Plantation. Perhaps she could find some old friends there. It would be solely a pleasure trip because no one there would have known Gabe. She would rent a saddle horse and go there alone.

Chapter XIX
Fern Haven revisited

It was a bright September day when Essie set out from Atlanta to find Fern Haven Plantation. She took the road east toward Decatur. Beside the roadway the fields, once neatly tended, were now weed infested. Even in a few patches where a scrubby crop of cotton had recently been harvested and a few bolls of white still remained, the weeds were abundant. Between the road and the fields the brush stood shoulder high to Essie's horse and crowded the trail, leaving a narrow clay path. Invading armies had trampled down the undergrowth, but now the plants were straightening up and taking over. She traveled over ten miles before she reached country which seemed familiar to her. At a rock-pillared entrance to an old cemetery, she paused. She knew this place. Yes, even though the wrought-iron fence which had enclosed the grounds had been removed to supply the cannon foundry, she knew this place. Pensively, she sat on the grey-roan horse peering into the ancient graveyard. Years ago, she mused, a tall iron gate stood here bearing the letters: "Eternal Peace." Tall grass crowded against the tombstones. Years of neglect pressed heavily against the leaning stones. Several fresh mounds of earth testified to the war's casualties. A familiar marble stone reigned over a family plot of several graves enclosed by a low stone fence. The large letters chiseled in the marker spelled out the name "Lovell." Beneath it and to one side was the name "Claire, beloved wife and mother." Claire?--elegant, unflinching, steadfast, arrogant Claire--resigned to earthly dust! What of Master Tom? Beside the grave of Claire were two other fresh mounds of earth.

Near the cemetery, stood the old wooden church, the doors flung open, the shutters hung askew or were fallen off. Tantalized by curiosity, Essie tethered her horse and ascended the rotting steps. She peered in, recalling the former cared-for condition of the old building. As she walked down the aisle, she fancied again how that the eyes of the proud southners had rested upon her. At the Lovell family pews, she paused. The gate stood open. Strands of wool clung to the rough, peeling paint of the wood. Sheep had taken refuge there from the weather. Somber thoughts of the Lovell children came to her--children once so carefree and naive, now subjected to the harsh, warring world. So shocking was the experience that she turned and fled from the building. Dared she go on to Fern Haven?

At the plantation, the long carriage entrance she had known so well had a strange appearance. Shaggy, swooping pine branches threatened to strike her as she rode along the curved driveway. When she came to the place where she anticipated a view of the mansion, her heart sank! Only the blackened stone foundation lay where once the great house had stood. Four tall chimneys rose forlornly above the ashes. The absence of the house allowed her to see across to the back yard and further to the curved row of slave shanties. How strange things appeared! A black woman had heard the approaching horse and was coming toward the visitor.

"It's Leona," exclaimed Essie. She spurred her horse forward, halted, and sprang from the saddle. Leona rushed to her with outstretched arms.

"Essie, dear Essie," called Leona as she embraced the mulatto. Then holding the younger woman at arms length, she drew back to gaze into her face. "Essie, you're the first good thing we seen in months. All what comes to us is bad news and trouble." She clutched her apron, brushed across her wet eyes and pinched and rubbed her nose. Seeing Essie scanning across the estate, Leona said, "Ain't hardly nobody left here no more. Most all th' niggers done left now that they're free."

"Mas'er Tom and the family?" Essie continued to search with her eyes.

"Mas'er Tom's here somewheres. He goes roamin' 'round the plantation all the time. Sometimes he's gone for hours, an' ain't really been nowheres. Oh, Essie--he's so lonely! He just mopes 'round. He'll be glad to see you. He allus liked you Essie."

"But the children, what about the children?"

"They've growed up an' gone. Ned an' Simon is both dead in the war--Battle of Pine Mountain. News of it kill't poor

Missis Claire--that an' the damn Yankee soldiers overrunning the place. First time, they comes gallopin' in here scarin' us half to death. Missis Claire--she hurries out onto the porch. She looks straight at 'em an' says, 'You, sir, appear to be the officer. I beg you not to allow your men enter my house. We'll give you food, but I beg you, leave us enough to survive.' That officer an' his twelve or fifteen men just push Missis Claire out of the way an' ransack through ever'thing. Dirty scamps took what they wanted, threw down, turned over, and crushed most ever'thing else. They tore into boxes and trunks and demanded keys for what was locked. Missis Claire were beside herself. She rung her hands an' cry, 'specially when one of 'em struck young Mas'er Simon's oil-painted pi'ture with his sword. In the kitchen I done roasted a chicken an' a duck. Them damn Yankees grabbed up th' birds whole an' tore at 'em with their teeth like starved dogs. They kept clammorin' for whiskey. Took all we had. What wasn't drunk, they splashed on th' carpets.

"In th' yard, they took all the chickens an' turkeys they could ketch, stuffed 'em in gunny sacks an' rode off. Poor Missis Claire--she wus fairly give out. She took to her bed, most nigh sick. When Mas'er Tom come home, Missis Claire can't tell what happen, so done in she was. She just sob an' groan.

"Next mornin', here comes another passel of Yankees. Mas'er Tom begged 'em to go away 'cause we already got raided. They just laugh an' don't pay Mas'er Tom no mind. They rifled ever'thing--the sideboard, takin' the silver knives, spoons, an' stuff--ever'thing! When Mas'er Tom say we ain't got no more whiskey, they gets so mad they done turn over th' old liquor case an' smash it. Missis Claire she screams an' throw her arms into th' air like she done lost her mind. Them damn Yankees don' care 'bout that for nothin'. They just stampeed into ever' room. Such cussin' an' blasphemin' come out'er their mouths like you never heerd in your life! Out in the yard, they cleaned out the smoke house--took ever'thing. What poultry wasn't took before got took. What wasn't took, them lousy scamps shot at an' tried to kill. Missis Claire--she so upset she can't control herself. She clings to Mas'er Tom. Part of th' time she's holdin' him back, an' part of th' time she's eggin' him to fight. At first, mas'er try to stop them rascals. Then one of 'em hit mas'er on the head with the butt of his rifle.

"When they done left, Missis Claire were plumb crazy. She set on th' floor an' scream an' groan. Me an' Mas'er Tom fix her a bed in thet first shanty, where ole Joe an' Aunt Eliza used to live. We figure if them damn Yankees come again, I kin hold her quiet an' keep her from knowin' they come. It didn't do no good though. Sure 'nuff, they come th' third time, this time at daybreak. Missis Claire were asleep. I heerd 'em whoopin' an' hollerin'. Mas'er Tom was sleepin' in the big house. He come down to th' slave shanty to protect Missis Claire. 'What you hidin' in there?' sez one o' th' Yankees, an' give mas'er a fierce shove to th' ground. Mas'er Tom he picks up a long stick of fire wood an' clubs it down atop that soldier's head, jest as he come to Missis Claire's room, an' her in her night clothes a'screamin' bloody murder! Lord help us! It were awful!" As she told it, Leona sniveled and sobbed, wiping her tears on her apron.

"They carry off th' unconscious soldier what Tom hit. I thought they was goin' to kill Mas'er Tom! One Yankee raise his rifle to shoot! Missis Claire she hung onto Tom, an' with such outlandish screamin' she beg for his life. She fought anyone who come near her. Clean out of her mind she was. 'My two sons are in General Polk's army. They'll avenge what you've done to us,' she scream.

"'General Polk died at Pine Mountain,' shouts one of them soldiers.

"'So did our two sons,' cried mas'er. Poor Mas'er Tom, he so frantic an' desperate, he don't know what he's sayin'. Missis Claire she scream an' faint in his arms, like she don't know we done buried th' boys three weeks 'afore. We carry her into th' cabin.

"When Mas'er Tom an' me come outside again, th' big house is in flames. 'Now they won't come back no more," sez Mas'er Tom. 'Ever'thing's gone.' We both set down an' cry. Oh, Essie! To see so much hurt done to Mas'er Tom makes me cry over an' over.

"Three days later Missis Claire died of pneumonia. She done took a bad chill bein's she were exposed to th' early mornin' air during th' raid--an' her in her night clothes. Poor Mas'er Tom!" lamented Leona, "he ain't got nothin' like he once had." There had always been a close bond between the old black slave and her master. Now they bore their desolation together.

Essie put a sympathetic arm around Leona. "But where are the girls? He still has them," said Essie.

Leona shook her head sadly. "Long time 'afore the war, Nettie married a young man working for th' gover'ment at th' port of New York. She done died seven years ago during childbirth. Olivia married a young man from Mass'chu'etts. His family got woolen mills. Course she ain't been home since th' war begun. Neither do Clara. Her husband is a Yankee banker in Phil'delph'a. Poor Mas'er Tom! His girls done married damn Northerners; no wonder he's so lonely." She sighed. Then she brightened. Coming across the field strolled a slender figure, his head held high. He moved slowly, steadying himself with a walking stick.

Essie watched him intently. How proud he is, she thought. Proud?--what had he to be proud of now? Still, now more than ever, to him it was essential that his demeanor should reflect pride and dignity. Tom walked thoughtfully and slowly, unaware that he was being watched. His imposing manner was so inherent to his character that, whether he were alone or in a crowd, it was all the same. He bared his soul to no one.

The black servant took Essie's hand and confided quietly, 'Don't show him no sympathy. He can't take that." She looked toward Tom and smiled. "Handsome as ever, ain't he?"

Essie nodded. Tom handled his walking stick as a stylish accessory, carefully disguising how he relied upon it. His hair, still full, was totally white. His complexion was tan and unblemished. He was formally dressed, but his frock coat was frayed at the cuffs and pockets.

A mulatto man of middle age appeared from the shanties and went to meet Tom. The younger man appeared to give solicitous attention to the older man.

"It's Buddy Lovell," murmured Leona. "He tries so hard to be worthy of Mas'er Tom's favor."

Buddy Lovell! Out of Essie's memory came the picture of the young mulatto who flitted about Fern Haven. "He's Mas'er Tom's boy," the black folks had divulged with delight. To Buddy Lovell black folks paid a residue of the respect they held for Mas'er Tom.

"If only Mas'er Tom could let hisself go. He keeps holdin' back," said Leona. "Tom ain't got nobody except Buddy, an' Lord knows, Buddy is hungry for his pappa's love. It's that old arrogance white folks got."

"Poor souls," lamented Essie.

"Don't fret, Essie. Tom ain't buried yet. Sometimes it takes a whole lifetime for people to wake up an' learn to live. He'll come around to it some day."

When Buddy and Tom saw that Essie and Leona were watching them, they separated. Buddy stole away and disappeared among the shanties. Tom came forward and exclaimed with delight, "Oh, Essie, you came back to see us! How fine you look! Lovely as ever. I often wonder about you."

"I've been living in Missouri. I came to Georgia to search for my husband. Slavenappers took him from me twenty-eight years ago. My son is in Atlanta, working for the Freedmen's Bureau. I couldn't resist coming to Fern Haven."

"The war has been cruel to us, Essie. Too bad you have to see us like this," said Tom Lovell. "But our fortunes will soon improve. First, we need to rebuild the manor."

"It pleases me to see you looking so fit, Master Tom. I'm sure you will soon have things restored."

Tom smiled. He went on to enumerate things which he planned to do. Sorrow filled Essie's heart, for she knew he had neither the physical strength nor financial resources to fulfill his dreams--oh, they weren't really dreams--only Tom's eternal pride. Essie chose not to inquire about Tom's family, and after a short visit there seemed nothing to do but say farewell.

Leona walked with Essie to her horse. "Will you stay with him, Leona?" Essie asked.

"Lordy, yes! I can't go so long as he needs me." She sighed. "An' I guess I need him just as much."

Essie took her hand. "You were kind and good to me when I first came to Fern Haven. I'll never forget you, Leona."

"I'll pray to th' good Lord that you find your man. Goodbye, child," said the old Negress.

As Essie rode away she turned her eyes again on the old plantation. How sad it was to see such degradation and ruin! Her heart was heavy. Farther along on the road, she saw Tom plodding across a field. He was walking toward the beauty spot where the wild ferns grow. There he would have an idyllic rendezvous with his dreams of the past.

Chapter XX
The Reunion

Essie returned from Fern Haven more discouraged than ever. Symbolic of her depth of despair was the destruction all around her. As she rode through the streets of Atlanta, she was forced to turn and weave in and out around the rubble before her. Damaged buildings were being demolished. Workers were constructing new edifices to replace the old. What, she wondered, had led her to think that Fern Haven would be the same as it had been years and years ago? What a mistake she had made to leave Missouri! She had searched everywhere, searching every black face, searching, always searching. Gabe was not here! He could be in Alabama or Texas--anywhere in the wide Southland. Lord, help me, she thought, he could be...dead!

She rode to the livery stable where she had rented the riding mare. The attendant took the horse from her. Sadly she turned to leave when an unexpected figure caught her eye. Back in the shadowy inner part of the building a large black chap was pounding on a piece of iron. It was Biddle, who years ago had been the blacksmith at Fern Haven. Now he was old and obese. But it was Biddle, sure enough. Essie rushed to him. "Biddle, Biddle, it's me, Essie!" she cried.

The big black fellow stared blankly. They had not been close friends at Fern Haven.

"It's me, Leona's kitchen helper at Fern Haven!"

He scowled at her. "Don't remember," he mumbled.

"Sure you do. You remember me. I was there about twenty-eight years ago." While she was so excited to see someone she had known, how could he be so indifferent? "I just came back from Fern Haven. There was practically no one there except Leona and Master Tom." Glumly Biddle gave a slight nod of his head. She was about to move on but asked one last question: "Where'd everyone go?"

"I don'no. Ever'one doin' what they can. What they was learned to do on the old place, I reckon." He stared at her disdainfully.

Essie left him. How grumpy and unfriendly he was! She attempted to cross the street. Dray wagons, loaded with bricks and timber, lumbered past her. The sound of construction crews, hammering and sawing, shouting and dropping timbers from loaded wagons was everywhere. Atlanta was rebuilding. Her thoughts went back to the Cherokee mission, to the building of the school, the noise of the workers, sawing, hammering and ...Gabe! Suddenly, the words of old Biddle came to her, "Ever'one doin' what they can. What they was learned..." She fixed her eyes on the laborers. Gabe was here somewhere! He was using his skill as a builder. She knew it! She hurried to seek out every workman, to investigate every man-made sound. Frantically she rushed from one construction site to another! Scrutinizing every black body. Searching, searching! It was evening. Workers were leaving their jobs. Lord, she prayed don't let the darkness come. And then she saw him! It was Gabe! walking into the street, turning to leave his work! "Gabe! Oh, Gabe," she cried.

The huge black man paused, he turned around toward her his denim shirt slung over his glistening ebony shoulder "Essie?" he said simply. She ran to him and threw her arms around his sweaty body. He stiffened. She clung to him. He made no response. "Essie, Oh, Essie," he muttered in a tone that showed no passion, no rapture. Almost, there was sorrow in his face. "Essie, I thought you was gone forever," he said sadly.

Essie's arms dropped to her side. Stunned by his lack of tenderness, she stood helpless and dazed. He stared at her. His face was cold and tense. Was there agony in those dark eyes? Silently he turned from her and walked away down the street "Dear God," her heart cried within her, "have I waited all these years for this?" Tears flowed down her cheeks. Transfixed, she kept Gabe in her blurred vision.

A boy, perhaps twelve years old, ran to the black laborer "Hello, Papa," he shouted and clasped the huge rough hand

Essie's heart sank. She wavered and tottered the long way to her room. She threw herself across the bed and wept.

Later, with tears and sobbing, Essie told it all to Caleb. Her heart was broken. "Gabe has another family!" she wailed.

Caleb, too, was perplexed, brokenhearted for his mother's sake. "But he is my father," thought Caleb, "He may spurn Mother, but he has no right to deny me. If he has another son, I have ..a ...half brother!" Caleb determined that he must find them. But how could he meet and talk to his father? He did not want to accost him on the street, nor trail him to his home. Yet, Caleb wanted to talk confidentially, face to face, with his father.

It was the end of a tiring workday. Gabe gathered his tools and carried them to the workshed. The foreman of the job met him and talked for a few minutes about the progress of the construction. Then the foreman said, "This note was given to me. I was told to pass it on to you, Gabe. I hope there is no bad news."

Gabe took the paper and unfolded it. Years ago Essie had taught him to read. The message: "To Gabe Forbes, You are asked to come to the Freedmen's Bureau immediately after you leave work today. It is imperative that you come. Signed, District Supervisor, Freedmen's Bureau." Gabe was perplexed. What could it mean? First, he would have to meet his son Paul.

It was with trepidation that the large, handsome black man entered the office. At his side clung a twelve year old. Gabe presented the note to an agent at the counter. A fine-looking young man was summoned. "Come into my office," said the District Supervisor. "Just have a seat there, Mr. Forbes. This young fellow, I assume, is your son."

"Yes, sir," said Gabe timidly.

"Do you have other children, Mr. Forbes?"

The man faltered, "Don't know for sure. They's just Paul, here, that I know about. I had others, but...."

Caleb's heart leaped within him. His father had known of his mother's pregnancy at the time when the raiders had stolen him away. Was he thinking about me? thought Caleb. "Do you have a wife?" asked Caleb.

"No, sir."

"Mr. Forbes, you have this son. Is his mother deceased or separated from you?"

"Yes, sir."

"Then, there are only you and your son living together? Is that true?"

"Yes, sir," said Gabe.

"Mr. Forbes, this is a personal matter. Would you rather that the boy wait in the other room?"

"No, sir. Ain't nothin' he don't already know."

Caleb studied his father carefully. He was mascular, but When he spoke of his son there was a unique gentleness to his tone. "Mr. Forbes, this office has information concerning a woman who claims to be your wife. Her home is in Missouri. Do you know about this?"

Gabe caught his breath. He hung his head. Agony tensed his face as a hard and painful struggle went on within him. He made no reply.

"She was separated from you about twenty-seven years ago. She has mourned that loss all this time, living in hope that sometime you would seek and find her. She traveled with the Cherokees across the country and endured tremendous hardship. Always, you were in her thoughts."

The black man raised his eyes, questioning. They were full of frustration and the expression of a crushed spirit. "How you know this?" he asked, with a shade of anger in his tone.

Caleb continued, "Do you know that she bore a son, your son, and raised him to manhood? Recently, she journeyed to Atlanta seeking you. Did you know that when you saw her and spurned her, you broke her heart?"

"Dear God!" he uttered in a tremulous gasp. He turned his face and brushed aside a tear which trickled down his cheek. "How do you know all this?" he asked. He rose to his feet. His voice reflected the resentment he held for this personal line of questioning.

Caleb was slow to reply. He felt a tension gripping his own heart. His love-sorrow for Gabe was overwhelming. He could not understand what the man was going through, nor why, but he

284

could continue the deception no longer. He stepped close, facing him. "I am your son! Essie is my mother!"

"My...son! Dear God..." The stalwart man broke down. "Oh, God, dear God!" he exclaimed, and threw his arms around Caleb. He was completely overcome with emotion. Finally, when he was able to break away from his son, he stood gazing at him in tearful amazement.

Caleb, too, dried his eyes. "Will you turn away from me, like you did Mother?"

"No! Oh, Lord, what have I done? Lord help me, what have I done to Essie?" he cried. "Take me to her. Oh, God! Take me to her!"

"Yes, Father," said Caleb. Then he realized how their dramatic meeting must have confused the boy. Caleb bent down, put his hands on the child's shoulders, and said, "I'm your brother Caleb. You can't know how glad I am to have a brother."

"M'name's Paul," said the boy shyly.

The three of them, Caleb and Gabe, with Paul between them holding to the men's hands, proceeded to Essie's rooming house.

Essie received them quietly, not knowing what to expect.

"I'm sorry, Essie, that I hurt you," said Gabe. "I'm so confused and ashamed. I would never want to hurt you, Essie. For a long time, thoughts of this kind of a meeting haunted me. Finally I gave up hope. I thought we'd never see each other again. After I was taken away from you, I lost all reason to live. The men who took me were beasts, too terrible to tell about. The leader of the gang kept me for hisself. He had a little farm--a slave-breeding farm. He owned a few slaves, mostly women. He kept me locked in a little shack. His business was--well--to raise slave children to sell. Ever' so often he brought wenches to me. I--I was supposed to breed 'em--make them have a baby. Lord, how I fought. When I rebelled, they kept me chained. Lots o' times I was horsewhipped. Sometimes I played like I was sick. I wished that I was sick and that I'd die. The women were lucky--most didn't live very long. The plantation boss turned me into a beast--a dumb stud-ox. I wanted t' kill 'im. Finally we rebelled. We killed the driver what whipped us. One of the wenches stabbed the owner in the back with a butcher knife. All the niggers went wild in celebration. Now, I thought, I can go to Essie. I tried to run away but got caught. I was taken to a new plantation. Later when the war ended and slaves was free, I found Paul and his mother. You see, Essie, I'm too defiled to be your husband again. I ain't the man you knowed before. Go back to Missouri and forget about me! But know this, Essie, I loved you--I still do. Your love kept me alive all these years."

Essie was in tears. "No, Gabe," she said, "I'll never go back to Missouri without you. I love you," she sobbed. "At last we're together again!"

"No," Gabe said firmly, "I can't leave Georgia. I have a son here. Paul's mother is here. I can't leave them."

Stunned by his words, Essie stared at Gabe.

Caleb, too, was shocked. "Then--you live with this woman?" he asked in dismay.

"Oh, no! I only found her after the war ended. Nelda is in a hospital now. She's very sick. Poor Nelda! Paul and me is all she's got. She needs us. Go back to Missouri, Essie. Forget about us."

Essie did not leave Atlanta. She bid Gabe goodbye, but she could not leave. After a week of torture and anguish, she went again to find Gabe. She met him after his day's work was over just as she had found him the first time. "Gabe," she implored "I want to see Nelda. If I can just visit with her a little while, I'll be satisfied. I promise I will do nothing to hurt her. Perhaps can help her."

Gabe gave no reply. He studied her, wondering about her request. He could find in her no trace of enmity or jealousy.

"Let me help, Gabe," she begged earnestly. "This poor woman don't need to know who I am. I'll not tell her."

Although he was not sure it was the right thing to do, Gabe could not resist her entreaty. He told her how to find Nelda.

The following day, Essie hired a driver to take her to the hospital where Nelda was. She introduced herself as a friend of Gabe's. "We were once owned by the same master," she said

286

slipping into a chair at the bedside. "I wanted to know if there is anything I can do to make you more comfortable."

The sick black woman smiled at her. "Don' need nothin'," she said. "The Lord been good to me. I prayed to Him and He done give me ever'thing I pray for. I ain't no slave no more! Praise th' Lord! I brung lots o' chilens into this worl'. An' He let me keep one for my own. Then He done sent me a man to help me." Nelda attempted to raise herself in the bed. Essie extended her hand for her to grasp. Nelda's thin hand was scarred and gnarled. Her little movement gave her great pain. Her whole body was distorted, her joints swollen and red.

"Got the rheumatism--an' gout," Nelda explained. Her face showed twinges of pain, but only instantaneously. Her glowing smile refused to be vanquished by hurting. "The Lord done let me keep th' son Gabe gave to me. Don't matter now what happens. My Paul gots his daddy now. Comes to see me ever' day, Paul an' Gabe does. No, ain't nothin' I's needin'. Gabe is so good. Only man I ever love. 'Course he don' love me like I loves him. It don' matter. Don' matter."

Essie rose to go. "Thank yo for comin', honey," said Nelda

Two days later Essie packed her things and boarded the train for Missoui. To her mind came haunting visions of Nelda on her bed of affliction. If her heart held any trace of envy as a result of Nelda's hold on Gabe, such a feeling was nullified by her sympathy for her. Essie's mind was settled. Gabe was doing the right thing, the only thing he could do under the circumstances. She wept as the train pulled out of the station. Only Caleb was there to see her leave. She had not told Gabe she was leaving nor bid him farewell. She bore her sorrow as she had always done, bravely and alone. Would she ever see Gabe again? She would leave that question unanswered.

Caleb watched the train pull out of the station. He saw the tears in his mother's eyes and his heart was heavy. It seemed to him his pity for his mother was everlasting. That he had, at long last, found his father gave him little comfort. Caleb would stay in Georgia to continue his work. Perchance, in his dealing with the black folks of Georgia, he might unwittingly be serving one of his own half brothers or sisters. On their behalf he felt added

287

sorrow. He resolved to treat all people with kindness and gentleness, such as he had learned from his mother. They are all a part his family. "Created of one blood," as Essie would say.

Five months later Essie pushed Mary Stanton's wheelchair onto the front porch where she could enjoy the warm October sunshine. Essie then returned to the kitchen where she was preparing to bake a couple of apple pies.

Mary's feeble sight and muted hearing soon were attracted to a carriage approaching on the road. When it came to the front of Stanton mannor she observed that behind the coachman sat two black men and a black youth. "Land sakes, who can that be?" she mused. From the halted coach two men stepped down and made their way toward her. Only then did she exclaim, "Caleb, praise the Lord, it's Caleb!" But before she could summon Essie with a jubilant shout, Caleb sprang upon the porch and embraced her, nearly lifting her out of her wheelchair. Awaiting on the steps and holding back so as not to intrude on such an affectionate welcoming, the black man held the boy by the hand.

"Caleb, dear boy," said Mary, "you're just about the most beautiful sight I've beheld in ages. And just look at you! Such an important, distinguished man you've become! Wait till Benjamin sees you. He'll bust the buttons off his vest." In her joy she wanted to turn to the two strangers on the steps and boast that Caleb was her boy, had been almost since his birth. Instead she said, "Oh, forgive me. Caleb, invite your friends into the parlor where we can visit more comfortably."

Caleb said, "Oh, Mistress Mary, this here's Gabe Forbes and Paul. Gabe is my father. First let me explain about things. Father came when I insisted that he should be here for my marriage to Sarah. Is Sarah here?"

"Gabe Forbes!" exclaimed Mary Stanton, "I've heard tell of you over these many years--ever since Essie first came to us. But Essie said nothing about your coming to Missouri. No Sarah's not here. She left a few minutes ago to visit her mother She'll be back shortly. She's all a-dither about the wedding."

Gabe nodded respectfully and said, " I wouldn't a'come, but Caleb begged so hard. I hope my being here will be all right

288

with Essie. I wouldn't want to hurt her. But I did want to be here for my son's wedding. That's why I came."

"Hurt her! Nonsense!" said Mary Stanton, "Gabe Forbes, you'll get a grand reception from all of us. Come into the parlor. Caleb, push my chair inside, will you please. Make yourselves comfortable in there while I call Essie."

"Essie, Essie," she called to the kitchen, "come quick. Caleb's here! Caleb's home."

Essie sat aside a pan of apples she had been peeling and hurried toward the parlor. Caleb met her in the hallway and threw his arms around her.

"Mother, you got my letter, didn't you? I came home to marry Sarah like I wrote you I was going to do. And, Mamma, I brought two visitors home with me. It's all right, isn't it, Mamma?" He gazed into her eyes seeking the answer.

Essie looked around his shoulder into the parlor where Gabe Forbes and his son Paul sat timidly huddled together. Essie gasped, her body grew limp. "Of course it's all right." she said in a wavering voice.

As they stepped into the parlor Caleb said, "I wanted my papa and brother to be with me at the wedding. It was all I could do to persuade them to make the trip with me."

Gabe raised his head and stood up. "Oh, I wanted to come all right, but--but I was afraid it might be the wrong thing to do. I know I've hurt you, Essie. I want you to know it was not a thing I wanted to do. I hope that someday you will be able to forgive me."

"I have forgiven you, Gabe," said Essie. "My love for you would not let me do anything but forgive."

"Oh, Essie!" exclaimed Gabe. In spite of his embarrassment and lack of confidence, he threw his arms around her.

Essie could not respond. Her body was numb; her mind confused. What did it mean? She tried to listen to the things he was saying.

"We were battered and beaten by the events and the slavery we endured. Life has been almost too hard for us to bear. Essie, Caleb has told me about all you been through. Maybe you can understand how I was not able to come to Missouri until now. I

289

could not desert Paul or take him away from his poor sick mother." Gabe's voice seemed almost to fail him as he whispered, "Nelda died a week ago."

"I understand," murmured Essie, "Yes, we were robbed of the happiness we should have had together. We did what we had to do." Little by little she began to relax in Gabe's arms. She felt his strength and she knew that somehow his strength had sustained her through the many years she had been alone. They were together! Bound together by their endless love. She knew, even though he had not yet said it, that Gabe would never leave her again.

Later Essie took Gabe to the grassy place which was the Stanton family grave plot. "You see, Gabe, I, too, have a son you do not know about." And then she told him about Arley. She wept a little and thanked the Lord for Gabe who comforted her. Sadly she had laid to rest in the cemetery her last connection with the Cherokee people. At least, that was what she had thought. But when Evangeline and Bill's little half-breed son grew, Essie considered herself to be his grandmother-- it was her own little secret, which she never shared with anyone but Gabe--but, oh, how delighted she was to have the parents' consent to teach Jeremy Cherokee words and customs! With gentle sighs of remembrance, she often thought of Fawn and Kevit, who were the true grandparents of little Jeremy.

Essie and Gabe were supremely happy. Judge Stanton accepted Gabe as a part of his household and assigned him many jobs to do around his farm. Soon the judge gave land for Essie and Gabe to build themselves a little cottage. In addition, Gabe's skill as a builder brought him many jobs in the community. Perhaps the most satisfying work he was to do was to tear down Stultz's old barn, and in its place, using some of the old lumber and added new, he built a new church for all the black people of the area. It was a labor of love, and Caleb and Sarah postponed their wedding until the church was completed. At the wedding, sitting next to Gabe and holding his hand, Essie lovingly nestled her arm around Paul who sat on the other side of her. Caleb took the little black girl to whom he had first taught spirituals to be his bride. As Essie watched she knew that never was a woman happier or more blessed than she.

ABOUT THE AUTHOR

Lloyd Durre, author, teacher, artist, actor, merchant was born at Greenville, Illinois. He grew up in Wood River, Illinois, where his father had a plumbing and heating business. He attended Wood River public schools and graduated from Shurtleff College in nearby Alton, Illinois, receiving a bachelor of arts degree.

He has been employed as a department store clerk and an insurance salesman. He is married and is the father of two daughters and a son. In 1959 he moved his family to Springfield, Missouri. Later, in 1962 he became a teacher in the Branson, MO. high school where he taught art and American history. He also became the shepherd in the outdoor summer theater production of The Shepherd of the Hills. This presentation of author Harold Bell Wright's famous novel has been the nation's leading outdoor drama for forty years. Mr. Durre portrayed the role of the shepherd for twenty-seven years.